The Long Journey of POPPIE NONGENA

Elsa Joubert was born in Paarl and lives in Cape Town. Throughout her illustrious and very prolific career she has been awarded almost every prize for Afrikaans writing, some more than once.

Elsa's work has been recognised internationally as well as within South Africa. She was awarded the Winifred Holtby Prize by the British Royal Society for Literature, as well as being made a Fellow of the Society for the novel *The Long Journey of Poppie Nongena*, (originally published in Afrikaans as *Die swerfjare van Poppie Nongena*).

This novel was also awarded the W A Hofmeyr Prize, the CNA Literary Award and the Louis Luyt Prize.

The
Long Journey of
POPPIE
NONGENA

Elsa Joubert

JONATHAN BALL PUBLISHERS
JOHANNESBURG & CAPE TOWN
AND
TAFELBERG
CAPE TOWN

© Original Afrikaans published as *Die Swerfjare van Poppie Nongena*,
Elsa Joubert, 1978
© English translation copyright, Elsa Joubert, 1980

Originally published in 1978 under the title
Die swerfjare van Poppie Nongena
by Tafelberg Publishers.

First English edition published in 1980 in hard cover by
Hodder & Stoughton Limited
with Jonathan Ball Publishers (Pty) Ltd.

This edition published in 2002 by
JONATHAN BALL PUBLISHERS (PTY) LTD
PO Box 33977
Jeppestown
2043
and
TAFELBERG PUBLISHERS
28 Wale Street
Cape Town
8001

ISBN 1 86842 145 7

Cover painting by George Pemba
Cover design by Michael Barnett, Johannesburg
Cover reproduction by Triple M Design & Advertising, Johannesburg
Printed and bound by CTP Book Printers, Caxton Street, Parow, Cape

CONTENTS

To the reader

This novel is based on the actual life story of a black woman living in South Africa today. Only her name, Poppie Rachel Nongena, born Matati, is invented. The facts were related to me not only by Poppie herself, but by members of her immediate family and her extended family or clan, and they cover one family's experience over the past forty years.

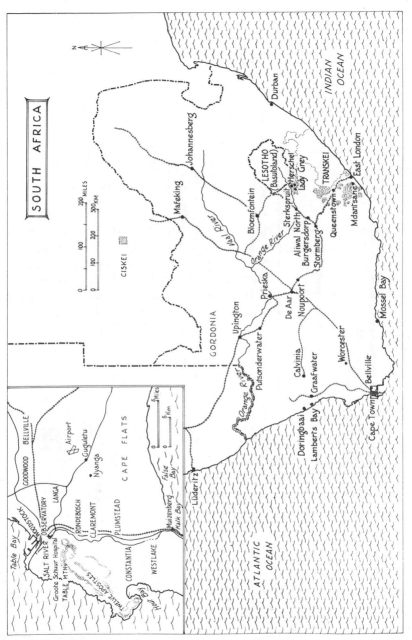

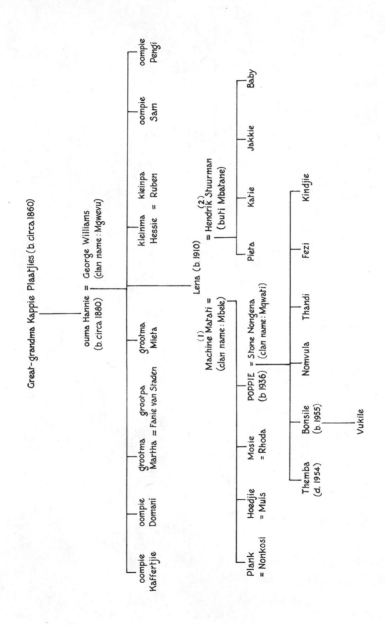

Great-grandma Kappie Plaatjies (b. circa 1860)

ouma Hannie = George Williams
(b. circa 1880)   (clan name : Mgwevu)

oompie   oompie   grootma   grootpa   grootma   kleinma   kleinpa   oompie   oompie
Kafferjie   Domani   Martha = Fanie van Staden   Mieta   Hessie = Ruben   Sam   Pengi
                                                                                      (2)
                                                           Lena (b. 1910) = Hendrik Stuurman
                                                                                 (buti Mbatane)

                                               (1)
                                      Machine Matati =
                                      (clan name : Mbele)

Plank   Hoedjie   Mosie   POPPIE = Stone Nongena   Pieta   Katie   Jakkie   Baby
= Nonkosi = Muis   = Rhoda (b. 1936) (clan name : Mqwati)

          Themba   Bonsile   Nomvula   Thandi   Fezi   Kindjie
          (d. 1954) (b. 1955)

                    Vukile

ONE

Upington

1

We are Xhosa people from Gordonia, says Poppie. My
mama used to tell us about our great-grandma Kappie, a rich
old woman who grazed her goats on the koppies the other
side of Carnarvon. Her second name was Plaatjies and she
had the high-bridged nose that runs in the family — our
oompie Pengi got it from her.

She told our mama about the old days and about the big
man, Dark Malgas, who was killed on the island in the Great
River, which they call the Orange River these days. She told
our mama about the rinderpest and the cattle and sheep that
died and about the English war or the Imfazwe yamabulu,
the war of the Boers.

We saw the Boers coming on horseback, she said, and we
fled into the koppies, herding the goats as we went. We left
everything in the huts and stayed in the koppies till the
white men had left. They didn't take our things. Everything
was as we had left it, but they ate all the mealie porridge in
the cooking pots.

And then Jantjie rode away with them as agterryer and
was shot dead in the war.

Jantjie, take the horses and flee, the Boer shouted when
he saw the English soldiers surrounding them, but by then,
old woman — so he came and told our great-grandma
Kappie — your child was dead.

Great-grandma Kappie only had one girl child, our
grandma Hannie. We called her ouma Hannie. Hannie
married George Williams, a shearer who worked on the
sheep farms. He was born in Beaufort West and his clan
name was Mgwevu and he died in the Big 'Flu of 1918. The
isibetho, ouma Hannie told us, was the plague that the Lord

11

sent us, the people were sick for three days and then they died.

Hannie had eight children by him. They were born on the sheep farms where their pa was working at the time. When he died, they were staying at Koegas, outside Prieska. But ouma Hannie had a hard time rearing the children and they moved to Vaalkoppies and they stayed on the lands at Louisvale where the Bushmen taught them to use a scythe. When the children grew up, ouma Hannie moved across the river to Upington, to get them to church and to put them to school.

The children were oompie Kaffertjie and oompie Domani and grootma Martha and grootma Mieta and Lena who was our own ma, and then kleinma Hessie and oompie Sam and oompie Pengi, ouma Hannie's last born, her dry-teat child, her t'koutjie, as the Namas say. Grootma means a sister of your ma that's older than she is, and kleinma is her younger sister. Oompie is uncle.

Ouma Hannie's children weren't at school for very long. Oompie Kaffertjie moved back to Koegas and worked as a farmhand, and oompie Domani went away to war, the Big War of 1914, and never came back. And the other children looked for work from Lüderitz on the coast to Upington, Putsonderwater, Draghoender and Prieska along the railway line.

All my aunts were married by force; that was the way the parents used to do it in those days. My mama didn't want my pa. He came to Lüderitzbucht to work on the boats, and then he saw my ma who was visiting with grootma Mieta. He walked behind her and the wind was blowing hard and he didn't stop walking because he had fallen in love with her. So he went to Upington to ask ouma Hannie if he could marry my ma.

Ja, he was a great talker, says ouma Hannie, and he paid a lot of lobola money for your ma, and that's how it was that he married her. His name was Machine Matati and his clan name was Mbele. His forebears came from the Ciskei but he himself was born at Mafeking.

Ouma Hannie was very strict with her children. She

12

wasn't at rest till they were married with lobola money, as well as in church. Then she settled down in the location of Upington and took in the grandchildren that her children brought to her, and reared them as she had reared her own. But our ma's children were closest to her heart, because our pa didn't look after us well. He left us on a Saturday morning and went to the office in Upington and joined up for the war, the war of 1939. He was sent away as a lorry-driver to Egiputa in the north and never came back to us at all.

Just like your oompie Domani, said ouma Hannie. But that was a different war, the war that was the first of the two great white people wars.

2

Lena's fourth child was brought to ouma Hannie who called her Poppie. She had another name as well, Ntombizodumo, which means girl born from a line of great women, and her mother added two more names, Rachel Regina as baptismal names, because she preferred the sound of the English to the more ordinary names like Lena and Martha and Mieta and Hessie which she and her sisters bore.

The three sons of Lena had English names as well, Philip, Stanley and Wilson. Perhaps it was Machine Matati from Mafeking, who went to war for the English, who chose these new names. No, says Poppie, it was not just our pa who was educated, our ma had some learning too.

But ouma Hannie called the child Poppie from Poppietjie which means little doll. And because her mother was away at work in far off Prieska, and because the child and her brothers grew up with their grandma, her words — Leave Poppie alone, or sshh Poppie, or give Poppie some of your milk — mingled with their play. The words, mingled with the clucking of the chickens they chased across the hot clay-smeared backyard, were caught up in the wind rustling the feathers of the red-brown fowls, swished with the sound of the top spinning in the sand. Because of that, the name stuck.

Ouma had no truck with English names. She called Wilson, the toddler who had to leave ouma's back to make place for Poppie, Mosie, and Philip she called Plank, and Stanley was Hoedjie.

They lived in Blikkiesdorp, which was Upington's shanty-town or location. All kinds of people, except whites, were living there. In those days nobody spoke of coloured or brown people. There were Basters who looked almost like whites, with long hair; and mixed Basters; Damaras who were black but tried to pass themselves off as Basters; Bushmen with the short bodies and big backsides, yellow skin and tight frizzy hair. Their Afrikaans was different, almost Nama, but everybody spoke Afrikaans, even the black people, the Rhodesian Africans and Xhosas and Sothos living there.

Ouma Hannie spoke Xhosa and Afrikaans. She scolded when the children wouldn't speak Xhosa. She said: Stop speaking Afrikaans, people who pass our house at night and hear you speak will think, Ninga malawu — you're all Bushmen. The Xhosa did not care much for the small yellow people.

Ouma's youngest child, oompie Pengi, used to tease her. He'd come home drunk, singing, and then he'd say: God, ma, just watch the way old George's child is singing. Then ouma Hannie would say: Pengi, you're making a noise, my head can't stand it. Then he'd say: But listen, ma, listen I'm singing to you. Then he'd start dancing, doing tap-dance steps — he'd travelled a lot, he knew the steps. Then he'd dance round ouma Hannie and say: God, ma, people say I'm not a Xhosa, I'm a Zulu. Then ouma would ask: Now why would they say that? And he'd answer: They say I sing too well for a Xhosa. You're no Xhosa, they say, you're a Zulu, go search for your pa. Ouma Hannie would reply: Go search till you find him, I don't mind. But it was just Pengi's joke.

14

UPINGTON

The fact was we couldn't speak Xhosa, says Poppie. Even now when my brothers and I are together, we speak Afrikaans, that's what we like to speak, that comes naturally, ja. My brothers had Xhosa names too, but in Upington we knew nothing about all that.

When Poppie grew too big to be carried on ouma's back, the safety pin was unclasped, the blanket dropped and she was put down on to the ground. Then Mosie left his place at ouma's side, it was Poppie who clutched her long skirts, and Mosie joined Plank and Hoedjie where they played behind the chicken coop on the heap of left-over sheets of corrugated iron. They clambered on to the old wagon, and followed the dogs, and got to know the sandy streets of the location. They went as far as the shops, and even further than the kraal where the goats were kept.

Our house was built partly of reeds and clay and partly of bricks. In front was a low wall and we liked to play and walk on it. Sometimes we sat on it to eat our food. Behind the house was a chicken coop and we liked to feed the chickens for our ouma. As long as I can remember we had a black and white goat in our backyard, tied to the wagon wheel with a thong. Oompie Pengi milked the goat and gave us the milk to drink.

Ouma gave us bread and magou. She would make very thin mealie-meal porridge and let it cool, then add a spoonful of fine flour to it and stir it well, but she had to have some left-over magou to add as well, because that made it go sour. We drank the magou or ate it with a spoon. We liked ouma's griddle cakes too, and umphokoqo, a crumbly porridge we ate with sour milk. At night we ate samp cooked with beans and meat.

My ouma never used a Primus stove, she did her cooking outside in three-legged cooking-pots over an open fire, and we liked to go with her when she gathered wood in the veld, because it meant that we could look for gum. It was not customary for the boys to gather wood, but they would climb the trees to get the gum for us. That's mine, that bit's mine, we would yell to them, pointing high up in the trees. The boys also hunted hares and shot at birds with their

15

catapults. Sometimes we would set out early in the morning, but if we only needed kindling for the cooking fire, we went in the late afternoon and did not go far into the veld. When ouma did ironing for the white people in Upington we waited till three o'clock in the afternoon to go.

Ouma would bend her knee to break the wood, giving us the pieces to drag to the stacking place where she tied it up into bundles. Then she twisted rags into small padded rolls for our heads. We had to hold on tightly to the bundles of firewood she lifted on to our heads. It was only when we felt the wood coming to rest on the pad, moving with our movement as we walked along the footpath, that we would stop clutching, that we trotted and danced. In the approaching dusk we could see the houses coming closer. The outside fires were burning, the people moving around the flames, the shadows lengthening and creeping up to the footpath.

Oompie Pengi had come home wearing his thick overcoat. He sat flat on the ground with his back against the wagon wheel and underneath his coat he hid a bottle. He turned on to his side, ducking into his coat to hide his head. He was groaning as if in pain, and then we heard the sound of his drinking, ghorr, ghorr, ghorr.

Plank lay on his back on the ground next to the fire. His legs kicked the air, in his hand he pretended to hold a bottle. He drank, he squirmed as if he had a bellyache. He was pretending to be oompie Pengi.

Ouma threw down her bundle of wood, took a stick and beat the ground next to Plank. Dust rose and was coloured red by the fire. Child of Satan, she screamed at him, child of the dog. Satan's child to mock your uncle.

Auk, he screamed, auk, and he clutched his backside, dancing around the fire, waving his arms and kicking his legs in such a way that we didn't know whether he was screaming or laughing.

Oompie Pengi was very close to ouma's heart, because he was her dry-teat child. But ouma was a God-fearing woman and it grieved her when oompie Pengi was drunk.

My ouma didn't have a bed, she slept on goatskins joined

together, flat on the ground, with a pillow and a few blankets. Ag, she slept so well, and I shared her bed. It wasn't hard at all, one sleeps well on a dung floor if one is used to it. In rainy or cold weather she used hessian bags underneath the skins to keep out the damp. My oompie Pengi slept on a bed in the next-door room, the room built of reeds and clay, but ouma and I slept on the goatskins and my brothers on hessian bags and blankets.

My ouma never went to sleep without saying her prayers. And at five o'clock in the morning she woke to pray, and she woke all of us as well as she knelt between us. She owned a Bible, though she could not read. But she loved to sing. We all sang together. And at night oompie Pengi prayed. At times when he was drunk, he prayed for such a long time that I fell asleep sitting on the floor next to ouma, and when I woke up he was still praying. But ouma never got angry with oompie Pengi for praying; when she wanted him to stop she just started singing. Then we would all sing together, Plank and Hoedjie and Mosie and I and my kleinma Hessie, if she was visiting, and oompie Sam and grootma Martha or grootma Mieta, if they had come to see ouma. They were all so fond of singing.

We had a cupboard with shelves in the kitchen. Kleinma Hessie could do paper cut-outs and she'd cut the patterns out of old newspapers and line the shelves. Every month she came from Putsonderwater to see our ouma, and she brought off-cuts of meat, or maybe flour or other foodstuffs. But when she left — this I remember well — ouma hid her prettiest stuff, because she complained: Hessie has long fingers, she loves my pretty things. But kleinma Hessie out-witted ouma and took what she wanted in spite of ouma's care.

When our own mama came to visit, we were happy because she brought us gifts, she was our mama. But we were not sad when she left, because she beat us. Ouma never beat us. We loved ouma more, more than our own mama.

Ouma Hannie earned her living by selling rags and bones. When she wasn't going out to work for the white people, my ouma always carried a bag, Poppie says. I picked up bones and took them to her and she threw them in the sack. Whenever we had meat to eat, she saved the bones to sell to old Solly. We searched for bones in the rubbish dumps of the location. Ouma would poke her stick in the rubbish heap and, scratching around amongst the ash and the old rusty tins and the garbage, pry the bones loose with the tip of her stick and scratch the filth away saying: Poppie, there's a bone for you.

When I was small I loved searching for bones with my ouma, I blew on the bones and wiped them clean and kept them in the small tin ouma gave me. She would settle the tin on the little cushion of rags on my head and we'd take the main road to where the white people lived. Plank and Hoedjie carried a big paraffin tin filled with bones, hanging on a stick balanced on their shoulders, and ouma carried a big bag on her head.

We would go up the steps to Solly's shop.

Old Solly will give you a penny for your tin of bones, Poppie, ouma says. Let go your hands from the tin.

And she'd say to Solly: Give the child niggerballs for the penny.

Plank and Hoedjie were given neither money nor niggerballs. They are big now, said ouma. But Poppie gave each of them one of her niggerballs. Ouma threw the empty small tin into the bigger one and it clanked as Plank and Hoedjie swung it. Then ouma picked Poppie up and fastened her on her back.

Poppie saved the last niggerball for Mosie. He was lying on the sack in the dark room, on the bed that he shared with Hoedjie and Plank. He was cold, his knees clutched against his chest, he had a fever, his forehead was shiny with sweat. Ouma pulled the blankets up around him, but he pushed out his arm to see the niggerball Poppie had brought him, blue like a bird's egg. He pushed it into his mouth.

Poppie licked the black stickiness from her fingers and her tongue, flat as a ladle, cleaned out the palm of her hand. It tasted sweet and sharply bitter and discoloured her tongue. She stuck out her tongue to show Mosie how black it was.

18

These are the memories that are still with Poppie, of her infancy with ouma Hannie at Upington.

3

Mama was working in De Aar for our keep, and ouma worked sleep-in with white people in Upington to help earn money for us. So Plank and Mosie went to live with kleinma Hessie and kleinpa Ruben at Putsonderwater, and Hoedjie and I lived there too, but with grootma Martha and grootpa Fanie who worked on the railway. We lived in the location close to the railyard. Early in the morning the oompies went off on a trolley to a far place on the railway line where they worked. We liked it so much when grootpa came home because he left us a chunk of bread in his billie can. It was a small blue pail with a lid in which he took magou and bread to eat at work. We would watch from the small koppie to see the railway trolley coming home along the line, then we raced to meet him, on account of the chunk of bread that we knew he had saved for us. That was good.

At the end of the month we used to go along with him to old Birge's shop, and watch him buy a bag of mealie meal, a bag of unsifted meal, sugar, coffee and roll-tobacco, because grootma Martha liked chewing tobacco and grootpa smoked a pipe. We'd load the bags on a wheelbarrow, and grootpa would give us sugarstick sweets. Grootpa Fanie was a true Xhosa, his clan name was Mkantini, but he could speak Afrikaans and he was fonder of us than kleinpa Ruben was.

But kleinma Hessie was always laughing and we liked her a lot. I remember when I was very small, at Putsonderwater, the sun darkening in the middle of the day. Then kleinma gave me a dark piece of glass from a broken bottle and said:

Look through the glass, Poppie, don't look at the sun with your eyes. Then the sun shrank till it looked like a half moon.

Poppie and her brothers went to school with grootma Martha's children. They crossed the railway line and walked a little way along the koppie to the church house. They walked single file along the chalky road, kicking at the dust which covered their legs with a fine layer of chalk. Mosie was the one who tired first, he dragged his feet to school. Plank capered alongside the track.

The teacher, Meester Riet, came to school on his bicycle, cycling along till his wheels bogged down in the sand and he lost balance. Then he would push the bike to the shady side of the church house and fasten the safety chain to the wheel. He knew that Plank had an eye on it and would steal a ride if he could. Even if he got caned for it.

Ag, there was such a pretty thing I saw at the school, says Poppie. I thought it was a plaything, that old-fashioned frame with the beads, it was so pretty. Then I saw the schoolmaster pick up a ruler and flick the beads. He told us: Count while I flick, one . . . two . . . three. Green and blue and white and red beads, bigger ones; and on the lower rung smaller beads. I couldn't take my eyes off them.

She sat on the floor and when the bigger children were busy writing on the slates on their laps, and she could hear the slate-pencils grating, he brought this beaded plaything over to her. His ruler was flicking the beads to this side, then to that.

Count as I flick, he told Poppie.

She was shy and her voice scarcely a whisper, then Meester Riet lifted her chin with his ruler, and said: Louder. And, as she had heard Plank recite at home, she chanted One . . . two . . . three . . .

Plank ran to meet grootpa coming with his billie can from the railroad trolley. The sun was drooping, the white chalky soil tinted yellow, black shadows creeping out from under the low bushes like lizards, and the long black shadows stretching from the foot of the electric poles made the poles look like men toppling. The veld had lost its bleak, barren look, glowing in the yellow light of the late afternoon, before night comes.

Plank called from far off to grootpa: Poppie is the cleverest one, Poppie can recite a verse.

They waited for her to catch up with them. She clutched grootpa's coat-tail to make him stop.

Come on, say your verse, said Plank.

Softly, but more clearly than at school, her eyes cast down, Poppie said:

> Klaas Vakie kom so sag soos 'n dief,
> Hy kom by die skoorsteen in
> Hy raak aan kindjie se ogies
> Terwyl hy saggies sing. . .

which means the old oompie sandman comes down the chimney and sends the little child to sleep.

Kleinma Hessie had been recited to earlier that afternoon and she gave Poppie gifts — a rag with which to wipe her slate, a small bottle to hold the water. Grootma Martha's life was too sparse to own such extras.

Poppie's slate was a broken one. The toddlers were given the broken slates. When they lost their pencils, they made slate pencils from bits of broken slate. But although it was broken, the slate was framed in wood, and Plank had written her name on the wooden frame. She carried the slate very carefully, to prevent the loose pieces from shifting in the frame. She never ran to school, because when she ran she could hear the pieces moving up and down in the frame and then her heart contracted from fear that the pieces should break into smaller fragments. So she walked slowly and did not join the other children when they jumped over ditches and hillocks on the way to school.

We crossed the railway line — those days they weren't so strict — we knew the trains, the freight trains carrying coal, the eleven down, the ten up. We didn't know what those names meant, eleven down and ten up and mail train, but we knew when to expect the trains. They were mostly goods trains. We liked to watch the goods trains shunt, quite close to our house; we liked to watch the shunters jumping

21

down to change the points, noticing who jumped well and
who ran well and who jumped back the fastest. When the
shunters jumped back into the moving truck it was terribly
beautiful. Plank and Hoedjie and Mosie and my grootma's
children used to point to the man and say: It's me that one
that jumps so well. They always fought to choose the man
who jumped the best and to claim: I'm *that* one.

I remember standing behind the house one day when the
trains were shunting quite close by, and the man in the coal
truck saw me standing there and he pushed out his teeth
at me. It was the first time I had seen false teeth, and I ran
away. I got such a fright seeing the teeth come out of his
mouth.

This is what remains in my memory of Putsonderwater,
the trucks and the cattle and sheep being shunted by.

We liked to gather coals along the railway line. The older
children carried bags and the little ones carried tins, and if
you saw a big piece of coal, too big to carry yourself, you
called one of the bigger ones to put it in his bag, but you
stayed with your find and you walked home with it and
you watched grootma take it from the bag and you watched
it burning.

Grootma Martha was sitting against the wall, on the sunny
side of the house. She sat flat on the ground, her legs
stretched out in front of her. Next to her was her sewing,
needle and thread and rags. She was patching grootpa's
khaki pants.

Kleinma Hessie called her: Come, sisi Martha, come
inside.

Grootma picked up her sewing and gave it to kleinma to
hold. She shook the dust from the hessian bag on which she
was sitting, folded it and took back her sewing before going
inside and closing the door.

Your brother-in-law has given his notice to the railways,
sisi, said kleinma. He's joining the Ethiopian Church. He's
putting on the collar.

Kleinpa Ruben and kleinma Hessie and grootpa Fanie and
grootma Martha were church-going people like ouma

22

Hannie. They were African Methodists, peaceful folk, who didn't drink. They went to church in the white building against the koppie where the children were given schooling, where Meester Riet was the teacher. And the preacher.

Meester Riet is a Sotho who has forgotten his tongue, kleinpa Ruben used to say: When the Basters and the Bushmen come to church, he preaches in three tongues, Sotho, Xhosa and Afrikaans.

Kleinpa Ruben could not speak Afrikaans, and he scolded the children when they spoke it. Don't speak that tongue, I am a Xhosa, he'd say.

That's why he did not like Meester Riet.

The Ethiopian Church stands for the cause of the Xhosa, more so than Meester Riet, said kleinma Hessie. They think much of the bloodline. They want your brother-in-law to take the collar.

Grootma Martha was a silent woman. She had no worldly goods, but she had eight children. Hessie was childless. She pitied Hessie who had so much but was so poor, and she felt it deeply that Hessie did not open her heart to her, did not tell her how deeply she grieved because she had no child. If buti Ruben became a preacher, Hessie would work in the church, and be called a juffrou which means teacher. Perhaps it was better so, it would comfort her in her childlessness.

Grootma Martha took down cups from the cupboard. I'll pour us some coffee. Ma will feel it if you leave the Methodist Church.

Ma can keep her Methodists, said Hessie.

Kleinpa Ruben went to Upington to be clothed as an Ethiopian preacher. Kleinma became a juffrou and wore special clothes for church, a skirt and long black blouse and a blue collar that looked like a bib. She sewed a piece of brown hide to her head-dress.

Kleinpa Ruben held the church meetings in his house, he preached all night long and they sang hymns. Mosie sang in the choir, he wore a long white cloak and led the procession to the house. All night long kleinpa preached and

23

kleinma preached and Mosie in his little white cloak sang until he collapsed into sleep.

Hessie's singing is wearing her out, said grootma Martha, she is as thin as a rake, and I never hear her laughing any more.

And still she did not bear a child.

4

Ouma Hannie tired of her work in Upington and arrived at Putsonderwater.

Bring Lena's children, she told Martha and Hessie, I want them back.

Martha gave Hoedjie and Poppie back to ouma Hannie and kleinma Hessie brought Plank, but she begged: Leave Mosie with me, I have no child in the house. Ouma Hannie had quarrelled with kleinpa Ruben when he joined the Ethiopian Church, but she took pity on her daughter's childlessness and said: Keep him with you.

They went to the station in a donkey cart. It was the first time Poppie had ridden in one, and sitting on the seat she was level with the trucks of the goods train. The donkey cart trotted along the track next to the railway line and she could see the heads of the sheep through the bars of the trucks and the little horns peeping through the wool. When the train ground to a halt, the donkey trotted past it and Poppie turned her head aside to avoid the stoker catching sight of her.

Kleinma Hessie came to the station to see them off, she brought the children some sugarstick sweets. The smaller children fought each other for the sweets, but the bigger ones pretended not to see, they stuck their hands in their pockets and hitched up their trousers as they had seen their pas do, and they watched the line to see if their train was coming.

It was a long wait. The children clambered into the compartment and out again, and Mosie was shown the inside. It was the old-fashioned kind of compartment with no aisle but the door leading straight on to the platform. Plank leaned out of the window, the sugarstick stuck into his mouth. He clung to the window-frame as the train started moving. And when he shouted goodbye to Mosie he lost the sugarstick. It fell from his mouth.

When ouma left Upington for some time, says Poppie, she let the house and the tenants gave the money to her neighbours. But oompie Pengi caused trouble. He'd collect the money from the neighbours (because it's my ma's money, he said) and use it to buy drink.

This time he used the money to buy a new guitar.

Plank's fingers knew music, as oompie Pengi's did, and when they got home, oompie Pengi said: My old guitar, that's yours now, Plankie.

The old guitar was made from a long narrow syrup tin, and strung with thin wire.

The house is like a pigsty, said ouma Hannie, do I always have to work my hands to the bone when I come home?

Oompie Pengi hung the cord of the new guitar round his neck. With the palm of his hand he stroked the strings lovingly.

Poppie moved nearer, quietly following oompie Pengi and Plank to his room. It had a different smell to ouma's room. The big red ants crawled up the clay wall, and burrowed tiny tunnels along it. Ouma would strike at the wall with the side of her hand, then blow away the crumbling clay.

Oompie Pengi took down the old tin guitar from the hook on the wall, and handed it to Plank who plucked at the strings. Oompie Pengi's feet heard the beat, he discarded the new guitar, giving it to Poppie to hold. His body came to life, his arms, outstretched like wings, moved up and down like a bird in flight, his legs jerked from the knees

25

downwards, the heels dragging and the toes tapping out the beat. His dancing raised the dust from the dry dung-smeared floor. Bars of afternoon light were streaming through crevices in the reed roof. Small insects, trapped in the light, seemed to be struggling to free themselves, but could not escape.

Plank felt the beat of the music taking hold of him too, his body started moving to the rhythm of the guitar. The feeling spread from his fingers, the gut of the strings became fire burning right down into his belly. He groaned, slow groans emerging from his mouth, capturing the beat, like a song that hurt.

Oompie Pengi took life easily, says Poppie, he was good fun. One couldn't be mad at him, even if he took the rent and spent it all. If ouma scolded, he joked back at her and then he had us all laughing, and that was that. Buti Plank took after Pengi, but buti Hoedjie was quieter by nature, he hated us to tease him, he lost his temper, but not old Plank, not him, as long as he had his music, he didn't mind the teasing.

Hoedjie didn't join his brother in Pengi's room. He went to the backyard where the outside fire had died down. He kicked at the dead ash, and talked to no one.

Come, come, we are tired out. Ouma Hannie scolded the two who were making music and keeping Poppie standing like a pillar holding the new guitar in her arms.

Come, come, get done with it. Put down the guitar on your oompie's bed, Poppietjie, and draw your ouma some water.

Ouma heard the cackling of her hens.

I feel like eating chicken's meat, she said. Tomorrow, Pengi, you must cut the red one's throat.

Poppie was a big girl now. When she finished her home-work, she helped ouma. She ran errands to the location shop. If Ben Mansana's daughter Emily went along, they were even allowed to go as far as old Solly's shop. Emily's father was a Xhosa, and he owned a café in the location,

26

but her ma was a Bushman, with a big bum and a flat yellow face with wide flat nostrils.

Poppie's other friends were Miriam and Nomsolono, both Xhosa girls. When they finished helping ouma they sat on the low wall in front of the house, where it was cool, and plaited each other's hair. It takes a long time to plait the short frizzy hair; the Basters have longer hair that they can plait and tie up with cotton rags. Sometimes the bigger girls showed them how to use black cotton to part the frizzy hair and to plait the spanspek or sweet melon pattern with the little plaits lying neatly in rows on the skull. Poppie and Miriam couldn't manage it on their own, their fingers were stupid, they plaited untidy little ends that stuck out like horns.

Fetch us your ouma's church stockings, Poppie, the big girls urged her, then we'll plait your hair ever so beautifully.

Ouma wore stretch stockings which, cut into strips, would have a grip on the short hair.

Don't give them the stockings, said Miriam, your ouma will kill you.

On Saturdays we liked to go to the cattle and goat kraals just outside the town to pick up dung and fill the tins and old dishes ouma gave us. Outside the kraals we could gather as much dung as we liked, but some people were strict and didn't allow us to go inside the kraals. We like to smear the floors of our house. If the floors are rough and uneven, we mix the dung with black clay, because the clay binds the dung, then we spread it thick over the floor, smoothing the broken parts. We make patterns in the wet dung, down on our knees with the palms of our hands, drawing wide circles with great sweeps away from our bodies and back again. We Xhosa people call these patterns indima or hand spoor. The Basters are not so fond of their dung-smeared floors as we are, they'll use a broom to spread the dung. We Xhosa people would never do that.

But oompie Pengi did not heed the hand spoor on the newly-smeared floor; he stumbled through the house, dragging his feet through the wet dung. He sat on his bed and we heard the strings of his guitar, which he plucked so sadly, so sadly.

Ouma prodded at the fire underneath the three-legged pot. To the dying ashes she added the dry dung that we had gathered, breaking kindling, and bending low to puff.

We didn't complain that oompie Pengi had spoilt our patterns on the wet dung-smeared floor.

Your oompie Pengi is grieving, ouma had told us before. He is grieving for Sonny Boy. Sonny Boy was the child oompie Pengi had by a mixed-blood woman who left him a long time ago and settled in Draghoender. Those days your oompie Pengi danced so well, said ouma, even better than he dances now. He travelled to far places and learned the different steps. But that was before Sonny Boy and his ma left him. Ja, said ouma, oompie Pengi is grieving for his little Sonny Boy.

Smearing the floors with dung, that was our job every Saturday, afterwards we could play. Or we could go watch the witchdoctors and listen to their drumming.

One by one the doctors came from their homes, from this street one, from that another. Miriam and Nomsolono called me softly, beckoning with their hands, so that ouma could not hear us. They're going down that way to old sisi Makone's house. The house had been cleared of furniture and a great deal of beer brewed.

Old sisi's children were scalding the paraffin tins on the open fire earlier this week, said Nomsolono, and the wind scattered the ash near to where we were playing.

We followed the sound of the drums. Standing a little distance away from old Makone's house, we watched the people coming down the street. They were dressed in white robes, their faces smeared with white clay, the old man carried a kierie in his hand, the younger one a sambok which he switched at the dust on the road. The men mock-fought with their kieries.

When the grown-ups were inside the house, we moved closer, pushing in through the door. We liked listening to the drums and the handclapping. When the isangoma, the chief of the witchdoctors, entered the room, the sound died down. She prayed. The people started singing church hymns, the singing stilled their mind to the work. We liked the singing, too.

The isangoma was an old mama, she wore beads round her waist, arms and neck, and a hat made of skin, with strings of beads tied to it. She held a switch in one hand and a small stick in the other. Her face was shiny with sweat, she threw back her head, her legs started trembling and she fell down on her knees. But when the people started thumping their feet, she got up and danced in the centre of the group, with her eyes closed and her hands stretched out in front of her.

The men with the kieries shoved Poppie and Miriam and Nomsolono aside. Get out, they said. This is no place for you. You'll get hurt.

Outside in the backyard the son of old sisi Makone was tending the fire. He knew his mother was a witchdoctor, but he didn't mind.

Because of the dancing, he told Poppie, I get a lot of meat to eat and beer to drink.

When Poppie got home, she told oompie Pengi, the buti of old sisi Makone is building a big fire. The medicine people are dancing.

Ouma Hannie heard what Poppie was saying, but pretended not to.

She lifted the flat-iron from the fire, wiped it with a rag, and spat on it. The spittle spluttered off the hot surface. Ouma was ironing her white bib and white doek. She wore her church uniform on Sundays and to special services — a black skirt and red overblouse with white bib and doek. Thursday afternoons she wore the uniform to the women's prayer meeting. Ouma was a faithful church-goer and did not approve of the dances of the amagqira, the witchdoctor people.

Ouma's Methodist church was a whitewashed brick building and her preacher was Mr Tshangela. His wife was the juffrou of the Sunday school. But the children in the location knew of many other churches: the Lutheran Church, the Ethiopian Church, the Anglican Church, the Dutch Reformed, the Baptists.

Mr Tshangela preached in Xhosa and a lay preacher translated what he said into Afrikaans every Sunday, and on some Sundays a third man repeated his words into Sotho. On those days the church service went on till one o'clock in the afternoon.

The Afrikaans-speaking people brought their Afrikaans hymn books and the Xhosa people sang in Xhosa, and when they came down the steps at one o'clock they were still singing, they formed groups and carried on singing. They couldn't stop singing. They strolled down the streets, still singing, walking slowly, forming new groups and starting afresh.

Ouma Hannie joined a group. She loved the singing, it brought a deep satisfaction. When they passed old Makone's house, she did not mind any more that Poppie had told oompie Pengi about the amagqira's dancing. She had made peace with the fact that oompie Pengi stayed away all night at Makone's house, that he came home drunk, that he left again in the early morning to drink the last dregs of the beer.

Once the witchdoctor people too, were church-going, ouma told Poppie without anger as they passed Makone's house. But their dreams destroyed them, and they were forced to leave the church. They were told in their dreams to become amagqira, to learn the amagqira's dances and songs.

Like kleinma Hessie when she left our church? asks Poppie. . .

My God, ma, shouted Pengi, in Lüderitzbucht sisi Mieta is wearing the skin of the black devil on her hat, and sisi Hessie is wearing the skin of the brown devil in Putsonderwater. . .

He had swept ouma's cups and saucers and plates on to the dung-smeared floor. They crashed into small pieces, and the table staggered after them. Oompie Pengi was drunk, but the crash brought him back to his senses. He was sitting at table and ouma was sitting up straight on her goatskins on the floor. Poppie and Plank and Hoedjie pulled the blankets over their heads, because they knew the rages of oompie Pengi when he was drunk.

But oompie Pengi was ashamed when he saw the broken cups and he said to ouma: I'll build the fire myself, a huge fire, a fire as big as the whole of hell, and then I'll call mama's children, the whole lot of them, I'll fetch sisi Martha and sisi Mieta and sisi Hessie and buti Sam. I'll walk right into the fire of hell and the others will follow me. But sisi Lena is mama's sweetest child, she can stay behind with mama.

5

Nearly every month ouma Hannie went by train to her eldest son, oompie Sam, to fetch food for the family. Oompie Sam worked on the railways and lived in the Koegerabie location. He lived without a woman, in a shack made of two sheets of corrugated iron set up against one another. The shack became very hot because the sun beat down on it all day long. Oompie Sam slept on a wooden stretcher and, when they visited, ouma and Poppie slept on the ground.

Sometimes oompie Sam's friends who worked on the railway sent word that a cow had been hit by a train, and that ouma could fetch some meat. Then Poppie stayed away from school and went with ouma. The train stopped in the veld at Koegerabie and ouma got down with difficulty because she was a great big fat woman. She delayed the train but at last she was down and she could stretch out her arms to take Poppie and her bag. The guard helped her to get down.

Usually the meat wasn't so fresh when they got there, but once a cow was hit while they were staying with oompie Sam and he helped with the skinning and brought home the hind quarter. As Poppie watched, the meat started jerking, like a chicken whose neck has been chopped off with an axe.

She screamed: ouma, the cow is still alive.

Ouma laid her hand on the meat and said: It's still warm, that's why it is kicking so.

Oompie Sam gave most of his railway-rations to ouma Hannie: Mealie meal, boer meal and monkey-nuts. He was small and skinny and did not eat much himself. He drank, but not much. Every few weeks he came to ouma's house, and had a few drinks with Pengi, but when Pengi started making trouble he'd walk away or go to bed, he'd never bother to fight.

Oompie Sam dressed well when he came to visit in Upington, he liked wearing a suit. Ouma thought: He's wife-hunting, but if he was, he kept it hidden from her.

Both the brothers were neat on their persons, they liked their clean white shirts and neatly pressed trousers. In those days they liked wearing white canvas tennis shoes, so Saturday afternoons after work they sat in the sun in the backyard, cleaning their shoes. They scrubbed them with soap and water till they were soaking wet, then smeared them with whiting and set them to dry. When they were stiff with whiteness they put them on, and went courting in the location.

Oompie Pengi was the one to make the beer. And when he was tippled and oompie Sam had left him and gone courting, he'd call Plank and his friends together and tell them to sing. Then he'd tap, he'd tap dance while they sang, he'd teach them to tap, sing along with them the whole night through and play his guitar: *Hitler kom van ver af, die boere skiet hom nerf-af, nader na die pale toe*, which was an Afrikaans song left over from the war, and which means Hitler comes from far away, the Boers are shooting him to Hell and back. They'd sing together all night long.

Or he'd wake up ouma Hannie and say: I'll show mama

how the medicine people dance, and he'd grab a kierie, and jerk his body this way and that and hit his knees together and throw his head back and pretend to be in a trance. He was very light of heart, oompie Pengi, and he'd mimic them to make ouma Hannie smile.

Your oompie Sam has forsaken me, he'd tell Plank. Come and dance with your oompie Pengi. But when Plank preferred strumming his guitar, when his fingers would not let go of the strings, he'd scream: Can't you hear me, you devil's child? Have you lost your ears, or are they stuck up your arse?

But ouma did not approve of the wild dancing in the witchdoctor way. She didn't like the swearing either. This is a Christian house, she'd say. It is God's house. I'll call the police. I'll call old Pieterse to come and lock you up.

Then oompie Pengi dropped his kierie. God, ma, if you call old Pieterse, I'll knock him down. You can go call a white man to lock me up, but no Damara baboon will lay hand to me.

Ouma Hannie said: Ag, Pengi, why are you such a worry to me? When will you find peace for your soul?

Oompie Sam started courting a girl of mixed blood from Soutpan who was visiting her sister in Basterhoek, and when she left for home he followed her to Soutpan.

Now, who would have thought it of buti Sam? asked oompie Pengi sadly. That bitch will be the end of him. She'll make him see his arse.

This was the time when Poppie's mama came from De Aar, where she was in service with white people, to have a rest in ouma's house. She told ouma that the father of her children was no more. He had died in the war.

Other people in the location said: But the war is long since past, and Machine Matati is pushing a new bicycle down the streets of Mafeking. But Lena didn't bother to listen to their stories.

He never looked after my children like a father should, she told ouma Hannie. I have no tears to weep for Machine Matati.

This was also the time when a letter came from kleinpa Ruben from Doringbaai, a fishing village on the west coast.

Dear mother, kleinpa Ruben wrote, it goes well with us, I hope it goes well with you. A body that has been stricken with illness is my wife's. A body that needs help is my wife's.

Kleinma Hessie had a hard life with kleinpa Ruben, Poppie says. The Bishop of the Ethiopians sent him from one place to another, and only at Calvinia was there a building for the church. In Doringbaai he built a corrugated iron church behind the barracks. In Nababeep the people lived in small round huts made of sacking. There were few converts and he couldn't be dependent on them, he had to work by day, at a garage in Calvinia, on the railways in De Aar or in the fish factory in Doringbaai, and at night he led the services.

At Doringbaai kleinma Hessie became ill.

At Doringbaai she could tell mama how hard her life had been.

Because ouma Hannie got a fright when she received the letter, she forgot her distress that Hessie had left the Methodist Church, she called Pengi and Sam and Lena to her and said: It is my wish that Lena goes to Hessie to look after her. And whatever will become of my little Mosie?

They had had no word of Mosie for a very long time.

Poppie must go with Lena, said ouma.

And so it came about that only Plank and Hoedjie were left with ouma and oompie Pengi.

Lena and Poppie went by train, via Hutchinson, to Calvinia where the railway ended, then by bus over the Cold Bokkeveld Mountains.

I was so scared when the bus drove over the high mountain, says Poppie. They told me: We have to cross the Cold Bokkeveld Mountains to reach Klawer near the sea. I looked through the window, it seemed so far to go down, it looked so dry and dead down there, I felt we would fall down the mountain. As the bus took the corners of the pass, it swayed from side to side and I thought the back end of the bus would never catch up with the front and if it didn't crash into the mountainside it would go over the edge. Where the road branched off the bus stopped and my mama and I clambered up the slope and sat behind a bush to relieve ourselves. The wind blew very cold against my buttocks, and my nose started running and my eyes watered.

When we reached Klawer, it was flat country and I was no longer scared.

The fish factory sent a lorry to fetch the people from Klawer and Lena and Poppie went along with the others. They sat on the back of the lorry with their suitcases and bedding that had been taken down from the roof of the bus. Their eyes watered, no longer from the mountain cold, but from the dust that rose in clouds from the dirt track on which they drove. They sat flat in the truck with their legs stretched out before them. Mama pulled Poppie away from the rim of the lorry and pressed her head deep into her lap to protect her from the dust. At times when the lorry went over a ridge her mother's body was lifted completely off the floor, to sink back again as the lorry steadied itself. The driver stuck his hand through the window and waved at them to reassure them, but the passengers screamed at him: Hoi, hoi, slower, man, do you want to kill us?

At Doringbaai a child stood waiting for them. Poppie did not know who it was, till mama told the people getting down from the lorry: That's my boy, that one over there.

And to Poppie she said: Ag now, don't you know your brother, that's Mosie, over there.

Then she recognised his face, but his body had changed, he was much taller than her. He carried their suitcases and mama hoisted the bedding on to her head. The road led up an incline and when they reached the top, she saw a stretch of water in front of her.

That's the sea, said Mosie.

Why are the people sitting in the water, she asked,

35

because she saw the rocks and the black sea-birds sitting on the rocks and she thought they were people.

He put down the cases and pointed. They're birds, man, not people.

But Poppie was too stupid to understand. She thought they were people till she saw them flying away in a flock.

Kleinpa and kleinma stayed in the factory barracks, rows of rooms built of corrugated iron. The factory bosses gave some families two rooms, others three.

Kleinma's bedroom wasn't the way Poppie remembered it from Putsonderwater. There was scarcely any furniture in it, the bed's mattress and springs rested on four wooden boxes and had gone slack so that it sagged to the middle and kleinma lay in a small heap in the middle of the bed underneath the grey blanket. Kleinma was thin and she seemed to have shrunk. She got out of bed when she saw her sister Lena, and in her nightdress, on her bare feet, the kopdoek awry, she came to her and flung her arms about her.

Ag, my little sister, she said, now I'll get well again.

Mosie boiled water on the Primus stove and made them some tea.

I've left school, he told Poppie. I'm looking after mama now. I gather wood and I cook the food and I sweep the house. Mosie called kleinma Hessie mama because he had lived with her so long. Going around with kleinpa Ruben to do mission work for the Ethiopian Church had spoiled his schooling. He hadn't been able to finish a single school year. Poppie already had more learning.

The factory manager sent for Lena when the fish catch increased. You can't sit at home, he said, we need you because we can't keep ahead.

I'm feeling better, said Hessie, I'll get up to make your midday meal, Poppie can walk with Mosie to take your food.

They walked over the sand dunes to get to the factory, a wooden building on the water's edge. Poppie wasn't scared till she got inside. Then she started crying, the wooden floor was old, it wobbled as she walked, and through the cracks between the floor-boards she saw the dark water moving, reaching at her, being sucked back again. She screamed at Mosie: Take me away from this place. The water will get me.

Mama brought fish from the factory and when Poppie saw Mosie eating the fish, she ate some too, because she had never seen fish before.

But Lena didn't get on well with her brother-in-law. When Hessie was well again, and when the people told her they paid more money at the fish factory at Lamberts Bay, she decided to leave.

I'll let Mosie stay with you, she told Hessie, if you put him back to school. In the afternoons he can help you, but he must get some learning too.

7

Poppie and her mama went from Doringbaai to Lamberts Bay in the factory boat. But Poppie was scared to get into the fishing smack waiting in the shallow water to ferry them to the boat. The fishermen shouted at them: Hurry up. Lena gave the suitcases Mosie had carried to the beach to the fishermen, the roll of bedding they passed along by hand. She tucked up her dress and waded in. When she was seated in the smack, she held out her hands to Poppie, but Poppie wouldn't move.

One of the fishermen picked her up under the armpits and carried her out. She kicked and beat her hands against his face and her body writhed against his, but when she saw the water splashing his legs she clung to him, arms and legs clasped around his body, she wouldn't let go even when the people in the smack tried to ease her in.

Mosie, she screamed, but the tears and water splashing her face dimmed her sight.

The waves caught the smack and lifted the prow and the little boat heaved and dipped and heaved and dipped. Poppie felt an illness as she had never felt before. She just said: Mama, and then Lena grabbed her and shoved her head over the side. The fishermen rowed to the bigger boat, eased the smack alongside, made it fast and told Lena: Step on the motor-car tyre hanging alongside. The sailors will grab your arms.

They pushed at her from behind, and others caught the tyre to keep it still, and others tried to ease the smack, and she stepped and reached out her arms.

Grab the woman, shouted the fishermen. They dragged her on board. They picked up Poppie and bodily handed her over.

On deck Lena crawled to her bundle of bedding, unfastened the blankets and drew them over her and Poppie. The fishermen brought buckets for their vomit and stood watching them and said: Now this is what you call being seasick, because Lena didn't know what was happening to them. A fisherman fetched his flask of coffee from the engine room to give Lena something hot to drink, but she could not get it down. With every dip of the boat her stomach rose in her throat.

At first they could still see the coast, then it was water wherever they turned their eyes, they lost direction and didn't know where they were being taken.

When they approached Lamberts Bay, the engine was cut and they drifted close to the jetty. Now Poppie was no longer afraid of the water rising and falling under the boards of the jetty, as she had been afraid in the factory of Doringbaai. Many people and children had come to watch the boat coming in. She moved her legs and stamped her feet on the jetty to get warm, and she felt: I'm better than the other children because I've come from far across the sea. I'm strong now.

The fisherman took her ma to the factory and she was promised work at once. They gave her two rooms in the barracks and the key. You can go now, they said, to get settled before you start work.

The wind was blowing hard and the sand was swept along the road in gusts and hurt their legs and got into their eyes and mouths. Poppie kept her eyes shut against the sand and clutched her mother's dress and stumbled along after her. She dragged the suitcase her mother had given her to carry. Lena carried the bedding on her head and the other suitcase in her hand. The place was empty of men, because the boats were out, but one of the women shoved a young boy forward and said: Can't you help the auntie carry her stuff?

The barracks were rooms built of corrugated iron, adjoining one another, set up in the sand with no separate gardens or backyards. The children crowded in the doorways to watch them pass. Lena pushed open the door to their room and they went inside. It was so dark that Poppie got scared and would not let go of her mother's skirt, but Lena said: The room is dirty and blackened by smoke. Don't worry, I'll whitewash it.

She put down the suitcases and bedding, undid the straps and sorted their things. She used an old rag to start cleaning up and wipe the windowsills free of sand.

Ask the auntie next door to lend us a broom.

She gave Poppie a small saucepan she had brought along and said: Get us some water. Poppie went to the outside tap and the children of the barracks gathered around her and said: We'll show you where to fetch wood. They took her over the sand dunes and she brought home her first load, carrying it on her head.

Then a neighbour brought them a fish: You can pay me later when you have started earning money.

After all the vomiting at sea Poppie was very hungry.

ELSA JOUBERT

Lena built a small fire behind the barracks room and they
fried the fish. Poppie licked the bones clean but she wished
for the bread she had eaten at kleinma's.

Later in the afternoon when the boats came in the men
returned from the harbour; some were drunk, some carried
bottles of wine and as they walked they took a pull at the
bottle. Lena watched them: This place is rough, she said to
Poppie, but you can see there's plenty of money around.

One of the children who helped her gather wood was the
same age as Poppie and she was called Katrina. She spoke
differently to the Basters at Upington, she slurred her r's
and said: Farrh away. The next day she took Poppie along
with her to the Roman Catholic school. You must go, said
Lena, any school is better than none.

Katrina had a light complexion and longish hair drawn
back tightly behind the ears and plaited with rags into two
stiff plaits. She walked with a loose gait, her knees jerking
and her backside quivering. Her dress which was too long
for her was tied up with a belt, and she wore two white
bangles on her arm. She didn't carry a slate to school, the
children didn't stand in a row as Poppie used to do, but went
inside the church house and dipped their fingers in a small
dish of water on the wall. Katrina showed Poppie how to
dip her finger and to touch the wetness to her shoulders, her
forehead and her stomach.

If you do it rrhong, you sin, Katrina told Poppie. She took
her by the hand and pulled her inside and said: Look what
I do, copy me, then you won't do sin.

Poppie watched her bob in front of the statue of the lady
set up on a table at the end of the room. Her face was like
a doll's face, with red spots on the cheeks, the white doek
on her head wasn't tied properly but the ends hung loosely
on her shoulders.

She's the Lorrhd's ma, said Katrina.

Mister Jacobs taught them, the bigger ones and the
smaller ones together in one room. Once a fortnight the
Father came from Vredendal to bring new exercise books
and new slate pencils and to listen to them reciting the Hail
Mary in Afrikaans. They all slurred their r's like Katrina:

Wees gegrroet, Marrhya vol genade, die Heerh is met u, geseën is u onderrh alle vrrhoue, geseën is die vrrhug van u liggaam, Jesus Heilige Marrhya, Moederrh van God. They liked to chant it while they played hopscotch games, balancing a pebble on their toes and jumping from square to square without dropping it.

They liked going to school because Mister Jacobs was a kind old man and was never angry at them.

Although they were church-goers, says Poppie — Catholic or Methodist or Anglican or Dutch Mission Church — the Xhosa people kept strictly to their own traditional Xhosa beliefs as well. And the most important of these beliefs is the abakwetha, or the man-making ritual.

I grew up with these customs. I took food to a young buti — when he was um-kwetha — he's now living here at Nyanga, but he was a child then. . . That was shortly after I had arrived at Lamberts Bay. I went with his little sister, Nosokolo. They lived in the rooms next door to us, her mother was a packer in the factory and her father a fisherman. Three of the boys went together to do abakwetha. They go into the bush to do the ritual, and that is why we call it going to the bush for short. A coloured man went along with them, he was called Dickman, but he was half coloured, half Xhosa, as we say of the halfblood or mixed people; his real name was Mzwandile, and another boy, Freddie, went along as well.

Young girl-children take them their food, this is our custom. We walked far into the bush, carrying the dishes of food on our heads, mealies or porridge or meat and bread, and sour milk in a pail. The first eight days after the ritual they may only eat red mealies, nothing else. On the eighth day a goat is slaughtered and after that they can eat all kinds of food. And every day we took them something different. When we reached the secret place in the bush we were not allowed to enter. We shouted to tell them we had come. Then the men looking after the boys and teaching them would come and fetch the food from us. We liked taking the food because we were always given some of it to eat.

We were really very ignorant, we never knew what they did to the boys in the bush, that they cut the foreskin to make men of them. We just knew it was abakwetha. The boys' heads were shaved and their faces smeared with white clay and they were led away from the location quite naked, with only their blankets covering them. We liked watching the older men dancing and mock-fighting with their kieries and singing all the time as they took the boys from their parents. Sometimes they really hit out at one another and we liked that. Lots of beer was made and the women danced and had a lot to say about it all.

And when the boys were brought home eventually, they had new blankets but only their eyes showed as the men crowded around them. It was great feasting when the boys came from the bush and we saw that all had survived.

Plank went to the bush from Lamberts Bay, after he and ouma had joined us there, and Hoedjie went from Cape Town, and Mosie went from George where kleinma Hessie was then staying. He always felt himself to be her child. And after Plank had been to the bush we who were younger no longer called him Plank, but buti Plank, to show respect. Buti not only means brother, it means someone older and more worthy than you.

Poppie and Nonsokolo reached the end of the track. Nonsokolo was carrying the dish of food on her head, Poppie had the pail of milk in her hand. They called out: Ma-kwedin! Ma-kwedin! Poppie shivered from cold; it was still very early, the sun had not yet risen. Ngqoziya! We hear you! came the answer from the bush. Ngqoziya! somebody was shouting, fiercely and cruelly. A man in a coat, kierie in his hand, appeared from amongst the bushes, he hit at the bushes with the kierie, clearing his way to them. He took the dish and the pail, and said: Wait here.

When he returned the empty dishes, they knew he had left them some food. They felt by the weight of the pail that some magou had been left as well. They started running along the track, making their way home. The sun had risen. They hid behind a rock and ate the food, chunks of bread dipped in the sour, runny porridge. They sucked the sour wetness off the bread, then dipped their hands in the pail, scooping up what was left, running their fingers along the sides of the pail and sucking up the sour magou.

Tonight my ma is cooking samp and meat, said Nonsokolo.

When we were children we ate wild figs and sour figs that are fleshy and dark brown, with pips, and other fruit growing wild in the veld, and bokhorings or goathorns that are wild runner beans clinging to the bushes.

We filled our pockets with the goathorns and munched as we walked.

We went to the beach and gathered shells from the rocks and filled our tins. Then we'd make fires along the beach and boil the shells. We liked watching the little bodies inside the shells cringing; they were alive still and as the heat reached them they shrank. We dug out their flesh with pins, and ate the black mussels and the flesh of round shells that crawl backwards like snails. Ag, but the flat kind of shell that clings to the rock surface, you have to be quick, touch him and he is clamped to the rock. We used knives to pry them loose, we'd watch and wait, and while they were still on the move we thrust in our knives.

We ate lots of crayfish. A child would come and say: They're working crayfish at the factory, then we'd rush from school straight to the factory, to eat the legs. They only had use for the tails and they threw away the shells, they made guano from the shells. So we fetched the shells and legs. Ag, we enjoyed it, we were never chased away for eating the shells and the legs.

9

Shortly after we went to live at Lamberts Bay, Poppie tells, mama started living with the stepfather. I couldn't stand

43

ELSA JOUBERT

him. His name is Hendrik Stuurman, but they called him
Hennie.

Mama had left Barrel's factory to go to work at Jaffet's
factory and shortly after she started work, he came to work
there too. He came from Nababeep in the north, in the
copper mountains. We heard there was a strike at Nababeep, a clash between the Rhodesians and the Xhosas, quite
a war, and he was one of the men who fled and came south
to find work. Quite a number came to Lamberts Bay. He was
born at Sweetwater near Lady Frere in the Ciskei, a real
Xhosa, with his little finger chopped off at the joint according to the tradition.

He taunted Poppie, and later Plank and Hoedjie, when
he was drunk: You grew up with the Hotnots — by them
he meant the coloured people — you don't know who you
really are, if you're Fingos or Xhosas. You're Fingos, he
would scream; the Fingos were of lower caste.

I never liked him, says Poppie. I called him oom. It
angered him. Then I called him oom Mbatane, because his
Xhosa name was Mbatane. Later on Plank called him buti,
by way of respect, and I called him that as well. We never
called him pa, not up to the present day.

He couldn't stand it when I spoke Afrikaans to my ma.
At that time I couldn't speak Xhosa at all, only Afrikaans.
I could understand Xhosa up to a point, but not speak it.

Later, when I was living in East London I dreamt that I
offered my hand to my stepfather. Now I pray to the Lord
that He will cleanse my heart from all ill-feeling towards
him. But he caused too much suffering to my ma. I still
can't offer him my hand. He never beat her, but he was
mean and jealous and false. Even when she fell ill he was
too mean to buy medicine for her, it was up to me and my
brothers to buy medicine or to give her money to see a
doctor.

The truck from the Doringbaai factory brought kleinma
Hessie and Mosie to Lamberts Bay, on their way to Upington to visit ouma Hannie.

She saw that Lena was heavy and that the man living with
her in the barracks room had no liking for Poppie, or Poppie

44

for him, and she said: If you give me money for the train
ticket I'll take Poppie back home with me.
Everywhere in the room stinking of tobacco and wine she
saw the man's belongings strewn about.
Shame on you, she said to Lena.
Lena wept.

10

Poppie and Mosie went with kleinma back to Upington.
They travelled by train. Mama gave them enough money to
buy cool drinks along the way and enough food to eat.
There was bread left over when they reached Upington and
Poppie stood at the chicken pen and called the chickens to
eat the crumbs that she strewed on the ground. Mosie
clambered on to the old wagon: I still remember the wagon,
he said.
Plank had left school and was working as a bricklayer. He
was fifteen years old. Poppie, sitting next to him at the fire,
watching him break the firewood with his hands, felt like
a stranger with Plank, thinking: Can these big rough hands
be my brother's?
Hoedjie works at the co-operation as a messenger boy,
ouma told them, but I am not happy about it, he should be
at school.
Hoedjie was thirteen years old and had only passed
standard three. This was as far as Poppie had learnt.
Oompie Pengi is drinking too much, said ouma to kleinma
Hessie. The devil is eating his heart.
Sisi Lena's children must get out of the house, he shouted,
it's my house, this. He talked wildly, waving his arms about.
I am selling this house. I want to get out of this location. You
must go, he yelled at them.

Ouma Hannie put on her black skirt and red overblouse and white bib and doek and took Poppie and Mosie to the Methodist Church. The new preacher was Mr Manda, a short little man with a wrinkled face. He took Poppie's hands in his and spoke to her in Afrikaans. He joked and laughed till his little eyes disappeared amongst the wrinkles. He took her to where the Sunday school class met in the corner and the children sat on their low benches.

Hasn't Poppie grown to be a big girl now, he said. But the children were strangers to her.

When your oompie Pengi was a child, he was a church-goer too, said ouma as they went home. When he cast away his church, the drink took hold of him. Kleinma Hessie sat at the table on a chair, but ouma sat on the floor and offered a prayer to the Lord. Oompie Pengi left his bedroom and joined them. But he was drunk and shouted: This is my home, this one. It is I who shall pray.

Oompie Pengi started praying, the words pouring from his mouth, but with the words came the swear words, the unholy thoughts from oompie Pengi's stomach not his heart, and ouma wanted to stop his prayers. So ouma started to sing a hymn, but he would not allow her hymn. Ouma prayed to the Lord while Pengi was praying: Ag Lord, don't listen to my child, she said. Close your ears to his words.

It was nearly dawn when Poppie, who had fallen asleep in ouma's bed, heard kleinma calling ouma: Ma, ma, the house is on fire.

Ouma tried to rise, she pushed her hand against the wall to support her body and give strength to her arms, because her legs were troubling her and had become weak. When she was up she could see sparks flying overhead, coming over into their room from Pengi's room, because the rooms had no ceilings.

Pengi's room, made of reed and plastered with clay, was burning.

And Pengi, sober now, had fled, but looking back as he ran, he saw the fire was spreading to the rest of the house and that people from the adjoining houses had come to fight the fire. His fear grew and now he was afraid to leave, so he turned back to hide under the wagon in the yard.

The next morning ouma Hannie called the police to take Pengi away.

He wept and begged ouma: Forgive me, mama. My mama.

It is too late to weep, Pengi, ouma said to him.

Ouma went to court when Pengi's case was heard and she watched him being led away to the cells, but he did not turn his head to look at her or at his sisi Hessie.

Ouma wouldn't leave the courtroom, she stayed sitting on the bench for a long while after all the others, even the policeman, had gone. She prayed to the Lord: Look after Pengi.

Then she left for Lamberts Bay with Hessie and Lena's children, and she never saw oompie Pengi again.

They travelled by train from Upington to De Aar and Hutchinson and from Calvinia by bus to Graafwater and from Graafwater to Lamberts Bay.

Mama was glad to see them, but she said: There's no room for you to stay with me and the man.

Don't let that bother you, sisi, said Plank. Plank was fifteen years old, a man now. I'm starting work on the boats. You watch, they'll give me my own house in the factory barracks, then ouma and Hoedjie and Mosie and Poppie can live with me.

The coloured people's location was called the Gebou or Building, but in the factory barracks the Xhosa people and the coloured people lived together.

Let it be so, said ouma.

She sent Hoedjie and Mosie to the Catholic school.

For Poppie there was no more schooling because she had to look after mama's new baby who had been born while they were away. Mama went to work in the factory and brought the child to Poppie: Your ouma's legs are plaguing her, she's too old to look after a young red baby.

The child's name was Veleli, but they called him Pieta, and after Pieta, Katie was born, and after Katie Eric, whom

47

ELSA JOUBERT

they called Jakkalsie, or Jakkie, which means little jackal.
Poppie loved him as if he was her own baby.

From her ninth year Poppie took care of the children
mama had by buti Mbatane, but she never stopped reading.
She read all Mosie's schoolbooks, and he taught her the
songs he learned at school. She sang them as she went about
her work, carrying a child on her back.

I wasted my time at the Catholic school, Mosie says later.
I couldn't get ahead, it was just play school. Then ouma sent
us to the Dutch Reformed Mission school where the
coloured children went. They put me back to Sub B, which
is a baby class. But I was too clever for Sub B, so they pushed
me on to Standard One, and I carried on till I reached
Standard Five. Hoedjie only went as far as Standard Four.

And we just had to get *Die Jongspan*, Poppie says. It was
a children's newspaper; we bought it every week at the
shop. It was written in Afrikaans which was our language,
ja. Hoedjie and Mosie and I read about the Pokkels, the
twins that got up to so much mischief, and Tarzan and the
stories of Jakkals en Wolf, which are stories of the Fox and
the Wolf. There was a puzzle page and we took a pencil and
joined up little dots according to numbers, and then could
see the picture of a dog or a lion or an elephant taking shape.
Ag, we liked that so much.

I looked after mama's children until I was thirteen,
because at thirteen the factory took children to work as
cleaners.

Two

Lamberts Bay

11

There were two kinds of jobs in the fish factory, says Poppie. Some were cleaners, others packers. The cleaners gutted the fish, scraped them, cut off the fins, head and tail and threw them into wire trays for the men to take away. The men washed them in cement dams filled with water, and threw them on to the packers' tables. The packers put the fish into tins, a machine fixed the lids on, and then the tins were thrown into a big sieve pot on wheels ready for the steamer. The steamer could take four of the big iron trolley sieve pots at a time.

At what time we started work? Now, that was just when the boats came in. The boats put out from about five o'clock or sunset. If the fish was very far out, they left earlier, at three in the afternoon. The quicker they got to the fish, the quicker they turned back and the sooner the factory whistle was blown. Even at three o'clock in the morning. Even at one o'clock. And then we had to get up and go. There were no electric lights in the location, we walked in the dark. When we were still living nearby in the barracks they called Pampoengat, it wasn't so bad, but when they put us out of the barracks, that is when they moved out the Xhosa people, it was a long way to walk. Sometimes, when the fish was very plentiful, the whistle went at one o'clock, and we only got home eleven the next night, we worked without stopping from morning to night to morning again; no we didn't stop at all.

There were two factories, old Mr Barrel's factory — our people called him old Umbombo because of his big nose, our people have the way of giving nicknames — and Mr Jaffet's factory way beyond Malkop Bay. Him we called ou

51

Mehlomane, which means four eyes, because he wore glasses. I worked as a cleaner at Barrel's factory. We knew the difference between the two whistles, we knew whose whistle had gone. Mr Jaffet's people knew when they had to start work and the others as well.

You got paid according to your tray. You had a ticket pinned to the shoulder of your overall and you got a punch for every tray you filled. Those days it was one shilling a tray, and you could make up to two pounds a day in full season. But the packers earned the most, more than fourteen pounds a week.

We liked working at night, though we got so tired, that when the whistle blew the second night as well, we certainly did not feel like going to work again. But there was no way out of it. I remember one time when everybody got really tired. It was the third day and there was no end to the fish. The boats were so full you could see the heaps showing. The fish got mushy in the boats; there was so much, we couldn't keep ahead at the factory. They weren't so clever with the cold storage yet. The foreman in the factory, old Marinus, saw the people were staying at home on the third and fourth day and he drove his lorry to the location to round us all up. Ag, but it was a fine time, because the shops were waiting and they knew people would have lots of money to spend. Things were cheap then and the money plentiful. We ate very well when the fish was in full season.

At that time my best friends were Meisie and Ounooi and Katrina who later had a child by buti Plank but he didn't pay damage money for the child because she wasn't a Xhosa. She was a coloured girl. Meisie was also a coloured girl who came from Port Nolloth. We all worked at the factory.

Lunchtimes we walked to the café to buy grapes or a peach or a banana or a bottle of cool drink to have with the bread we had brought from home. The big boys made up to us when we took shelter on the shop's stoep against the wind, but we paid no attention to them. As we walked back to the factory we would put our arms round each other's waists, lean back against the wind, and break into a little trot, because the wind pushed us along. But by three

o'clock, the wind used to die down and the afternoons were
quiet. At sunset there never was wind.

12

Sunday afternoons when our housework was done, we
went to the beach. To the sandy beach or to Malkop Bay
where we liked to play in the water between the rocks.
Mosie dived into the sea from the high rocks and the boys
caught small fishes with hook and line.

Mama wouldn't let us take the little ones to the beach for
fear of the sea. But we could take them to the veld, Pieta and
Katie and Jakkie. Jakkie was a lively child and Hoedjie's
friends especially liked him and took him everywhere with
them. He looked like a little girl with a stocky little body and
a round face. His hair was longish, more like a Baster child's
hair than a Xhosa.

Hoedjie left school and became a waiter at the hotel. He
wore a white cap and white jacket which he washed and
starched himself, and black trousers and white shirt and a
small black bow-tie. He was a quiet boy but the girls liked
him a lot. Especially the coloured girls even though he had
a very dark complexion. He had oompie Pengi's high nose
and his blackness.

Buti Plank's work on the boats was heavy. It was dangerous. The weather was treacherous at Lamberts Bay. One day
it rained, the next day a terrible wind. The east wind came
overland and when it blew you couldn't see a thing in front
of your eyes for the dust. And if it wasn't wind or rain it was
the mist, and the boats could not put out and lay waiting
for the mist to lift. Then everything came to a standstill.

But ag, it was so sad when the sea got rough and the boats
were still out and we gathered to watch the boats struggling

back to the harbour. It was so sad, standing on the break-water, not being able to help. It was rough sea at the breakwater, many boats sank and the people were drowned.

When the weather was really bad, the foreman gave us off, then we gathered and watched all the time. We would count the waves and after the sixth wave, when the sea quietens down, a boat would try to get through. When they managed it, we who were standing on the breakwater, clapped our hands and shouted.

Meisie and Ounooi and Katrina and I liked to go shopping.

The first shop from our location on the way to town was de Waal's shop and butchery and further along was old Swarthoed's. He was an old man with many children, but we only knew baas Hennie and Miss Baby. We liked his shop, we bought milk from the old missus and fresh bread which she baked. But my ma liked old Heunis's shop as well.

On Saturdays the fruit lorries came to the location. Tractors, lorries, wagons, anything on wheels brought water melons and sour milk and buttermilk and fruit from the farms.

Old Attie brought bundles of wood on his tractor, figtree wood that my ma was very partial to and bought from him for a shilling a bundle. All the white people came from the farms to sell their goods. Every Saturday the location was packed. Old Sarel's stuff was the best, but expensive. He had the best plums and peaches. Old Missus Maria with her big bonnet sold milk and buttermilk and sour milk in drums. She was very fond of us. When we were moved from the barracks they followed us to the location to sell their goods.

Ja, it was a fine place when the fish was in season and money was plentiful. When the merry-go-round came to the town we rode on the swings and the little horses. We could buy a ride for a sixpence. I only liked the swings. I didn't like the big wheel which took you through the air upside down. And when the season was finished, well, the fine time was over.

The friend I liked best was Meisie. She was tall and thin

and very pretty with a light complexion and blue eyes and long black hair. She looked quite different from her mother, auntie Lena, who was a Bushman woman with a big bum and a short body and yellow skin. Meisie's father was a white man who lived in Port Nolloth and sent word to her when he came to Lamberts Bay. Then he stayed in the Gebou location in another auntie's house, auntie Poenas. But he didn't sleep in her house, he slept outside in his motor car.

When he sent word to her, she asked me: Come along with me, Poppie, I'm scared. He was sitting in an old-fashioned black Ford motor car, and she got in beside him and they sat talking. I was scared of the white oom too, but after a time Meisie didn't mind him. The people said it was of longing for Meisie that the white oom came to Lamberts Bay.

Xhosa men were fond of Meisie. In the shop they called to her: Mé-si. But auntie Lena was very strict with her and told her: You must never marry a Xhosa man because they always let you down. Auntie Lena had been living with Uncle James, a Xhosa man, in the Pampoengat location, but he left her and married a Xhosa girl in Cape Town.

The coloured girls liked Xhosa men, but Xhosa girls never went with coloured men, it was against our belief.

Ouma Hannie was strict with Poppie. She taught her to respect the traditions. Poppie walked along the beach with her friends. She dragged her feet through the shallow water, holding her dress bunched up between her legs. It was quiet down at the sea, the beach deserted. But Poppie was keeping an eye on the setting sun, watching the sunlight reflected on the water. She must be home before sunset. That was the custom of her people. Katrina and Meisie knew that it was so.

If there is a daughter in the house, Poppie told them, an old woman cannot light the lamps. This is our custom. That's why a Xhosa girl cannot stay away till sunset. She lights a lamp for every room, every day of the week, and she cooks the food. Ouma tells her what to cook and she

55

cooks it. My brothers have nothing to do with the house-work, it's against our custom for the men to work with the food. Ouma is strict, too, about church-going. She sent to Upington for her removal papers. Sundays we put every-thing aside and go to the Methodist Church which is held in the barracks. This is what ouma taught us. It is our duty to go.

Before ouma died, I was enrolled as a prayer meeting girl and clothed. I wore a white blouse and a black skirt with a black beret, black shoes and stockings and a red bib.

13

Ouma walked with great difficulty and had stopped visiting her friends or going to the shop. She sat in the sun with her darning, and as it grew hot, moved to the shade. A friend from Calvinia sat with her, they talked of Damara people they knew, and Griquas.

Ouma had trouble with her legs, says Poppie. Tiny little water blisters appeared on her skin, old wounds from her varicose veins troubled her. The doctor gave her pills and told her to swallow them with lots of water. Ouma com-plained: Now for what must I drink so much water.

Ouma is longing for oompie Pengi. She says: Hoedjie looks like Pengi, but Plank takes after him. Plank sings the way Pengi used to sing, he plays his guitar like his oompie. He has made lots of money on the boats but he still plays his oompie's syrup-tin guitar.

He has also started drinking, like his oompie Pengi. He brought liquor back into our house, says Poppie. It was the way of the fishermen to drink, having so much time on their hands, sitting around doing nothing, so they drink.

Buti Plank had plenty of money and he moved them out of the barracks house and built a house close by of corrugated iron, next to auntie Lena's house. Poppie liked living next to Meisie. In the evenings Poppie and Hoedjie and Mosie played card games with Meisie, catcards and snap. Buti Plank did not join them. Ag, stick your cards up your arse, he'd say, when he came home drunk.

Friday nights buti Plank used to go out, he went down the street listening for the sound of guitar or gramophone and people dancing. He had many friends, and they opened their doors to him.

Come and join us, Plank, the coloured girls called as he passed by. They were drinking too. Their bodies moved beneath their tightly fitting dresses. They took a pull at the bottle, their bodies were scented and their brown legs shiny with oil. It was mostly because of girls that Plank got into fights when he was drunk. Mosie and Poppie were the only ones that could calm him down.

We were sitting at auntie Lena's place, says Poppie, playing cards, then they called to us: God Almighty, old Plank has started a fight again, they said. Then we dropped the cards and ran to where we heard the noise and the shouting. Come, buti, we would say, and we'd take him by the arm. When we were with him the others were no longer scared, they'd help us lead him to the street.

Go call old Zulu, they'd say. Old Zulu was a Nyasaman who worked on the same boat as Plank and who also had a way with him.

Look, brother, look, your little sister has come to fetch you home, he would say.

When he was really in a bad way, and his eyes cleared and he saw that he had been brought home, it used to come all over him again, and he'd struggle to free himself.

Go to Hell, crawl up your bloody arses, he'd scream at Poppie and Mosie.

But all the fighting exhausted him and he'd lie down on his bed.

Bring the straps, said Hoedjie. We'll strap him down till he falls asleep.

Don't strap me down, pleaded buti Plank, but he was too weak to stop them.

Don't strap him down, Hoedjie, pleaded Poppie and Mosie. We'll guard him, we won't go to sleep, we'll sit beside him all night long.

Ouma started talking to him: Come now, you must sleep. You must stop making this noise.

Soon he would be snoring.

That's what started Hoedjie and myself going out at night, says Mosie. We fooled ouma. We'd say: We are going to the bioscope, then we'd start looking for Plank. The boys knew us. When they saw us coming, they didn't touch Plank. They'd tell us, don't worry, he's safe.

Then ouma would ask us: Where's Maplank, and we'd tell her: At Shakana's place.

Is he wet? ouma would ask, which means drunk. No ouma, we'd say, not wet nor warm, but perhaps just a little bit so. But ouma kept asking: Has he got a wet tooth, which means is he drinking a lot, and we couldn't lie to her any longer: Yes ouma, he has.

Buti Mbatane, the stepfather, gave the advice to strap him down when he was drunk, and buti Plank never forgave him for it.

When he wasn't drinking, he was very gentle, says Mosie. But drunk nothing could hold him. He smashed everything up, he had a fire inside him. Once when he was fighting, the other man fetched a kierie. Buti Plank took it from him and broke it with his hands: Am I a snake that you have to hit at me with a stick? he asked him. I am not a snake. The other man couldn't do anything. Buti Plank hit with his fists, he didn't carry knife nor kierie.

It's because of your fighting, ouma said to Plank when he was sober, that I'm being thrown out like I'm a piece of dirt.

It isn't because of buti Plank, cried Poppie. She was sad that she must leave auntie Lena and Meisie and Katrina. But it was not because of buti Plank's drinking.

It's because of your drunkenness and your fighting with the coloured whores, screamed ouma.

It isn't because of him, cried Poppie. Why are mama and buti Mbatane also being sent away? And why can auntie Girly and oom Kolie, who are drunk all the time, stay behind?

We had to leave the barracks place, tells Poppie, they gave us ground outside the town. They built us something like a squatters' camp and we had to go and live there. Only the coloured people could stay behind in the barracks, the Xhosas had to go and live separately. It was a new thing that the municipality started. It was when they wanted to separate us from the coloured people and let us live apart.

I'll build you a hell of a house, my little sister, buti Plank told Poppie. He bought new sheets of corrugated iron at the shop, and wooden posts to take along to the new quarters. Ouma took some money from underneath her church clothes in the wooden box and gave it to Plank to help buy the posts and the corrugated iron.

She resigned herself to moving because the Methodist church which was nothing but a room in the iron barracks would also be taken down and a new asbestos church would be built in the new location.

I'll hire a lorry to move ouma to the new house, said Plank.

They were given a plot next to Lena's and that made ouma feel better. Perhaps your oompie Pengi can come and stay with us too, she told them.

14

But before she could let oompie Pengi know, and before their house was taken down for the move, ouma Hannie died.

She became ill and lay down on her goatskins on the floor and did not get up again.

It is too much for Poppie, said Lena, to work in the factory and to look after her brothers and nurse her grandma. She's not even fifteen years old.

So Lena left her job at the factory and came to stay with her ma. For four weeks, while the poison from the sore place on ouma's leg spread through her body, Lena looked after her, and then ouma's mind started wandering. She talked about Pengi and Martha and Mieta and Sam and Hessie. Lena sent Hessie a message with the factory lorry to Doringbaai and Hessie came to Lamberts Bay to help look after ouma.

Ouma was delirious. I've lost the button of my red church blouse, she was moaning, nobody will sew a button on for me. She lay with her eyes closed and her lower jaw trembled like someone wanting to cry. She lifted her arm from underneath the blankets and stretched out to them. Her hand trembling, she was pointing at the chest in which she kept her belongings, in which her church clothes lay neatly folded. My button has gone, she moaned, I have lost it. You must tell the juffrou to bring me a button from Cape Town.

We'll tell her, ouma, said Hessie, she'll bring you a button.

She was dreaming and her tongue moved in her mouth as if searching for moisture. Her arms gripped Lena and Hessie and she tried to raise herself. I see a high tree, she was saying, a tree without end, it is growing higher and higher to Heaven. The tree is bending down towards me, the branches are reaching down to me and they say: Your time is not long now.

Her hands clung to Lena and Hessie. Although her body was emaciated, the grip in the hands was strong.

They are telling me to tell you — and those standing round her bed thought ouma was speaking of the angels — they are telling me I must tell Martha: A God-fearing woman does not chew tobacco.

Sing to me. Sing, Guide me, O Thou great Jehovah, she begged when she had sunk back on to her goatskins. Her mouth was trembling, and her voice was so soft they had to bend over to hear what she was saying.

They sang to her. Plank and Hoedjie and Mosie and Poppie and Hessie and Lena and Lena's young children and the neighbours who had joined them and the woman from Calvinia and her sisters of the church.

Three days later she died.

But I am still going to build our house, said buti Plank after the funeral. I am not moving in with sisi and her man. Poppie can look after us, me and Hoedjie and Mosie.

Mama gave in to them, because Plank's plot was right next to hers and she could keep an eye on Poppie.

We don't live together under one roof in peace, Plank said. My ma's man is, how shall I put it? our opposition. He is against us and we are against him.

15

Buti Plank was working on the trawlers and sometimes he stayed away for as long as three months. He worked the stretch to Lüderitzbucht and back, and there he found the girl he wanted to marry. He went with other trawlermen to her father's house because her father was also a fisherman; there were four sisters, but he liked the middle one.

When she got pregnant he came back to mama. Where are my father's people? I must send them to talk to the girl's family. I want to marry her.

At Lüderitzbucht was a man who carried the clan name Mbele. He had been at the wedding of mama and Machine Matati.

Go and see him, said mama to Plank. He'll be your spokesman.

So it came about that Plank paid his damage money and

his lobola at the same time, and married the girl and brought her to Lamberts Bay. Her name was Eugenia and she belonged to the Catholic Church. Mama gave her the in-law name of Nonkosi.

But mama was not satisfied with Nonkosi. She's too lazy, mama said, she lolls around all day. Mama watched from her house next door.

My God, Nonkosi, you're no fucking good, move your arse, shouted Plank when he came in from work and the food was not ready. Nonkosi, if I'd known what a fucking no-good you are, I wouldn't have married you, I would have married your mother or your sister.

But Nonkosi wasn't angry at him, she just laughed. When he wanted to hit her, she moved out of his way.

Poppie and Hoedjie and Mosie were fond of her. She was a friendly girl and she talked to us and the house wasn't quiet and empty any more when we came home.

And we didn't go to sleep — we'd stay awake if we saw that buti Plank had drunk too much wine. Friday evenings we looked after Nonkosi. Hoedjie and Mosie and I slept in the front room, and buti Plank and Nonkosi in the back room, and we kept awake till we were sure that buti Plank was asleep. If Nonkosi gave a single cry, we were there to help her. Then we would stop buti Plank from hitting her. So he never got a chance really to hit her. If we stopped him, he listened to us. He was always very gentle with us.

A white nurse came to help her and the child was born in the house. Buti Plank was drunk but she didn't mind so very much. Not long after the child was born she went back to her people in Lüderitzbucht. But she never told them about the hitting. Roman Catholic people don't get on with Methodists, that was all she said.

We never saw Nonkosi or the child again, says Poppie.

16

You must give some thought to getting married, Poppie, Nonkosi had said. Poppie was past her fifteenth year and fully developed.

Ag, it's just the old men that come courting Poppie, said kleinma Hessie. Life on the road with kleinpa Ruben had been too much for Hessie; she had joined her family in Lamberts Bay to work in the fish factory.

Poppie pulls up her nose at her boy friends, said Mama.

Does mama want me to say yes to these old men who ask for me? asked Poppie.

Mama did not see eye to eye with Poppie about her suitors.

One morning early I'd gone to gather cow-dung near the white people's kraals, to smear our floors. As I was picking up the dung — it was still quite dark — I heard someone greet me: Molo, which means, Morning.

I got a fright and, looking up, saw it was an old man in a long overcoat. They called him Mahamba ngenyawo which means someone who goes barefoot. He asked me: How is it going with you, and I answered: It goes well.

He said: Poppie, I have come here to talk with you, because I want to ask your parents to marry you.

He was an ugly old man, with an ugly long face, a pitch-black old man, a Zionist with bands of wool round his neck and round his foot. I looked him up and down. But I said nothing and went on gathering the dung.

He said: Don't you hear what I am saying to you?

Then I said: What is oom saying to me?

He said: I want to come and ask for you, to marry you.

I got cross, but I didn't want to show him that I was cross, as old men have a way of just grabbing you. I took my tin and put it on my head and went home. When I got home, I told my ma nothing, but I went to Meisie and told her the whole story. We laughed so much. Afterwards the old man sent people to my people to ask for my hand.

But my people said: We have no child in the house. When they say that it means that they don't accept him.

Later on we were very naughty. Meisie and the other girls and I started laughing and teasing the old man whenever we saw him on the streets.

Then my ma scolded Meisie and me. You must stop it now, he is a grown-up person, and he tells me he doesn't know what he did wrong to come and ask for your hand. It's no joking matter.

After that it was another old man. Old Bey. This old Bey had been staying with another auntie whose name was Nongono. She already had grown-up children and I was much younger than them. But he left the auntie and came to ask to marry me.

My ma had sent me to the shop one day. I walked by myself — I don't know where Meisie was that day. I was walking along the road and this old uncle comes along and he says: Molo, Poppie, and I say: Molo. He asks: How are you, and I say: Fine, thank you. But he doesn't stop and he says: I have come to talk to you, I want to ask your people to marry you. I looked him up and down, at his cheeks. He was of the Baca tribe that mark their boys' cheeks with cuts while they are still very young. I looked at his cheeks and I said nothing and walked on.

The old man sent kinsmen to my ma's kinsmen to ask for me. They promised him that he could have me, but I was fed up. I talked to my kleinma Hessie and complained: I don't want that old man. He is too ugly, with those marks on his cheeks. He's too old for me.

Kleinma took me away for a holiday to Upington.

It was in December and she had something up her sleeve, because they were all set on getting me married.

She knew a young man who came from Boegoeberg, a Mister Malgas. Before we left, she had written to this young man's people to arrange a meeting. She told me about it on the train. He's such a good young man, she said, and a church-goer and a good worker.

In Upington she pointed him out to me when we were

walking in the street, but I didn't like him at all. I wouldn't answer when he spoke to me.

Kleinma was angry at me. You have no manners, she said.

I don't care, I said. I thought kleinma helped me to get out of marrying the old man at Lamberts Bay, but now she wanted to marry me off to another man I didn't like either. We stayed in Upington until February and then we came back to Lamberts Bay. There it came about that I met the man I married.

17

At first I really didn't like him much, says Poppie, because he came from Herschel in the Ciskei and I wasn't used to the people who came from the land, as we said. His oldest brother, Witbooi, lived close to us with his wife Muriel, and he came from Herschel to visit his brother. He got a job at the factory as boilerman.

I saw him in the factory, but I never spoke to him.

Come walk with me to buti Witbooi's house, Poppie, said Nikiwe. She came from Herschel too, and worked next to me in the factory.

His younger brother is visiting him, said Nikiwe. Ulitye is his Xhosa name, but they call him Stone, and the coloured people say ou Klip which is Afrikaans for Stone.

I don't feel like it, I said. I'm not used to the people that come from the land.

But on Sunday after church Nikiwe and I were walking together and they followed us; she started talking to them and joked with me. At first I didn't take any notice of him, but then he started writing me notes. He gave them to his brother's girl child to give to me, on the sly. I was then sixteen years old.

Dear Poppie, Ndiyaphila. It goes well with me. I hope it

goes well with you too. I have had my eye on you for a long time. I ask you nicely, please answer this letter. Ndiyathanda. From Stone.

I didn't answer his letter. Nikiwe came to plead with me. Please, won't you send a word to Stone? Won't you come to the beach with us this afternoon?

So we went walking along the sea. The butis would wait at the corner of the road, and follow the girls, but when we got to the beach every boy walked with his girl. Then we came back in the late afternoon before sunset, before it was time to light the lamps. Ag, we only held hands, and we were very careful of our parents. We didn't let our parents get to know about the boy friend, we kept it secret. If they were to find out, we'd be given a hiding. I wrote my notes at bedtime and sent them to him with my little stepsister. If later the children told tales about you, you denied everything they said.

We grew used to one another.

He wrote to me: Dear darling, it goes well with me, I hope it goes well with you too. Why didn't you meet me yesterday? I waited at the roadside till six o'clock, from half past two. I waited and waited and now I am cross with you. Will you come Sunday next week? Stone.

Then I wrote back to him: Dear buti Stone, it goes well with me, I hope it goes well with you. I couldn't come to meet you because of the wind, then we had visitors after church and I had to work till late afternoon, there was no chance to get away, ngothando, with love from Poppie.

His clan name was Mqwati and he spoke real Xhosa. He couldn't speak Afrikaans because he grew up in the Ciskei and worked on contract on the sugar plantations in Natal and then went to that place where they dig for lime, it's called Taungs, and at Prieska he worked on the asbestos mines, but there they spoke Fanagalo, which is a mixture of all the languages. From talking to him my Xhosa got much better. And he learned to speak Afrikaans at Lamberts Bay.

He was quite short, only slightly taller than I, with a trim little body, short hair like mine and a light complexion, lighter than mine. He was a neat man, and dressed smartly.

Those days men liked to wear grey flannel trousers and striped double breasted suits. On Sundays he always wore a suit.

He was quiet by nature and not as lively as the other boys. We grew very fond of each other. As we were walking on the beach he would say: I want to marry you, but then I laughed at him, because I didn't think of marrying at all yet. When we were together and he kept talking of marrying me I wouldn't listen to him. I was still very childish. Then he would become cross with me. I was only sixteen, he was twenty-four.

One morning Meisie and I and my two brothers were standing in front of our house, singing. It was early Sunday morning. We stood outside combing our hair before going to church, combing and singing. Meisie knew all our Xhosa hymns. We stood at our front door and I could see his buti Witbooi and two other men coming down the road towards our house. Meisie and I got a fright and ran inside because we knew at once what these strange men were coming for.

They stood outside, waiting to speak to someone. Only Mosie was there and he couldn't speak Xhosa, but he could follow it. They asked him: Where are the grown-ups?

The grown-ups are in that house, he said, pointing to mama's house.

Go and call them.

He called: Sisi!

When my ma came outside she had a fright too, because she didn't expect to see these strangers.

But come inside, she said, and took them to her front room.

I don't know what they talked, because I wasn't there. I made tea and served them, it was early, about nine o'clock that morning. I became very cross, because there was nobody I could talk to. Meisie wasn't on my side at all, she knew I didn't want this thing to come about.

Then my ma called me inside and kleinma Hessie asked me: Do you know this man, this Stone of whom they are speaking?

I don't know him, I said.

You are lying to me, you know him, said my mother.

But I kept on saying I don't know him. I was angry and they were angry as well. They said: How's it now, you don't know the man and we see you walking together; every day when you go to the shops he joins up with you.

I went outside and I wept because they said: You are going to marry this man. You wouldn't have the other one, now you are going to take this one.

I don't want the man.

You're going to show us, you're getting married to the man, this walking out thing is something of the past now.

It was a very troubled time because I didn't even dream that I was going to marry him, I thought it was just a game and then he was serious. I didn't think he'd send kinsmen to ask for me, because we never talked it out. If a man likes you, he sends his kinsmen, he doesn't consider whether you want him or not, he sends them to ask for you. Those days we were very stupid.

Then my mother sent for my father's people of the clan name Mbele, who also lived in Lamberts Bay, because so it is in the Xhosa custom: if your son goes to the bush, you send for his father's kinsmen, and if your daughter gets married, even if your mother is living with another man, she must send for her own father's kinsmen.

You must come back later, my ma said to the strange men. First I must send word to the child's kinsmen.

Then they had to talk out the lobola business. Two men from my father's side came, and the stepfather was present, but he had to keep quiet, he could only listen. They came back again on a Sunday to my ma's house.

Everybody, also Meisie and Katrina and Nikiwe, was very glad that the man sent to ask for me to get married. So I didn't know how to get out of it, he was my first boy friend, I was still very childish.

He paid more than a hundred pounds for me. He worked and saved up and his elder brothers helped him. If a family is of one mind on something, they help each other.

He didn't pay everything at once, he would bring twenty pounds at one time, then thirty, till he had paid all that was demanded by the kinsmen, only then could he get married.

We didn't really know the people from Kaffirland, Mosie explains, but we got used to them. Because when we didn't know their Xhosa names, we gave them Afrikaans nicknames. Stone's friend's cheeks were marked in the tribal way with long downward scars, so we called him Snoek, which is a barracuda fish. We said: The snoek bit him in the face. The straight tall one we called Stokkiestyf, which means something like stiff as a yardstick, and a very black one we called Metjiesbek which means match-mouth. Stone we called Doodgooi, because of his thick pair of lips. Doodgooi means heavy and lumpy. At first we were dissatisfied that our little sister should marry a man from Kaffirland. We had heard of the hardships there, but when they became fond of one another, we couldn't stand in their way. We didn't know the place where he came from, we had only heard about this place called Kaffirland.

18

Stone took a year to pay off the lobola.

Sunday afternoons they walked to the sea and sat on the rocks and watched the waves break. He was very quiet as they sat watching the waves, but she was content, she brought him the shells and pretty things from the pools. They walked to the café at Malkop Bay and bought ice creams. Poppie gave her mama all the money she earned at the factory, but now she asked to keep some for herself and bought new clothes. Those days we wore flared skirts and check dresses, it was the New Look. And we always liked to plait our hair and to walk bareheaded.

Lena started buying Poppie's trousseau: clothes, pots,

kitchenware, blankets, sheets. The lobola money paid in instalments didn't cover her expenses. Poppie's earnings were added and her brothers gave her money as well. Mama badly wanted to buy Poppie a kitchen dresser and a table for a wedding present. It was customary for the husband to buy the bed.

Stone brought her a signet ring and the engagement was celebrated. Lena slaughtered a sheep and served ginger beer and cake and tea to the visitors. Shortly afterwards the signet ring broke.

Lena bought a second-hand long white wedding dress and a veil from a white woman in town for ten pounds. She went by weekend bus to Graafwater and from there by train to Cape Town to buy blue voile in a shop in Salt River for the second dress. A coloured woman in the Gebou location made the dress, a long dress like the wedding dress with a blue doek coming to a point in the neck.

Four months after the engagement they were married. It was a Wednesday to allow the minister to come from Cape Town, because at that time their church had no regular minister. The wedding lasted two days and the people stayed away from work to come to the feast.

First we had the business of the choirs, says Poppie. The man's kinsmen sing in the church and then the girl's kinsmen. The day when the banns are called the choirs start practising, three weeks before the wedding. On the wedding day, when the bridegroom steps up to sign his name, his choir starts singing. And when I step up to sign, my choir sings. And they sing a special hymn when the minister signs. After the church service the choirs sing and dance at the church door and everyone claps hands and dances, and they won't allow the bride to get into a car. Unfortunately on my wedding day it started to rain, so there had to be a car for the white dress.

Buti Plank was Poppie's bestman and Nofgali, a Xhosa girl, was her chief bridesmaid. There were two small girls with long lace dresses walking behind her. Stone also had a bestman and bridesmaid.

The first day the wedding feast was held at Lena's house.

70

The people walked there in the rain. They stood in groups outside the house under their umbrellas. Lena had slaughtered an ox and it was roasted outside. Beer and brandy and bread and porridge were served with the meat. Stone and Poppie sat on chairs in Lena's sitting room, together with the bridesmaids and bestmen, and the guests passed in and out of the house the whole day long. Later on the sun came out and the umbrellas were put away, but when it started raining again later that evening nobody minded because they had been warmed by the beer and brandy.

When you are wearing the white dress, they are very strict with you, says Poppie. You may not look around you or laugh. No, you may only look down, you may not talk, you must remain silent. You mustn't look sullen or cross, you must have a pleasant expression on your face. The man sits with you and if he is a smoker, he may once in a while go outside to smoke. But he too must stay silent. The bridesmaids may talk and you may answer softly if they ask you something.

The first night after the wedding Stone and his people went back to their home. Poppie slept in buti Plank's house and mama and kleinma Hessie stayed with her. The second day they dressed her once more in her white clothes, they combed her hair and prepared her as they had done the first day. Through the window she could see the people coming down the street. They were dancing and beating drums. They were bringing Stone to fetch her. The second day the feast was held in the house of the in-laws.

Buti Witbooi had slaughtered an ox and a sheep and Muriel had made the beer and bread and porridge. The rain had passed and the sun shone brightly. There was so much food at buti Witbooi's that the neighbours had to store some of it in their houses. Poppie sat on a chair in the strange sitting room. Towards afternoon they took her to the bedroom and dressed her in the blue voile dress. Then she went back to her chair. They brought her a cool drink because she didn't like beer. Buti Plank had long since left his bestman's chair and had joined the drinkers outside. She could see Mosie and Hoedjie nowhere.

71

At sunset, she heard the children shouting outside. They were telling her little stepsister, Katie: We are tired, come, let's go home now.

I'm not going home yet, said Katie, I'm waiting for my sisi, we'll go home together.

Only now when she heard Katie speaking did Poppie know that she was never going home again.

Buti Plank, she started. . . but he was no longer sitting on the chair next to her. Hoedjie. . . Mosie. . . nobody was to be seen.

Don't cry like this, sisi, Katie tried to comfort her. She saw the tears running down Poppie's cheeks and wept with her.

What have I done now, Katie? asked Poppie.

Then the in-laws comforted her and said: We are going to dress you in your makoti clothes.

They took off her blue voile dress and dressed her in a long dress made of German print, put a short little Scotch shawl round her and buttoned it in front and wound a black doek round her head. She was unused to it and it kept on slipping down. Now she was a young married woman, a makoti.

Come back to the sitting room, they said.

Now the feast was over and the elders sat waiting; the respected old men and old women of the man's clan and her clan. The women sat with the hands folded round the breasts or resting on their knees. The men leant on their kieries held between their knees, or sat up straight in the way of old men on chairs that had been carried into the sitting room. Poppie and Stone and the bridesmaids and bestmen were told to sit at the table.

This was the ukuyalwa, says Poppie, the time of telling-off or admonition, when you are told how you must live together, how you are expected to behave.

You are different people now, the old men said, new people.

You must look to the family of your husband, and you must know you have become their child, the old women told Poppie.

You must know you are the child of your in-laws and you

must be ready to help when trouble comes to them, the old men told Stone.

You who have become a wife, they told Poppie, you must not tear apart the family into which you have married.

This is the hardest part of the Xhosa wedding, the saddest, because they talk at you till you are weeping in the sitting room. You and your husband sit at the table and the old people sit around the room, they sit in such a way that they can watch you all the time.

And all the stuff and clothing that you had to bring along as bride is carried into the room. Piece by piece it is held up for everyone to see, you must show every bit of goods you have brought. And if the husband's people are in a mind to complain, if they see you lack something which should have been there, the trouble starts. Then your people have to put a hand in their pockets to add money to what you have brought. They call every piece by name: Your pa's coat, your pa-in-law's coat. The man's sisters must be given a present each, even if it's only a doek. They call out what they want. They say: We have paid lobola, we want something in return.

The many people that feasted have left. After sunset only the elders remain, those that give you the telling-off. It's an awful thing to have to listen to. You have to weep. You take it so much to heart that you are almost sorry you ever had the thought of getting married. Your husband is upset too, he hangs his head. It is sad for everybody there, because as the elders sit watching you they think: These young people don't know what they've let themselves in for. Then you see them starting to weep along with you.

It lasts an hour, and then it's done with.

Then the sisters-in-law take you outside and lead you to another room. They bring you a plate of food and try to make you eat something. They stay with you till late. When it is quite late, they take you to your room and say: This is your and your husband's bed, you are going to sleep here with him, and this is your room.

Buti Witbooi had added a small room made of corrugated

iron to the back of his house. There was only place for a bed and a dressing table in the room.

Then when all the people have gone to bed and his kinsmen have left, the man comes to you, while your heart is still heavy with the words that have rained down on you, because you know you have not married only the man, you have married into his family. From now on you are under their roof.

A makoti has to rise at five o'clock every morning, says Poppie. They expect you to work for them. You can't let them get up and you lie abed. The first morning after the wedding they expect you to bring them early coffee and tea and water to wash.

Sisi Muriel came to tell me who drank coffee and who drank tea. But I wasn't allowed into the room where her husband slept, she accepted it at the door. Then I made breakfast for the men who went to work and fed the children. I washed and ironed everyone's clothes and they watched me all the time to see whether I'd been brought up correctly.

If my mother-in-law had been there, she would have taken me in hand, but it fell to sisi Muriel to show me their ways. The Xhosa clans have different ways and beliefs, and I had to learn the ways of my in-law clan. My father-in-law's name was Ntozimbi which means ugly, because he was very ugly as a baby. But now I was not allowed to use his name-word if I saw something ugly. And my mother-in-law's name was Nomaqabaka, which means somebody born in cold weather, so I wasn't allowed to use that word any more either, I must use another for cold weather. So there were many things you were taught.

After a week the in-laws gave Poppie her new name, Nonkosinathi, which means The Lord is with us.

This is the end of your girlhood, says Poppie. The new name leads you into your woman's life. The new life. It makes you feel like a woman. If the in-laws were to call you by your girl-name you would feel rejected. It would seem to you that your marriage had failed.

And another thing, a woman may not walk bareheaded in the yard of her in-laws without risking her marriage. We don't wear the kopdoeks for pleasure, we are forced to wear them. They are uncomfortably cumbersome if you are not used to them. When I go to mama's house, or the house of my brothers, I take off the doek. But outside in the street I have to wear it. My own people may see me bare-headed, but not my in-laws. If a woman walks bare-headed at her in-law's place, she is naked before the izinyanya, which means the old people lying under the soil, the forefathers who must be respected.

After the marriage I no longer called my husband buti Stone, but buti-ka-nombi, which means buti of his brother's daughter. And later mama called him mkhwenyane which means son-in-law, and Plank and Hoedjie and Mosie said swaer which is the Afrikaans for brother-in-law. An in-law is never addressed by his true name, that is our custom.

After my marriage I was too shy to see my mother. I was shy because of the long dresses I had to wear. I wouldn't see her for a long time, about two months, and we were living so close to one another. The first time I went to the shops after my marriage my husband's sister walked along with me and when we passed our house, my mother did not recognise me. The previous time she had seen me was in the white wedding dress and she did not know me in the new get-up.

The in-laws were satisfied with Poppie's work, and Stone was satisfied. If you have children one day, he would say, you must bring up your children in just the same way as your ouma brought you up.

She didn't go back to work in the factory, but stayed at home and took her husband his dinner every day, bread and fried fish, or samp and beans and meat, or umphokoqo with sour milk in a pail. He sat waiting for her to bring the food, great dishes of it, because he would not eat alone. His friends shared his food and they said: Your wife cooks better than the girls on the land. He was proud of her, and of the way she fitted in well with them. If you are a good cook, it

75

makes the man's heart soft for you. If he eats well, he thinks of you as the best wife.

A month after their marriage Stone told his buti he would like to have his own house as their room was too small.

Nonkosinathi, I have spoken to buti about our house, and he says it is well so, he told Poppie.

He received a plot from the municipality and his buti helped him to build a one-roomed house from corrugated iron and wooden boards. He laid out a small garden and planted mealies and pumpkins and carrots. Her ma could give them the kitchen dresser and table and some chairs.

Only after two months, when she had fallen pregnant, did Poppie go to visit her ma.

I fell pregnant at once. I was stupid, I can't tell whether I was glad or not, says Poppie, it just came to be that I was pregnant.

Can I come and stay with you to have the baby? she asked mama.

She was shy of her brothers, too. They were still living alone, and mama cooked their meals. But after she had moved into her own house, Mosie and Hoedjie started coming to see her. And Meisie still remained her best friend.

19

At the end of the year when he got his leave, Stone wished to go to Herschel where his father and mother lived.

Poppie is going to Kaffirland for Christmas, mama said to Plank.

Plank was drunk. Sisi, it's your fault, he said. You were in such a hurry to get her married to a fucking raw Kaffir.

Shut your mouth, mama answered. Did you want her with child, like the girls you go around with?

My little sister is a good girl, said Plank. You pushed her too much.

They paid lobola and she's churched, mama replied. It's right that she goes to visit her in-laws.

Poppie was content. Stone was good to her. He borrowed a provision basket from buti Witbooi for the journey. Mama baked her a loaf of bread, and cooked a leg of mutton. Buti Plank gave her money to buy the things she liked to eat: Sunrise toffees, cream caramels, ginger nuts, Marie biscuits and Assorted and a bottle of Oros.

It was a long journey. From Lamberts Bay by bus to Graafwater, by train to Cape Town. They stayed over the day in Cape Town and caught the evening train. The next night at one o'clock they changed trains at Stormberg for Burgersdorp, and at Burgersdorp they walked over the high bridge to catch the train to Aliwal North and at Aliwal North they changed trains for Lady Grey.

Such a slow train, Poppie told mama later, I never saw before in my life. And such a strange country, I have never seen such a strange place, and all those mountains.

At sunset of the fourth day, they arrived at Sterkspruit and took the bus to Herschel.

It was such a funny bus, it looked like an old lorry. I was very uncomfortable, because I had to sit with people who had red blankets wrapped around them. It was the first time I had seen such people and now I had to sit next to them. The bus shook terribly, everything was covered in dust, I was not used to such roads.

When we got down from the bus I thought we had come to a location like ours. But there was nothing, only a few round huts, two or three built together and another two or three a little way off.

The sun was setting behind the mountains, shadows lengthened. Far away up in the mountains Poppie saw a light.

Now what is that over there? she asked Stone.

It's a house, he said.

What's a house doing up there on the mountain?

There are people living there.

77

They walked along the road and on both sides were the mealie lands, and on the road the small herds of cattle. And the strangest thing to Poppie were the young boys wrapped in blankets.

It was the first time I had seen naked children wearing blankets, herding the cattle with kieries in the hand, and I was terribly scared of the cattle because I wasn't used to them.

The hut was full of people when we got there, because they had heard we were on the bus. My father-in-law, my mother-in-law and my father-in-law's sisters sat one side of the hut. They sat in the dark in long dresses with heavy doeks on their heads. They had spread a small mat on the floor for me to sit on, on the side opposite to where they were sitting. It was very unpleasant because a huge cat came to sit in front of me and I could do nothing because my ma had told me when you're makoti you're not allowed to hit the cat or the dog or the children of your in-laws. And the cat was sitting right in front of me and I wondered why had he chosen that place to sit.

They asked me how it went with my parents. I kept quiet, my husband spoke to his people. He sat on a chair, because he's a man. He didn't sit on the side of the hut where I was sitting, he sat with the men. Where I was sitting was the side of the women. My father-in-law's sisters and sister-in-law and wife who had been taken up into the family's beliefs could sit with the men. But newly-married women aren't allowed there and they may not greet the father-in-law by hand, though the aunties came over to greet me by hand.

I was scared of the strange people and didn't look around too much, for the hut looked so dark and frightening, lit only by a tin lamp standing near the dishes. It was a horrible place, I'm not used to such houses.

But I kept quiet because my ma had taught me how to behave myself with my in-laws. There wasn't any furniture, only clay seats against the walls and a clay built-in cupboard where the dishes were kept. The roof was pitch black from the smoke of the open fireplace in the middle of the hut. The fire wasn't lit, being summertime when they cook outside.

But when it rains they cook inside the hut. There was a small round hole for a window; when they went to bed they pushed papers or a cushion into the hole to close it, and when they got up in the morning they pulled out the cushion to open it.

They brought me food, a kind of sour mealie porridge which they called inqodi, but I had never eaten it before and I couldn't swallow it. I tasted it and left it and my sister-in-law took it away.

Our child is tired, they said, and so we went to sleep.

Buti-ka-nombi and I and my little sister-in-law and other people slept in the one hut. I had brought my own sheets in my suitcase, ja, and I made up my bed on the small reed mat which they unrolled for me. We slept on the floor, but a week later the bed my husband had sent by rail arrived. He knew that his parents did not sleep on a bed, that's why he had sent the bed from Lamberts Bay long before we left.

The next morning I went outside and looked around expecting to see a location such as I was used to, but I saw nothing at all. Only huts and mealie lands and peach trees, and the houses not even close together, but in groups of three or four, at a distance from each other.

In the other hut behind us another old auntie lived, my father-in-law's second wife. And then there was oupa Melani, my father-in-law's father's youngest brother — I liked him very much, he was a great one for jokes — and my father-in-law's stepmother, an old ouma whom they called gogo Nomthinjana. My husband's eldest brother's child, Xolile, whom I knew from Lamberts Bay, also lived with them. But the one I liked best was my little sister-in-law, Lindiwe.

Lindiwe took me to the donga, which is a kind of gully they use as a toilet. On the way back she showed me the fireplace and the kraal, built of stone with clay used as mortar, different from the kraals at Upington which are built of dry thorn branches. Behind the rondawel I saw an orchard of peach trees and prickly pears and chickens and a pigsty.

Now we have to fetch water, Lindiwe said.

And that to me was very strange too, because we had to walk downhill through the long grass, and I didn't like that at all, I am scared of snakes and spiders and I was wearing the long dress and couldn't see where I was treading. But I had to go. I carried a pail and she carried a pail and a round dish.

For what are you taking the dish? I asked.

To scoop the water with, she said.

I thought one tapped water from a tap and now here there was no tap at all.

We walked downhill, to the donga where the soil had been washed away. It was difficult to climb down. Lindiwe went first and I followed her. Then I saw why she took a round dish along. The water oozed up from the bottom of the donga, we had to scoop up the water with the dish and throw it into the pail.

Lindiwe told me: We are the first to come, now we put down the dish and leave the pail and we go home. If someone comes after us, she may not take the water that has filtered up, because our dish is first in line. She must fill our pail and put it on one side and then she can help herself.

This fetching of the water and climbing up the donga with the pail on your head was a very uncomfortable affair. Ouk! When it rained, we had to take off our shoes.

This was one thing that puzzled me: when it rained the people took off their shoes.

I asked Lindiwe: Why do you walk barefoot when it rains?

Not to spoil our shoes, said Lindiwe. We must save our shoes.

But I kept on my shoes. Only when I climbed down the donga did I take them off, so as not to slip in the mud. I was scared of all the rain and the thunderstorms, but not terribly scared. I was born like that, nothing ever frightens me very much.

The country was so different, with all the mountains around us. Before the sun set the mountains threw such long black shadows, and then the place where we were living was in the shade. But over the other side, on the far-off slopes, the sun was still shining.

Lindiwe, I asked, how can you people live here for ever? It is to me such a strange thing to be in the shade before the sun has set.

Far away in the mountains we could see huts and the smoke curling up from them, then it was time for us, too, to make a small fire in front of our huts on which to cook our food.

The food was quite different. We had to grind the mealies by hand. And that sour kind of porridge I was given the first night, I wondered what kind of food that was! Early in the morning Lindiwe called me. We knelt on the grinding-stone and pressed the mealies down till they were mashed, then we wet them again. We ground them to a fine mash. In Xhosa they call it ukokola. And we left the soft dough lying in warm water overnight. It went sour and we boiled it up the following morning and this is what they called inqodi. It seemed to me a lot of work; in Lamberts Bay if we wanted sour porridge, we added tartaric. It was their chief food, like tea. If somebody came visiting, they gave him a dish of inqodi to drink.

I learned how to bake bread in new ways: straw bread, and water bread. I wanted to see everything and learn as much as I could to be able to tell my people all the new things I had seen.

Lindiwe took Poppie to the fields along with the other women. They put a long pickaxe in her hands and showed her how to hoe. But she was clumsy, the hoe was too heavy for her to use.

Sisi, you are chopping out our food, said Lindiwe. But she was not cross, she was laughing. She showed Poppie how to chop out the weeds and not the mealies.

Poppie found it too hot in the fields in the long dress. She wished she were Lindiwe who was only a few months younger than she, but might wear the short dress and go bare-headed. The doek on her head irritated her.

Go home now, said her mother-in-law. She saw to it that Poppie didn't work too hard. Go and rest in the shade.

ELSA JOUBERT

When you are rested, you can prepare our food and bring it to the fields.

She took care of her because she knew that Nonkosinathi was with child. Shortly after she arrived, her mother-in-law had asked her: How many months far are you gone?

Poppie cast down her eyes and stared at the big black ants carrying small twigs to their holes. It was shortly before the rains came. She answered so softly that her mother-in-law had to repeat her question.

Four or five months, I think.

Then the mother-in-law fetched a herb which she called isicakathi and put it into a jam tin filled with water. It looked like grass. If one plants it, it will grow, she said, but now it must be left standing in water. Every morning you must drink some of this water, Nonkosinathi, and every evening before you go to bed.

Stone's childhood friends came from Bloemfontein and Johannesburg for the holidays and there were many wedding feasts. When he had finished working in the fields, he took off his boiler suit and put on his best suit and went out with his friends.

We Xhosa people have different ways, says Poppie, the men don't take their wives along when they go out, you must be content to stay at home.

I was curious to see everything and went around with Lindiwe. We took sacks and walked to the mealie fields to chop dry mealies for firewood, or to gather dry dung, or wet dung to smear out the house. But I was only allowed to smear out one side of the hut. Only she who is related by blood is allowed to smear on the men's side.

We walked a long way to church. One week we went to Lindiwe's church, the Apostolic church, and the next week to my husband's church, the Methodists. If the service started at eleven o'clock we had to start walking at nine o'clock. It was in another ilali or location.

I kept my shoes on when I walked, I couldn't stand going barefoot.

Don't the thorns prick your feet, I asked Lindiwe.

We're used to it, she said.

My father-in-law had been married in the Xhosa way, but his children were baptised in the Baptist Church.

They believed strongly in the Xhosa faith. They prayed terribly much. We could not eat until they had prayed. In the way of all people who believe in God we all gathered together to pray before going to bed. Sometimes they were a bit drunk, then they would fall down on to their beds, but even if it was only the Our Father, or a Nkosi sikelela osiphekona, which means, Father bless this food we have been given, which is actually a mealtime prayer, before they could sleep, they had to pray.

My father-in-law had worked as a shearer in the Free State, and married my mother-in-law in the Free State, but here at his home yard he kept very strictly to the Xhosa faith. They were not really what we call raw people, but like all Xhosas he set great store by his own customs and beliefs. And the old people liked drinking their sorghum beer called mqomboti. They watched to see whether I had been brought up correctly by my parents, whether I knew precisely the time when I must make tea or coffee, or the time to light the lamps.

My father-in-law didn't speak much to me. I was shy of him and they had taught me not to say his name. He took in all the old people to live with him. The ouma whom we called gogo Nomthinjana I loved best, she was always cross, but still she was full of fun. This old ouma had been a witch-doctor, but she was old now, and her power had left her. She used to doctor people and help them.

Dadebawo Nozasi who came for a visit at Christmas, was also a witchdoctor. They told me she became very sick because she didn't do what her dreams had told her to do. She went out of her mind, but she would not submit. But then when she got too ill, she went to study under a fully-trained doctor, an isanuse. They don't do wicked things; a witch, or what you call an igqwira, is the one who does the wicked things, but she became an igqira, a doctor who helps people.

I saw many witchdoctors in Kaffirland. They wore white

beads around the feet, around the head and on the arms.
They study in the same way in which a nurse studies. When
you are a probationer you have one string of beads and the
further you go, the more strings are added till your arm is
covered up to the elbow, and then you wear a string of
beads round your head and a second one, till you are fully
clothed and then you are an important doctor. It's the same
as a nursing matron who is given her stripes.

In the evenings we could hear them playing the drums
in the huts and dancing. As I was makoti, I was not allowed
to watch them, but Lindiwe and I stood outside in the
moonlight and watched the dancing from far off and
listened to their beer-drinking and singing and drumming.

Mama wants me to come and have my baby with her, said
Poppie to her mother-in-law. Poppie wasn't happy any
longer in Kaffirland, she wanted to go home. Mama sent a
letter to the post office and said: We are longing for you to
come home.

When Stone's holiday was done, they got on the bus, and
changed to the next bus and travelled by train for three days.

Early in February they arrived in Lamberts Bay. Mama
and Mosie and Hoedjie and mama's younger children
fetched them at the bus stop. It was hot and the wind had
risen and blew the sand against her legs. It was nice to smell
the fish again and the guano factory.

The people themselves smelled of fish.

Where's buti Plank, mama? asked Poppie.

He's at sea, says mama, but he sent a message that he'll
bring you a fish tomorrow.

20

Poppie's baby was born in mama's house. Old Martha
Horings, the midwife, a coloured woman who lived with a

Xhosa man, helped her. It was a little boy and Poppie called him Themba which means Hope. His English name was Andrew. During the first winter, at five months, he died of whooping cough.

I don't know what it was that year, says Poppie, but all the people's small babies died. I can't say it was especially hard in the houses made of corrugated iron, in the cold weather and the thick mists, because after all my ma had all her babies there and reared them. That year was just a bad year, many died, coloured and black, and were buried in the graveyard.

Poppie didn't realise that the baby, who was feverish and breathing heavily, was so very ill, till her sister-in-law came to her and said: Cover the child and take him to your mama's house.

Before the early hours of the night people began arriving and taking their places in the sitting room. Mama stayed with Poppie in the bedroom, the sister-in-law and the neighbours were there too. Give the child the breast, said mama. Poppie tried but the child would not take the breast, even when she tried to press the nipple into its mouth the lips stayed slack. The eyes remained closed and the child had stopped crying. Mama took the child from Poppie. Early the next morning the child died.

The men stood outside in the yard. Xhosa men are not men who weep, says Poppie. The father of the child stood with hanging head, the other men tried to talk to him. He bought a good little coffin and the women covered it with white cloth. All the people stayed with me, they did not leave me alone one minute, till after the funeral.

Ag, but then it was so sad to be back in my house again. When I came in from outside it seemed as if I saw the child lying on the bed, or when I was in the backyard I seemed to hear him crying inside the house. Meisie said I should come back to work at the factory, but my husband would not let me go. He was earning four pounds a week and things were not so expensive and he said: It is enough for us to live on.

They taught school at Langa, in the church, and Pieta and

Katie started school. Pieta was eight years old when he started. Mosie had already left school and was working at a garage in the village, but he didn't want to stop learning so studied for his Standard Six with the Union College, by post.

This was the time when Meisie married a coloured man of Dal Josafat, Sammie James. Auntie Lena gave her a big wedding, first in the Catholic church and then a dance in the Gebou location. They lived in auntie Lena's house.

A few months after Meisie's marriage Poppie's second child was born. Ouma Martha Horings stood by again, and once more it was a little boy. Poppie called him Bonsile which means: We have proved something, something has been mended. His English name was Stanford and when she was nursing him, or when she and mama played with him, they called him by the Afrikaans name of Klonkie. Now when she spoke of her husband Poppie called him tata-ka-Bonsile, which means father-of-Bonsile, by way of showing him respect.

21

When Bonsile was one year old, we came to Cape Town.

Two white men walked through the location and told us we could go where we wished, but we Xhosa people had to see that we leave Lamberts Bay. The longer we stayed, the more we were caught and taken to the police station, even while sitting at table at night eating our supper.

The people were angry. I grew up here, said Mosie, I'm not leaving. I've got a good job at the garage and I'm studying with the Union College.

LAMBERTS BAY

Buti Mbatane had worked at Lamberts Bay for twelve years, and before this at Lüderitzbucht. Where to is it that I must go now? he asked.

Before her child's birth Poppie saw in a dream that the white paling round ouma's grave had broken down and weeds were growing over it. Hoedjie and Mosie helped her to make it neat again. Must we leave the grave for the weeds to grow? she asked. And my baby's grave?

The men may stay, the policemen said, but the women who lie around doing nothing, waiting for full season to start work at the factories again, must go. Back to the places from where they came. Or look for work elsewhere. They said: This part of the country is a coloured preference area. Too many black people are coming from the tribal lands to work in the Western Cape.

When it was not full season, says Poppie, the people locked their houses and went to Tulbagh or Paarl to pack fruit. When they came back to Lamberts Bay they were homeless because the municipality had burned down their houses. The houses were built of wooden boards and sheets of corrugated iron, lined with cardboard. It took only one match for the house to flare up and burn down.

The house across the road was burned down. Poppie saw the coloured policeman help the white policeman carry the stuff from the house: an iron bedstead, a cupboard, a kitchen table and a few chairs, some broken down, a few pieces of crockery, tins and paraffin cases. The policeman had kicked the door down, it swung in on its broken hinges, when he struck the match.

The children gathered in the street to watch.

Before he drove off the white man asked the women who had joined the children in the street: Do you know the people who lived here?

Yes, we know them, they said.

Well, then you must carry away their stuff and keep it till they pitch up again. It can't be left standing in the street.

Poppie and the other women carried the stuff away.

When he came home from work, tata-ka-Bonsile dragged a few sheets of iron from the burned-out rubble. He dragged it to his yard and built a lean-to as a shelter for the people's belongings.

When the law became so strict that they were burning down many houses at Lamberts Bay, we started to think about leaving, says Poppie.

One day a policeman, whom they called Adonis, came to my house where I was hanging washing on the line. He was new at Lamberts Bay, a coloured man, and he did not know me. He asked: Where is your pass?

I said: I don't have a pass. My mother has got some papers, ja, but I never had no papers myself.

Then he said: You must come with me to the police station.

I put my child on my back and went with him.

There were other women waiting at the police station who had been caught too. Oompie Japie, a policeman who had known me from my childhood days, saw me and asked: Now for what have you come here, Poppie?

I was upset, I said: They catched me, oompie Japie.

Then he said: Ag no, child, you go home now.

I went home, but the other women had to stay behind. They were keen on catching the women. The men who were working, could stay.

Many people started leaving. Mama left in 1955. Some went to Cape Town on the lorries, others went to Tulbagh or Worcester, others went by train to Mossel Bay. My stepfather said: The Xhosa people are being pushed out of Lamberts Bay, it's better to go. First we were pushed out of the barracks, now we are being completely sent away.

A white man held a meeting in the location: A special town called Nyanga is being built for the Bantu people on the flats near Cape Town, he said, that's where you must go.

But the people were scared of going to Cape Town because of the stories they heard of the skollies. The schoolteacher tried to give them courage: In Cape Town it's not as rough as they tell. The skollie, he's not going to grab you by the shirt and say: Now you, you've had it, and stick a knife into you. There's no such thing. It's you yourself who'll get trouble if you look for it.

Buti Plank did not mind going because he had worked along the coast, southwards to Hout Bay. Hoedjie left his job at the hotel and went along with mama.

I didn't want to leave, Mosie says. My boss at the garage said: Don't go, man, let your ma go, you stay behind, you can send her money every month. But I said: No, where my ma goes, there it's my place too. I had many friends, too, white children. Jannie Koertse worked in the butchery, I helped him after school, and Ferlands, when he needed someone to take his cow to graze and bring it back in the afternoons, I helped him out, and so we became friendly. I was sorry to leave Ferlands and Jannie Koertse and Tredoux. My boss in the garage was just as sorry to let me go.

At first Poppie stayed on because tata-ka-Bonsile did not want to leave his job at the factory.

I can't let him stay alone here, Poppie said to Meisie. He's so fussy about his food, and he's fussy about clean clothes. Every day he brings his boiler suit for me to wash. You know the way I have to wash and iron his clothes. I can't go away and leave him just like that.

But she was homesick for her mama and her brothers and later on, when she was the only woman left in her street and all the houses around her had been flattened, she couldn't feel at rest. Early in 1956, a year after her brothers and her mama had left, she packed up to go.

At sunset one evening tata-ka-Bonsile walked with her to the bus stop. He carried her suitcase and she carried the parcel with the child's milk and food and a fried chicken and a loaf of bread she was taking to her ma.

I left my house just as it stood, and gave my things to coloured people to look after. I didn't find it hard to go, because the place wasn't the same any more. The way all the people had to leave, it made you feel they didn't want you there any more, there was no other way but to go away too. And I was glad to go to my mama and my brothers.

The train was very full, but the Lamberts Bay people who travelled with me in the bus to Graafwater, helped me with the child and the suitcase. We got into the third class compartment. The child luckily was very restful and slept all the way. At De Hoek we liked to look out and watch all the black Rhodesians who got on the train. They had very loud voices and strange ways. I suckled the child after De Hoek and then he slept until we reached Cape Town.

THREE

Cape Town

Mama had written to tell Poppie to get off the train at Bellville. But there was nobody at the station to meet her until
she heard a strange woman mention her name.
Your ma sent me, she said. Your ma is at work.
At the factory? asked Poppie, thinking of her mother at
work in the factory of Lamberts Bay.
She's doing housework, the woman replied, she's what
we call a char.
The woman carried her suitcase and they walked to the
bus terminus. Poppie looked up at the double-decker bus
and was scared.
I'm not getting in there, she said. Not with the child on
my back.
The woman prodded a child sitting on a downstairs seat.
Get up, give the sisi your seat, can't you see she's not used
to climbing upstairs.
Poppie's mama was living in a location near Lansdowne
Road, called Brown's Camp.
Your ma hasn't got her own house, the woman told her.
She's rooming with people from Lamberts Bay.
From the bus Poppie watched the locations they were
driving past, the houses all alike, row upon row. Hauk, she
said. Look at these houses. Why is there no house for my
ma?
Wait till you see where she lives, the woman answered.
It's not like this, it's still raw.
Where the bus stopped, they started walking. The streets
came to an end and they walked through stretches of sand.
The shacks were hidden amongst the bushes, and behind
the shacks they could see sand dunes. There were no adults

around, in the backyards children played, the bigger children carrying small ones on their backs, the small boys playing in sandy patches amongst the stones. One of the boys recognised Poppie. It was Jakkie. He came closer to her, but was too shy to greet her at first. He had grown taller and thinner and his round baby face had changed.

Molo sisi, he said at last, walking alongside her. The woman with her took a key from her handbag and unlocked the door of a house.

This now is sisi Nonceba's house, she said. There's nobody at home, you must wait here till they come back from work this afternoon. My house is the one opposite.

It was hot inside the tin shack. There were four rooms — one of the two bedrooms was rented by mama. Lay your child down on her bed, said the woman.

When they were alone Poppie called Jakkie to her. To make him feel less strange, she opened her basket and gave him a leg of chicken to eat. Stay with the baby, she said, so that I can go outside to rinse his nappies.

Mama's bed took up all the space in the room. At night another mattress could be squeezed in between the bed and the wall; it was now set upright against the wall.

Poppie was weary. She lay down on the bed and waited for Pieta and Katie to come home from school. They were happy to see her.

Sisi, they asked, have you come to stay with us?

Yes, I have come to stay, said Poppie.

We like it here. We go to the Dutch Reformed school, and we have made many new friends.

They were hungry and Poppie gave them what remained of the food she had brought. She saved some chicken for mama.

Katie had to take off her school uniform and put on old clothes before she started cleaning the house. I do mama's share, she told Poppie.

Mama came at dusk. She had to travel by two buses and a train to get home from work.

My, see how big my baby has got! she exclaimed when she saw Bonsile.

Mama was weary too. I don't like this rooming business, she complained. We were brought here to Cape Town, and now there's no housing for us. But old Mbatane has managed to get an erf in Elsies, and he is planning to build us a shack. They call the place Elsies because the people were moved from Elsies River, said mama. All the people you see around us were moved from somewhere, now they call the new parts after their old homes like Kraaifontein and Jakkalsvlei.

Mama made them a pot of tea. Mbatane is working at a garage, she said, but not being married to him caused a lot of bother, so we got married two months ago in the Native Affairs department, to qualify for an erf.

Mama sighed. They were still sitting in the kitchen but would have to move to the bedroom shortly. It would be cramped in the bedroom. You must try to live in peace with Mbatane, Poppie, mama said.

There won't be trouble, mama, said Poppie.

But our marriage was blessed in church, said mama who was defending Mbatane. In the Dutch Reformed, because they haven't built the Methodist in Jakkalsvlei yet.

And my brothers, mama? asked Poppie.

Hoedjie works in the bar of the Carlton Hotel, he works late.

Mosie has a job with Jews in Camps Bay. He has dropped his name of Mosie, they call him by his English name, Wilson.

What kind of job?

He's a houseboy. It's a sleep-in job, which is much better because we've no room for him to sleep here as well.

But is that not woman's work, mama? Ouma Hannie had reared them so strictly, the girls do the housework, they gather wood, they smear the floors.

Don't ask me, said mama, ask him yourself when he comes home on Sunday.

The next morning when the others had gone to work and the children to school, Poppie and Hoedjie were alone.

I'll wash your clothes for you, Hoedjie, she told him, your nice white waiter's jacket.

95

I don't wear a white waiter's jacket in this place, Poppie, said Hoedjie. I work at the wash-ups, I clean the glasses. I don't like the work, they are always shouting at me.

When Poppie tackled Mosie on his Sunday off, he made excuses. There are other women in the house to do the woman's work, he said. A cook and a housemaid. And a driver called Major. We're four who work for the Jews.

But what do you do for them?

Other work, said Mosie. He didn't like being questioned. He wouldn't tell them that he washed the kitchen floor and polished the stoep. He was angry at Poppie for asking.

It's not that I was so mad about taking the work, he said. I also said to myself: That's woman's work they make me do. But here in Cape Town if you don't take a job you get no pass. So I had to take what I could get, because of this pass business.

The pass business was something quite new to Poppie.

You know we had no papers in Lamberts Bay, said Mosie. How could I know we have to have papers in Cape Town? If they had told us about the papers, we would have been prepared like. But they just said: Go to Cape Town, there's place prepared for you in Cape Town, they kept shouting — go to Cape Town, go to Cape Town. So we go. And now we're here, now they mess us around. We must do this, we must do that, nothing comes right.

Actually my brothers didn't have so much trouble getting work, Poppie says. Their names could be entered on to mama's house-card. But because I was a married woman, I couldn't get on to her card. Buti Plank fixed his pass, and he sailed with the fishing boats from Hout Bay to Lamberts Bay, Lüderitzbucht and Walvis Bay. We only saw him every few months.

But our greatest problem was getting somewhere to live. Even when buti Mbatane had built his shack in Elsies River and they moved in, it was overcrowded before they had settled down. They only had two rooms and mama and buti Mbatane and their three children lived there and Hoedjie came in at all hours of the night from the hotel, and slept during the day, and buti Plank when he was home from sea, and I and my child moved in as well.

After a few months of living alone in Lamberts Bay, tata-ka-Bonsile chucked up his work, broke down the tin shack with his two hands, and stored the stuff and went to Eendekuil where he knew some people. He was looking for a place to work where I would be allowed to come and stay with him, but the pay was very little at Eendekuil and so he couldn't take the job. In Moorreesburg he couldn't get work either. He was very discouraged and got on to the train to come to Cape Town where I was. He didn't tell us he was coming, he just arrived one day. The two-roomed shack was so crowded that a few of us went to sleep with sisi Anna who lived close by. She also came from Lamberts Bay. But it didn't work out well.

Then one day another auntie, sisi Violet, a Cape Town woman whose husband also belonged to the Mqwati clan, knocked at mama's door.

We have heard that people from the district of Herschel have moved into this house. It's not according to our way that a son-in-law stays in the house of his wife's people, she said. Mama poured her some tea and she spoke again: My husband says the buti of his clan must leave and come to live with him.

Their house was not far away from mama's house, also in Jakkalsvlei. Jakkalsvlei was only bush and sand and small footpaths leading through the bushes to shacks made of corrugated iron. The streets were made later. Tata-ka-Bonsile agreed and we moved from mama's house to the house of his clansmen. But I wasn't happy there.

I don't get on with this sisi Violet, Poppie complained to mama. Our ways are different. She isn't my mother-in-law, why must I listen to her? And she has so many children, there's no place for us to sleep in her house.

23

Poppie thought: There is no other road for me, I must go find a job. There's no place for me to sleep here. Mama has no other small child now, she can look after my baby. Then tata-ka-Bonsile can stay with his sisi Violet and I'll take a sleep-in job.

We can't all stay with you, mama, said Poppie. And at auntie Violet's place we don't get on.

Mama agreed. The baby can stay with me, she said, but now what will I do the day that I go to char and the madam says I can't bring the child along?

Poppie didn't care. Then Katie must stay out of school and look after my baby. As I looked after mama's baby.

The auntie next door knew about a job and took Poppie along with her, first by bus and then by train and then by bus to Constantia. It was a sleep-in job at a plant-growing nursery. The woman didn't pay much, six pounds a month, but Poppie thought: We'll see how it goes, till tata-ka-Bonsile finds work. The work was hard. There were nine white people living in the house, the man and his wife and his wife's sister and her baby and five more children.

It was then the first time she and tata-ka-Bonsile and the child were living completely apart. It was the first time in her life that Poppie slept alone in a room. She was nineteen years old. The room was the end one in a barrack-like building occupied by the black garden labourers. At night she could hear them talking and laughing and fighting. On Saturday nights the noise went on the whole night long.

Stone was uneasy when he brought her back on Sunday evening after her afternoon off. Must I leave you here alone with all those men next door to you? It makes that the room isn't so quiet, she said. But they don't come and bother me.

At five o'clock the workers in the rooms next to hers rose. They went outside in the dark, emptied their bladders in the bushes, stuck their heads under the water taps. The smoke from the fires where they cooked their mealie porridge started curling up. An old man was always the first one to break the kindling and poke at the ashes.

At six o'clock Poppie had to be in the kitchen. The work in the dark of early morning was the best time for her, with the garden workers gathered round their fire and dawn breaking. She boiled water on the Primus. Then she took coffee to the nine white people. Cups of coffee to the three grown-ups, mugs to the children, and a dash of coffee in the bottle of milk for the baby in the cot.

It was strange to her to go into the rooms where the white people slept. The woman, still as a corpse, on her side, the blankets pulled up high over her shoulders, the man on his back with his mouth open, his chest bare. It was as if everything was dead in the room when she went in.

Draw the curtains, Rachel, the madam said as she put down the cups next to the beds. She worked under her English name.

But the moments when she stood in the dark, not knowing if they were awake or asleep, were to her the strangest.

The work was heavy. The white woman stood behind her back and said: Come, come, come, haven't you finished yet? The woman's sister, who lived with them with her baby, unlocked the kitchen door in the mornings, because she woke up early and was in the habit of lying in the dark, smoking. Poppie could see the little red spot of the cigarette moving in the corner where her bed stood.

Clean the ashtray for me, she'd say. She had gone back to bed after unlocking the door, and the child had fallen asleep with its bottle of coffee.

While the adults had breakfast, the baby sat on its mother's lap, pushed forward on her knee so that the cigarette should not burn it. The child hit at the table with its arms and hands and splattered porridge to all sides.

Wipe up, Rachel, before we step in it.

She had to make the beds and clean the floors while the people ate, and put away the children's things lying around. The man left his pyjamas lying on the floor. She picked them up and folded them. It was just the pyjama trunks. Before she went to the nursery, the madam threw all the washing

99

in a pile in the passage. She looked through the washing that the children had left in the bathroom the night before and added it to the heap. The sister brought the pail full of nappies.

Poppie washed by hand in the cement washtub in the yard. She heated the water in pots on the stove and carried it outside.

The sister was very particular about the nappies. I like my nappies to be white, she said, snowy white.

I had to bleach the nappies, and sprinkle them with water every now and then, says Poppie. Every day there was a heap of washing, because there were school-going children in the house. I think there were five of them and there wasn't a washing-machine. The madam did the cooking herself, but I laid the table and prepared the vegetables. After lunch I washed the dishes and at about three o'clock I could leave the kitchen to have a rest. At four o'clock I started the ironing. While I ironed, the madam did the cooking. They ate dinner late at night, and at nine o'clock perhaps, I finished up in the kitchen.

I worked till I couldn't work any more.

I got sick at the work, but the madam said to me: You can't be sick here, you must go to Nyanga, I'm too busy to look after a sick person. But I was never flat on my back, I just felt the pain in the lower part of my body. Then she'd say: Work has never made anybody sick. It hurt me very much when she said that, because I was still young, but the work was just too much; she had so many sheets to wash, and every day school clothes and nappies.

The children weren't naughty, they were just like other children. I was used to children because I come from a big family, but they didn't know how to do anything for themselves and they messed up the kitchen when they came home from school. I was fond of the little girl, Chrissie. In the afternoons when I was ironing she used to come and talk to me. Then she told me how many servants her mother had had, and how her father hit the maids if they didn't want to work; I think it was a coloured servant, who drank a lot, that he used to beat. But when I was there he must have quietened down a lot, because I never saw him beat anybody.

Her mother never liked the children to gossip with me. Sunday nights, after my time off, I had to come back. After I had seen my child and given my mother the stuff I brought her, then my husband and I had to come right back, we couldn't sit down to talk, the place was too far out. No more than a half an hour, then we had to leave again, perhaps when the child had fallen asleep or Katie had taken him out of the room to give me a chance to get away.

From Nyanga we took the Claremont bus, then the train to Wynberg, then the bus to Constantia.

The bus conductor got to know her.

Come, come, he'd say to Poppie when she got on the bus on her afternoon off. He was a coloured man, and spoke Afrikaans to her.

Don't you 'come come' me as well, said Poppie. Where I work it's 'come come' from the moment I get up.

He was kind to her and used to wait when he saw her hurrying to the bus stop.

She had grown accustomed to the electric trains and wasn't frightened as she used to be when she first heard the sighing bang of the doors or the shrill whistle. She liked the train, it gave her a moment of rest, her body folded into the movement of the train, she closed her eyes. A few moments of rest between her jobs, the white woman who was for ever thinking up new things for her to do, and the time when she arrived at mama's house.

At the bus stop at Claremont rows of people were waiting. The faces of some had become familiar to her. The weather had changed, the wind was blowing and a fine mist, like the sea mist, swept past them, transforming itself into wetness on their faces. She pressed her bag to her bosom, and raised her arm to protect her face. The warmth of bodies and human breathing came to her. Molo, she greeted those whom she knew, but there was no chance to talk, because she dared not lose her place. She was first in the queue when the buses arrived to take home the five o'clock city workers.

It was nearly dark and close to six o'clock when she arrived. Her ma was working in the kitchen and the children sat around her while she prepared their food. In the light of the Primus stove Poppie could see their faces turned up to her. Her eyes searched out her child, sitting on Katie's lap. Katie sat flat on the floor with her back against the wall; she picked up pebbles from the floor and dribbled them through her fingers to keep Bonsile's attention. Poppie put down her bag and picked up the child.

Son-in-law! Ma called at the kitchen door and tata-ka-Bonsile came in from the backyard.

He's been waiting for you ever since he came back from work, mama said.

Has he then got work?

No matter how much Stone had tried, he could not get a permit to work in the Cape.

He stood next to her, and she felt his body against hers as he took the child from her. She did not want to talk about his work in front of his people-in-law.

Mama poured them tea and they sat down at table.

Where is Mosie? Poppie asked, because he too was off on Thursdays.

He is singing tonight, mama said. The church group asked him to come.

Strange feelings were taking root in Poppie's heart. Tell him he can sing for my part too.

What is this that you have against Mosie, asked mama. She did not know the new tone in Poppie's voice.

They are four servants working for two people, I am one working for nine. And she started to cry. I'm tired, mama.

She did not drink her tea, but took the child back from her husband, felt if his nappy was dry, then gave him back to Katie.

I must go now, mama, otherwise I won't catch the bus.

The baby cried.

Take him to the room, mama said to Katie, so he doesn't see his ma.

Poppie gave her mother the bread she brought from work. Stale bread could be soaked in coffee; the children would like that. She also handed her mother a few onions and potatoes that the old man working in the garden had given her as a present.

Can mama wait till the end of the month for the money?

Stone went back with her. First the bus, then the train, then again the bus. There were long waits, but they didn't mind, it gave them a chance to talk.

All along she had been against his leaving Lamberts Bay and coming to Cape Town but he had said: How was I to know that I would have such trouble getting a permit to stay here?

But now he told her: You keep your mouth shut about me, I have got my permit.

How did you get it?

I have taken contract.

She didn't need to ask what contract. She knew. All the black people knew it was what you took when you couldn't get anything else, when you had to take something to stay on in the Cape. It was at the dairies at Philippi, near Nyanga. The work was hard, people couldn't stand it, their fingers became sore and swollen and the glands in their armpits swelled up.

It is not far to go, said Stone, because he knew how hard hotel work made life for Hoedjie, who had to walk home in the middle of the night when the buses had stopped. I can get there on foot. I start milking at four o'clock in the morning, and we milk till two o'clock. When the milk cans are brought back, we start washing the cans. Five o'clock I can be back at the house.

It is before she gets home. Yes, but he starts at four in the morning. And she? She starts at six o'clock. And she works until. . . Until nine o'clock, but it is not the same thing. Poppie was not used to arguing with tata-ka-Bonsile. She was ashamed to think she was talking to her husband in this manner, but she thought: I know the Cape better than he does.

There was no other work, said Stone. Because I have come

103

under contract I can get a plot and build a house for us.

How long will that not take!

How long would it take if I had not come under contract?

Yes, but the dairy work, it was the last thing . . . you are used to better.

It was after ten when they reached her room. From the room next door they could hear the talking and laughing of the men. He looked around him. The rooms were built of brick, with a ceiling, and whitewashed on the inside. It looked the same as when he was here last. There was no sign that anyone else had been there. He knew the blankets, but felt ill at ease in the dim light of the bulb against the ceiling. It made her look different, and made him feel different. They had never gone to bed by electric light anywhere else.

The voices of the workers in the room next door still worried him. But they were voices speaking a language he knew, so that made him feel more at ease in the white people's place. But at the same time he was jealous. He felt a powerlessness come over him.

From now on you shut your mouth about my work, he said.

The light at the corner of the building burned all night, and even when he had switched off the light in the room, it was not dark, but dully lit by the glow coming through the thin cotton curtain. This dark was not the dark they knew.

He slept with her. All night, it seemed to her, he was on top of her. It felt to her as though his body had grown thin.

He neglected himself when he stayed alone in Lamberts Bay, she thought. And he is going to neglect himself again, even more so with this contract work.

When the night was old, two, three o'clock, he got up. He felt afraid to be there at night in a place where he did not belong. The noise in the room next door had died down. The light outside was still burning, but a strip of shadow ran down the length of the outside wall. He was careful to stay in the shadow on his way to the gate. The dogs started barking at the big house when the animals heard him fumbling at the gate. But before they could make too much noise he had slipped through. He began running down the street.

Whenever he saw motor-car lights approaching from far off, he hid in the moon shadows of shrubs. The closer his running brought him to the main street, the more often he had to duck, moving from one dark pool to the next. He was uneasy, he wanted to get out of that neighbourhood.

Near to the shops he met a night watchman warming himself at a fire he had lit in a broken drum. The man was also a Xhosa, and Stone gulped down the mug of lukewarm coffee he offered him. That way, the night watchman showed him, down the hill and then you're at the station. He saw the light of the approaching train, and reached the platform just as the doors opened. He got into the last coach. The train was empty, with an early worker here and there. Only when the coach doors shut, and the train started moving again, did he feel safe.

Ever since he had arrived in the Cape, he had felt unsure of himself. Any moment the police might stop him and ask: Where is your pass? And then take him in. And even if he were to go back to Lamberts Bay, they could arrest him there as well.

The return half of the ticket he bought with Nonkosinathi was clasped in his hand. When the conductor came round, he could give it to him.

The workers on the opposite benches were sitting sleeping, their shoulders hunched forward, their bodies shaking with the movement of the train.

Stone fought the urge to sleep. He put his arm on the windowsill and rested his head on his arm. When the coach door opened and the conductor shouted: Claremont! the tiredness had not left his body.

At the station bus stop the bus from Nyanga had just pulled up, bringing in workers on their way to the city. He was the only passenger to go back to Nyanga. The lights in the buses were still on, but showed up more dimly in the greyness of the day which was starting. He sat up front in the bus, his head lowered, but he jerked it up, putting sleep

105

away from him. He was uneasy about the new work. When the bus stopped at Nyanga he made his way past the queues of people waiting and started to run. There were no buses to the Philippi dairies, he had to go on foot. The quickest way was over the dunes through the bush. From kayas or shacks built under the bushes men crawled out on the way to work, paying no attention to him. Light rain was sifting down.

The lights were on full strength at the dairy, shining on the pools where the first workers had hosed down the cement. The white man wearing gum boots splashed through the wetness. He had put on his thick overcoat.

You're late for work, he said. But he left it at that. The boss boy will show you where to start. And from now on, come at the time I told you to come.

I think he was afraid you were not pitching up, said the man working next to Stone. After all the trouble with contracts and permits he gets very angry if the people don't pitch up. But you'll have to watch the coming late from now on. The boss knows: When a Kaffir has worked for a few days you can start shouting at him, they don't leave the work if they are going to lose a few days' pay.

Sundays and Thursdays I had the afternoon off, says Poppie, but Constantia was so far, when I got to the location the sun had already set. Just half an hour together, then we had to leave, when the child was asleep, or my sister had taken him to give me a chance to get away. So my husband was not satisfied that I should work there, and as he was now earning as well, I left after four months.

24

Stone was given a plot in Jakkalsvlei, one of the sections of the Nyanga location. There were several sections where people could build houses, Browns Camp and Elsies, and Kraaifontein and the Dutch Location named after the Dutch Reformed school. Emasekeni, one of the old locations, was built of corrugated iron, like the others. But the ones called the Old Location and the Mau-Mau were built of bricks. Many mixed people lived together, especially Xhosas with coloured wives.

Jakkalsvlei was hidden amongst the bushes, built against a little slope, and behind the houses you could see the sand dunes. Close to Stone's plot a church was being built of bricks.

Hoedjie came to help build the house.

If buti Mbatane bothers me, I'll move in with you, he said.

Hoedjie was still a gentleman when he came to Cape Town, says Poppie. The girls of Lamberts Bay loved watching him, dressed up in his white jacket with his white cap on his head, balancing the tray on the palm of his hand and serving beer or tea on the stoep of the hotel. He had a way of slipping the tip from the tray into the front pocket of his pants. It was good fun watching him; he was a showman.

But he disliked the work at the Carlton Hotel where his job was washing glasses in the scullery, where the fat barman was rude to him, and he had to walk a long way home at night. He left the hotel job and went to work in a Jewish factory in Bellville and there he got into bad company. He started drinking with his new friends.

The house was built bit by bit and as Hoedjie helped them carry the sheets of corrugated iron Poppie smelt the liquor on his breath. Buti Plank, the fisherman, was always drinking, says Poppie, but here in the Cape drink got hold of Hoedjie too.

Mosie also came to help build the house. I never liked this houseboy business. When your house is ready I'm coming to stay with you, little sister. The Jewish man I work for, this Mr Green, is going to help me. He says with my Standard Six certificate I can do better in his factory.

The house was not ready yet, only the walls of corrugated iron were up, and the roof was fixed, when they moved in. A man from Lamberts Bay brought her wedding dresser in his van and the table and chairs which she had left with some coloured people.

Now only buti Plank must still join us, thought Poppie, and it will be like when we were at Lamberts Bay.

There was only one room in the house, but they managed.

25

With the child on her back she walked to the dunes to gather wood. On the footpaths people passed her by, dragging wooden boards or sheets of corrugated iron.

You must take care, the woman living in the house across the road, told Poppie.

She was a big woman, stouter and taller than Poppie, dressed in a long dress and pinafore of German print. Poppie knew her by sight, she was the neatest of all the women living there in the newly-put-up houses. She was always clean and kept her children and her yard clean, which was a hard job, because she sold coal. Every week the coal lorry came and unloaded a few bags of coal in her yard, which she would shovel into a rough shed made of corrugated iron and sell by the pail and half pail to the people of the neighbourhood.

Poppie bought coal from her. The winter was nearly over, but on the Flats the cold persisted. The rain kept on, right up to November. In the evenings Poppie lit a fire in the konka with the firewood she had gathered in the dunes. When the coals were glowing in the brazier she carried it into the house.

You must take care, the stout woman — her name was Mamdungwana — cautioned Poppie. Take along some of the bigger children when you go to gather wood. And watch where the children go. There are many skollies in the dunes.

Stone liked some heat to be still in the konka when he got up in the early hours to go to the dairy. He warmed his hands before leaving. He was no longer feeling well. As he had been warned, his fingers had started swelling from the continuous milking, the pain crept up to his armpits and the glands in his armpits became swollen.

At that time the contract was very strict, says Poppie, if you broke your contract, you were caught and they locked you up.

Mamdungwana talked of courage to Poppie and gave her advice. They saw each other every day. She was also a church-goer and took Poppie along to her church. Poppie no longer went with mama to the Methodist church, because at Lamberts Bay Stone had changed and become Anglican and she had to join up with him. Mamdungwana took her to the Nyanga Holy Cross church of the Anglicans.

Tata-ka-Bonsile made me to leave the Methodists, she often complained to Mosie, and now I go on my own to the Holy Cross, because he has no more spirit left for his church.

Mamdungwana gave her advice: You must get papers, sisi. That's why it went so badly with you in Constantia. If you don't have papers, the white people do just what they want with you.

How do I get papers? Poppie asked. As the wife of a man under contract it will be hard for me.

Come to Woodstock with me, said Mamdungwana. If they made you come from Lamberts Bay by force, they must give you papers.

The man in the office of Native Affairs sat behind his table and listened to her story, looked at her mama's file and gave her a paper. It was the first time that Poppie had a paper with her name, her plot number and a date.

It is for three months only, said the man, then you must come back for an extension.

Three months seemed a long time to Poppie then. Her heart lifted.

We are not going home now, she said to Mamdungwana.

I want to go and show you old Ben Menjane's shop in Salt River.

They took the bus. Old Ben did not know her, but she knew the shop. She showed Mamdungwana the rolls of cloth, the blankets stacked up right to the ceiling, the boxes of shoes, the crockery.

Here my ma and I came to shop when we were living in Lamberts Bay. Here my ma bought all my wedding things.

With the papers in her bag, Poppie felt that Lamberts Bay lay behind her, that she was now one of Cape Town's people.

She bought them two cool drinks and she paid the bus fare back to the location for both of them.

26

Now that she had the papers, it wasn't so hard for Poppie when tata-ka-Bonsile began talking of breaking contract. One day he came home and said: I told my boss to sign off my pass, I'm not going back there.

His fingers were swollen and stiff, he could hardly bend them to bring a spoon to his mouth. His work was slowing down.

I'll go to the office in Langa and show them my fingers.

She spoke to her ma: Will mama look after my child for me, if I get a char job and work by the day?

Mama agreed. Mama was not working at this time and it was only at night that the stepfather made trouble for her if she looked after Poppie's child.

A church-going woman whom she knew, told Poppie of a job at Bellville, charring for a Mr Pullen who had a garage and lived above it with his sick wife. She only needed to take one bus, seven o'clock from Nyanga, to arrive at

Bellville by eight. Mr Pullen was an elderly man whose hands were stained with black grease. You can leave again by three o'clock, he said. There's not so much to do. And on Saturdays you can leave by twelve. The pay was two pounds five shillings per week, and even paying bus fare twice a day left her with more than she had earned at Constantia.

It was a good time for us, says Poppie.

At the office it went well with tata-ka-Bonsile too. The white man had already told him that he would have to go back to the country, to the Ciskei, because he had broken contract, when a black man came into the room and put down a form on his table.

Wait, said the white man to tata-ka-Bonsile after he had read the form. This wood factory needs a worker, I'll give you another chance. If you are given the contract at the factory in Bellville, then you may stay on.

This time the work was not so hard. He worked as toolboy to an electrician. He worked there till he got sick again.

After Poppie had been given her papers, and tata-ka-Bonsile had got a better job, the house in Jakkalsvlei began to feel like their house in Lamberts Bay. Tata-ka-Bonsile liked gardening. He worked over the sandy soil with ash from the fire and with mqomboti bran which she begged off beer-making people as manure was scarce. He started planting vegetables, potatoes, cabbages, beetroot, beans, mealies. And Poppie learnt to look towards the mountain like the Cape people, and when clouds started gathering about the mountaintop she would say: Look, the weather is turning. She loved telling Mamdungwana about her first house at Lamberts Bay. Her brothers got to like Mamdungwana too.

Four o'clock in the afternoons she would get back from Bellville, fetch Bonsile from her ma, do her washing at home and cook. While tata-ka-Bonsile had been staying with sisi Violet, when Poppie worked sleep-in, he had neglected himself and become thin. Now she cooked the food she knew he liked. But he remained a poor eater, Poppie says.

After three months she went back to Woodstock and the

ELSA JOUBERT

white man in the office asked: Have you got a job, else I
can't give you extensions. I've got a job, she said. Mr Pullen
signed the papers she was given for him to sign and he
posted them back to the office.

Those days the permit story wasn't so difficult, says
Poppie. And when I left Mr Pullen because I was going to
have a baby, the office gave me three months to stay at
home.

When you go to work again, come back here to have your
pass signed, the white man said.

I left the job at Mr Pullen's because of the baby and so I
had to stay at home to look after it. The child was breast fed
and it's hard to give a suckling child to someone else to look
after. This child was only four months younger than my
ma's last child, her girl child called Georgina, whom we still
call Baby. Poppie's child was born in the house. A Xhosa
district nurse, nurse Bam, helped her. It was a girl and they
christened her Rose in the Holy Cross church. Her Xhosa
name was Nomvula, meaning child born on the day it
rained.

It was during that time that Mamdungwana and I got so
completely used to one another. I went to see her often and
she came to see me. And when she was in bed with 'flu, I
would clean out her house and cook her food. After a while
it felt as if we were sisters born. If she was having a baby and
the pains came in the night, I was the first one to be called.
When the nurse came, I was already there, I had boiling
water prepared and put everything she was going to need
together. She helped me in the same way. If I was having
a baby, she was the first to be called. *Then* my husband
would go to call my ma. Then they'd call the old Makhulu,
who lived next door. Then everybody was with me to help
me if something should go wrong.

We looked after each other's children when we went to
work. When the baby was a bit bigger, I went to char for
Mrs Graham who lived in Bishopscourt, three days a week,
and she paid me twelve shillings and sixpence a day, that
gave me about eight pounds a month. The other days I
stayed at home and then Mamdungwana went to work.

112

When I was heavy with the next baby, Hoedjie went to the bush to do his abakwetha. Mama was there when he left, but not when he returned. Mama had gone to work at Wolseley, for the fruit season. My ma was forced to work because of my stepfather being so stingy. What he did with his money we never knew. But he wouldn't spend it. Mama had to buy her children's school clothes herself and pay for their food, and we helped her. The stinginess was the worst thing about my stepfather.

When buti Hoedjie returned from the bush, we didn't have a big party because that was the time of what they called the potato boycott. The people were told not to buy potatoes, because the story did the rounds that a white man in the Transvaal, in some place they called Bethul or Bethal, where they plant a lot of potatoes, had killed a black boy and buried him in the potato field. The A.N.C. men used to come to the houses to see if we were cooking potatoes. If they saw potatoes in the cooking pots, they threw out all the food into the yard. It was all right to cook meat and other vegetables, but no potatoes. This trouble was the reason why we did not give a party for buti Hoedjie.

There was too much unrest in the location.

The baby was again a girl and nurse Bam helped me once more. I had the child christened Agnes and her Xhosa name was Thandi.

It was at this time that they came around the location to say that all the women must come to the Nyanga Hall in the bachelor quarters to have snaps taken and to get pass books. The new law had come which said that the papers must go and women must carry pass books.

But the pass books didn't give the trouble, says Poppie, because everybody got them. The biggest thing was the extension, the permission to stay here or to work here. If you didn't have the right to stay here, even if you had the book, then the book was no good to you. And even if you had the right, then you still had to go to the office after a time to change your pass, because the time they had given you ran out. And if you went to a new job and the previous

white people had signed you off, it was back to the office
to discharge the pass as well.

27

Old Makhulu who lived next door to us — makhulu means
grandma — shared her house with a witchdoctor woman.
The witchdoctor woman was quite old, but she still worked
a lot. Many days I saw Bellville registered motor cars parked
in front of her house, which meant that it was white people
who had come to buy medicine to get pregnant, or to be
helped in a court case, or to win at horseracing, but mostly
it was to be cured of the sickness of their nerves.

Old Makhulu had the same clan name as my father,
Mbele, and that's why we felt as if we were family. Her
house was a broken-down affair, boards and sheets of
corrugated iron and sacking stuck together any old how.
When the wind tore bits off, buti Hoedjie tried to mend it
for her with wire and pincers. Buti Hoedjie stayed with us
for long stretches of time, and when he became angry at
buti Plank he left us for mama, when the stepfather got his
goat, he came back to us.

Mosie and buti Hoedjie added a second room to our house
and then they stayed with us permanently.

Of tata-ka-Bonsile's brothers only one came to Cape
Town, his name was Spannerboy. He had gone to look for
his brother at Lamberts Bay and worked there until he was
sent away to Cape Town, where he got a job on the boats.
He also moved in with us. Witbooi never came to Cape
Town, he was sent to Tulbagh and from there back to
Herschel where he died.

Mosie went to night school in Nyanga and there he met
Johnnie, whom we called Johnnie Drop-Eye because of his

bleary eye. He came from Springbok. My father, he said, trekked through that part of the world with his sheep and his goats, from Bitterfontein to Klawer, and nowhere could he find a place to stay. Johnnie came to the Cape and here was no place for him either. Then Mosie said: Come and stay with me in the room I've built on to my little sister's house.

When buti Plank came home from the sea he moved in with us too. Now I was completely happy. Until buti Plank and buti Hoedjie fell out with each other about the drink. The eldest had too much to say about the second eldest, he wanted to play the big boss. Then he would say: Old Hoedjie, you are drinking too much.

Then buti Hoedjie would answer: But you're the big boss and you drink more than I do, buti.

One day Hoedjie came home from work: He'd bought a new hat and put it on his head, and had his wages in his coat pocket. Quite close to our house, while walking along a footpath in the bushes, he was attacked by skollies. And he told us: My little sister, I found myself up in the air, they had picked me up boots and all, and stole my hat and my money and my jacket. They wanted to pull down my trousers, but some of them said: Leave him, we know him, it's bra Hoedjie. Then they let me go. Fortunately he wasn't knifed. Bra is short for brother. And if they don't feel like saying buti, the young ones in the location say bura.

Another time buti Hoedjie arrived home wearing only his underpants; they had stolen everything else, and Mosie had to give his brother some of his clothes because he had little of his own.

You'll never possess anything because of the drink, buti, said Mosie.

I have finished with the drink, said Hoedjie. From this day on I've done with it. But he cheated us. When we thought he was at his job, he would sit drinking at the Jabulani hall. All day long. I make him food to take to work, then he sits drinking beer at the Jabulani till he's dead drunk, and he comes home at nightfall, food and all. Sometimes he gave the food to the skollies.

115

One day .Plank saw him at the bus queue, looking this way then that way, slowly advancing when the queue moved, but so restless, peering this way, that way. And then he left his place and made for the Jabulani. Plank followed him. I am not fighting you, he told Hoedjie. But you're getting up right now. With all this nonsense of yours I'll be late for work. It was a Friday. But still buti Hoedjie cheated buti Plank. After Plank's bus had left buti Hoedjie again abandoned the queue and returned to the Jabulani.

That night they sat waiting in Poppie's house. She sent Mosie to tell mama that Hoedjie hadn't returned from work. People get worried on Friday nights in the location when someone doesn't come home. Perhaps he has been knifed, perhaps the skollies have attacked him, maybe the police. Every weekend brings its trouble. One weekend three corpses were picked up in their neighbourhood.

Mama has to know, Mosie, Poppie said.

Mama and Mosie went to the police station but couldn't find him. Mosie took his money to phone all the hospitals but he wasn't there either. At last they found him in Philippi's police station. He'd lost his pass, his wages, everything he had. The man is robbed, Mosie said, cleaned out.

On Monday mama told Pieta: Stay out of school and take this money and go and pay Hoedjie's fine.

And when he came home that afternoon, mama asked: Where's your dompass? But he couldn't say. Pieta, asked mama, did you ask the policemen where's his dompass?

They said they don't know, mama, said Pieta.

But that night one of the men who had been arrested with buti Hoedjie, a man who hadn't been drunk but had been arrested because he carried a knife, came to tell Hoedjie the story. When they brought you in on Friday night, you were very drunk. The police asked you: What's your name. Then you answered: What the hell is that to you? Then the policeman said: Take out your pass book that I can see your name. They beat up buti Hoedjie because he answered: Take your own dompass and shove it up your arse.

CAPE TOWN

Black policemen were throwing their weight around with people those days. They took his pass book by force and tore it up, and the wages in the book they put in their pockets.

This is what the knifer came to tell us, mama told Poppie, but whether it is the truth, that I don't know.

He went home with the fellow with the knife, and they got drunk together and it's at his place that Hoedjie met this Muis woman of whom he got so fond.

My brothers gave us a lot of trouble with their drinking, says Poppie, but they were full of fun when they were drunk. Tata-ka-Bonsile liked their joking. He was a quiet man, but he was fond of his brothers-in-law and their light-hearted, fooling, joking ways.

It makes me feel better, Stone told Poppie. It helps me forget my stomach.

28

The work at the wood factory was not hard, but Stone's health still worried him.

I go to work in the mornings, he told Poppie, and from twelve o'clock onwards the pain starts. It's not a vomiting or a stomach-working, only the pain, like a hand pressing into my belly, something gnawing at my insides.

But then you must see a doctor, Poppie said.

The factory doctor gave him pills, signed him off work for a day, then two days, and then said: I'm tired of your complaints, your stomach has nothing wrong with it.

Tata-ka-Bonsile was a nervous man, says Poppie, he was nervous about his job and about me and the children, and about himself. Later on he became short of breath. In the afternoons when he came home he complained of feeling

117

cold. Then I'd give him warm soup or warm food, as you would give someone who is ill, but he never felt like eating much. He was never a big eater, but he spoilt his health when he was staying with his clan people and I was working sleep-in.

Then I told him: The factory doctor is tired of you. We must go to a private doctor.

On a Saturday morning we went to a white doctor, a Dr Smit, in Lawrence Road in Athlone, and he took his time to examine him thoroughly, we were very satisfied with him, ja. He said: You have got T.B., but it is only a small spot, starting in the left lung.

The location people said: We told you, the people working at the wood factory all get T.B. But Poppie answered them: You are talking nonsense, my husband didn't even work in the factory, he was toolboy for the electrician.

Dr Smit gave him a letter and took him off work completely. At the factory they gave him papers to sign to apply for the disability grant. At first it was three pounds ten shillings a month, then later another pound was added. All the T.B. people were given the grant. It was the same as the old people's pension.

Three times a week Stone went for treatment to the clinic, in a corrugated iron house near Elsies, where the nurse gave him injections. She came to Poppie's house and said: You must all come to the clinic to be examined.

Poppie and her children took the bus to Philippi to be X-rayed. At first they were all right but when Nomvula, then a little girl of two years, got ill, the doctor said it's T.B. too and she had to have the injections as well. When her father went to the clinic he took her along. She was very quiet and good with her father.

Poppie was working as a char with Mrs Stevens.

But in the afternoons when I got home, says Poppie, I saw that the place on the skin where the injection had been given, had formed a little knob and something watery was running out. I showed it to the nurse and she stopped the injections and only gave pills. And cough mixture and cod-liver oil, and for months on end the milkman came

118

every day and brought us two pint bottles of milk free. We were given brown bread for free, every day I had to fetch a loaf at Mr Katz's shop. He became angry when the bread heaped up and became stale because I didn't have any big child to fetch it, and it was a long walk to his shop, especially on the days when I charred. Then they took away the bread. Every Wednesday I went to the clinic, and was given a card with which to buy seven and sixpence's worth of groceries at the K.T.C. shop.

But Stone didn't get well.

You're doing wrong, tata-ka-Bonsile, said Poppie. The doctor told you to rest. Now you work around the house all day long.

He walked to the dunes with Bonsile. He cut Port Jackson branches and made palings to enclose the yard. He plaited the green twigs and made a pretty fence. It was not hard work, and Bonsile, who was five years old, helped him, but before long the sweat was streaming down his face, and his strength had left him.

If you don't rest here at home, said Poppie, you'll have to listen to the doctor and go to hospital.

This angered him. You want me to go away so that I can die and you can marry some other man. Nobody comes from the hospital alive.

But when his condition weakened, he knew there was no other way. One day he walked away to the clinic and when he returned, told Poppie: So, I have booked a bed in the hospital. You'll like it very much to stay alone.

That's good, said Poppie. I'm getting tired of being scolded at the clinic about your not going to hospital.

They also scolded her about the loaves of bread which she did not fetch at the shop.

We are trying to help you, said the white nurse. And is this the thanks we get?

If you don't want us all to die, said the black woman next to Poppie to the nurse, then you are forced to help us. Because you pay us so little.

Those years the money was miserable.

119

Sunday afternoon buti Hoedjie arrived at Poppie's place.

They were sitting on the sunny side of the house, enjoying the low autumn heat. But Stone had his jacket collar turned up and a coat thrown over his shoulders; the children were playing in the next-door yard and Poppie had her youngest at the breast. She was glad to see Hoedjie because he hadn't been sleeping with them. Mamdungwana had told them that people had seen him hanging about this Muis woman all the time.

How is it you all sit like this? buti Hoedjie asked. Don't you know about all the trouble in the location?

He sat down on a small wooden box. People are going to strike because of all this trouble with the passes and the permits when we visit Langa. And for a pound a day wages.

I heard about the meeting, said Stone, but I have no strength to go.

I don't feel for this meeting, Poppie said. She's not complaining. She has a pass and her ma has one, and each of her brothers. Mosie never runs into trouble; it is only buti Plank and buti Hoedjie who get into trouble when they are drunk because they lose their passes or haven't the papers on them or don't have them stamped in time. Twice last month she paid buti Plank's fine to get him out of gaol.

He was very contrite afterwards. He wept and returned the money she had paid. I was drunk, my sisi, he told her. She then put the matter out of her mind.

Poppie took the child from the breast. Well, forget about this meeting, my buti. She cooked food and he shared their meal.

Little brother-in-law, buti Hoedjie said, I hear you're going to hospital. It's the will of God, Stone answered. I am booked in, and they will let me know when there is a bed available, ja. He was fond of talking Afrikaans to his brothers-in-law, he was now so proficient, he did not want to talk any other language with them.

Now it is God's will, Poppie said, but he doesn't talk about all my uphill time with him before he went to book himself in.

Stay with us tonight, buti, Poppie invited Hoedjie after they had eaten. With the location so disturbed it is better for you to stay off the streets.

Mama's house was not far from where the meeting was being held.

I'll go to mama's place and see how they feel about it.

It wasn't the question of whether you felt in sympathy with the strike or not, Poppie explains. A strike is like that. If you are inside a strike or outside, your face shows nothing. If you're not on strike you are in danger, because people think you're a spy.

The people marched to the police station the first day and brought their passes — some burnt them, others threw them on a pile. I stayed at home with the children and my sick husband.

They said the pass laws were too hard and the money too little. Those days the police would knock you up, even twelve o'clock at night and come into the house and demand: Iphi dompass? which means, Where is your pass? If they found somebody without a pass they locked him up. Or if you lived in Nyanga and you visited your people across the road in Langa and you had no permit for this visit, they'd stop you in the street and then it was into the cells at Philippi, just like that. That is why people went on strike, because the police were too hot with the people in the location.

Now if they think you are not with them in the strike, they burn your house.

Monday afternoon the man Major who was the driver where Mosie worked, knocked at Poppie's door.

Has Wili gone to work? he asked. They called him Wili at work because of his name Wilson.

Yes, Poppie answered, he is not very serious about the strike.

Then you must make a plan so he can come home safely

121

this afternoon, Major said, else he's going to walk right into big trouble at the bus stop. The strikers are beating up people coming back from work by bus.

Poppie took money from the dresser and gave it to Major: Take the money for the bus fare, she said. Go find Mosie at his work. Tell him he must not get a bus.

Major took the money and went by train to Cape Town, from there he went to Mosie's work place, but when he got there the foreman said: I let them go earlier this afternoon, because they're restless. I saw Wili walk to the station.

But Major did not see him on the station and a man whom he knew, told him: I saw Wili get a train. Maybe you'll find him at Langa station.

The trains were not as full as usual at going home time, people were quieter and watching each other as if they were afraid. At Langa station there were policemen wherever you looked. Major saw Mosie and, pressing through the crowd, he took him by the arm: We must get away from here, buti. We're not of the Cape people, let's keep ourselves outside of their trouble.

As they left the station they saw the permit house burning, the house where you went for a permit if you wanted to go from Langa to Nyanga. First the black smoke and then the red flames and the noise of the wood crackling and the shouting. The people around them gave way for fright. Near them the police wanted to go this way, then that, just like dogs not knowing which to bite.

Major said: We can't go this Langa way to Nyanga. Nor the other way round. They heard the sounds of shots fired by the police; in the people around there was a movement, as if it had grown out of the earth.

I didn't know if they were pressing us forward or trying to go back, Mosie remembers. Then we were swept down the street by the crowd. We moved with the stream of people running as if they were following their own legs.

We ran down a lane near the station, other people came running from it.

God, Poppie, he told Poppie. Then the thing was right in front of me.

It was near the station in an open place that the crowd pushed up against a car in which a white man was sitting. Somebody shouted something, somebody else started pushing the car. Quickly more people joined in. I nearly got shoved over the roof of the car. They took it by the sides, it was over, it was lying on its roof. The white man was out and yelling to his friend somewhere. Somebody shouted: He is from a newspaper! The white man was bending down, covering his head with his arms as the people started hitting him, when the car began to burn.

God, Poppie, it made a noise like 'WHAAA' when the petrol on the ground exploded.

The fire and the heat pushed the people back. Or maybe the blood on the man's head, running through his fingers. Maybe a stone, or a broken bottle that hit him.

I felt a cold wind in my stomach. I thought: God's truth, they're going to kill him. The man next to me I knew, but his face had gone all funny like. I didn't know his eyes. He had a stone in his hand. We were drowning in the noise but I shouted at him. I wanted to take his arm and stop him. Major pulled me away. They'll finish you, he shouted, and I didn't listen.

Then Major pulled again and shouted: Come, Wili, the dogs. They're bringing the dogs.

People ran so fast, they ran over each other. Women were run over, then children, but they got up and ran again. We ran as if we had an electric charge in us. The white police stopped beside the white man lying in his red blood on the road. The black police followed the people running down the lanes, hitting everybody with their kieries. *Wham, wham*, I heard the police hitting and the people shouting. The white man from the newspaper was carried away, they said.

What happened to his mate I don't know.

Mosie and Major went by a roundabout route through the Port Jackson bushes to Nyanga. Late at night they knocked at Poppie's house and she opened the door.

Inside Mosie's friend Johnnie Drop-Eye was also waiting

123

for them. She closed the door quickly and listened to Mosie's story. The whole location, she told him, already knew about the newspaper reporter. He had died. The people killed him with stones and bottles.

From that time on Mosie stayed at home. He was frightened he might get beaten up. Those who went to work and came back by bus were beaten up badly. It was from that time that Mosie decided to study with the Red Cross and St John's Ambulance.

The strike lasted for three weeks.

We had a difficult time, Poppie tells, but it was not too difficult. Hungry but not starving. Bread lorries came into the location, and white people brought food, mealie meal and milk for the children. If they saw white people bringing food, they let them in. There was very little paraffin, but we went to the dunes to get firewood, dragging back dry branches.

During that time mama was working in a fruit factory in Wolseley, because it was the season. But when she heard about everything, she was worried and came to Cape Town to see what was going on. When she saw all the men sitting at home, not being able to work, she said: Somebody must earn money. This old thing of mine will see to it that everybody just dies of hunger before he'll give us a penny, the old bastard. If I only knew where the old miser hides his money, we would not have it so difficult, she told Poppie. She then made as if she were going to the dunes to get wood, but she took a bus and returned to Wolseley.

The worst worry was about your own people. About tata-ka-Bonsile who was coughing and could not get his injections at the clinic, about mama's children walking like stray things all over the place, until Poppie told Jakkie: Come and live with me and bring Baby along, and Katie, too, because she has to look after Baby. Also about buti Hoedjie who didn't care a damn when he was drunk and told the police: Stick the dompass up your arse, but told the same thing to the strikers. But she was worried the most about buti Plank who might come in from the boats and get beaten up by the strikers because he had been working.

On whose side her stepfather was she did not know. He was a two-face, people said. He preached in church but did all kinds of wicked things. And the more mama was made to suffer because of him the more he said: Man, I love my church very much.

During that time churches were in danger, Poppie explains. The people wanted to set fire to them. I remember our mfundisi at the Holy Cross church getting men to guard the place at night. They could not sleep, not for three weeks because of this threat to burn the churches. The people felt they were suffering too much and how come the churches received so much money? Everybody had to be the same.

When are you going to church again? mama used to ask buti Plank or buti Hoedjie.

And Plank would answer: God, sisi, what'll I be doing in a church? They take you like a chicken and pluck all the feathers round your arse hole. And I am not for this bare-arse business.

This was the way people felt and how they were talking. And lots of people who had a lean time, felt that the ministers were pushing them in the same way as the whites. While people were walking up and down in the streets the minister would be out warning against all this disturbance. So they felt: The minister is with the white people in this thing, making our life miserable. I never heard them say God was a white man because they understood about God, but they said: There is pressure on the mfundisi that he should do what the white men tell him to do. Others said people gave money to the church and the church did nothing for them. There was no difference; all the churches were in danger, the strikers did not want to know anything about God.

Mosie guarded the church with the others and with the mfundisi. Night after night. For Poppie this was cause for both gladness and fear — gladness because he was helping, but fear that for this the strikers might turn their hate on him.

The second week of the strike the hate and death came to Poppie's street.

She saw it with her own eyes.

It came during the night. When the murmur of the anger came, she could hear it distinctly. From afar, and all the way closer. Mosie wasn't home, Johnnie Drop-Eye had gone as well. When the growling and thunder came down her street and came past her house she went to the door and called to tata-ka-Bonsile: I am standing here because I have to be ready to open the door if Mosie comes or Johnnie. But they didn't come to her house. She saw they were young fellows, all carrying kieries. They went across the street to the house of Mr Mfukeng, the shopkeeper.

Come out, Mfukeng, they shouted. Come out, we want to see you.

They wanted to break down the door. One of the young men struck a match and the low flames sprung up in the night and died down again as the grass in front of the house burned.

Come on outside, Mfukeng, we'll burn down your house over your head.

They were young people and had known Mr Mfukeng from the time that they could first walk. They had been to his shop hundreds of times. It was therefore as if they were frightened when he opened the door and they saw him standing in the doorway.

Get out, he shouted at them. Get out, you swine.

The young men slowly backed away, some picked up stones and threw them on the roof of the house and at the fowl-run round the back where they heard a cackling start up in the darkness. Mr Mfukeng was still shouting and they backed away, then left at a slow run.

The fire was eventually put out. The silence came back. Poppie left the window and lay in the dark, waiting.

The next morning they were back.

Mr Mfukeng left his house early, pushing his bicycle. Carefully he looked up and down the street as he walked the bicycle to the gate in front of his house.

He came across the street and talked at the window of Poppie's house.

Molo, neighbour, he greeted Stone. I am going to look for the people that wanted to burn houses at night. They talk Sotho because Mr Mfukeng is a Sotho, and Stone, who came from Herschel near Basutoland, knew Sotho. He pushed his bicycle on to the house of some other Sotho people in the street, and went inside.

There the young people of the previous night found his bicycle. This time they came with a motor tyre and petrol. Poppie heard the shouting and came out to see. She heard shots being fired — maybe policemen or soldiers shooting people, she thought. She started running to fetch her children in, when she saw the thick smoke of the burning tyre and the bicycle in the fire, the glint of its spokes visible through the black smoke.

Mr Mfukeng must have fired from the door, Poppie explains, because the revolver was still in his hands when the young people took him. It must have been the revolver which made them go out of their minds. They hit the revolver out of his hand with kieries, then they attacked him about the head with kieries and bottles, they hit him with bricks and he pitched forward, there in the street near where the bicycle was burning on the burning tyre. He got up from the ground, and turned down the street like he wanted to get away, his arms above his head to keep away the kieries' blows, till somebody threw a brick at him. It hit him in the back, making him stagger. Still he staggered on, but stones were now raining on him, some against the back of his legs. Then he pitched forward and lay all stretched out on the street, his arms in front of him. Even so, he did not lie still, there on the sand of the street. He crawled on, dragging his left leg behind him. And now it was stones and bottles and every kind of object raining down on him as he crawled slowly like a snail.

I cannot move, my feet are stone. I can see his blood on the road, but I cannot do anything.

A woman who lived near me and was family of Mr Mfukeng ran from her house and threw herself on the man lying in the street. The crowd stood back and did nothing to this woman.

He was not dead yet. The older people went to the shop to call his wife and they brought a stretcher and pulled him on to it. Mr Mfukeng had many wounds, his blood shone. They picked him up and carried him into the house of the woman who had thrown herself on him, then they tried to get a doctor. He was a white doctor and he came with the Saracens, he couldn't have come by himself. But by the time he got there Mr Mfukeng was finished, already dead.

This now was one of the bad things I saw with my own eyes.

This Mr Mfukeng was a very quiet man. He once asked my husband to work with him in his shop in Nyanga, because of tata-ka-Bonsile also speaking Sotho, but he could not take on the job because of his sickness. His wife worked in the shop as well. He was a very neat man, very light in colour, very fond of a suit and a hat. When they killed him it was the first time I heard he was C.I.D.

The police fetched away his wife the same day he died; they fetched her with a police van, her things were put in another van. They were afraid the people would kill her as well.

Buti Hoedjie had gone for a walk up against the dunes that morning, and he saw what was happening in the street.

It was the shooting with the revolver, said buti Hoedjie. The people were uncertain before, they only wanted to burn the bicycle. He shot in the air to frighten them; then the young ones knew why he carried a revolver, because he was C.I.D. Only white people and black policemen carry revolvers, and maybe coloureds.

Poppie's hands trembled while she poured tea for buti Hoedjie and tata-ka-Bonsile. She had drawn the curtain in front of the window, because she did not want to see Mr

CAPE TOWN

Mfukeng's house. All day long the curtains remained drawn. She cooked something on the Primus, even though it was a waste of paraffin. She did not have the courage to go outside and cook over an open fire.
There were rumbling noises in the street, now a jeep, now an army truck. From the time of the murder it did not stop, day in, day out.
And then there was the noise at night, in the sky above your head. They went out in the backyard to have a look. It was a helicopter flying low, a strong light shining from underneath it. Bonsile grabbed Poppie's dress, shouting: Mama, I'm afraid.
I think they are throwing the light on the bush to see whether people are holding meetings, buti Hoedjie said.
They stayed in the backyard, close to the wall, in the shadow. They did not want to see Mr Mfukeng's house.
We thought it would be burned down that night, Poppie explains. But people's anger against him was finished, they did not come near the house. Only very much later, people who did not know Mr Mfukeng, or how he died, came to live there.
They killed him, using bricks from a church being built not very far from his house. That church was never completed. It is still standing like that to this day, half finished.
The feeling against the black police was fierce. From that year, 1960, people started murdering the police, because they were reckless. If they saw a black policeman walking alone, they killed him. Then the council moved the black policemen from their homes and let them live on one side, by themselves.
At Lamberts Bay I had seen teams playing kierie-hitting and how they beat each other and how they became angry. Here in the Cape I knew about the skollies and the bodies found in the bush after the weekend, even three at a time. At night we had trouble with my brothers, buti Plank and buti Hoedjie, walking about, drinking and fighting. Then we had to hire cars and take them to hospital. And the police came two, three o'clock at night knocking on our doors asking to see dompasses and permits to be in Nyanga. And

if the police were drunk, they would tear up the permits in front of my brothers' eyes and take them to the station so that they had to pay five pound fines which were pocketed by the police. I have seen a lot of ugly things but this was the first time that I had seen people kill somebody with their bare hands.

It was not for fighting or for money or because of drunkenness, it was something different. It was the worst thing I have seen, when they killed Mr Mfukeng, because he was C.I.D. and they hated him.

31

The strike in Nyanga lasted for three weeks, but after this time we heard the people of Langa were already back at work. When the police wanted to finish the strike, they started hitting everybody with samboks and kieries and rifle butts to make them return to work.

The people marched to the police stations, the Cape Town gaols were full. I had heard they marched to demand Kgosana; he had a reputation for saying terrible things at the meetings. He was a university student but they locked him up. The people marched to set him free, and the day they let him go he disappeared and escaped.

The last day of the strike the location was filled with policemen and soldiers. An army jeep went round the location and a man with a microphone said: The strike is over, people must return to work. It was early in the morning, not yet eight o'clock, when a helicopter came low over the houses and they spoke over a loudspeaker: You must return to work, it is now over.

After eight they came back again, the army jeep and the helicopter, and now they were saying something different:

The people who are still in the location must return to their houses and stay there. Nobody is allowed to go anywhere, not to the shops or nowhere. Now the entrances to the locations were shut off and we had to stay in our houses. And when I went to the outside tap to fetch water the white policemen said: You must turn back, but I kept on and fetched my water.

Through the windows we could see people being loaded into police vans, and those who could find no place inside had to follow on behind. It was a rainy day, and they walked in the rain. They went from door to door and every man they found not working they hit and loaded on to the army trucks and took to the police stations. We were afraid they were going to shoot them.

Later they also came to my house and we saw what they meant about people not going outside in the streets. It was so that they could beat the men right out of the houses. One would be knocking at one door, then another door, knocking everywhere, white and black policemen. They hit out with kieries and nobody could get away. They filled my house and wanted to take my husband, but I showed them the doctor's papers. The white policeman read the papers and told the others the man is ill, leave him be.

Buti Plank had such a big fright when he saw the men being loaded in the vans, that he hid in the fowl-run before they came to our house. He lay on the ground and pulled sheets of corrugated iron and sacks over himself, but the police found him there when they saw his feet sticking out from underneath.

Two policemen dragged him out, the one took his arms, the other his legs. His body dragged on the earth, his jacket dragging up round his neck. The fowls were going mad inside the fowl-run and while they were dragging him outside some of them sat on him and shit on his clothes. He did not fight, his only fight was to keep his body like a dead man. Chicken feathers were in his hair and he spat and blew to get the down out of his mouth and his nose. He spat and he swore terribly.

It was great fun for the children to see the grown-ups

131

running away from the police. I remember my youngest stepbrother Jakkie killing himself with laughing when they dragged buti Plank out of the fowl-run. Jakkie was ten years old. Katie did not laugh, she was carrying Baby and looked away from this dragging business. But Jakkie and the other young boys laughed as if they wanted to kill themselves; holding their stomachs, lying on their backs in the sand and kicking in the air, making as if they were buti Plank being dragged away by the police.

When the police hit buti Plank into the van with their kieries, the children were still laughing.

Poppie screamed: Stop that laughing! Stop that or I'll kill you.

Tears were running down her cheeks. It was different from the laughing when we were young and oompie Pengi was lying there drunk. It was not the children's strike, it was the strike of the grown-ups. And the children laughed about it. They laughed when their tatas and their oompies and their elder butis hid underneath the beds or behind the clothes in the clothes cupboards or in the toilets and the fowl-runs and were dragged outside.

It was 1960 and the children were ten years old and nine and eight, or maybe eleven. And others were younger, but they remembered.

It wasn't the sort of thing for children to see, Poppie says. They lost their respect.

FOUR

Poppie's pass

After the strike Poppie went to the clinic to ask if the bed in the hospital was still free. The doctor said: Yes, Stone must come.

But Stone was again unwilling and accused Poppie: You want to get me out of the house.

She took him to the clinic and went along in the bus to the hospital in Westlake, but he wouldn't speak a word to her. She walked with him up to his bed in the ward and helped him undress, but still he didn't speak a word to her.

You can come on Sunday afternoons to see him, the nurse said.

A month after the strike, Mrs Graham went back to England and Poppie lost her char work. To get her pass fixed before taking on a new job she went to the new office in Nyanga, two old brick buildings where white people had formerly lived, now fixed up as an office.

They gave me an extension for six months, but after six months when I went back — I didn't have a job yet because with a sick husband and small children at home it was too difficult — now Mr Strydom looked at my pass and he said: You don't qualify for the Cape, you must go away to the Ciskei.

It was the first time that I had heard such words. I thought: They brought me here to the Cape, they wouldn't say such a thing now. I didn't think it so serious, I thought: Perhaps it is just his way of speaking.

Mama, said Poppie that night to her ma — but she made it sound like a joke, because she didn't believe it — mama, they want to send me to Kaffirland.

Mama didn't take it seriously either. But still she said: Then you must see that you get a job. If you've got a job, they can't send you away. Katie must leave school and look after your children.

Poppie wouldn't have it that Katie should leave school. I'll manage by myself, she said.

135

She went to work for Mrs Scobie at Rondebosch for eight pounds a month.

When the clinic heard that I had a job, they took away the disability grant because a person working doesn't qualify for the grant. So the job meant only four pounds extra to what I had been having, but working helped me to change my pass.

The work at Mrs Scobie's was inconvenient. She worked sleep-out, from eight in the morning till five in the afternoon, she cooked in the afternoons and put the food in the warming oven for the four adults who were at work, the parents and two children. She worked from Sunday right through the week. Sundays Mrs Scobie's other married daughter and husband and two grandchildren came to dinner, they ate till two o'clock, then she didn't leave the kitchen till after three.

Sunday was the only day I could go to Westlake to see my husband, says Poppie. It's beyond Retreat, past Pollsmoor, and on Sundays the buses were few. When I got there, it was too late, past visiting time. As I came down the road I'd see my husband standing inside the gate, waiting for me. But the gates were locked and we'd have to stand talking through the bars. That's where he started getting jealous. Where were you? he asked. With whom have you been carrying on? What are you doing all the time, while I'm stuck away here?

Sometimes he started weeping. He became thin and weak.

It was also very difficult because I had no one to look after the children. Mosie and Johnnie Drop-Eye stayed with me, and buti Plank off and on, but they were at work. When the weather was bad, buti Plank came home from the boats. When he wasn't drunk he was as gentle as a woman with the children.

But other days I had to leave them in the house. The little boy, Bonsile, was in Sub A but the others did not go to school yet. When I left them there, I hid the matches — because children like playing with matches — and locked them in the house. I'd say to the neighbours, I'm going to my job, keep an eye on them. I kept the boy from school and he looked after the other children well. He was seven, the girl five years and the youngest two. Later on they got used to staying alone, because I told them, I don't want other people's children in my house when I'm at work, because I lose my stuff, the children carry things away. Now they are content, and I leave them bread and cold tea, everything cold, they must eat it cold.

The hardest thing for me was when the children got sick. You leave the children well in the mornings and when you come back in the afternoon, you find one is ill with a cold, or earache, or feverish. By then the sun has already set, but you've got to leave the other two again and walk with the sick one to hospital, that was the hardest. And the houses we lived in, they could take fire so easily, they were only pondokkies of corrugated iron and wood. At work, I used to think perhaps: Has my house burnt down? And have the children run out in the street? Sometimes when you got to Claremont station, you'd hear them talking of a child run over by a car, then you'd get a fright that makes water of your body, and you'd be in a hurry to get home to see if the children were all safe.

The boy was a quiet child, like his father, but he was a good child, fond of his little sisters, not fond of fighting or naughty like. The little girl was four or five years old when she asked me in Xhosa — the children in the location didn't learn much Afrikaans — she asked me: Mama, who does mama love, me or Thandi. Then I got a fright, because I didn't think a child of mine would ask such a thing. I didn't know what she had seen, Thandi was about two, they were close together in age. Then I said: No, but I love both of you. Then she said: Oh, I thought mama loved Thandi more.

It gave me a fright, because she was too young to ask such a thing. What made her ask it, I don't know. I was always tired and worried when I got home, perhaps I didn't always treat the children right.

Your buti keeps talking about Muis, said mama. Muis was half-coloured, half-Xhosa. After the strike it seemed she'd dropped him. Now they'd made up again. Mama didn't often come to see Poppie, she worked sleep-in and, when she was off, had to see to her own house and children.

She's not the wife for buti Hoedjie, said Poppie.

Mama sat at the table on a straight-backed chair. She rubbed her hand over the table, the table which she had bought Poppie in Lamberts Bay. She's a hard worker, said mama.

Forget the hard work, mama, I don't like her ways. I had a good look at her when she and another woman came here to see Mamdungwana. She works for a month or a week, they say she can't keep a job.

Perhaps she'll help your buti, said mama.

But who are her people, from where does she come? We only know she hasn't got no people, and she grew up in a reformatory at George.

But mama's heart was for Muis. I can't help it, but I already love her. It's surely because of her hardworking-ness.

Poppie wouldn't go to the wedding. Buti Plank was on the boats at sea, but Mosie went. Poppie wasn't pleased that he went. That thin girl with the legs like sticks, I can't stand her, she told him.

Mosie thought: My little sister is jealous that her buti is leaving her for another woman. Even if he gives her so much trouble.

They were married in Rylands, in the house of the minister of Muis's church.

It's not the place for our people that, said Poppie, the Indians and coloureds live there in brick houses, but the Xhosas must live in pondokkies.

The only comfort for Poppie was that buti Hoedjie didn't need to pay lobola for such a cast-off orphan child.

POPPIE'S PASS

Mama gave them a party and Hoedjie and Muis roomed with her. But after two weeks she left mama to stay at another woman's house. Then she started drinking with Hoedjie.

And where now is the woman that's so hardworking? Now mama can see her for what she is.

She is good to Hoedjie, mama kept on. But she's just like kleinma Hessie was, she's got long fingers and she can't keep her hands off my things.

Perhaps that's why she was sent to the reformatory, she is a thief.

Keep your mouth, Poppie, said mama. She never had no ma or brothers like you had.

Kleinma Hessie wrote: When Mosie has to go to the bush, he must come to us, he was always like our child.

Kleinma Hessie had gone back to kleinpa Ruben, who now was the Ethiopian preacher in Knysna.

Because mama worked sleep-in, she felt it was better so, that Mosie should go to Hessie. The stepfather said he didn't feel like taking Mosie's bush ritual on his shoulders. Mosie was glad to go, because he was nearing thirty.

Come along with me, he said to Johnnie Drop-Eye. But Johnnie wouldn't go, because he had been converted to the Zionist Church and was an office-bearer and at that time the Zionists said: We don't go along with the bush ritual, it's a heathen custom.

After Mosie had come back from Knysna, things weren't the same between him and Johnnie, says Poppie. When a boy has been to the bush he can't be on the same footing with those who haven't been. Johnnie felt all my friends have become men, excepting me.

I can't go around with you any more, Mosie, said Johnnie Drop-Eye. I can't go to the bush either, because of my faith. I'll always be the small boy, although I'm your age. Boys that haven't been to the bush show you respect, but they call me the old man who is still kwedini. I am going away to a place where they don't know me.

He suffers a lot, said Mosie to Poppie. But he's decided

139

to take the train for Durban. Perhaps he'll fit in better with the Zulus, whether he belongs there or not.

34

The winter after she had finished a year working for Mrs Scobie, it became too hard to leave the children early in the dark, cold and empty house, with only spread bread and cold tea. When the children got whooping cough she made up her mind to leave the job.

When she came to the office in Nyanga to change her pass, because her work extension had run out, Mr Strydom said: As the law stands now, I must give you a phumaphele. That's what they say in the location for: You must get the hell out, you must go away.

The law was strict that the wives of men who had not been in the Cape fifteen years or hadn't worked ten years for the same boss must be sent back to their homes.

But where to must we be sent back? said mama. They brought us to Cape Town from Lamberts Bay.

Mama had trouble with the pass too, but she used hard words when she went to speak at the office.

Do you want to send me to Kaffirland? I belong to this land with these people here. I was born here and grew up here. My husband worked in Lamberts Bay from 'forty-five. I have no knowledge of Kaffirland. For what must I go and live with those raw people? Must I go and eat red mealies in my old age?

They gave mama's pass a stamp for a six months' extension, and later for a year. But Poppie was not so lucky.

Her stepfather threw words at her: I told you you would have trouble when you married a man from the raw country. But he was lying, he had never gone against her in her marriage to tata-ka-Bonsile.

POPPIE'S PASS

You don't qualify for the Cape, said Mr Strydom. It was again this thing about the Cape being a place set aside for the coloured people, the thing of getting the black people away to where they came from.

She tried to tell Mr Strydom about Lamberts Bay, about the house built of corrugated iron in Jakkalsvlei. The contract. About the children. Her husband in Westlake hospital.

We know your story, said Mr Strydom. It's here in your file. We know it as well as you do. You don't qualify for the Cape, but because your husband is sick, we'll give you two months' extension.

After two months she was back again. And then she got a month. And after a month, a week. After the week, when she brought papers from the welfare, they gave her two months. From Observatory to Nyanga, from Nyanga to Observatory. A month, then three months, then a week. She spent her days sitting at the pass office.

Why do you put this heavy load on my shoulders? she asked the white man.

He talked more gently. With the back of his hand he beat on her papers. I can't help you. It's the law. It is written here. We are helping you too much as it is.

Then he raised his voice. Don't argue so much. Again he struck the papers with his hand. Here it's written. Here. Read so that you may know.

But in spite of that he gave her a paper with a week's extension. To take back to Observatory to have the extension stamped in her pass.

I don't know how this thing comes about, Poppie said to mama. They don't give me the permit because tata-ka-Bonsile is so sick and can't work. But then they give me the extension because he is sick and they are sorry for me. Now I don't know if his sickness helps me or stands in my way.

Mama named some people who'd come to the Cape after they had, and who had been given exemption passes.

Some people manage to fix everything, she said, they buy the passes with money. But when once your papers are wrong, it is very hard to get them right again.

Look, said Poppie, if the office in Nyanga has chased you away, even if the man in Observatory feels he wants to help you, he's scared to do so, in case the office in Nyanga thinks you've bribed him.

Poppie's trouble came through her husband, Mosie says, because they said: This man is from the homeland. If he's from the homeland he must go back there. But you can't force the man, because the white people need him to work for them, so the wife must go. It was the same thing at Lamberts Bay — the woman must leave.

Poppie kept on. Every month, every two months, depending on her extension, she went to Observatory, to Nyanga.

It's working on my nerves, she told mama, I have the same pain in my stomach that tata-ka-Bonsile had. Am I going to get sick? What will become of my children? But she kept on.

She was heavy again.

At the clinic the doctor who had sent her husband to Westlake, asked her: How's this? Your husband is in hospital and you're pregnant?

Poppie was shy to answer. Once a month he gets a weekend off, she said.

Then we'll call the baby Weekend, said the doctor.

He gave her a note to Mrs Retief, the white social worker who had helped her with the hospital papers and the grant papers and who worked with the T.B. patients' families.

A fourth child? That's not so bad, Poppie. How old are you now?

Twenty-six, said Poppie.

Don't lose courage. Every baby comes from the Lord.

If you look at her, Poppie said to mama, you'd think Mrs Retief is a hard-tempered woman. She's got such a long face and a big body and her voice is hoarse like a man's. But she's a woman of faith. If the Lord sends another mouth He will also send a crust of bread along, she says.

Mrs Retief had helped her with the pass. Once when her extension had elapsed and Mr Strydom had said: This time I will not extend it again, Poppie took the bus to Bellville to

Mrs Retief's house. Mrs Retief lay sick in bed, but when Poppie spoke to her, she got up and phoned the office to give the extension. She got work for Poppie in Bellville, but Poppie couldn't take it, they wanted to pay only three pounds a month.

My God, Mrs Retief said when she heard this. God help us. Don't lose courage, Poppie, we'll look for something else.

35

Sunday afternoon at the Westlake hospital the sister said to Poppie: The doctors think it's better for your husband at home, you can take him back today. Here are his pills. He is not making progress, maybe he is longing for his family.

God forgive her, but her first thought was: It is one more mouth for me to fill.

When she got to his bed in the ward, he was dressed and ready. His clothes hung loosely on him. He had never been a stout man, but she had grown used to him in his night clothes; dressed in his suit, he seemed to have shrunk. He was shaky as they walked down the passage.

Buti Plank was surprised to see him. My God, brother-in-law, you have shrunk to nothing. We must put some fat back on to you.

He helped them every week with fish, and money earned on the boats. Stone's own brother, Spannerboy, also helped when he came from the boats, and Mosie too.

Stone wasn't so partial to fish as his brothers-in-law who had grown up at the sea. He would eat a small piece and then push it away. Poppie started cooking food for her husband behind the cooking shelter, the way she remembered his mother had cooked on the land, she made inqodi

ELSA JOUBERT

to drink and baked water bread. One day he would eat and
the next day he wouldn't touch the food.

During the day he would try to keep himself busy. The
second room had still to be lined with wooden boards. Then
he would take the hammer and nails and start nailing the
boards, but soon he grew tired.

When the disability grant had been taken from him, Stone
started doing handwork in hospital, plaiting baskets and
making trays, as a means of earning some money for his
children. There he had got to know a witchdoctor man. A
week after his discharge from hospital, the witchdoctor man
knocked at their door.

Tomorrow I'm coming to doctor you in my way, he said.

Poppie lay watching him from the settee where she was
resting. Has he ever earned any money with this doctor
business? she asked. His shoes are tied with wire and his
shirt is in rags. No man, here in my house, he won't get
money. He wants to practise on you.

Poppie didn't believe in the witchdoctor people, but
Spannerboy believed and old Makhulu and the witchdoctor
woman who lived with the old grandma.

The witchdoctor woman had started dancing again on
Saturday nights. She put on her long white dress, strung
beads round her neck and the small of her back, and bound
shells round her ankles to make a noise as she walked along
the dirt road. And when she saw children watching her, she
stamped her feet and did fancy steps. She was on the way
to a house in Zwelitsha Drive where they danced. Poppie
hated the witchdoctor business and wanted to stop the
children dancing after the witchdoctor woman.

Thandi was not yet four years old. She bound a towel
round her body and clapped her hands above her head and
twisted her bottom. Her dancing was different to that of the
other children, she twisted her bottom in the way of the
witchdoctor woman. Nomvula stopped dancing and
watched Thandi following the witchdoctor woman down
the street. But Poppie grabbed the child in her arms and
carried her back to the house.

You stop this now, she shouted at the children, one

144

doesn't make fun of older people.

We're not making fun of the ouma, cried Bonsile, we are just doing like the ouma does.

Leave the children alone, said tata-ka-Bonsile.

Poppie was angry. I'm a church-woman, do you hear. I don't have part in this kind of thing.

And when last were you in church, said tata-ka-Bonsile.

It's you with your jealousy that keeps me away, she wanted to answer back, but she kept her mouth shut.

The ouma is also a church-goer, said tata-ka-Bonsile. And to that she had no reply. When she collected for her church and asked Makhulu and the witchdoctor woman, they'd take out their money and pay their tickets. They never missed out.

If the white doctors can't help you, you must try the tribal doctors, said Makhulu to Stone.

Poppie remembered what ouma Hannie had told her, right at the end of her life. It's like an injection needle, Poppie. The doctor can kill you with it, or make you well. As long as he makes you well, it is good. If the witchdoctor woman can help a person, it is also good. It is a kind of faith. But it is not my faith.

This she had said in Lamberts Bay when she was close to dying. And now tata-ka-Bonsile kept on with this witchdoctor thing.

You should have let the old man doctor him, buti Plank said when she chased the ragged old man from her house.

So she couldn't go against them when old Makhulu came to tell of a clever witchdoctor man, a Mr Mkwena. And when Spannerboy, home from the sea, said he would give the money for it, tata-ka-Bonsile answered: Now you can't stop me again.

They walked a long distance to the other side of Nyanga where Mr Mkwena lived in a council house. The house was built of bricks, whitewashed, and a low wall was built round the garden with a cement footpath leading to the front door. Built against the house was a corrugated iron lean-to, and the young boy who opened the door to their knock took them there. Before they walked round the house, Poppie looked through the open front door and saw the furniture and the wireless and the artificial flowers and the glassware on the sideboard.

The lean-to was his surgery, where he kept his medicines. On the shelves were canned-fruit bottles with roots and bits of shrubs and leaves and seedpods in them, and next to the bottles coils of hair and jackal tails and bones and broken animal skeletons, on the floor in a corner an intact snake skin.

They sat waiting on two low benches but Poppie felt ill at ease. I don't like this kind of thing.

You must shut up when the man comes in, tata-ka-Bonsile said.

She knew she must not speak, it's akuthethwa eyezeri — when someone works with tribal medicine nobody may say a word.

I'll hold my mouth, she says, but it's a nonsense thing that you are doing. She wished to take tata-ka-Bonsile's arm and lead him home. The Lord is not in this place, she wished to say to him.

But he sat waiting and she waited along with him.

The witchdoctor was a lean man, with a long neck and a sharply pointed face, very dark of complexion, with close-set eyes. He kept on twitching his eyes. He wore an ordinary suit and tie, the white string of beads he wore round the wrist under his cuff was the only sign of his being a witchdoctor.

He sat on a stool opposite them and asked them without looking up: Do you want short news or long news?

Stone had the feel of the five-pound note of his buti in his pocket. Long news, he answered.

First the doctor got up and walked out, but he came back after a while. Then he sat down and pulled a stool closer and put down a lamp on it. The boy lit the lamp and put down a small mirror, the kind a woman carries in her handbag, and a paper and a pencil beside the lamp. Then the doctor spoke words we could not follow, lifted the mirror, turned it round, looked into it and then made pencil marks on the paper. He started speaking. After a time I couldn't listen any more, mama, said Poppie, he spoke such non-sense, and tata-ka-Bonsile just kept answering: Siyavuma, siyavuma — yes, yes — to everything he said.

He said tata-ka-Bonsile had been poisoned, not here, but in his home country, a clansman had put the poison in his food. We must go home, he said, and tell all the family to gather at our house, and Monday at hanging sun they'll see him drawing out the poison.

On Sunday Stone went to tell his whole clan and Monday at sunset they were all there, they waited until dark, but the doctor man didn't turn up.

Tuesday tata-ka-Bonsile went to ask him: And what now? Monday isn't a good day, he said, I'll come tomorrow.

But the next day the clansmen wouldn't come the whole distance again, then it was just buti Spannerboy and Makhulu and an old man Majola, living opposite us, and buti Mosie and I were there to watch, says Poppie.

Light more lamps, he said, when he came, there must be enough light for you to see the poison.

Then the man started shaking. He said to tata-ka-Bonsile: Take off your shirt. Come here and kneel in front of me.

Then he took the razor-blade to cut tata-ka-Bonsile. I hate that kind of thing. He cut him across his stomach and pressed the cut to keep the blood back. He took a tobacco pouch from his jacket pocket and loosened the thong with his teeth. He took from it a horn, I think it was a springbok's horn.

Bring a glass jar, he said, so you can see the poison.

He pressed the horn on the cut and started sucking it. He sucked and he sucked. Nodding his head, he said: Hmm, this poison is very old and strong, it won't come out.

Buti Mosie and I looked at each other and I thought, now if I were a man, I'd kick the witchdoctor, but we weren't allowed to say a word, because we'd be spoiling his work.

The doctor man took a wire from his pocket and scratched in the horn and threw something into the jar: Hauk, look what's come out of his stomach. The others went nearer to look, but Poppie wouldn't go. I'll make us some tea, she said.

147

And so, so what is it that came out of your stomach, she asked tata-ka-Bonsile when the people had left. Aren't you going to lie down, other days you are in bed by now.

She looked into the jar and turned it over on the table. It looked like dog's or cat's hair that had been mixed with grease to form a little ball.

Nothing came out of your guts, says Poppie. If anything had come from your guts, your guts would have been cut up, you would have been in a flat faint, and I would have had to rush you to hospital to have your guts stitched up.

Shut your mouth, tata-ka-Bonsile shouted at her. Shut your mouth about my affairs. Or is it that you want me to die so that you can marry the pa of the child in your belly?

That man came to rob you, said Poppie.

He was shaking so much with anger she made him sit down on the bed.

Was that thing really in the horn? she asked.

Yes, said tata-ka-Bonsile.

Can't you see that the man took a wire and scratched it out of the horn. Are you so stupid?

She helped him to undress and lie down.

I was made a fool of, he said to her at last. I'll go to him tomorrow and demand back my money.

You won't get it back, said Poppie. But it was your buti's money, I'm not worrying about the money.

Was it the right thing for you to lower the witchdoctor in your husband's eyes? mama asked her.

Because Stone stayed sick. After three months he went back to hospital.

Buti Mosie told her: Sisi, you are heavy again, you must leave the char job. I'll look after you. 'Cause your children are my children.

My buti, you are past thirty. The time will come that you will take a wife to you.

Poppie had heard stories that buti Mosie was keeping company with a girl from the St John's Ambulance classes but she did not question him about it. She and buti Mosie were alone now; buti Plank was away on the fishing boats

and buti Spannerboy had gone to Tristan da Cunha islands
with the ships, and Johnnie Drop-Eye had left them and
where buti Hoedjie and Muis were living nobody could say.
And even when the boats were in, there was so much fish
that buti Plank remained living at Kalk Bay. He had moved
in with a coloured woman whom they did not know.

Let me keep on working, says Poppie, everything can't
rest on your shoulders, my buti.

36

Of an evening old Makhulu brought a strange man to
Poppie's house, a small man, half coloured, half Xhosa.

I look to help an old man, he said, an old man with the
clan name of Mgwevu. By the help of the Lord I am well
now. When I lay in hospital next to him, the old man asked
me: When you leave, my little brother, ask around after my
people, my people here in Cape Town. People with the clan
name of Mgwevu. Then you tell them their oompie Pengi
from Upington lies sick in the Groote Schuur hospital.

The small man held his head askew, enquiringly. I was
told a daughter is living here whose mama when she was
young, had the clan name of Mgwevu. So the old woman
brought me to you, sisi.

Poppie felt her legs grow weak under her. She sat down
at the table, tears started running down her cheeks.

Sit down, Makhulu told the strange man. I'll make some
tea.

She gave Poppie tea to drink, with sugar. It's the shock,
she told the old man. This sisi was very fond of this uncle
Pengi, but she thought she would never see him again.

I must go to mama, said Poppie.

Your mama works sleep-in.

149

I must go tell my stepfather so he can telephone mama from his work tomorrow.

The strange man walked with her from Jakkalsvlei to mama's house.

This is far out of my way, he said, but she didn't hear him. They kept close to the houses, across the street it was bush. And behind the bush the skollies hid. They came slinking along the dirt road, their gum boots making no noise, and before you knew where you were, they grabbed you. Here Poppie did not walk at night. But tonight she sees no bush, nor her mama's church which they pass, nor the bus road, nor the street with the lamp posts. She sees nothing till she stands in front of mama's house.

The people here will walk back with me, she told the old man.

Her stepfather was asleep, but the children were still awake, doing school work.

Go fetch your father, Poppie said.

Buti, said Poppie, you must phone mama. Her tears started again. Like Makhulu, the children were unused to their sisi's tears. Their father didn't argue either.

Oompie Pengi is in the Groote Schuur hospital.

Pieta and Jakkie walked home with her. She lay awake, worrying, till she thought: By now they should be safely home.

Buti Mosie came home late from his classes. Why didn't you wait for me, sisi?

I was in too much of a hurry, buti, I never thought of waiting.

The next evening they filled the big lift at the hospital: mama who got off from her sleep-in, Mosie, Poppie, Pieta, Katie and Jakkie. When they were all standing round oompie Pengi's bed, buti Hoedjie also showed up. Mama had sent him a message.

At first they didn't know oompie Pengi. And the tiny, wrinkled little man in the big bed under the grey blanket, did not know them either. Till mama went up to the head of the bed and put her hand on his shoulder.

Pengi, she said, this is Lena.

150

His bright eyes wandered around the bed.

And this lot?

These are the children you chased from your house when you burnt it down.

He seemed to like Poppie better than his sister Lena. Perhaps he took Poppie to be Lena. She stood on the other side of the bed next to him and he held her hand. His grip was strong, it seemed to Poppie that it was ouma Hannie's hand on her fingers.

He pulled her nearer to him. My sister's child, he said. It's gone poorly with me: my mama threw me out, and now I had to live with this person, and then with that person. And then I got so ill in Upington. I dreamt I walked into a big house and out again, and outside a taxi waited. Then a man in a white coat opened the door of the taxi and said, old Pengi, get in. But I ducked back, I wouldn't get in and he drove away again. My sister's child, I was so sick and when I ducked back the taxi drove away. If I had gotten into the taxi, it was tickets with me.

What does all this mean, oompie Pengi? Poppie asked.

My God, it was Death, the man with the white coat who wanted me to get in.

He didn't talk much to the others and when they were leaving, he clutched Poppie's arm once more. Where then is my old Plankie? Isn't he coming to see his oompie?

The others had left the ward, but she remained at his bed. She told him what she has never told the others about her hard life. What have they got against me, oompie Pengi, that I must struggle so much? Oompie Pengi, I wear my feet out walking to the office. It's now almost five years that I am walking. But they won't give me the stamp to stay.

The next day she stayed away from work and took the train from Claremont to Kalk Bay to look for Plank.

From the station she walked to the fishing harbour. She pushed her way through the coloured people and saw a fisherman she knew from Lamberts Bay.

Where's Maplank? she asked. Where can I find him?

His boat is still at sea, but wait a little bit, sisi, he won't be long.

She waited on the jetty. She smelt the fish and the sea water and the diesel smell of the boats. She watched the first boats coming in past the breakwater. The fishermen threw out the shining snoek on the jetty and buyers started bidding.

One of the fishermen she had known at Lamberts Bay came to greet her. He bought her a cool drink and asked: Is life treating you well in Cape Town?

She did not speak to him about her troubles. One keeps them to oneself, this she had learned. If you fall out with friends, nothing stops them from going to the pass office and telling: That woman hasn't got extension, go check her pass. She stood outside the harbour café, sucking at the cool drink through a straw. She was glad to be near the sea again, to smell the fish and to hear the sounds of the boats and the fishermen. But this harbour was different to the one at Lamberts Bay. There the snoek was thrown out from the dinghies on to the beach and they could pick up their skirts and wade in the shallow water to the boats. Here people waited on the jetty.

Her ears caught the faint thug-thug of boats approaching, the sound changing as they cut the engines. Two boats came round by the breakwater to tie up alongside the jetty. The fish dealers pulled their lorries up as close as they could get to the fish being thrown out on the jetty. Poppie pushed her way through the people, because this one was Plank's boat, and he must see her.

There is much noise as the dealers bid, forty, fifty, up to eighty cents per fish. The baskets were emptied and the dealers' crates filled and carried on the lorries. People shoved her aside and the children who were fish cleaners swore at her but she kept her place till buti Plank had finished his work and came to her.

Molo, Poppie, he said.

His forefinger was thrust through the bloodied gills of a fish. He took a piece of string from his pocket and threaded it where his finger was, for her to carry.

152

POPPIE'S PASS

Molo, buti. She took the fish from him, carefully.

And this, buti? she asked, pointing to his head.

He had taken off his oilskin jacket, but the ends of his trousers were still pushed into his gum boots. He wore a woollen jersey and a woollen cap on his head. She was pointing at the white bandage which showed under the cap and at the back of his neck. His skin was shaved and painted with red disinfectant.

Carefully he touched his ear, as if it was hurting.

God, my sister, that Hottentot hit me with a plank, he got me flat on the ground. I chewed the ground. God, man, when I got up I said to myself: Ja, it's the same ear that won't hear.

She knew that ear had been hurt badly before.

Perhaps now that ear will hear when we talk about drink, my buti, said Poppie. Because she knew the fight was caused by drink.

I came to tell you, buti, that oompie Pengi is here. In the Groote Schuur hospital. He wants buti to visit him before he goes back to Upington.

He wouldn't believe her. You fucking well lie to me, he said.

I saw him last night, buti, that's why I come to find you.

So he believed her.

You hear? he says to his mates on the boats. You fucking well hear me, my bloody little oompie from Upington has come. You hear me, it's the oompie that taught me to tap-dance, that taught me to sing, nader na die pale toe . . . you devil, you bloody little oompie, said buti Plank. He had forgotten about his ear, he had forgotten about the fish, he held his arms as if he was holding a woman or a syrup-tin guitar. He hunched his shoulders and danced a few steps. Oompie Pengi, he said, tonight we tap-dance that hospital into its blue arse and back.

153

The month's extension that the office had given her had again expired.

I always struggled to get another extension, says Poppie, but I never knew whether they would give it or not.

She sent word that she wasn't coming to char. She left the children at home and walked to the bus stop. A thick mist covered the mountain and the whole of Nyanga, bringing dampness to face and clothes.

Are you going to the pass office? the other women at the bus shelter asked her.

They knew her. Sometimes, knowing that she would again be kept waiting the whole day at the pass office, she asked them: When you come from work, go into my house to see if the children are all right. She didn't care any more if they took her stuff; they must take what they wish. Or she asked them: Send your girl child when she comes from school to keep an eye on my children. Now that she was nearing her time, she worried, she saw ill-omens every-where, mostly she feared that the children would set the house alight. I feared fire, that was the worst, the house burning down, with them inside.

She went by bus to Claremont station and felt her time was very near. It was hard to walk. The clinic had told her the baby would come in the middle of the month. It was the beginning of the month. When the train pulled in at Claremont station, she pressed her heavy body forward with difficulty, clinging to the rail to lift herself. The door banged to behind her before she sat and she had to hold on to the seat before turning to sit down.

Only a few stations before they reached Observatory. She passed through the subway to the street taking her to Standard House where the papers are given for the pass to be changed.

Because of the rain, there were no long queues of people waiting outside in the street. All had pressed inside the building to get out of the wet, and were crowding the passages. She pushed in through the door and was shown where to join the end of the queue. The people moved forward inch by inch, for long stretches of time the queue did not move at all.

Poppie tried to wipe the wetness from the shoulders and sleeves of her coat. The coat was mohair, bought second-hand from Mrs Scobie. It was too small for her and pulled over the shoulders and didn't do up properly down the front, though being heavy, no piece of clothing would close in any case. Being big of build she did not show so much. The rain had soaked through the coat and down her back but she did not feel the cold. The passages were crowded, the air stuffy and warm, she smelt wet clothes and body heat. It was better to be inside with the others than outside in the rain.

When the queue started moving and the first people entered the waiting room, the women in front and behind her said: Go and sit on the bench there. We'll keep your place.

They said to each other: When one is nearing the end, it is hard to stand so long.

Right through the lunch hour they queued. Other women came and sat with her. Poppie talked, but not too much. Sometimes it was easier to talk to these strange women about the trouble with her pass than to her mother or her neighbours or her brothers. My husband's boss died, one woman told her, before he could work the full ten years. How could he now help that, tell me? I'm coming to speak for my child, another woman said, I want her to come back to stay with me. My husband is sick, said Poppie, that's why he can't work.

After lunch the white men came back and the queue started moving again slowly. At last Poppie was in the office, seated on the bench against the wall. Behind the big desk the white man sat.

He had her file in front of him. He paged through it, he saw the declarations, the letters, the forms. He paged through the file, let the pages fall back, discouraged.

155

I can't give you another extension. It is finished now.

He sees her eyes on his face, expressionless. Her mouth does not move to talk. He sees the heavy body.

Look there, there behind you. He pointed to the long queues of people waiting. Every one wants extension. Every one wants permits.

For what is the law there if we just give, give, give?

He drew a piece of paper towards him, wrote something on it, stamped it. Take it to Nyanga. I give you seven days, then no more. Nyanga must make the arrangements to let you leave beforehand.

Poppie knew what the arrangements were. Papers for the train ticket. To her husband's people. To Kaffirland.

You would go and marry a raw Kaffir, mama had said to her. You are the one that likes Kaffirland so much. I didn't know, mama, about the law. Could mama know about the law?

As Poppie took the paper and walked away, the black clerk said: She's near to her time, that woman. The white man did not answer. She heard the clerk quickly adding, as if he was afraid that he had given offence to the white man: But show me one that's not pregnant.

Then he let the next woman enter the room.

Mosie was sitting reading at the kitchen table. After work he passed by the Parade and bought a book to read. He saw that Poppie was cooking more slowly than usual.

Is it not time yet, sisi?

It's too soon.

But in the night she woke him. Go and fetch old Makhulu, she said.

The doek was off her head, it was the first thing she threw off, it made her feel hot, she wanted nothing to cling to her. She had woken up with the pain. If it is a boy child she knew it eats at the small of your back. Now it felt as if the small of her back had been broken in two, and with the pain a hotness all over her body.

When the pain had eased and the hotness drained away, she spoke to Mosie. The nurse's card is on the shelf, under

the teapot, buti. When you have called Makhulu, tell
Mamdungwana, let the man take you to fetch the nurse.
Mosie put on his trousers, his jersey and jacket. He knew
that since 'sixty nurses didn't come in the night unless you
sent a car. He saw that Poppie was holding on to a chair, she
stood quiet till the pain left her, one hand pressed into the
small of her back, the other gripping the chair. When the
next pain had gone, she slowly walked to the room.

From the room she urges Mosie: Go now and call the old
woman. But don't waken the children.

Makhulu was the first to arrive.

Come closer so that I can hold on to you, Makhulu, said
Poppie when the cramp came and she felt it was really
strong.

Makhulu stood beside the bed, and Poppie held on to her
forearm.

Mamdungwana had just thrown an overall over her
nightdress and put on shoes before coming. She asked
Makhulu: Is everything ready?

Makhulu stayed with Poppie who held on to her. Mamdungwana knew the house, she lit the Primus, put on water.
Where is the stuff you bought? she asked Poppie.

You must look in the suitcase.

By the time the water was hot, she had put out everything
the nurse would need, the wash-basin, the cloths, the Dettol
and soap and powder. From the top of the wardrobe she
took down newspapers and brown paper.

Put the paper on the floor, said Poppie, I can't lie on the
bed any longer.

She got down from the bed; Makhulu held her by the arm
to help her down. She knelt on the papers, on one knee, the
other leg stretched out sideways. The pains came, left off
for a while, came again. When they come again, without
leaving off, then you feel you have to help yourself, then
you start to push down.

The child was born on the newspaper.

It is a boy, said Makhulu.

They wrapped something warm round him, an old
blanket of one of the other children.

The afterbirth was not down yet, so Makhulu brought a wine bottle and let Poppie blow on it, but it was no use. The nurse arrived and took away the bottle from Poppie. She cut the cord and tied it, then made Poppie get back on to the bed, and worked with her until the afterbirth came. Makhulu held the baby, Mamdungwana was the nurse's hand, passing her this, then that.

Poppie named the child Fezi, but the nurse and the old women called him Weekend. He was a small, puny baby and cried a great deal.

Makhulu and Mamdungwana cleaned the house and gave the children food. Mama came from her sleep-in to see the baby and Mosie took mama to the bus stop in the early morning dark for her to be in time for her work. Mosie went to Westlake to tell his brother-in-law of the child that was born.

But Poppie did not have joy in the child or the people who were rejoicing around her. Her thoughts were on the paper in her handbag, still folded the way it was when she walked out of the Observatory office. Only she knew about the paper lying there.

She lay on her bed with a bitter feeling in her heart against her husband who had brought this thing upon her with his illness, against her brothers and sisters who did not know what was happening to her. As she moved slowly through the house, rinsed the child's nappies, cooked food, there was a darkness like a wall between her and the people with her. Pieta and Jakkie brought gifts from mama, a blanket, more nappies, Katie and Baby wanted to play with the baby like with a doll. She talked little with them. She gave Katie the nappies she had rinsed and said: Hang the nappies on the line. Six days she stayed inside the house, because a woman who has given birth doesn't at once go out among men. Only after six days did she fetch water again, or walk to the washing-line.

Tata-ka-Bonsile did not come on Sunday and sent word he was feeling worse and not allowed out.

She moved slowly from the house, outside to the fireplace, to the washing-line, to the tap; in the mornings she wished for it to be afternoon, in the afternoon she wished for it to be evening. She stayed away from her work and sent no message to explain.

The folded paper lay in her bag like a dirty thing she had hidden there. The devil tempted her: Ask the old witch-doctor woman who lives with Makhulu for muti against the folded piece of white paper. Let her help you the way she helps the white people with their court cases. And then fear overcame her: The muti would work against the child.

She had nightmares and rolled about in bed, she dreamt that a goat was to be slaughtered for muti, but the child was slaughtered, not the goat. She remembered a story from the Bible about a woman who was chased into the desert with her child and she remembered a child that was slaughtered, and now she screamed in her sleep.

Lord, she prayed, take these things away from me. But dear Lord Jesus, where must I go?

At other times long strings of curses that buti Plank and buti Hoedjie used went through her mind till she covered her head and moaned: Ag, Lord, God, help me. Take this sin away from me.

The nurse came every day for ten days to wash the baby but she had a lot of work and was in a hurry and couldn't do much.

The seventh day Mrs Retief came to see Poppie. Poppie heard the hoarse voice that she knew at the door. Mrs Retief pushed open the door and came inside.

And so, what is going on here? she asked.

She picked up the small bundle and opened up the blankets.

Well, well, so this is Weekend.

The child was small and skinny, the little arms and legs lay tightly pressed against the body, dark and creased as at birth. He was dirty and wet.

Give me a nappy, she said, so I can clean him.

Is Wilson helping you? she asked. She knew about Mosie, by the name of Wilson.

Poppie nodded.

159

So what's going on here? I don't know you like this?

Poppie went to the room where she kept her handbag. She took the paper from the bag and gave it to Mrs Retief.

Lord Almighty, said Mrs Retief.

Again she looked at the date. The seven days they gave you have passed. What are we going to do with you now?

She knew Poppie's story. She looked at Poppie once again: Poppie's face had grown darker, the hollows of the eyes were nearly pitch-black, she looked neglected, the house was dirty.

You can't leave, she said. Not with a husband in Westlake and a week-old baby. We'll have to ask for an extension. That's all.

Poppie shook her head.

Come along with me, I'll take you to the office.

Again Poppie shook her head. She drew back from Mrs Retief, she did not trust her either.

Mrs Retief didn't believe Poppie could be like this. You're not a stupid girl. You're quick to understand. What has happened to you?

Poppie seemed dazed and uncomprehending, afraid to leave the safety of the pondokkie, the four walls that enclosed her like the shell of a snail.

Mrs Retief knew that the pondok can be torn off her back the way children crush the shells of snails underfoot. She knew that Poppie knew this too, and that was why she was afraid of going to the office.

I'll come and fetch you, Poppie, said Mrs Retief. There is no other way out. I'll take you in my car, then it won't take long. I'll say you're sick, then they won't keep you waiting. Come. Come now. I'm coming tomorrow morning, hey? The sooner the better.

She lost patience. You know as well as I do that it won't help you hiding here. Come, behave like a grown-up person, and we'll have it fixed tomorrow morning.

Mrs Retief spoke and the office in Observatory gave her a month's extension and Nyanga stamped the pass.

I must get a job, Poppie thought when she had got her

160

extension. A job before the extension is finished. I can put the child on my back and try to get a job.

But Muis helped her out. She brought money from Hoedjie.

She played with the baby. Now watch this little Hottentot, she said, he doesn't let go of his auntie's finger.

She looked round her. Poppie's house had a different feel, nothing was clean and bright the way it was the first time she came there, the bed hadn't been made, the blankets on which the children slept just kicked to one side. The linoleum in the sitting room hadn't been polished. Her hands itched to get busy on the house.

She and Hoedjie hired a room in somebody else's house. Her industriousness burned in her hands.

Here, give me your nappies, I'll wash them for you.

When the nappies were on the line: Where're your cloths and your polish and your brushes.

She kicked off her shoes, put on an apron, carried furniture from the kitchen. She washed down the shelves of the dresser, scrubbed the table, scoured the pots, washed the windows. Then, while the stuff was still outside, she tackled the floor.

Ag, if you could have seen me, she told Poppie, ag, that linoleum mat in the passage of the Reformatory. Nobody could polish it like me. I tackled that mat and shone it like a mirror. Ag, that mat, it was the only thing that I had a heart for in that place. First the polish, and then with the hand-brushes. They praised me for that mat.

Now you come and sit down here at the table with the child, Muis said when she had done with the sitting room which was also the kitchen.

She tackled the bedroom. The smell of birth was still in the room. She hung the blankets in the sun, carried the bed and mattress outside, shifted the wardrobe and washed down the walls. When the room was clean and the bed made, she put on water for tea.

Mama always said you were hard-working, Nosamile, said Poppie. It was the first time that she'd used the in-law-name for Muis. Now I believe her.

ELSA JOUBERT

Now what is it to clean up such a small pondokkie, said Muis.

When the child was three weeks old, Poppie started charring again. She left the child with Muis. Muis was good to Weekend, till she started drinking again. But then Spannerboy's wife, Constance, came from the tribal country to visit him in Cape Town, and Constance could look after Weekend when Poppie went to work.

At Westlake the doctors asked Stone: What is bothering you? The spot on the lung had healed, but they saw that he was getting no better. They sent him to Groote Schuur in the van and there other doctors spoke to him: What is worrying you? they asked.

It's that my wife cannot get a pass and that my children have no one to look after them.

We think you should go home now. If you have a job and you are earning money for your children, your health will improve as well. The spirit and the body have an effect on one another.

Stone didn't understand everything they told him. Some days he felt he would rather stay in the hospital. He was afraid of getting on to the train, of the people on the stations, of the police. I won't be able to get a job, he told them.

The doctors tested his eyes and gave him spectacles. Wearing the spectacles he felt stronger. Come, give it a try once more. If you have a job, you will get better, they said.

One of his clan told him of a job at a garage in Goodwood where he was working himself. Giving petrol to cars wasn't such hard work, so Stone took the job and once again came to stay at home.

When my extension ran out, says Poppie, I was given another extension for two months, then for a month, then for three months. Since Mrs Retief had spoken to them, there were new words written on my file. I could read it myself, it said: Under investigation. The woman for whom I worked took me to the Black Sash people, but those people, they couldn't do nothing for me, because my husband did

162

not qualify for the Cape, that's why I had to go away. So they said to me I must tell my husband he mustn't leave that job before he's worked for ten years in the Cape. That's the only chance for me.

38

After oompie Pengi had been sent back from Groote Schuur to Upington, things started going badly with buti Plank.

He left the fishing boats and went to live with mama, but when he quarrelled with the stepfather, he moved in with Poppie. He and buti Spannerboy built on another room where Spannerboy and Constance slept. It was very small, only space for a bed, built of sheets of corrugated iron and lined with cardboard. Constance stuck pictures on to the cardboard.

Buti Plank drank a lot. When he was drunk, he spoke about oompie Pengi: He was a fucking real man, he was my tata, he was my buti. His wife walked out on him, just like mine walked out on me, she went away to Lüderitz, she stole his child from him.

He sang the songs that oompie Pengi had taught him, especially the song about Sonny Boy. As he sang, the tears streamed down his face. Every evening he spoke of Sonny Boy.

There my oompie lies in the hospital bed, and the taxi man, the Death man, is standing at his bed and he tells me: Plankie I long for that child of mine, Plankie, why did I let that fucking whore take my child. I'll go look for your child, oompie Pengi, I promised him.

Sonny Boy is a grown-up man by now, buti, said Mosie. He was already older than us when we were children.

I must go look for him, Mosie, said buti Plank. Then I'll go look for my child, the child of that girl I payed lobola for.

He started planning to go on the boats to Lüderitzbucht to search out the children. Sonny Boy is a grown man, it's *your* child at Lüderitz, Mosie told him. But Poppie comforted him: Come to bed now, my buti. It's just the drink that is hurting you so, when will you learn?

Stone was the one with the most patience for Plank. He gave him money when his money was spent. You helped my children, brother-in-law, now I must help you.

He was robbed till he had nothing left. One night he came home only in his underclothes, shoes, pants everything was stripped from him. Then Mosie went to his cupboard and gave his brother some clothes.

He spoke to him: Buti, I don't like it when you drink and hang round the streets. Drink and stay here with us. It's people like you that the skollies are watching for to rob.

But Plank swore at his brother. You think you're better, you think you're Mister Red Cross. Shut your bloody mouth.

Everything I say he knows better, Mosie complained to Poppie. When he's drunk, we can't talk properly. Meantime I want to tell him: Buti, how can you know anything that goes on? You're in dreamland the whole year.

Plank wasn't afraid of skollies, that was his trouble. But he was very frightened of spooks. One night he saw a baboon. He was drunk. He was walking with another man to Elsies, to mama, through the bush, from Jakkalsvlei through Kraaifontein location. And he said he wanted to pee. But as they stood at a bush peeing together Plank looked up from his pee and the other man had gone.

You bloody fuck, I said to him, but where I'm talking he's not there and I look round, and there sits this baboon. He looks at me, he grins his teeth at me. My little sister, said Plank, then the wine was finished right out of my head. Then the peeing was also finished. It was late, my little sister, past twelve o'clock, the moon was shining so bright, I was running away, fast, but I never saw that baboon again.

So we don't know if it was a witch's baboon or a veld

baboon or a drunkenness baboon, says Poppie. But from that day buti Plank didn't drink so terribly much anymore, and he didn't speak about Sonny Boy no more.

We thought: Perhaps oompie Pengi has died and he sent the baboon to frighten the drink away from buti Plank. We spoke a lot about oompie Pengi those days, and wondered if the baboon had been an omen that oompie Pengi was going to die. But then it was not oompie Pengi that died, but Pieta, mama's eldest son by the stepfather.

It was time for Pieta to go to the bush. Mama had put by her whole month's wages to pay for it, and the stepfather had spoken to his clansmen to come and do the work. But I suppose we spoke too much about oompie Pengi and it worked on Pieta. Pieta was fond of buti Plank. Don't teach the child to drink, mama had begged and buti kept his word to her, but he had spoken to him a lot about oompie Pengi and his guitar and how he tap-danced in his white tennis shoes and the black trousers with the pin-stripe. It was already a long time since oompie Pengi had been sent back to Upington, but Pieta kept thinking about him.

Sisi, he said to Poppie, I go to the bush one of these days, but before I go, sisi, I buy oompie Pengi a shirt and socks and send it to Upington.

Pieta was a big strong man, but he wasn't clever and had failed several of his standards and left school at Standard Three. But he was strong and when he hit out the skollies fell.

Pieta mixes with bad company, Mosie told mama.

A week before he died, he said to Mosie: Buti, see that guy, he bullied me when I was a young boy. Now look, I've got stronger and bigger than him, now watch I got him under me on the ground, and I keep him down, and he tries to make me scared with his mouth. Wait till I stand up from here, he says. But I say you talk too much, that time you talk so, that time is past now.

Mosie told Pieta: Little brother, take care, you must keep out of his company. Now that you're the stronger, you'll get a knife in your back.

On Friday after work I go buy oompie Pengi's shirt and

165

socks in Bellville shops, sisi, said Pieta. That way I get nice to match stuff. I'll be late back.

Friday evening I sat in my house, says Poppie. Buti Mannie, my husband's brother from Worcester, was with me. We were sitting at table, we had finished eating. Then about ten o'clock people came by, the girl's name was Mongbulu, and she had a boy called Ruben with her. They said, sisi, we come to tell you oompie Veleli — that was Pieta's Xhosa name — has got hurt. I got a bad fright, I asked: How did he get hurt. We dunno, they said.

They didn't tell me that he had been knifed and was dead. Buti Mannie went to Mamdungwana's husband. He asked: Come with me so that I can see where the child got hurt. I know him from Lamberts Bay days, I saw him grow up.

The girl and Ruben went along in Mamdungwana's husband's car and Mosie and the stepfather.

When they got there they found the child had been stabbed dead.

They stood around, they fetched the police. The police stood around and then a boy came forward, his name was Pepe. Pepe said: I know who knifed Pieta. We were together when he was knifed, but I ran away. They stuck him in the neck.

Pepe went with the police to the house of the boy who had done this thing and they caught him that same evening.

Three o'clock they were back at my house. My husband had been back too because he was working night-shift. He had gone after them. But they didn't speak to me about it. I asked if they had taken Pieta to hospital and they said yes. Next morning I got up early and went to my ma's house and only there I heard that he had been knifed.

Mama worked sleep-in with Mrs Louw. She dreamed. She dreamed she saw her child amongst the coloured boys, quarrelling. One of the boys is holding an axe. My child is a strong big man, my fine boy, my young tree, but the others come up from behind him and throw a jacket over his head and hold him and when he turns round, they stab. It was on a Friday night, coming from Bellville, in Nyanga East at the place they call Kraaifontein.

166

Then mama heard dogs barking in the lane outside her room, and she woke up, and she knew.

The child is dead, she said when they knocked at her window and told her to get up.

She did not shed a tear. I had a dream, she told Mrs Louw whom she went to wake up. And my child is dead.

Mr Louw took them by car to where Mosie and the stepfather directed them, but the body had been taken away.

He didn't come home from work with the rest, said Mosie. He first went to the Bellville shops to buy oompie Pengi's stuff, then he walked home alone. On a Friday night you mustn't walk home alone, not with your wages in the pocket, not if you've already had trouble with the skollies.

It was after this that buti Plank started drinking badly again, and never got to see Lüderitz or Sonny Boy or his own child.

After Pieta's funeral, Jakkie, the only boy left of those born to mama from the stepfather, came to mama and said: I am now leaving school.

He was in Standard Six and had wanted to get more learning. He was cleverer than Pieta.

I'll take Pieta's job, and bring home Pieta's money, he said.

Mama complained to Mosie: I don't like it that Jakkie must go to work. You must speak to him, Mosie.

But he wouldn't listen. He was sixteen years old.

So mama had no more hope of having an educated son. Only Mosie still read books. He went to first-aid classes at St John's in Cape Town, he sat the exam and got the Advanced Certificate and then the silver one. He taught people first-aid in the school building in Nyanga. He also helped with the classes in Guguletu and there he met Rhoda.

Actually I knew her mother first, says Mosie. She belonged to the Red Cross of Simonstown, they came to Cape Town to the Drill Hall, sometimes the Mutual, only later her daughter joined up too. Together we taught the others, we were teachers like.

Mosie wore a khaki gabardine uniform and medals when

167

ELSA JOUBERT

he went to class or when somebody died who had been a member and they attended the funeral. He helped many people. If he saw an accident on the street, he would stop the bleeding, or put on splints. Ouma Hannie had said when he was a child: Mosie must one day be a doctor. Now he threw in his weight with the Red Cross and St John's. He belonged to the Faking Club. They pretend someone is hurt, on the street or anywhere, and then people can come and see how they fix him up and by looking, they learn how to do it.

39

At the pass office there were new people behind the desks. The people in the queues were those that had arrived in the Cape after 1960. There were raw people, people from the tribal areas that got helped before her, and were even given houses.

What then have they got against me? Poppie asked herself.

It was for seven years now that she hadn't known longer ahead than two months or sometimes three that she could stay in the Cape. The longest extension had been six months. Sometimes she got nothing.

Once I stayed in the location for two weeks without a permit. I got used to it. If they were to catch me, my husband would just have had to pay the fine, I could do nothing about it.

Those years, 1966, 1967, the police were very hot, says Poppie. And a Mr van Jaarsveld came from the office in a combi to catch us and check our permits. When the children saw the combi they ran along the streets shouting, Jaarsveld, old Jaarsveld, here comes old Jaarsveld. Now we hid, under

168

the beds or in the wardrobe. Constance didn't have a pass. She was a stout woman, so I just put her up against a corner of the room and threw blankets and clothes over her. They ran a lot of people in and raided the houses.

And when the police lorries came, the children shouted in the streets: Umgqomo, which means petrol drum, because they looked like huge petrol drums. Or they yelled: Nylon, which was what they called the pick-up with the nylon mesh netting. Then people fled into the bushes and waited there till the police had finished their raid. Once old Jaarsveld told the police to surround Jakkalsvlei, because he wanted to clean it up of people without permits, but he arrived too early and we fled before the police turned up. We heard him shouting: I told the police to guard the roads, now all the fucking bastards are taking cover in the bushes.

When we had made the bushes it was impossible to catch us. And the children couldn't be caught either because they don't carry a pass.

More than once I hid because I did not have an extension. After the police, one black policeman and one white, were gone, we'd laugh and tell Constance she could come out from under the blankets. It was great fun for the children to see their pas and mas and aunties and oompies climb out of wardrobes and come out of lavatories. Luckily I was never caught, but this always running to hide was no life for me.

In 'sixty-eight when I came to the Native Affairs in Observatory, a Mr Steyn took my pass book and my files and my folders to the big boss and then the big boss said: This woman must leave at once. He wrote on my folder: She must leave at once. Mr Steyn was a believer, religious man, a man of much faith. He told me: If it is the Lord's will that you stay, then you will stay, and if it is the Lord's will that you go, then you will go. He was a man to talk courage into you, but he was a little scared of the big boss himself, he turned round two, three times at the door before he went into the big boss's office and then he now came back with the story: She must leave at once.

The woman for whom I charred told us to go to an attorney in the Volkskas building. He helped people who

169

were being chased away to get permits. My husband went along with me to the Volkskas building and the attorney came to Observatory with us. He spoke and we got a one-month extension, and then again two months. We paid him twenty-one rand.

The big boss can't help it that he can't give the extension, Mr Steyn told us. It's not him that wants the people to leave. It's the law.

40

Poppie went to church with her children.

Molo, sisi, the women said to her. Molo, she answered. She sat with the women. Most of them were clad like her, in a white blouse, with a turned-over collar, and a purple overblouse with a black belt, a black skirt, black shoes and stockings and a black beret. In front at the altar there were flowers and candles and the little mist of incense shed over the beakers and Bibles. It was a big church, and slowly the people filled the seats.

The preacher was in the pulpit. Wherever you go, he said. Wherever you go, the interpreter repeated in English, there the Lord protects you. If by day you go to your place of work, said the preacher, if by day you go to your place of work, repeated the interpreter. There the Lord will protect you.

Poppie listened to the words. When the devil is on your tracks, then the hand of the Lord comes to you and takes your hand. As Mr Steyn took her hand. If it is the Lord's will that you stay, you will stay. If it is the Lord's will that you leave, you will leave.

Poppie felt her soul was thirsting for the words she was hearing. Her soul drank in the words, she could scarcely remember them separately, they had sunk deep down into her soul. Only now she understood fully. She felt her heart grow big and strong. She wanted to tell of this blessing, it swelled up in her bosom, she wanted to sing it out to the congregation. When the singing started and her voice rose with the rest, it was as if she was being released from everything pent up within her breast, as if she had found peace in this release. Her body started swaying slowly from side to side, her eyes closed, her voice climbed up above the rest.

They were singing to the tune of 'Jerusalem, my happy home', a hymn that Mosie had learned at the Mission school in Lamberts Bay. Here they were singing the Xhosa words:

> Jerusalem ikayalam
> endithanayo
> wofeza nin umzamowam
> zundi phumle kuwe?

She was standing before the throne of the Lord, singing these words that He might hear her:

> Wabona nini amehlo am
> lomasango mahle
> nezi trato zegolide
> zomzi wosindiso?

She felt her head wet with sweat, as if a fever had been broken. When the preacher closed down the hymn and said: Now we want a few prayers, perhaps one of our sisters. . . she heard her voice praying. She knelt on the little mat in front of the bench and softly she started: Protect me, O Lord, that I do not perish before your countenance. Her voice got louder, words of hymns she knew poured through her lips: Lord we have gathered in your house, do not leave us by ourselves. We are here before your countenance. Show us your countenance, do not hide your face from us, O Lord Lord Lord Lord, take my hand.

Lord, Lord, take my hand. Ewhe, the women joined in, ewhe siyavuma Lord Jesus, have mercy on us, Dear Lord

171

Jesus come down from Heaven and join us, a voice started up shrilly.

Amen, said the preacher from the pulpit.

An old man had started praying. The men sitting together, held on to his words. The old men, their hands resting on the kieries held between their knees, listened with their eyes closed, he was speaking the words of their hearts, he was giving voice to what their hearts were begging of the Lord. Ewhe, they repeated. In the eyes of the old man who was praying tears were gathering, running down his cheeks in shiny wet streaks. He was praying for his children: Bring them to your temple, O Lord, fetch them out of the bush in the night when the devil of darkness is wandering. Bring them to the light of the street lamps, protect them with your kierie, beat down the servants of the devil.

Everything Poppie felt in her heart, was being said. She thought of buti Plank, of buti Hoedjie, Lord, protect them, Lord beat down with your staff everything wicked which approaches them, Lord come to us. She thought of her husband: Lord help him. She thought of Pieta: Lord have mercy on his soul. She felt strength rising in her as she repeated these words, she was strong once more. Life had not defeated her, she could get up again.

After the service she had to leave with the children, she was unwilling to leave the body of the Lord. The members of the choir were still singing as they left the church, the women in their purple blouses were singing as they poured out through the open door. The singing bound her to the other women, she was no longer alone. The Lord was with her.

When she got home, tata-ka-Bonsile was still asleep. He worked night-shift and came home at two or three o'clock in the morning. She started cooking. Peace reigned in the house.

The church is my mainstay, Poppie thought. As long as I remain true to the church, the Lord will be with me.

In 1967 Bonsile was twelve years old and Nomvula ten

years, and they were blessed in church. The bishop sat in front of the altar, clad in his purple robe, his hat on his head, his long staff in his hand and the children one by one came to kneel before him. He dabbed oil on their foreheads and laid his hand on their heads and said: I accept you, I lay hands upon you.

Poppie served tea and cake to her friends who came to congratulate the children, the two children received small gifts.

Poppie was satisfied.

I feel as if my desire has been fulfilled, she told mama.

Tata-ka-Bonsile was not able to attend the service because he was on duty at the garage. But he went along to buy the clothes, a white dress for Nomvula and a new suit for Bonsile. Although not a regular church-goer, he too was satisfied that the children had been blessed.

On a Sunday afternoon after she had washed and put away the dishes, Poppie stood resting at her front door. She saw a combi stop down the road, let a white girl get out, and then drive away again. The girl stood looking around her hesitantly, but as she caught sight of Poppie in her doorway, she approached her.

Good afternoon, she said.

She was carrying a Bible, holding it pressed against her heart, as if taking courage from it.

Good afternoon, Miss, said Poppie.

The girl looked around her, to Poppie's house, to the other houses.

Do many children live here? she asked.

She showed Poppie the Bible, holding it out towards her as if presenting it as a gift. Will you help me, I want to teach Sunday school to the children.

Weekend came out of the house and clutched at Poppie's skirt. The girl sat on her haunches and talked to him.

Do your children speak Afrikaans? she asked Poppie. She had been speaking Afrikaans all along.

They hear when you speak Afrikaans, Miss, but they are too shy to speak it themselves.

The girl pointed to the flat piece of ground in front of Poppie's house.

If the children come and sit here, I'll tell them Bible stories. She beckoned Thandi and Nomvula, who had appeared at the door too, to come closer.

Poppie knew about Sunday-school teaching in the houses of black people. She would like it very much to have Sunday school taught in her house.

Miss can come inside. Tata-ka-Bonsile is asleep and buti Mosie has gone out, the kitchen is empty.

She sent Bonsile: Go and call the children of Majola and ouma Vuyiswa. Tell them a school teacher has come and she'll teach the children Sunday school.

I liked it very much, said Poppie, to hear the children singing in the house.

The juffrou came for more than a year. After a while many children attended. Every Sunday afternoon after the lesson, she gave the children some little gift, a sweet to suck or a text, or a Bible picture or paper and some drawing chalk. If the children couldn't understand her, I helped her out and repeated the stories in Xhosa. She taught them English and Afrikaans songs.

The juffrou and I, we sat on chairs and the children on the floor at our feet. The children were quick at catching the tunes. Even if they couldn't understand the words, they loved the tunes. They loved to roll their arms as they sang the chorus: Running over. They shouted the words: Asa Lord loves me, asa heppie asa bie, my skaap is fula running ova. We always laughed at skaap, which means sheep instead of cup. The little ones used to jump up from excitement as they sang and stamped their feet, wanting to dance with the song. The juffrou was very fond of Thandi and of Weekend who joined the singing although he was only four years old.

Stone started complaining. All week long I have to work, Sundays I need my sleep. This screaming in the kitchen gets on my nerves.

You watch the clock when I go to church, Poppie hit back. I can scarcely talk to anyone on the road back, without you asking: Where have you been? To whom did you talk? Now that I have church meetings in my own house it's not good either. I will not tell the juffrou she must stop coming.

But the next Sunday afternoon while the juffrou was praying, Majola stormed into the house, dead drunk, and shouted at his children and took them by force and said: What is the white woman doing here with our children. Then Poppie knew: It is tata-ka-Bonsile who put him up to it.

Can't you do your own rotten work, she asked him, must you go behind my back and let another man do it?

I never told her to stop coming, says Poppie, but after Christmas the juffrou went away on holiday, and then she got a job in another town and in the New Year nobody came to take her place.

41

Why are you so jealous of your brothers' wives? mama asked Poppie.

Poppie couldn't take it that Rhoda wore long trousers the first time that buti Mosie brought her home.

One doesn't come to your in-law's place in long trousers, mama.

It's the new way, Poppie.

How would mama like a daughter who sits on my settee reading a book, in long trousers, while I have to do the cooking? She thinks she's better than us, she looks down on buti Plank and buti Hoedjie. She told buti Mosie he is wasting his money when he helps his drunk brothers. She doesn't want to have anything to do with them.

Mosie is different from his brothers, said mama. She suits Mosie.

Deep down in her heart mama is proudest of Mosie who is doing well at work, who sings in the church choir, and wears his St John's uniform when he teaches first-aid.

You have too much to say about your brothers, Poppie, she said. You must let them be.

Poppie was jealous because Rhoda and her mother had more learning than any of them, more even than Mosie.

This girl Rhoda doesn't treat me like she ought to. She thinks she's better than us. She doesn't fit in with us, mama.

But mama had worse troubles than Mosie's Rhoda.

Muis is at her tricks again, Poppie. She sells liquor, and she keeps company with other men. It comes of never having your own house but just renting a room. She has been how often to Groote Schuur hospital, but she can't get heavy. Now she has no child, no house, that's why she drinks.

And when Hoedjie was drunk as well, he nearly beat her to death because of the other men she went with.

And mama says I must let my brothers be, says Poppie. Then who will look after them? It's always me that's struggling with them. Now buti Plank is behind with his pass, now he's run in, now buti Hoedjie is in gaol and it's to me that they come for help. Right through the night it's at my door that they knock, two o'clock, three o'clock, in the morning, then the skollies are at them and I must jump up to open the door to them. Mama doesn't know how much trouble they give me, but I don't complain. I'm thankful I can do it for them.

But Muis is still going to get buti Hoedjie killed, said Poppie.

Muis ran away from buti Hoedjie and went to stay with another man in Guguletu. Don't go and search her out, buti, Poppie pleaded with him. She has left you for the other man, stay away from her.

But she knew she pleaded in vain, because a drunkard listens to no one. I knew this was going to happen from the start, she thought. Saturday night late she heard a knock at her door and opened it. It was buti Hoedjie, covered in blood. He stumbled inside and threw himself on her sofa.

Have you come from Muis? asked Poppie. She was frightened to see her buti in this state. He was pressing a rag against a deep wound in his head, his cheek was cleft open, his shirt had been torn and blood was streaming from his chest.

Poppie fetched more cloths and tried to stop the bleeding. His lips were swollen, he could hardly talk, but he nodded his head. Yes, sisi.

And it's her man that hurt you so?

Yes, sisi.

Stone was working night-shift, ten o'clock at night, till six o'clock in the morning. She was alone at home.

I'll get dressed, buti, and fetch old Makhulu to stay with the children. But how will I get you to hospital, buti, I by myself? By now Mamdungwana had moved to their new house in Zwelitsha and nobody else nearby owned a car.

I dunno, my sisi, said buti Hoedjie.

Outside in the street it is quiet, bright moonlight, every house in its own pool of shadow and behind the houses, the bush.

Tonight I'll be killed, thought Poppie. And then she resigned herself to it: What else is there for me to do? If I have to be killed because I am trying to help buti Hoedjie, then it has to be so.

She knocked at Makhulu's door, the old woman threw a blanket around herself and came at once. In Poppie's house they wound more cloths round buti Hoedjie's head and pulled on a cap to keep the bandages in place. As he got up he spat out a mouthful of blood. They tried to keep him on his feet.

Take him to Monk, said Makhulu, Monk is his friend. Then he can take over. If your sister is murdered tonight, it will be on your conscience, Hoedjie.

The loss of blood had weakened Hoedjie. He had no more strength left. Poppie took his arm and slowly, step by step, led him down the street. She had to hold him so he didn't fall down. Dogs barked, then it was quiet once more. Nothing moved in the white moonlit streets. As they walked Poppie did not look to left or right, she kept her eyes fixed on Hoedjie's feet slowly shuffling step by step down the dirt road.

Monk's home was made of hessian and tin. When his dog started barking, Monk pushed open the door. Evelina his wife and their three children were sleeping on the mattress in the one-roomed hut. There was no place for Hoedjie inside. Monk held him and made him sit down on the ground, his back resting against the building. His head fell on to his chest. He is dying, Poppie thought.

Monk went inside to put on his pants. Evelina came out too.

Poppie undid the knot in her handkerchief and took out twenty cents. You must take him to Philippi, she said to Monk, let the police phone an ambulance.

Is it the bloody bitch that's done this? asked Monk. He knew Muis.

He was looking for trouble, said Poppie. He wouldn't listen to me. Monk supported buti Hoedjie and they started walking to Philippi.

Have you now finished with Muis? she asked Hoedjie when he was well again.

Yes, my little sister, you were right, said Hoedjie. That whore is poison to me.

I hear she has gone to Umtata, said Poppie, with the man from Guguletu.

It is better so, said Hoedjie. If she'd stayed here, I would try again to get her back from him.

42

It was all in my file, says Poppie, that I came to the Cape with my husband, that I had a work permit before 'sixty. But he had not been here for the required fifteen years, and that's what caused the trouble. We had to keep going to the office. If he was working nights he came directly from Goodwood, and I came in from Nyanga and we met at the Native Affairs office at Observatory. Then we sat there till late in the afternoon, till he had to go back to work. Nothing was settled. We brought food, a loaf of bread, or a bottle of cold drink or a few bananas. Some days the big boss was not at work and so it was no use waiting, other days we saw him but he said: Now look, I'm not giving you a paper to have your pass extended, you must leave the Cape. One madam for whom I worked came herself to Observatory. I think she saw a Mr Stevens. I don't know what they told her, but she said to me: It's no use, Rachel, you'll have to go, you'll be given a nice new house with inside taps.

If you had a baby, you put the child on your back. My babies were all breast fed. Some days you got helped fairly soon, other days you sat from early morning till two o'clock when the white people went to lunch. Those years there was a man called Mr Bayi who showed us bioscope pictures of the Transkei, to interest the people in going there.

We didn't talk much to one another, we were too worried, everybody was uncertain. Was he going to hear: No, I'm giving you no more extensions? You are very uneasy as you sit waiting there. Some days you are given a letter with a week, two weeks, sometimes an extension for a month, but you know very well it's nothing permanent. Then you take the letter to the office in Nyanga and they stamp the month.

For close on ten years I struggled to get my extensions to stay in the Cape, says Poppie.

The same thing they said in Lamberts Bay, Mosie adds, the same thing they said here. The wife and children must go.

When they told my sister to go to the tribal land, she said: But my husband, he's working here, his children were born here, there is nothing for him on the land. So they said: He has his father on the land. But my sister said to them: That very same father is dependant on us, we send him money, how can we go and sit on his back? Now the Native Affairs sent a letter to the old man saying: Your child hasn't

179

permission to stay in the Cape, he has nowhere to go. As any parent would, he said: Let him come back to the land, there's room enough here. When my sister got back to the office they told her: You have got a place to go to, you can go back to the land. By now she was very tired, tired of the going every day, from one office to the other.

One day Mr Stevens threw my pass at me and said: What are you still doing here? You must leave the Cape, you don't belong here.

One day they sent for me and my husband, and then Mr Stevens took my house card on to which my rent was entered and he tore it into small pieces and threw the receipts at us and told my husband: Your wife should have left long ago. Then we turned back without saying a word.

Old Jaarsveld looked out through the window and said to me: You're going to Kaffirland, you're going to eat gubu mealies. We just looked at him and walked away. I went to ask the social worker, Mrs Retief: What must we do now, our house card has been torn up? Then she went to speak to the office again and we were given a new card.

Mrs Robson for whom Poppie charred, was dissatisfied. You stayed away the whole week, Rachel, she said.

Every day for a whole week they had to go back to Standard House in Observatory. Mr Steyn, the man of much faith, told her: I'll help you with the bus fare, Rachel.

Her mama knew people who rented a room in the house across the way. The woman's papers had been torn up in front of her and she had to return to the Ciskei.

She wept bitterly, said mama. She wept for days to leave her husband.

But Poppie said: If I have to leave, I'll not weep like that. Does mama think this is Heaven that I'm being sent away from.

180

43

Rhoda was pregnant or unzima, as the Cape people say, and Mosie eloped with her in the Xhosa way. He met her in Rondebosch when she came from work, and took her home to mama's house.

The next morning he sent kinsmen to the girl's parents to tell them: There is no need to look for the child, look our way. The child is with us. In two weeks' time we will come back to you.

The old men of the clan name collected lobola money to be able to give something in advance, and then returned to the girl's people and said: How much money do you want for her? Damage money for the pregnancy and lobola combined.

After they had paid up, she was makoti and had to wear a black doek and long dresses made of German print. Poppie sewed the dresses on her mama's sewing machine.

Even though she has no heart for it, if she wants her man, she has to do it, Poppie thought. She may be modern in her ways, but now she has to conform, because it is our belief. And how can she feel otherwise, because she's a Xhosa, she's not of mixed blood, she has been taught since childhood how to treat her in-laws.

Mama and Poppie and Katie got together to choose an in-law name for Rhoda; they named her Nokhaya which means: Woman of our house. When she had borne the child, they were married in the vestry of the Methodist minister in Langa. According to custom they had to live in mama's house, because Mosie had brought his ma a new daughter.

Poppie was pregnant too.

Mama, it's my last child, she said. I have a foreboding.

All her children were at school and learning well. Bonsile was in Standard Four, Nomvula Standard Two and Thandi in Standard One. Weekend had just started school. He was her cleverest child. Before he was three years old he said to her, look, mama, and he wiped the sand smooth and wrote a capital R with his finger.

ELSA JOUBERT

She suffered from high blood pressure. The doctor at the clinic said: Don't skip a visit, come regularly. We want to keep an eye on you. Along with the high blood, she got headaches. She went every week to the clinic till they said: Now you must no longer come to the Peninsula clinic, you must go to Groote Schuur hospital.

The office wanted to send her to the Ciskei to her parents-in-law. But she said to the man: I can't go to my in-laws with five children. They were taken away from the first place where I visited them, to a trust village, now they don't have big huts but small huts, and they live together with other people, how can I go there with five children?

I will not go and stay with my parents-in-law, said Poppie. I'll go away if you give me a house. From one house, to another house.

We'll let you know when we have a house for you, said Mr Stevens.

He stamped her pass for another two weeks, then he looked down at her body, at the uncomfortable arms, the swollen face.

When is the child due, he asked.

I am past my time.

He overwrites the two weeks' extension: Changed to two months.

It was the longest extension she had been given in the last five years.

Then my husband was very dissatisfied. I told him I had now just had enough, I couldn't take any more with this last child. The nine months I was pregnant, I spent all my time walking to the office and back from the office. So I told him, I couldn't stand it any more. I must go away.

It's no use arguing with me, I said to my husband. I can't go on like this, I can't talk any more. I felt that if there was a life for me somewhere else, I would go and live there.

The last Thursday at the clinic the white doctor examined me and said: You are past your time, you should have had the baby. Today I am not sending you home. Today we will induce the birth.

I was content, because I was by this time very tired of trudging up and down the hill at the Groote Schuur hospital. They put me to bed and started working with me. The pains began. The doctors stayed with me and examined me off and on, and later that night they said: Now we cannot wait any longer, otherwise things will go badly with you. We are going to operate. My husband had for a long time asked for me to be sterilised so they said, now we will sterilise you at the same time. You should not have another baby. He brought forms for me to sign, and the doctor spoke to the nurse and they pushed me into the room where they operate. And from then on I knew nothing.

It was a Caesarean baby, a girl.

Sunday afternoon mama came to visit her.

Muis is back, said mama. She had too hard a time in Umtata so she got on the train to come back. But she didn't have a ticket, so the guard handed her over to the railway police at Bellville and the police brought her in the van to my house.

And I suppose mama took her in, said Poppie bitterly.

What else could I do?

But she doesn't belong to us any more, mama.

If I didn't pay for the ticket they would have taken her to gaol.

And you forget that she nearly got buti Hoedjie killed. Mama knew the hard time I had with buti Hoedjie.

Poppie felt ill, this way of having a baby was hard.

I don't want to see Muis, mama, she said. She'd better not come here.

Poppie called the little girl Thembisa and her baptismal name was Beauty, but she called her by the pet name of Kindjie, which means little one.

44

With the new baby on her back, Poppie went to Native Affairs in Observatory.

As she walked from the station, keeping to the pavement of the narrow street winding through the white suburb, it started to rain gently.

Ahead of her she saw the big red building and the queues of people waiting. As they felt the rain, the queues started moving, people pushing to get under cover. The white window frames in the red brick building blurred in the rain, seeming to lose their outline. A nausea rose in her, she had difficulty in lifting her feet, in pushing on, she couldn't force herself to go towards the red brick building, to the corridors where the people stood and waited, to the smell of wet human beings, the heavy stench of a child's dirty nappy.

In her mind's eye she saw the small empty office with the big desk and the window raised, and the skinny white man sitting behind the desk, swallowing, gulping down his spittle as he looked at the paper put down in front of him, his white fingers with the short yellow hair on the backs twitching at the pencil while he read, already groping for the stamp lying ready at his side. The dates, carved on the ridges of the stamp, can be turned by a twist of his fingers without his having to give it a glance, he knows the feel of the dates, extension for one month, two months, three months, a year. Or nothing.

What's the matter? asked a passing white woman. She would have liked to help, but was unsure whether the black woman was drunk or not.

What's the matter? she asked again. Poppie held on to a lamp post with both hands, spasms passed through her body, tearing at her, her legs were shaking, the spasm rose, pushed up from her belly, her mouth opened, colourless slaver dribbling out at the corners, then her gullet jerked uncontrollably, and she doubled up retching. Not much came out, mostly bile.

She leant her head against the lamp post to which she was still clinging, her eyes closed, her mouth wet with the yellow bile that was still dribbling out.

The white woman saw that Poppie was really ill not drunk, and she took a white tissue from her handbag. Here, take it, to wipe your mouth. She pushed the tissue in between the fingers clamped around the post.

Mr Stevens pointed to the map with a stick. Now you must choose, Rachel, there's Ilinge near Queenstown, and Dimbaza near King William's Town, and Mdantsane also in the Ciskei but right next to East London.

I do not know these places, said Poppie.

Mr Stevens stopped her protest. Look, I want to help you. You have been used to town life since childhood, and I think it best that you go to East London. I've seen those other places, but let me be frank with you, you mustn't take them.

Is there a house for me? I won't be able to build a house like my brothers built me here in Jakkalsvlei.

We will give you a house.

And will there be school for my children?

There will be school for your children. Is it all right so, Rachel?

It is all right.

Then we put down your name for a house in Mdantsane.

Outside a woman she knew was waiting. Are you leaving, Poppie?

What can I do? said Poppie. I can't break the law with my hands?

45

By Christmas Poppie had not yet had news from the office.

Stone bought a sheep and he and his buti Spannerboy

and other relatives, also a man without a pass called Koopman, slaughtered the sheep in their backyard and skinned it. Poppie had given him the name of Koopman, he was a Xhosa but light complexioned, and to get a job, he had to pass as a coloured. Now what coloured name can I take, he had asked her, and she had said: We call you Koopman, and Koopman he stayed.

Buti Plank also came home on Christmas Eve.

They laid sheets of corrugated iron on the sand and the one man held the sheep while the other cut its throat. They held it carefully so as to catch up the blood in a dish, not to make a mess in the yard. Plank shouted at the little boys standing around: Go dig a hole, that we can bury the blood.

They milked out the entrails, Spannerboy saw to the fire, and they fried the entrails on the coals. When the carcass was skinned and the meat hanging, the men sat round the fire to fry the liver. Johnnie Drop-Eye was there too, he had returned from Durban and stayed with Poppie again.

The wind started blowing, and buti Plank raised the sheets of corrugated iron on which the sheep had been slaughtered to keep the wind from the fire.

Poppie brought food outside, porridge and bread. Constance was cooking in the kitchen, she had not yet returned to the tribal land.

Poppie saw that someone else had joined the men at the fire, and behind him a woman was sitting on her haunches. She recognised the skinny body. It was buti Hoedjie and Muis.

Molo, Poppie, how are you? said Muis.

I'm all right, said Poppie. How are you?

I'm all right too, said Muis. She got up to come nearer. But Poppie stopped her, turning away from her so that Muis couldn't reach out to the baby on her back. And this now? she asked. What new trouble are you bringing to us?

Why do you ask me such a thing? said Muis.

Mayn't I ask? Buti Hoedjie nearly got killed because of you, and now you see he's not dead yet, now you come back to see if they kill him off properly.

She put down the porridge and bread on the ground.

186

POPPIE'S PASS

Buti Plank told her: Shut up and leave the woman be. But she wouldn't listen to him.

Talk to her, brother-in-law, Plank told Stone. Poppie wouldn't listen to them. She was screaming: I don't want her here in my backyard. She must go. I don't know what she is looking for here, because my troubles are heavy.

She started weeping.

To see buti·Hoedjie again tagging along so meekly after Muis, infuriated her. If something happens to buti Hoedjie, she cried, then it's me who has to help him. She has now seen that buti is not dead yet. She's had enough of the other man, now she comes back to him. I don't want her in my house. And you can all go away too, she screamed at the people who were trying to quieten her.

Now old Hoedjie has left with Muis, and God knows where he'll spend the night, lying drunk under a bush, said buti Plank.

I suppose it's my fault.

Buti Plank didn't yet know what she had told the people in the office. He was looking for the bottle of wine he'd left in the kitchen.

Buti, she wanted to say to him, next year I won't be here. Who will look after buti next year, and after buti Hoedjie?

Yes, buti, she wanted to say to him, you worked so hard to build this house, and what will become of it when I am gone? And what will become of you when tata-ka-Bonsile has to move to the bachelor quarters and you have no roof over your heads?

Now she knew: The trouble is not only mine, it has come over them as well. That's why they were against me giving up hope, all these years. Try again, Poppie, they kept on saying, try once more.

Buti Plank will be sorry when I am gone, Poppie thought. Buti Hoedjie will be sorry too, when Muis has got him beaten up again and I'm not here to help him. And buti Mosie will be sorry when I am gone and Rhoda treats him badly, and looks down on his brothers, and refuses to help them when they are drunk.

You're jealous of your butis' wives, mama had told her once before, and see how nicely they behave to your husband.

It's not the same thing, mama, not at all the same, said Poppie.

On Christmas morning Mamdungwana awaited her at the church gates.

Why didn't you tell me? she asked Poppie.

Where did you hear?

The woman who was on the bus with you told me.

Mama does not know yet.

It's better you tell her yourself, that she does not hear it from strangers. Ag, sisi, where to are you now going?

It's only the Lord that knows, Poppie answered.

Then it must be enough for you that the Lord knows, said Mamdungwana.

Ewhe, said Poppie, but her heart was not in her words. It seemed to her that not only was she leaving her friends and her brothers behind but the Lord as well.

Christmas afternoon when tata-ka-Bonsile was working shift at the garage — he was glad to work on Christmas Day, then the white people are tipsy, he says, then they give good tips — she spoke to buti Plank.

They are sending me to Mdantsane near East London, buti. Your brother-in-law doesn't wish us to go to his people, he doesn't wish his children to bear the hardships of life on the land. That's why I chose Mdantsane, where there are schools.

Mdantsane, Mdantsane, I dunno nothing of this Mdantsane, why do you keep on talking of this bloody Mdantsane? Buti Plank was drunk, he didn't understand what she was trying to tell him.

You must go ask the office why I keep on talking of Mdantsane, buti, said Poppie.

Buti Mosie and Rhoda came to have tea with her and when Rhoda took the children to the café to buy cool drinks — the children had shown their oompie their school reports and he

188

had given them money to spend — buti Mosie stayed behind with her.

My little sister, how is it that I don't have your confidence any more? he asked her. Why is it that I must hear from strangers . . .?

I have been telling buti for a long time that I can't live like this any longer, if there is chance to lead a good life somewhere else, then it is better that I go there. If there is a life somewhere else for me, I had better go and live there in 1971.

I am also worried like, said buti Mosie. I have my troubles too. I cannot get a house, and this staying with my wife's people is no good. And for my sake, too, I feel like going to the office to say: Please, boss, we too are people of this country, we don't know another place, let us stay here, give us place to live, we don't want anything, only the right to stay here. But who will listen to me? My heart is heavy that you are leaving. We are children of one mother. We should stay near to one another.

Christmas night she stayed awake. She got undressed, but did not go to bed. Someone had to stay awake to unlock the door when tata-ka-Bonsile got home, to close it behind him, quickly, as soon as he was inside.

She kept his food hot in a plate on the saucepan of boiling water on the Primus stove. The stove was turned low and she had to watch it carefully. If the head cools off, the paraffin shoots from the nipple and sets it alight. This was the way many houses in the location had been burnt down.

The alarm was ticking. It was past two o'clock. She expected him at two o'clock, half past three at the latest. Often he had explained to her: If the ten o'clock boy does not pitch up, or if he's drunk, I have to stay on. It's no good sitting up waiting for me. Then she had replied: How must I know what has happened, it may be that you have been knifed, or beaten over the head or thugged, and are lying beaten up somewhere in the bushes, or there might have been a hold-up at the garage.

Buses didn't run at that time of the night. He had to come

189

by foot from Goodwood, and take a short cut through the bush.

She heard his step, unlocked the door and held it ajar for him to see the chink of light as he approached.

It was quieter tonight at the garage than on other Christmas nights, he told her. He ate the food she placed in front of him, the steam rising from the stamped mealies and dried beans. She heated water for his feet. While he ate she sat with him, when he had finished, they had tea together.

She shut down the Primus, and lit a candle. It was quite still in the room. The others were asleep. The candle was burning quietly, the shadows on the walls had stopped moving.

She must choose her words with care. If tata-ka-Bonsile got a shock, it could hurt him inside, make him get sick again and to take to his bed. She couldn't tell him straight what was in her mind, she must put it in such a way that the words seemed to come from him.

She talked about the children. He was fond of his children, sometimes it seemed to her that he cared more for the children than for her. She talked about the coming year. What if they stop giving me monthly extensions, what if it is in the middle of the school year, then I must leave at a very inconvenient time she tells him. And then what happens to our children's schooling?

He did not answer her. She pitied him. He cares for us too much, she thought, he always will be the first to see that a child needs new shoes, or a jersey. That is his nature. He looks after us well.

Then it is best that you leave early in the new year, he said, to give the children a full year's schooling.

But the next morning he had a headache and stayed in bed and Poppie fetched pills and remedies from Makhulu to make him feel better. As he got used to the idea of their leaving, he slowly recovered.

The week between Christmas and New Year, we talked: my mother, my stepfather, my husband, my brothers and me, says Poppie. Then we took the trouble on us. The second of January 1971 my husband went to Observatory and told the boss to get me a place as soon as he could, I now chose to leave.

On the seventh of January we got a letter: Come to the office, we have a house. We went, and after that I did not take much time to get my things ready, I wanted to get away from it all, I couldn't stand it any longer. So we packed up quickly. I gave my house to Makhulu, I asked at the office: Can we give the house to the old woman? Mr Stevens refused, because he said: She's a pensioner. Then I said, why can't you let her have the house because I didn't want to break the house down, it was built of iron sheets, but nicely built, lined with planks on the inside. I was too sorry to break down the house, and the old woman lived in a shanty affair. Then he said, all right give it to her.

My husband went to live in a brick house in the special quarters, the bachelor quarters which they call Mau-Mau. It was not far from the house my mother was given when she left Elsies and Mamdungwana's house after she had left the iron house in Jakkalsvlei. They called it Zwelitsha.

We packed the furniture and everything in boxes from the administration office. They give you everything, even the train ticket, sacks, bags, planks, everything to wrap your things in. You tell them when everything is ready, then the office sends a tractor or lorry and men to come and load your things and take them to Bellville. There they load them on a truck. They came in the middle of the week to load my stuff.

I left on the Sunday, the seventh of February. The whole family came to my house. My stepfather said a prayer and the church-women prayed and sang. They gave me presents or money, Mamdungwana gave me five rands and a piece of material. All the neighbours came. I didn't make a big party, but everyone came to me the day I left. They came to pray and give me money and cool drinks and cake to take on the train. Mama had baked enough bread and given us butter and cold meat and fruit.

We rented a bakkie to go to the station. My ma and my sisters came along, Katie and Baby. At quarter past six the

191

train pulled out. My baby was only a year and three months, but the others were big, Bonsile was almost sixteen, Nomvula thirteen and Thandi twelve. Buti Hoedjie was there and buti Plank and buti Mosie and Rhoda. Rhoda brought her child along and buti Mosie carried the child on the arm. My girls were so fond of their father, they just kept at his side all the time. And Bonsile and Jakkie walked along the platform looking at the trains. The church-women came by bus to see me off, because there was not room for them on the bakkie.

My husband could have come with us if he had wanted to, the law doesn't mind, but if he went along he would have had to be a new boy again, and we knew people who came back from East London and told us: There's no work there, you stay idle for a year or eighteen months before you find work, or you have to buy work from the foreman. My husband couldn't risk it, because the children had to be kept at school and he had to earn money for us. So he decided to stay at his job here. What the law wants is for the wife and children to leave and the man to stay.

I didn't feel so badly as we pulled out of the station. I must be honest and say: No, I didn't feel badly at all, because I was fed up of the law, I could not stand it any more. I didn't even see the point of going to the office any more, because every day it was the same story: We don't want you here. What are you still doing here? I am going to make you eat gubu mealies in Kaffirland.

I didn't cry when the train pulled out of the station. For what must I cry? What can you do, if you can't go one way any more, then you take a road the other way.

FIVE

The Ciskei

46

Poppie didn't find the train journey hard. She was used to all the long journeys from Lamberts Bay to Upington with ouma Hannie and kleinma Hessie. The children were old enough to look after Kindjie when Poppie wished to sleep. They travelled third class in a coach with green seats, not wooden benches, but harder seats than in the second class. With them in the compartment was a woman with two children, going to Aliwal North but she hadn't been sent away, she was going visiting. They travelled through Sunday, and arrived at De Aar on Monday where they could walk around and look at the shops and she bought the children cool drinks. Up to Noupoort Poppie knew the country, but when they turned off at Noupoort, when the coaches on half the train were hooked off and pushed back and shunted on to a new line, when the train whistled in a new way and jerked the newly-hitched wagons to life behind him, and set off on a railway line that she could not see, the old life fell away from her.

Night fell and the conductor came to switch on the lights. The children's faces looked different in the jolting train under the lights. The two girls sat on the bench opposite, next to the woman from Aliwal North and her two children. Thandi's face was thin. She had the high nose bridge of her great-uncle Pengi. She was tired, half lying on the bench she tried to sleep with her head against Nomvula's shoulder.

Kindjie was asleep on her ma's lap, one leg dangling, sucking her thumb. As the lips relaxed in sleep, the thumb dropped from her mouth. Poppie took her hand and held it in hers. Fezile sat hunched up against her. Although he was seven years old, he never let go of her. Even when she went down the corridor to the washroom he clung to her dress and walked with her.

At four o'clock in the night they stopped at Queenstown and heard the people on the way to the Transkei getting off the train to continue their journey by bus. After that she did not sleep again. Shortly before five, before the washing room was occupied, she got up and went to wash herself.

Bonsile had not talked to Poppie since he heard that she had agreed to leave Cape Town. He sat next to her, staring out of the window as though he could see more in the dark than his own reflection in the glass.

There is no reason why I must leave, he had said. I will stay with my father. Buti Spannerboy had agreed: Leave Bonsile behind, he can live with me, he is sixteen years old, he is grown up.

Do you think they'll keep him at school if he's no longer registered on my house card? Poppie asked.

There are many children like me whose mothers have been sent away, Bonsile said.

Where do you think to live when buti Spannerboy is away on the boats and your auntie has been sent back to the land?

With my father, he said.

It's too rough in the special quarters, said Poppie. When your father has to work night-shift, they'll mess with you.

But above all Poppie had felt: I am tired. I am not going back to the office to ask for permission to let my child stay on here at school. And her heart hardened against him. If she had to bear this trouble, why not he?

But he was on the train with her against his will. He ignored the new things he was seeing, the new country, the lushness, the new people. Poppie did not pay him attention. He had to snap out of his mood if he felt like it, she couldn't be bothered.

You are not going through to East London, the white conductor told them. Your tickets only go to Arnoldon, there you must get off.

He knew their type. It was not the first time he had to put

people from the Cape off at Arnoldon, people who had no idea where they were going. They were like a stone you picked up in one place and put down in another. His face showed nothing of his feelings, but he seemed to pity them and retraced his steps before entering the next compartment.

You must give the paper to the station master at Arnoldon, he told Poppie. Arnoldon is the station for Mdantsane.

And then, when Poppie did not answer, he asked: Have you still got the paper?

She took it from her handbag and showed it to him.

Bonsile wasn't paying attention to what was being said. Here, you, the conductor told him. You'll have to move to get all your ma's stuff from the train. We don't stop long at Arnoldon.

They got off at the tail end of the train. Not on the platform, but on the red earth of the veld. The grass grew tall with long, fat blades. The heat beat up at them from the earth.

Come away from the train, Poppie told the children.

Steam spurted heavily from between the wheels.

Bonsile decided to make a move. He handed the cases and parcels to Poppie and Nomvula, Thandi held Kindjie. The whistle went as he clambered down the steps. The guard who had been watching them as he clung to the train, one foot on the step, one dangling in the air, waved his flag. They watched the tail of the train disappearing.

Some of their stuff had been put down on the grass, the rest on the red soil. Thandi sat down with Kindjie on her lap. A strange kind of sweat was gathering on Poppie's face and on her body. It came from the heat steaming up from the damp earth and pressing down on them from the sky.

Get up from the grass, she told Thandi.

She looked up at the sun. It is still high, a strange sun sifting through a thick mugginess. The closeness comes into your body when you breathe, it brings a tightness into your chest, it makes you feel you can't get enough breath.

We must get into the shade, she said.

If each of them carried his share and she and the girls put the cases on their heads as well, they'd manage. They

walked slowly to the station building. The station master
spoke to them through the small window and took Poppie's
paper. He told the black man behind a desk: Phone up the
location office and tell them more people from the Cape
have come. And he told Poppie: They'll send a lorry to fetch
you. You must wait here.

It was the lunch hour, so he pulled down the shutter of
the window. Poppie felt shut out: Now I've lost my papers
too, she thinks, but it didn't bother her.

What must we do with the stuff, ma? the children asked.

Behind the station building there was some shade, but not
much, because the sun was high. She picked up the suitcase
she had put down when she gave her papers through the
window and put it back on her head. They stepped down
from the stoep and she opened the roll of blankets and
spread one on the red earth. She did not trust this earth;
it looked dark and wet. Then she lay down on the blanket,
her head on her bent elbow. The children didn't know their
ma in this mood. They sat themselves on the blanket.
Poppie kept her eyes slightly open to watch Bonsile.

Where are you off to?

I'm going to pee, ma.

You stay here, she shouted at Fezi. Let Bonsile go alone,
you just stand here and pee against the wall.

The girls were thirsty. They took a mug from the bags
and searched out a tap. They brought her some water, but
she couldn't swallow the lukewarm stuff.

Did you let the tap run first? she asked.

It stays so warm, ma.

The children's foreheads glistened with sweat. There was
still some bread in the carrier bag, but they were not hungry.
Poppie felt food would choke her.

Long after the window shutter had been opened and the
white man had returned and several black people had
walked by, greeting her but not stopping to talk, the lorry
came to fetch them. The white man came outside and gave
her papers to the black driver.

Molo, nikosikazi, the driver said. He was an elderly man,
she greeted him, but had no feeling for him in her heart, he

was part of this heavy thing that she had to bear. She got in front with him, the small child on her lap. The children climbed on to the back of the lorry. As they pulled off, leaving the station behind and taking the tar road to Mdantsane, the movement brought the children to life again. She heard them talking at the back, clutching the suitcases and packages when the lorry took a sharp corner.

It was not far to go, through a gate and then they were in the location. This place is not like the Cape, she thought, everywhere is uphill and downhill. The houses are of brick with bigger plots than at Nyanga, mealies in front of the houses and at the back, and right round the houses.

I saw plenty of hills from the train, but I did not know it was such a hilly place we were coming to.

She saw women wearing the big folded doeks on their heads like her mother-in-law wore in Herschel. They wore long dresses and strings of beads round their ankles. Wherever there was a flat open space, schools and shops and churches had been built, but the houses were built any old how, uphill and downhill. It seemed a very inconvenient kind of place to Poppie, but the soil was rich, which was why the mealies grew so well.

The driver took her to one of the flat open spaces to the office.

Do you come from the Cape? the black man behind the desk asked.

Yes, said Poppie.

He gave her her house number and handed it to the driver as well, adding: It's now too late to fill in a house card; you must come back here tomorrow so that we can write down everything.

The children were waiting on the lorry and the boys in the street were talking to Bonsile, pointing out the school.

The old man got into the driver's seat, and as they drove, he asked her about the Cape with curiosity, and with some envy. I hear the money is good there, he said. His clothes looked shabby for a driver. She looked down at his feet struggling at the brake as they went downhill. His shoes were tattered. In the office the people waiting had also asked her about the Cape. We hear there is much work and much money, they said, and they looked at her clothes, from her head to her toes, until she felt embarrassed. A woman said to her, I come from another location, Duncan Village, and they've given me a house here, but she looked terrible to Poppie, sick and starved and clad in rags.

Poppie felt strong: Stop when we come to a shop, she told the driver. I want to get milk for the child and fresh food.

She kept fifty cents in her hand as she put away the change, and when she got back in, she gave it to him: Buy yourself something to eat on the way back.

He let go of the steering wheel and took the money with both hands, as a child would accept something from an older person. She felt embarrassed at an old man taking it from her like that.

They left the older part of the location and drove into the newly-built section, left the tarred road for a dirt track and then stopped. He helped the children to unload the stuff, then turned the lorry round in the track and drove away.

She and her children stood in the road, their belongings piled around them. They looked at their house.

There were no other people in the street where the lorry left them. This way, that way, wherever they looked, they saw no one.

The sun is setting, mama, screamed Nomvula. The sun goes down on the wrong side, mama, he's going down where he has to come up, mama, he must go down that side of the mountain, and look what he's doing now.

At first it seemed very raw, that place, says Poppie, because they were new houses. There were rough pieces of cement lying in our way, and the earth was all dug up, and the grass around the house was overgrown. I felt very heartsore because the place was strange and I knew nobody. I felt, really, I'm now quite thrown away. When you get to a strange place it is nice if someone meets you. There I was just put in a new house with my children, but there was nothing there, no people yet in the houses next door, no doors inside, only a front door at the front and a back door at the back. But the house was clean, there were cement floors and panes in the windows, but no ceilings, you had to put them in yourself. There was a water pipe in the kitchen but you yourself had to buy the tap and fix it. The house stood on the slope, there were three steps inside.

Yes, it felt very hard when I walked round the house and saw there was no other person living near us.

We had been put in a desolate place.

Loneliness was all round us.

47

Bring in the things, Poppie told Bonsile.

The children walked round the house, looking for the nearest outside tap in working order, jumped over the building rubble to the other empty houses, peered in at the windows, but when the sun slid lower and the shadows between the houses lengthened they became afraid.

Bonsile carried the stuff in. He put everything in the back room and Poppie did not go against him.

We must open to get a draught, he said.

Their voices were loud in the empty house.

A woman who lived near Poppie in the Cape and had been sent to Mdantsane before her, had written to tell her: Bring a Primus with your hand baggage. Poppie opened her boxes and put the Primus on the floor. She took the small saucepan she had bought with the fresh bread and milk, and boiled some water. She made tea on the floor. She crumbled bread and added it to the milk in Kindjie's bottle.

The children were tired and went to sleep on the blankets. It was too hot to cover them. The little one couldn't settle down, sweat gathered on her forehead. Darkness fell fast. After the noisiness of the evenings in the location in the Cape, and after the noise of the train wheels under her head at night, it seemed to Poppie as though she had come to lie down in her grave here in this closed-up house.

Bonsile had carried his blankets into the next room. He had matches with him. She heard a match being struck, and saw the small glow against the roof before it died away. He was not wasting matches, just off and on he struck one, as if deep in thought. She was content that he had moved to the next room, without asking her first, just taking his blankets and going.

Long after he slept, Poppie still lay awake. Her mind told her: My children and I are lying here quite helpless. We can be murdered. Skollies may be roaming around, who will hear if we call out in this desolation? She had hidden her money between her breasts, would that stop thieves? How often had she not heard the skollies shouting about a woman they had mugged: Milk the cow, milk the fat teats of the cow. They knew the hiding place. They'd scream: Empty out the fat teats.

But these fears — even for her daughters who were ripe to be plucked — did not seem to take hold of her. As she lay there sweating in the close, half-completed house — they had shut the windows out of fear — she felt the emptiness of being completely alone, discarded. She felt some part of her had been lost.

She was tired, but sleep wouldn't come to her. She thought: I have been cast aside by my people. They allowed me to come here, alone. My husband and my mama and my brothers stood on the station platform and said goodbye and together they walked away from me. When the train left the station they walked away together. Now my heart has deadened towards them.

It felt as though her heart had also hardened towards the Lord. If the Lord wills, you will stay, if the Lord wills, you will go, the white man had said, but the Lord had not willed that this trouble should be taken from her.

Was this why she could not say, tonight before she lay

202

down with the children: Lord, watch over us in this strange place? Why she could not say before they ate the bread and drank the tea: Lord bless this food? And against Bonsile, her child, her heart had hardened so that she wanted to say to him: Go your own way, I don't care.

She heard someone groaning. She thought it was some-one outside, groaning, like the night when buti Hoedjie had been stabbed and he stood outside groaning, waiting for her to open up. Who could be wandering between these empty houses? she thought. But before fear took hold of her, she realised that it was she herself who was groaning. It was her own body giving voice to her pain. She tried to still the sounds, but her body started shaking, like someone with fever. She drew a blanket around her and the shivering subsided.

And as her body calmed down, quiet came to her heart. She thought: I am here now. They tore up my papers in front of me. They took me from the house my husband built for me. They took me from my husband and my mama and my brothers. They can do what they will, but I am not dead yet. Now I go forward. I go forward with what I have kept, and that is my children. And the first thing I must do, is to see that my children get their schooling.

Then she could sleep.

When daylight came she got up, lit the Primus stove and cooked porridge for the children to eat before they went to the new school.

48

I was thinking why had they put me in a house on the dirt road. There were three empty houses on the tarred road, but they had to give me the one on the dirt road. So I decided

I wasn't taking that house. I wrote down the numbers of two other houses 3351 and 3353.

I told Bonsile: Get up and dress, for you must go alone this morning and take the children to school.

We knew where the school was, just opposite the office in NU 3. There wasn't a school yet in NU 6 where they put us. The children had to walk a long distance to school. I unpacked their school clothes. The girls wept, but I said: I can't go with you, I go to the office, because I don't want this house.

I gave them food and told Bonsile: Take the children to school and take along the papers the principal gave us.

When they had left, I tidied my things, put the baby on my back and locked the house. Outside I saw that some more people had arrived. They were unloading stuff at the house next door. It was the woman from Duncan Village bringing her things. She was called Mantolo. She asked me: Are you satisfied? I said, No, I want to change. I don't like the house.

I walked along the tar road to the office. Mr February, the man in charge, wasn't there, but the others told me: You must take that house, there's nothing wrong with it, don't come to us with your Cape nonsense.

It isn't nonsense, I said to them, you don't give me the house for free. I rent it, and I won't stay in that house.

I waited the whole day, but Mr February didn't come to the office.

Thursday I again went, and found Mr February.

What? Aren't you written up yet? he asked me.

I am waiting for you.

Then you must come to my office.

Inside the office I told him: I don't want to rent that house. It's on the muddy side of the street. I want a house on the tar road.

The house is all right, the houses are all the same, said Mr February. What's the difference?

The difference is that in the rain you walk through mud to the house.

I've written the other number in your card.

I kept quiet but I stayed put.

All right then, I'll do it, he said, and scratched out the number on my card and gave me the house I still have.

Then I was very satisfied and went home.

Mantolo asked me: Did it come right? I also want to change. But when she got to the office Mr February chased her out and said: Go home.

Bonsile also didn't think they'd change me. The people at the office thought they wouldn't change me. It made me very satisfied that they did change me.

After a week they started filling the place up. They brought in people any old how. If the houses stayed empty, the skollies messed them up, and took out the panes to sell. Many people came from Duncan Village which was a slum and being broken down and Punzana location, others from Mossel Bay, and Beaufort West and Noupoort. Cape Town was only given three houses a month.

Two weeks later Poppie's furniture came by goods train. A few times she had gone to enquire at the station. Once the old man who drove the lorry picked her up, because it was long to walk. The white man at the window would tell the black man at the desk: Go through the papers. See if Nongena's stuff has come yet.

The fourth time she went it had come.

The old man and a helper brought the stuff on the lorry and Bonsile and school friends helped to unload. Poppie cooked for them on the Primus. The boys enjoyed unloading furniture of new arrivals, pulling off the wrapping, and throwing handfuls of straw at one another. Poppie made tea for the old man and this time gave him a rand tip.

The furniture looked strange in this raw cement house, the dresser and table and chairs from the Lamberts Bay days, and the bed. Nothing was left to put in Bonsile's room.

Fezi, do you want to sleep with Bonsile? Poppie asked Weekend. At school they called him Fezile and she got used to it. But Fezi wanted at first to sleep with her and his sisters.

I stayed at home and cooked and worked and did the washing. My children were unused to the place, they slid in the mud and messed their clothes. It was too difficult for me to get a job there. I had no friends to care for the baby. I felt it would harm my children if I was away all day. They had to walk a long way to school. There were no buses, the place was too raw. I got up at five o'clock to get something hot into them. It was a long walk home, too, and I didn't want them to come home to an empty house and no cooked food. They were often cold and wet, because it rained terribly that summer. The whole Mdantsane was sluits everywhere that overflowed when it rained.

I didn't have many friends. One can't really get used to the East London people because they feel: What are the Cape people coming to live here for? They always had something bad to say about us. They called us the Amalawu which means Bushmen. My children couldn't speak Afrikaans as well as we could when we were children at Upington, because in Nyanga they didn't hear it so much, but they could understand it. And they spoke it to the people of De Aar and Beaufort West and Mossel Bay and Richmond who were also resettled in Mdantsane. So we were called the Bushmen. Some didn't say it to your face but behind your back. They said their children wouldn't have a place to live, because the Cape people were being given all the houses. And it wasn't easy to ask someone to mend something for you, or to put on a door, because you had no one of your own. Ag ja, they were not bad people, but you didn't feel at home with them, so you kept to yourself and your children. The children got on well, they all went to school together and the East London children wanted to hear about Cape Town, but the adults were different.

The church was a long way away, two bus trips. My house was in NU 7 and the church was in NU 1. I couldn't go every Sunday. The children told me when the minister held services in the school for the people living too far to go to NU 1. They also came to tell me when other Cape children arrived, then I'd go and see if I knew them.

Nomvula said that Roksie had come from Cape Town and was in her class, so I went and found her carrying in stuff and I greeted the people of my stepfather's Mbatane clan. Roksie was the daughter of a coloured woman and a Mbatane, we called him Monday. But I didn't know the woman sitting in the house. Sister, she's your sisi, this one, she's Mbele, said Monday to me.

Later I found out that he had left the coloured woman in the Cape and brought this Mbele along, she was his second wife. But he brought his children too. They lived near to us. Cape people stick together.

My best friend was sisi Emily who lived in NU 3. She came to see me shortly after I arrived. She was a widow put out of Cape Town, but her daughters had passes for Cape Town, her son and grandchildren too. So it was with the passes, one gets a pass, the other doesn't. So she was living alone in Mdantsane. She knew old Makhulu, who had written to her that I was coming.

The old people who were resettled had a hard time in that place. You struggled to get a car to take the sick people to the doctor. The doctor refused to come because of the bad road. The old people couldn't walk so far, uphill and downhill. Many died.

In NU 3 four houses were joined for a clinic. We took two buses to get there, first to Highway and then further. We had to get up at five o'clock in the morning to get there in time; they only took the cards from one to eighty, and if you arrived after seven it was too late. At the hospital in East London you had to be there before six o'clock. They also had numbers and if the numbers had all been given out, it was no use.

We bought our groceries at O.K. or Ackermans, and took the bus back, and the last bit we walked carrying the plastic bags and the boxes on our heads. It is fourteen miles from Mdantsane to East London. There were no street lamps, only posts. The lights came later. A few months after we arrived, the tractors started levelling the ground, and cleaned up the stones and pieces of cement blocking the yard. Then we could start to garden and plant mealies.

Poppie had brought her sewing machine along but material was too expensive in East London. She wrote to mama: Here I pay too much, can't mama get me stuff from the tip?

Although she'd never been herself, Poppie knew all about the tip, about people coming from as far as Worcester and Paarl, to get off-cuts and other stuff at the city's rubbish dump. It was too dangerous for her. How many children had not been killed dashing in front of the huge tip lorries to grab the stuff, getting under the wheels when the tractors were levelling the rubbish? But the skollie children went, fighting over pieces of material, reels of cotton, zips, buttons. They say one woman even found a new sewing machine on the dump, but she was waiting for it. A man she knew had put the machine with the rubbish he was sorting at the factory. The women who didn't work and the skollie children fought to get at the stuff and to fill their plastic bags.

Can't mama send me tip off-cuts, Poppie wrote. She meant mama to buy them from the skollie children. But mama took Jakkie and Katie and Baby and herself went to get the stuff on the dump. A man from Cape Town brought a baleful on his bakkie, bundled together and bound tightly with wire. As Poppie unpacked it the children sat watching, except Bonsile. He wandered around the streets at night, and Poppie couldn't stop him. So she made clothes for the children from the off-cuts, then used what was left to make children's suits, skippers, pants, girl's dresses, and sold them to make money.

She began to get around more.

Many kinds of people lived in Mdantsane, Poppie explains.

One day I went to Mamtshawa's house and there I saw a man, and I said to myself: This man looks a lot like buti Monkies. His real name was Mongezi but the coloured people called him Monkies. He got a surprise when I asked him: Aren't you buti Monkies?

From where do you know me? he asked.

I know you from Lamberts Bay.

He was in too great a hurry to talk, but I asked him: Where is Stafie, your wife?

Stafie is in Stompneus Bay.

Stafie is a coloured woman, they had many children, when I left Lamberts Bay they were still together. And now as he left, Mamtshawa told me: I know this man, I see him walking up and down, he's a mailer.

For whom does he mail?

He carries drink to the shebeen queens, wine and Jabulani beer, one queen gives him fifty cents, the other gives the same.

This surprised me, because he'd been a trawlerman in Lamberts Bay and had a lot of money. He used to play the guitar in the Apostolic church. Now he was a mailer, which is a low job, he looked quite different, not much body to him and with tattered clothes.

I remember a Xhosa woman came to search for him in Lamberts Bay: I'm your mother, she said, you are my little boy that left me when you were small, but he answered: I don't know this auntie, it's not my mother, my mother died long ago. The auntie's nose looked just like Monkie's nose and it was bad the way he killed her words.

We thought he did so because he had taken a coloured wife and Stafie looked down on the Xhosa people and couldn't speak Xhosa, and because he had fear in his heart that he would be sent from Lamberts Bay. I thought it was his mother's tears that had brought him to this state. I told Mamtshawa about the mother whose words he'd killed. He got a fright when he saw I recognised him, he said: I'll be back soon. But I never saw him again.

Poppie regularly heard from Cape Town and tata-ka-Bonsile sent them money. He never missed a fortnight, twenty or thirty rand a time. The postman brought the money and she had to sign for the registered letter.

Only for the postman and for the office where she paid her rent did she have to show her pass. Because here in Mdantsane no one asked for it, and no one was run in for not having one. And when the Umgqkomo lorry came down the road, no one ran away. Only the boys who were playing dice along the road or on the empty plots gently dropped the knives they were carrying into the tall grass, so that the police who searched their bodies could find nothing.

We picked up plenty of knives in the long grass, says Poppie.

As the location filled up and all kinds of people were thrown together and life became rough, it was so dangerous that people were being shot at inside their houses and forced to throw money out of the windows. These skollies were children who'd left school after Standard Four and Five, and could find no jobs.

50

Poppie had been in Mdantsane for a year when mama wrote to her: Your husband has experienced a hard thing — his buti Spannerboy was knocked down by a car.

I was sitting in my house one Sunday afternoon, she wrote, when a man knocked and told me: A relative of yours has been run over in the big street. Baby, Jakkie and I then ran after this man, in the direction of Guguletu and from a distance we could see the people standing around him. When I got there I tried to speak to him, but he was mumbling and talking like a man who has lost his mind. So they took him to hospital where he stayed for three weeks. And then he started getting the fits. A doctor sent your husband to a lawyer for his brother, and the lawyer is now working on the case that your buti Spannerboy may get some money for the accident. They operated on his head, but it is as if he has become a little blind, and because of the fits he cannot work any longer.

Poppie also received a letter from tata-ka-Bonsile: My buti's wife is returning to Herschel, but my buti has to remain here for news about the insurance. My buti's wife will come by East London, and it is in my heart that she takes Nomvula with her to the land. My father and mother are getting old and they would like to have a grown child with them to care for them.

The letter was a shock to Poppie. I came to Kaffirland to this place with schools for my children's sake. Must all this trouble now be in vain?

I am not for it that the child should be sent to your father and mother, she replied in a letter to tata-ka-Bonsile. Things on the land are too rough. It is too raw there. That's why I came to this city place. I won't allow them to have a hard time on the land. They must get their schooling first.

The time she herself had spent on the land came back to her, the games she used to play with her little sister-in-law, the fires outside, the shadows when the sun disappeared behind the mountain but you could still see the sunshine on the hills opposite.

I don't want to let her go, sisi, she told Emily. I've had enough trouble in my life. I wish to give my children a better life. My children were born in Cape Town, they are not used to the land.

But Emily was not with her in this matter. The sisi is old, Poppie thought, the sisi herself wants one of her grand-children with her here in Mdantsane, but her children in Cape Town don't send a granddaughter to her. Why should I send my child away?

But tata-ka-Bonsile's letter had disturbed her peace of mind. Sisi Constance who is returning to the land is fat and strong, she told herself. She must see to the old people. And for her part she decided to take better care of sisi Emily. She sent her daughters regularly to help their sisi Emily with the small jobs in and about the house.

She did not hear from tata-ka-Bonsile, whether he agreed with her in this matter. She waited with anxiety for Constance to arrive, fearing Constance would tell her: I am taking Nomvula to the land. Then she would have to let her go.

Towards the end of the year bad storms struck Mdantsane. It rained for seven days on end, day and night. The children went to school in the rain and came home dripping wet. On the seventh day the wind and thunder became very fierce and two corrugated iron sheets were torn from the roof of the house. Poppie and the children were very frightened because they did not know such storms. They left the house to spend the night in Mamatola's house behind them. When they went outside they sank to their knees in the mud.

The next morning everything was quiet, the storm had passed. Bonsile went to the council to report the broken roof and the council had all the damaged houses fixed, but it took a long time to mend the roads and bridges.

Buti Mosie wrote to Poppie: We heard the news on the wireless, and we thought your house had toppled over on to you. My brother-in-law was so worried he became very sick. He came from work and he couldn't talk. His friends came to call me to come, they were trying this witchdoctor business on him, but I said: Come, let's take him and rush him to the doctor. So while we were sitting in the doctor's waiting room, he started undoing his shoelaces and making with his hands like somebody working with money and counting out change, all the while saying: Yes sir, yes sir, how much, sir? So we asked the receptionist to take the man through to the surgery right away. We then told the doctor: Look, we think this man has lost his mind like, as they call this kind of thing. 'Cause why he received a letter from East London about his wife's house which was broken above her head by the storms, and then the nerves went all over him because of this thing. The doctor examined him and said: Yes, it's a nervous breakdown. He was an Indian doctor. He gave him an injection and pills, and then we could go. Halfway home I could see him starting to look here and there, all around us, and when we reached the house he looked about and said: Molo, brother-in-law, as if it was the first time that day that he saw me. He went to bed and when he woke up he was all right.

Mama wrote as well: Things are all right now with my son-in-law. Mamdungwana is looking after him. Buti Spannerboy is living with Makhulu now, because the buti's wife went back to Kaffirland last month.

When Poppie received the letter it was the month's end. So sisi Constance did not come by way of East London to fetch Nomvula. Ag, in spite of the news of tata-ka-Bonsile's sickness, the heaviness is lifted from my mind, Poppie thought. I can carry on with my life again without the fear that Nomvula will be taken from school and sent to the land.

She wrote to tata-ka-Bonsile: Don't be heavy in your heart about us. The council fixed up the damage to the house. We did not get hurt in the storm. The thing that must come first in your mind must be your own health.

During this time the St Francis Anglican Church was built in NU 8 and Poppie could go more regularly to church again. Bonsile did not like church and Thandi even less. It was only Nomvula and Fezi and Kindjie who liked going with Poppie to the house of the Lord.

51

After two years had passed tata-ka-Bonsile sent word that he was going to the land to do the ritual ceremony for his two elder brothers that had passed by, buti Witbooi and buti Damon. They had been dead for ten years and it worried his father that the goats had not been slaughtered for them.

On the way to Herschel, he wrote, I will visit you in East London.

Poppie did not tell the younger children that their father was coming. She took only Bonsile with her to the station. They waited at the far end of the station in the open veld where they had got off the train when they came to this place. It was the first time in a long while that she and Bonsile were alone together. For the occasion she bought him a pair of long pants and a green skipper. He had the build of his father, only he was more thickset, like herself. He had passed his seventeenth year, he was no longer the child he had been when they left Cape Town.

You have been a good help to me here in the new place, Bonsile, she told him while they waited. Your father will be satisfied.

He was not a child of many words. He did not answer her.

They watched the railway track filling in the distance, and they heard the noise as the train approached. Some way further up the line from where they were standing, tata-ka-Bonsile got off and waited. He was wearing the same clothes he wore the day he said goodbye to them in Cape Town. But the clothes seemed too large for him. He turned around before he stepped down and took the parcels and suit-cases someone handed down to him, as if he had no strength. Bonsile got on to the steps of the carriage and took the luggage out of his hands. They knew that he had been ill that day after he heard about the storm in East London.

Poppie approached him. Tata-ka-Bonsile turned around to face her.

Molo, he said.

Molo, she said extending her hand. Although it was a warm day, his hand lay cold within hers.

She took some of his luggage and put it on to her head. Bonsile carried another suitcase and walked ahead of them, then came tata-ka-Bonsile, with Poppie following behind. They started walking even before the train had pulled out.

It is quite a long way before we get to the place where the buses are, Poppie said.

It is well.

He was satisfied with the house. He was glad to see the

furniture again. He touched the table and the dresser that he knew so well.

Are you living well at the place where you are now? Poppie asked.

They treat me well.

Mamdungwana writes that you visit her.

She also treats me well.

And how is it with mama and buti Plank and buti Hoedjie?

They used to live here and there, but then they moved in again with old Makhulu, in our house. She looks after them well.

Buti Spannerboy?

He is still waiting for his money.

And buti Mosie?

He waited for two years, and then he got his own house.

Mama had written to her telling about it, and she was glad about buti Mosie and Rhoda who were expecting another child. But a bitterness had crept into her heart now that her husband was with her.

Everybody is all right. Everybody has houses. And us? I who have to stay so far away with strangers. Everybody is getting along without me.

But tata-ka-Bonsile was satisfied with the house. While she was preparing food she showed him the mealies she had planted. It was now a year since the bulldozers cleared the area all round the house and they could start gardening. Tata-ka-Bonsile touched the soft beard of the corn. He parted the leaves around the cob and pressed with his thumb against the kernels. When you can't any longer press milk from the kernels with your fingers, the mealies are ready for picking.

This is a good stand of mealies, he said. Nonkosinathi, these mealies are ready for picking, can you cook us some?

She felt ashamed of the weeds between the rows of mealies. In the country it is the women who have to hoe in the fields. I am on the go all the time she said, I cannot see to everything.

I can also work now that I am here, tata-ka-Bonsile said.

215

When Nomvula and Thandi came home from school, she sent them to fetch Kindjie at a neighbour's place where she had left her. Kindjie was very shy with her father, but after a while she followed him everywhere. The children watched him all the time, afraid that he might leave again.

He opened the parcels, the suitcases, and showed them the clothes he had bought for them. It was only the shoes that didn't fit. Poppie had sent him the sizes, but these had not been right.

Bonsile took off his long pants, put on his old clothes and worked with his father in the garden. The other children had been around him during the afternoon, trying to help. But she could see, not long after bending and hoeing he would straighten up, tired. Then he would look at Bonsile, at his muscular legs filling his short khaki pants, the thick arms and the thongs of muscles under his skipper. The boy has become a man, he thought.

That evening when they had eaten, tata-ka-Bonsile said: Bonsile must come along with me to the land. Poppie lifted her head at table where she was busy stacking the plates.

Go to the land with you? she asked.

This is a big thing that I must do, he said. My tata let me know that he is waiting for me; he is old now, he must do it before he dies. We must fetch back my brothers who have passed by, they are waiting for us.

Poppie could remember that her mama after ouma Hannie's death in Lamberts Bay had asked the men of the clan-name to come, and they had bought an ox and made a makeshift kraal of planks and thorn-tree branches in the yard at the back of the house. She and her stepsisters had helped mama make beer. They'd baked bread and cooked samp mealies and made the sour magou drink with yeast and cornmeal and water, and the men had slaughtered the ox.

Meisie had asked her: Why are they doing it? It costs money and you are a church-goer. It is a heathenish thing that you are doing.

There are equally heathenish things that you do in your Roman Catholic Church, she'd told Meisie. We do it to bring

216

back somebody in the family who has died. This is our belief and our custom. We have a word that all those present must say: Makabuye. You must come back. Then we feel we have done the work that we should do, and he that has died can come back and live with the people of the house. So if my grandmother feels that she has not said or done something before her death, she can return in our dreams and tell us what she wants done.

Poppie didn't argue when tata-ka-Bonsile had to spend money for an ox for his dead brothers. His father received a pension, and he had also put aside money. She knew that it was something that must be done.

But this matter of Bonsile going along to the land, that was something new. The boy looked at her to see what she had to say about it.

The old men of the clan will be there, tata-ka-Bonsile said. They will get up and tell the young men of the work they do. There will be lots to do for young men like Bonsile. They must watch that they may learn.

Poppie was still standing at the table next to the basin and the dishes that she must wash.

Let him go if he wishes, she said. If he thinks he is so clever that he can do without his schoolwork.

They could hear from the tone of her voice what she was thinking. She wiped her soapy hands with the dishcloth. From the wiping of her hands, from the movement of her arms, the set of her shoulders they could see what she felt.

Tata-ka-Bonsile was tired. He wanted to go to bed. We will talk tomorrow, he said.

The girls slept in the living room, Fezi was with Bonsile. There was a sadness in her that this matter of Bonsile must rear itself between them on their first evening together. But he would be with them another two weeks. Things would be all right again.

The next morning she told tata-ka-Bonsile: The teachers send letters every other month to the parents of every pupil about a meeting to be held at the school. And when we are there, they tell us why they have let us come. If there are children giving trouble, they will talk to the parents. Then

217

they explain there must be co-operation between the parents and children. For that reason we must do nothing to cause the child being sent away from school for no reason whatsoever. The teachers themselves do the ritual during the weekend or only in the holiday time.

She explained it nicely to tata-ka-Bonsile. If she talked gently to tata-ka-Bonsile then he listened to reason. But it distressed him that his son wouldn't be able to do the ritual with him in the land.

It is well like this, he said, then I will go alone.

He stayed only two weeks on the land, and then he came back to East London to say goodbye to them. He spent a day at home with them and brought them mealies and two pumpkins from the grandmother.

How was it there with your pa and your ma? asks Poppie.

It was good.

He looked in better health. His eyes were calmer but he was still thin.

Mama is getting old, he said. It is difficult for her still to be carrying water and making fire.

Poppie knew what would be coming next.

She asks that one of my two daughters come to live with her.

Is there going to be trouble between us again, Poppie thought, here at the last, when we must taste peace and happiness? Must she again battle for her children?

Nomvula? she asked.

Or Thandi. The grandmother does not mind. She only wants two strong arms and legs.

If I submit, Poppie thought, it will have to be Nomvula. She felt an anxiety about Thandi, why she did not know.

As she stood there pouring tea for tata-ka-Bonsile, she felt a weakness coming over her. It was the same weakness that she felt after the birth of her last child. Her hands holding the teapot had no strength, her eyes clouded over. She closed her eyes and bent her head, as if she were praying for strength.

But I told my mama, she heard tata-ka-Bonsile's voice coming as from a distance, that my children must first finish

with their school. I am not going to have them experience
the hardships of the land, not now. One of the girls living
near them must help the old people.

He is not going to have Nomvula or Thandi sent away,
Poppie realised. She raised her head. The weakness drained
from her. She poured the tea. The clear brown tea filled the
cup. She also poured herself a cup. The cloud disappeared
from her eyes.

Her voice was quiet when she spoke. Is your mama
having a difficult time with only the girl living next to them
to help her carry water and make fire?

It is my father's sister's grandchild. My father's sister
is still strong, she can let my mama have the child.

Dadebawo Nozazi's grandchild? she asked.

Yes.

And buti Spannerboy's wife? asked Poppie.

She thought of the fat Constance she had hidden in the
corner of the room under the blankets during the time of
the raids. She could help, couldn't she?

She lives in the next ilali, in the next village. She can help
too, tata-ka-Bonsile said.

My tata was sorry not to have seen his grandchild, was
the only reproach that she heard him making about Bonsile,
but he says we must promise that he comes to the land when
he is of the age to do the bush ritual.

That is well, said Poppie. And she was glad she could
promise something because the matter of the girls had been
cleared up and taken away from her.

52

On a Saturday afternoon Poppie put on her Sunday clothes
to go to the funeral of a schoolteacher. It was a year since

she had seen tata-ka-Bonsile. She knew people by now. She had sat with the corpse the previous night.

Leaving the house she met two men at the gate who greeted her.

Molo, Nkosikazi.

Molweni, Poppie said. Where are you going?

We came to the number of your house, they said.

For what have you come here?

Something has gone wrong at our place and the spoor leads to your house. There's trouble with our daughter.

Then she knew what they meant. But she kept her peace.

I am sorry, she said. I am on my way to the funeral, you must come next week.

They also knew the teacher, Miss Xiniwe. One of the men said: That auntie was my teacher too, in Sub A, so we'll come another day.

After the funeral she went to buti Monday, who was of her clan, to tell him: There's trouble, brother-in-law. You must be my spokesman. Bring buti Blaauw with you and come talk to Bonsile and ask him what he knows of this business.

The Blaauwens from Beaufort West stayed close to buti Monday, they were people who, like them, spoke Afrikaans and those that spoke Afrikaans stood by one another in this new place.

On Sunday they came and sat in the living room and said: We are here to speak to Bonsile. Poppie went to the kitchen and busied herself there. After talking to Bonsile, the men allowed him to leave and called Poppie.

He was honest, buti Monday said. He takes responsibility.

The girl's kinsmen must come again next Sunday, so we can discuss it with them, me and old Blaauw.

Poppie wrote to tata-ka-Bonsile. Men came to the house, and I asked my stepfather's clansmen to speak for me.

The next week she wrote: They ask damage money, as much as you can send. The girl is an orphan child. She goes to school with Bonsile, she is in Standard Eight in the same class with him. The people asking the money say they reared her and now she's pregnant.

Poppie asked Nomvula and Thandi: Do you know the girl?

Her name is Xoliswe, says Nomvula. I see her at school, but I don't know her. She's not of our kind, mama, but she's clever, she has much learning.

Poppie never spoke to Bonsile about the girl, or the baby she was carrying; it was not their custom.

Tata-ka-Bonsile sent forty rand and she gave it to buti Monday who took it to the girl's people.

53

At this time a great loneliness and longing again entered Poppie's heart. She felt: I am far from my kinsfolk. I must care for my children, but I am a woman alone. What will become of us?

If some time passed without bringing a letter from the Cape, she felt heartsore and filled with resentment. If the letters came from her stepsisters or from Jakkie or from mama or Mosie, the heartsore deepened. They have made a life without me.

Some days the homesickness was like a pain in the pit of her stomach. She would come out of the shop and see the silhouette of a man, see a certain movement of his body and think it's buti Plank. Another time she mistook someone else for buti Hoedjie. Hearing the men's voices in church, it seemed to be buti Hoedjie singing. She closed her eyes and said to herself: It's buti Hoedjie I hear, then for a few moments the longing was stilled. Till she opened her eyes again.

The church was her comfort.

Nomvula was grown up, she was sixteen years old with a ripe body. She loved to put on her best frock and go to church with her ma. The little ones also liked to go. It was only Thandi who always put forth excuses, her shoes were wrong, the dress was not good enough. She had to beat Thandi to get her to church.

This was the age people came under the influence of the amafufunyana spirits, says Poppie. They entered your body and dwelt in your belly. At parties they took hold of you, especially if you were a young married woman or young girl, and made you leave your body so that they could speak from your belly. It was an evil thing if it took hold of your child, it forced her to leave school, and put an end to her learning. It was quite different to the work of the witch-doctors.

That was why I beat Thandi to get her to church. If I see you at one of those parties, I'll kill you, I told Thandi. It is the spirit of the devil that goes into the people, the seven demons the Bible tells us about.

One day, I touched at sisi Bettie's house on the way back from church. Thandi and Nomvula were with me. A girl was sitting on a chair, and she started passing wind and jerking her head this way and that.

What's the matter with the child, I wondered.

Sisi Bettie got up and threw a piece of white material — it looked like a lace curtain — over the child's head and drew the curtains of the room. Ja, I thought, this surely is amafufunyana. I was glad for Thandi to see it, because I knew it was all put on, it was the girl herself speaking in the hoarse voice.

Sisi Bettie stood by saying: Yebo, which is the Zulu word for that's right. And then the girl called the other girl, Mbuiswa, who had joined us, and told her her fortune.

Ja, but wait till she tries to tell our fortunes, I thought, because us she doesn't know. That will prove if amafufunyana means something. But she sat jerking around in the chair, farting all the time, the lace curtain covering her face, and never a word she said concerning me or my children.

I told Thandi: Now, can you see it's all nonsense? She wanted to impress us, but she only tells fortunes of people she knows. There she sits lolling around, rolling a zol

222

(which is a dagga cigarette) and she's half drunk and the amafufunyana is all rubbish. You stay away from those parties, do you hear? You come to church with me like a Christian person. Even the witchdoctor parties are preferable, because the doctor people sing and dance and clap their hands and it's something quite different.

Since Poppie had had to pay the big sum of damage money for Bonsile, she could force him to come to church with her as well.

I'll lock the house, she'd say. If you go your own way, you can sleep outside tonight. And tomorrow as well.

He was keen on his school, and scared his mother would lock away his books and school clothes as well, so he went to church with her. But the heaviness of spirit did not leave her. It overshadowed every day. She knew it had to do with Bonsile, not the girl whom she had never seen, but Bonsile himself. Dreams plagued her. As a child she had dreamed a lot. Poppie was born with a caul, mama had told ouma Hannie, we must attend to her dreams. But since the birth of her children, she had stopped dreaming.

Now she had a dream which stayed with her for weeks. She dreamed she was alone in a room and a thin, dark-skinned woman entered. She knew the woman, but could not place her. She was laughing at Poppie, mocking her and said: Your son Bonsile will never be an heir. And when Poppie wished to ask: Who are you? she faded away and disappeared. When she woke, she tried to place the woman, because it was not a stranger to her, but she could not. She only knew: Bonsile was mentioned by name, and the woman mocked me.

For weeks Poppie watched Bonsile leaving the house and returning. She lay awake at night waiting for him to come in. Christmas and New Year passed, having no meaning for her. Only in the church did she find comfort. She spent nights singing, she would come home from church in the early morning, with hoarse voice and inflamed eyes, to throw herself on the bed and sleep, leaving the cooking and housework to the girls.

Bonsile will never be an heir. Was it a warning? Was it

223

a punishment because she refused to send her daughters to the parents-in-law on the land, because she rent asunder the family who received her as a daughter? Or did it go back further? If she had let Bonsile stay in Cape Town, would all this have happened?

Once more tata-ka-Bonsile sent damage money. Because of the second lot of damage money tata-ka-Bonsile could send less for themselves, and nothing extra for Christmas.

She told the girls: There is none left for Christmas clothes.

At night she went to bed with fear in her heart, in the mornings she searched the night for the face of the woman, but never again did she appear to her.

Then I got sick, says Poppie, and went to the Frere hospital in East London. The doctor examined me but said: Nothing is the matter with you. Every day I felt my strength growing less. I could not swallow my food. I went back again and the woman doctor told me: Stand in front of the mirror and see if it's a sick person looking back at you.

She gave me pills for my nerves and said I mustn't worry so much.

Emily advised her: Get a job, Poppie. It will take your mind off the children, and you'll worry less about money because you will be earning.

School fees took much money, the children at high school paid more than thirty rand each, and at the lower primary and higher primary schools they paid from five up to fifteen rand.

Bring Kindjie to me, said Emily.

Poppie was more used to the place by now, and thought: With the white people of East London I'll get on too.

You won't get on with them, someone else told her. The Cape people don't get used to the jobs here. The money is less, eighteen rand for a sleep-in job, less if you sleep out. If you want to earn more than twenty rand, you must work in the garden, and wash the motor car, like a man. And the white people treat black people differently here. The Cape people can't stand it.

I'll give it a try, said Poppie.

Have you got papers? asked Emily. She showed her Cape

Town pass book to Emily. It was dirty and torn.

You must get snapped for a new book, said Emily.

I'll get snapped on Monday, when the Lower Primary school starts, I'll wait till the younger children are at school, then I'll get my papers fixed.

Sunday morning after church, a child from NU 3 brought Poppie a note.

Poppie opened it and read: Dear Friend, it goes well with me, I hope it goes well with you. I want to let you know that Xoliswe's pains have started and we took her to Frere hospital, from Mrs Mabi.

Poppie showed the letter to Bonsile when he came in late that night. He was embarrassed and said nothing. Did you know about it? she asked. No, said Bonsile. Well, she's gone to hospital. Now we have to wait and see.

In a week's time Bonsile would be going back to school to study for Standard Nine. In a week's time Xoliswe would also have gone back to school.

That's why the damage money was so high, Poppie thought, and she, too, regretted that the child would not be able to go. The people who reared her, said: It's a child with learning that was spoiled. Poppie found it hard that her son was the cause.

54

Monday morning I went to the small office at the gate they call Igati, says Poppie, and they asked where I had worked before and wrote it down and gave me a stamp to take to the big office in East London.

When I got back my feet were tired and I felt like a cup of tea, I took bread from the sideboard to cut myself a slice. I sat at the table eating, when I saw the postman coming through the garden gate. It gave me a fright because my husband had written the former Friday and sent money by telegram and I fetched the money on Saturday. He can't be sending money again, I thought. What on earth is this telegram about?

It was from mama and said: Your husband is very ill, expect money.

My fright grew, because I know when they say: Expect money, it means they have sent money for you to come home. I knew at once something had happened to him. Perhaps he was stabbed or run over, as things happen in the Cape. My fear was so great that I left the bread lying on the table and took the telegram and walked across the road to a neighbour who had people living in Cape Town too. Mr Majola.

Look what I got, I told him. Then I started weeping.

No, don't weep, he said, no bad thing has happened. Your ma would not send the telegram direct to you.

My ma would not send it if he were just ill, I said. I feel that something bad has happened.

I sat with them, waiting. And my other neighbours joined us and Majola told them about the telegram. They knew what a telegram meant. But they comforted me: Don't be afraid, nothing has happened, they said. They waited through the night with me. But no money or telegram came.

On Wednesday a man called Zikali arrived from Cape Town. He entered my gate and said: I've come from Cape Town with Majola's relatives. Your husband is sick, he's in hospital, your ma told me to bring you with me when I go back.

But I'm not going today, he said, and not tomorrow. I'm driving back on Friday.

I knew he was lying to me, and said: So if you are leaving on Friday, so I leave by train tomorrow.

It's no use, he said, I'll be in Cape Town before you get there.

It doesn't matter, I'll go by train.

I took the girls and Fezi and asked sisi Blaauw to take care of them. Bonsile could stay alone at home, I took

226

Kindjie and went to the station to buy a single ticket to Cape Town for that night.

But as I stood in my bedroom another telegram came from my eldest sister-in-law in Johannesburg, asking: Where will Stone be buried?

They had sent word directly to her that her brother had died but to me they only said: Expect money, your husband is ill. But I had known in my heart that he was dead, that is why I would not wait until Friday to leave. I sat in the train and knew there was nothing more to be done, my husband was dead, and I must try to get back to Cape Town.

As I sat there waiting for the train to pull out, Zikali came to me: How can you leave by train, when your mama sent me to fetch you?

I'm not getting off, I have bought my ticket.

But the auntie in the compartment with me said: My child, this is a wrong thing you are doing. Get down for your children's sake. This man can't drive back alone to Cape Town with your children.

Zikali took my ticket and explained it to the station master and he returned the money.

I went back with him to my house and the neighbours came again and watched with me and prayed and sang.

They stayed with me till three o'clock in the morning, when Zikali fetched us. We sat through the night praying and singing and drinking tea, and when the car came they accompanied us to the car and stood there singing as we drove off.

We had no trouble on the way. Once he was stopped by traffic cops, I don't know where it was, and was given a ticket. Close to De Doorns, I think it was. At Worcester his lights failed, it was an old car, he took a chance to travel so far in it, and we had to travel through the mountain pass without lights. But two white ladies in a Johannesburg registration car just ahead of us, I think they realised we were having trouble with the lights, because they stayed just ahead, lighting the way, till we got to Paarl. Then they drove off.

When we got close to the airport, at the bridge, his car

stopped. He had no more petrol. It was about half past ten. But it was close enough for him to cross the bridge on foot and go to Section 4 to Mosie to get petrol. They ran back through the dark with the cans, the children and I waited in the car, it was a very dangerous spot, close to the coloured location, where the skollies roam at night. But what could we do but sit and wait?

Zikali drove to my mama's house and picked her up, and took me to my own house where Makhulu was still living, and buti Plank and buti Hoedjie with her. My people said a prayer and then said: Poppie must get some rest.

Mama stayed with me all the time, and buti Spannerboy. It is our custom. If someone has died their people stay with them, they go to work but after work, they come back again, they sleep in your house, all the close family, till after the funeral. I saw the cut on buti Spannerboy's head, and his eye was bleary, it had gone quite blind.

Saturday morning when the people heard I was back, they stormed the house, they were so glad I had come because buti Spannerboy had made arrangements for his buti to be buried in Herschel, but I said: No, I have come here to bury him, I can't go back again to Herschel. Buti Spannerboy said: Your father-in-law wants him to be buried there, but I said, let my father-in-law come here to bury him. You brought me here from East London, I am not going back to Herschel.

We had a difference of opinion, because the land's people like to take the corpse back to the land, but my own people and some of his kinsmen said: No, his home was here, his wife and children have come from East London to bury him here.

My husband's clansmen arranged the funeral, my only duty was to go to Goodwood to get his papers and to the Tom Boydell Building in Cape Town for his unemployment fees. But his clansmen arranged the funeral and bought the coffin.

On Wednesday evening buti Plank came home from the boats. Is it with this trouble on me that I see you again, my buti, said Poppie.

But it was not for her to speak much. She must sit in the bedroom with her mama on the mattress on the floor. The furniture had been carried outside and put under plastic.

When Mamdungwana could, she left her house and joined them. Her other friends came when possible. Everybody helped, they gave a hand to ouma Makhulu who was cooking on the outside fire, they went to the shop to buy food, stamped mealies, potatoes and vegetables. Buti Mosie came to shave Poppie's head, and the heads of her children and Stone's relatives.

In the backyard the men slaughtered a goat.

A neighbour made the black dress for Poppie to wear to the funeral. And always the men were standing round the house and not leaving them alone, clansmen, old ones, grootmanne, men in groups, waiting round the house.

Friday night the wake was held.

The women sat on the mattresses in the bedroom with Poppie. She was tired from weeping, from talking, from the disagreement with the clansmen of Stone. But when Lindiwe arrived by train that afternoon the trouble had lifted from her. It was still the same little sister-in-law who had taught her to scoop up the water in the dongas and grind the mealies to flour. She shook hands with her. Molo, little sister.

Lindiwe started weeping. The women brought her food and tea.

Friday afternoon after work the men crowded out the front room. This furniture too had been carried out and benches brought in for the old men to sit on. The preacher read from the Bible, the old men joined in: Ewhe.

From the back room Poppie listened. She heard buti Plank's voice join in the singing. He has known these hymns since childhood, Poppie thought, now his mouth is unused to them, his lips are struggling to get the feel of the words. Buti Hoedjie was singing too. Buti Mosie prayed. Right through the night the men kept up the singing. In the back room the women had become quiet, and it was not for Poppie to speak much. Off and on someone came from the front room to where the women were sitting and condoled with her. They shook hands. Then Poppie wiped her eyes with her handkerchief.

Where are the children sleeping? she asked once. With the neighbours, the women replied.

The singing was different to the all-night hymns in church. The voices were pressed together in the front room. They were singing for tata-ka-Bonsile who was dead. In the same room where she had told him four years ago: Now I cannot take it any longer, now I go.

But this time it was he that had gone.

In her handbag, pressed in under a corner of the mattress, she had put the telegram which came to East London: Where will Stone be buried? She had also put there the note she received before leaving: Xoliswe's son was born Monday, she was cut open for the birth.

She had told no one of the child. Not even Bonsile. Let them first bury tata-ka-Bonsile. Then she would gather her thoughts again and make further plans.

Slowly she started giving heed to the words of the hymns the men were singing. Silently she joined in, shaping the words with her lips, her body started to sway, where she was seated on the mattress, leaning against the wall. She moved from side to side.

Our sisi is coming to life again, Mamdungwana told mama.

Later on they helped her to go outside to the toilet. The men standing around made way for her, they stood back and mama cleared the path for her. The oil lamps didn't give enough light, so candles had been lit as well. Some of the men who'd grown tired and others who were slightly drunk were lying flat on the backyard path. They were drawn to the wake by the hymns which they knew from childhood; even those who were somewhat drunk joined in the singing, and prayed.

Walking back from the toilet, Poppie saw that dawn was glimmering behind the houses.

What is the time? she asked mama.

Mama owned a watch. Almost five o'clock.

Inside the men were still singing. Those that had slept were refreshed, the spirit moved them. They talked about death, recited Bible verses and prayed for brother Nongena. For tata-ka-Bonsile. Still Poppie could not believe that this noise and business and this being back in Cape Town was real. That she could see buti Hoedjie and buti Plank and buti Mosie again, but that she might not speak to them. She seemed to be dreaming. Dreaming? Then she remembered her own dream. Bonsile will not be an heir. The dream foreboded the death of his tata. Ag ja. This thought brought peace to her heart and she felt: So it had to be, it could have been no different.

The women brought her hot sweet tea and bread. She swallowed the tea but couldn't get the bread down. Outside the men were sitting round the fire, they poked their sticks at the embers, setting alight small twigs with which to light their pipes. Buti Plank had joined them. She wanted to be with buti Plank. But it was not for her to be with the men. The women took her back to the inner room.

When the full day had dawned, the people who lived close by went home and the ones that had come from far were given water to wash, and they stood outside splashing their faces and rinsing their mouths. They spat out the water on to the plants.

Old Makhulu made a new fire. She poured coffee. Mamdungwana swept the house.

Still the people came, still the mournful singing was to be heard, its slow beat lamenting the dead man. Poppie tried to think about tata-ka-Bonsile, but she could not remember his face. What came to her more strongly was the suffering she had to bear, the troubles that had come to her while she was living in this house.

When the children started gathering in the street and the

231

people came from their houses to join them, mama knew that the hearse had come.

It is the coffin, Poppie, she told Poppie who was now dressed in her black clothes, sitting in the room on the mattress.

The undertakers struggled to get the coffin through the small front door. Her brothers had prepared the benches on which the coffin must be laid. The women in the inner room heard Mosie tell the undertakers: At half past one you must be back to fetch the coffin. They heard the wheels of the big black hearse turning on the dirt road, heard the gravel being crunched as it pulled off again. The children that had made room for it group together once more.

The hardest part lies ahead for you, Poppie, said mama. But he looked nice when he died, I was with him to the last.

No, it is well, mama. I want to see him.

The brothers and the men of the clan Mqwati opened the coffin in the front room, and only after they had seen the corpse were the women allowed in.

Poppie bent over the coffin. And the feeling of heavy grief left her as she saw the small, dark face, the sharp nose, the lips and mouth. Ag, dear Lord Jesus, she wants to say, is this you, tata-ka-Bonsile? Her fingertips touched his forehead, so cold. She touched his face, as if touching the face of a stranger, his cheeks, his mouth as if it belonged to a stranger. His cheeks were sunken, his face had become small and sharp.

The colour has turned, said mama, who was standing on the other side of the coffin. See how dark his temples are.

Bonsile had his turn with the men, now the girls came. They were weeping. Katie and Baby supported Nomvula and Thandi, Rhoda had picked up Kindjie for her to see her father.

The room filled. By twelve o'clock there were so many people that the preacher announced: We are going outside for the service. Bring the coffin out. They picked up the coffin and carried it out, bringing the benches on which to put it down.

In the street the cars that had come to drive the old people to the graveyard were waiting. Mamdungwana's husband had brought his car, Mosie his. Friends had put their wreaths in the cars.

Because tata-ka-Bonsile of late was no church-goer, mama had explained to Poppie, we could not hold the service in the church, but the preachers are coming to the house, from the Holy Cross church and from my Methodist church as well.

When they had done praying and singing, the hearse fetched the coffin.

He would have been glad to be buried from his house, Poppie thought. And now clear to her mind came the image of tata-ka-Bonsile in his weakness, hammering away at the wooden boards inside the house. Bringing planks from the factory where he worked and helping Hoedjie and Mosie to build the house.

Slowly they followed the hearse. In their black clothes the children felt strange with her. To her too they seemed different, clad in clothes lent by neighbours. Bonsile walked with the men. He searched out Jakkie, mama had told her, but Jakkie was the only member of the family not allowed to attend the funeral. When his brother-in-law died he was doing the bush ritual, and had only just come back, he still had the red clay smeared on his face, and was not allowed to come near strangers. Poppie longed for Jakkie, my klonkie with the curly hair that I looked after in Lamberts Bay she thought. She started weeping. Bonsile was pretending to be grown-up, he kept at the heels of his oompie Plank and oompie Hoedjie and oompie Mosie.

The hearse took the turning to the graveyard. The people carrying wreaths shifted them from one hand to the other. The women moved closer to Poppie, dragging their feet through the sand. It was a Christian funeral, they were singing softly, they dragged the sound like their feet, their bodies swaying to the rhythm of the song.

The preacher had taken off his hat, but held it to shade his head. He had the Bible in his one hand, with the back of the other he wiped the sweat from his forehead. The children in their borrowed clothes went to the edge of the grave to peer inside. They were pushed back as the clods started falling.

Poppie and mama went home by car. Mama led Poppie to the dish of red mealies set out alongside the footpath, for her to take a handful and eat, she led her to the basin of water set out next to it for her to wash her hands and dry them on the towel. Then she and mama and the stepfather waited in the front room and the people returning from the graveyard washed and dried their hands, took the mealies and ate them. In the front garden, in the backyard, all over, there were dishes of mealies. Then they came to mama and Poppie and the stepfather waiting in the front room. One by one they shook hands and Poppie said: Thank you.

56

Saturday night the sisters-in-law slept with Poppie, but Sunday morning mama came to see her.

Tata-ka-Bonsile wrote that his stomach was still troubling him, mama, Poppie said. But he hadn't taken to his bed. How did it come that he died?

You know about his stomach trouble, said mama. The doctor Lazarus in Langa thought he had an ulcer and gave him a letter to Groote Schuur hospital. But when he got to Groote Schuur they X-rayed him from all sides, but they couldn't see it. Then he was sent to the Conradie hospital, but the doctor asked him: What is bothering you, I can see nothing in your stomach. He said it bothered him that he was living alone and his wife and his children were far away. Then the Conradie hospital told him: For that there is no medicine.

After that he went to an igqira, a herbalist, said mama,

and the man gave him medicine they call ukugapa. When you have swallowed it, you fill your stomach with water, then they push a feather down your throat and you bring it all up. The man gave him the medicine and an enema. And as I hear the story, the medicine was too strong for him.

He went on a Sunday morning to the igqira, drank the stuff and stayed there all day. Many people stay in his yard. When they've taken the medicine and had the enema they must stay to go to the toilet. He got so weak there, he fell asleep in the yard. When he woke he was still weaker and the igqira sent him by car to the bachelor quarters where he lived. Johnnie, who lives with him, says the whole night long he had to get up and go to the toilet, and later on, Johnnie says, he was so weak he held on to the wall as he walked. Then Johnnie got up to help him, ja.

Early morning Johnnie called Makhulu and she called sisi Mamdungwana and the sisi came along to tell me. I tried to help him, I made Oxo and tried to get him to swallow it, because I could see he was very weak, and I sent Johnnie to fetch the real doctor, Dr Mantagisa. Very early, the sun wasn't up yet, the doctor came and asked tata-ka-Bonsile: Have you taken Xhosa medicine?

He was very weak, but he said: Yes, I've taken some.

His stomach worked blood. He didn't vomit, only worked down. The doctor was angry that he had taken the Xhosa medicine and gave him other stuff to drink and an injection. I am going home, he said, but if he gets worse, call me at once.

Tata-ka-Bonsile held my hand and said: Ag, it was a good thing I tried to do, it was not my death that I sought.

And that was all.

I tried to get him to swallow some glucose water, I lifted him by the shoulders and tried to hold the spoon to his mouth, but by then the man had died.

By that time his brother had come, and the neighbours, and Mosie and his wife. Dr Mantagisa gave us a death certificate and he called the undertakers. They took him away to the morgue and then I sent you the telegram, Poppie.

Poppie was not satisfied. She and mama and Miriam, the

ELSA JOUBERT

sister-in-law who had come from Johannesburg, and sisi
Lindiwe waited in the kitchen for Johnnie Drop-Eye to bring
the box and the case containing tata-ka-Bonsile's belongings
from the bachelor quarters. There was not much to bring.
A spoon, a mug, a knife, a plate and a few blankets and
pieces of clothing. Mama took the medicine from Groote
Schuur and Conradie and the doctor and burnt it on the
outside fire.

Poppie unpacked the few pieces of clothing, unfolded
them, touched them gently and folded them again. These
are old clothes, she told mama.

The clothes we took to the morgue to lay him out in, said
mama, were better.

Poppie thought of the money he had sent them every
fortnight, and the forty rand damage money he'd sent for
the child of Bonsile. Then she remembered about the child
and took the note from her handbag which read: Xoliswe's
son was born Monday, she was cut open for the birth.

My buti has been given back to us, said Lindiwe.

They compared the dates. She was taken to hospital on
Sunday, but she could not give birth, so they had to cut her
on Monday.

The child was born on the day my son-in-law died, said
mama.

He must pay lobola for the girl so that we may have the
child, said Lindiwe. The forty rand was just damage money.
It does not make a Nongena of the child.

But when his oompie Spannerboy went to talk to him
about the child, Bonsile said: I don't want to lobola her. I am
a schoolchild. I want to complete my studies. The girl has
no people, she's a cast-away orphan child. If you want the
child she'll give him to you.

If she's a cast-away orphan child, who were the men that
came to talk damage money? asked Poppie.

They aren't her kinsmen, said Bonsile, she grew up with
them. I'm not paying them lobola.

I lay my husband's death at the door of the igqira, said
Poppie.

236

Why don't you go see him? mama said. Talk to him, tell him he killed your husband. It will lift this heaviness from your heart. What do I seek from him? asked Poppie. I don't believe in those people, what now can he tell me?

You can make a court case, said buti Mosie.

She remembered the attorney in the Volkskas building, but he brought back troubled memories. She considered the Black Sash people and the Legal Aid that Mrs Retief once said would help her. Johnnie took her to the office in town where black people were given free legal aid.

The white man behind the desk was angry at first: You go to the herbalists and then we have to mend matters. He pushed his work aside and pulled the telephone to him. He phoned up the Guguletu police station.

They know of your husband's death, he told Poppie. They are looking for the death certificate.

They waited, they heard the voice of the police sergeant speaking.

The white man put down the telephone. The certificate states that chest trouble caused his death.

It's not true, said Johnnie. I heard this Dr Mantagisa say: The igqira's medicine kills you off, but you still go to him, you must stay away from him. And I saw the man dying that night, how his stomach worked blood till he had no strength left.

The white man answered: What can I do? The certificate says chest.

Poppie picked up her bag and got up. It's bribery, she said. The igqira bribed the doctor, or even the police.

Against bribery she had no power.

The igqira is rich, she said, the people fear him. He has ears where we don't. He hears talk of the court case my husband's brother will make and he gets chest trouble written on the death certificate.

It's a serious thing you are saying, said the white man. If you can bring me proof, I'll take up the matter.

It'll be no use, said Poppie. In the location they say: Money speaks, and I have no money to bribe. Leave the matter be. My husband is dead.

237

The white man looked at Johnnie.

He hung his head, at a loss. Master must rather leave it be. If the police hear about this, it will cause trouble. They'll demand where's your pass, where's your permit. We don't feel for more trouble. Leave it alone, master. And if it ever gets to the court, they'll twist it in such a way that we won't even know what it's all about. We don't hold it against the herbalist, he only tried to help, sometimes his medicine helps a person, but this buti's illness was too deep for him.

Poppie thought: I am here in Cape Town without a pass, I must stay as far as I can from the police.

You mustn't blame tata-ka-Bonsile too much, said mama. He just tried to help, and found his death.

Poppie did not blame him. Her feeling of attachment to him grew. Perhaps because buti Plank had gone back to sea and apart from the money he gave her, he could do no more to help her; and buti Hoedjie had moved in with another coloured woman. Buti Mosie was good to her and said: You and your children must come and live with me. But he was busy, too, every night with his volunteer work, or choir practice or overhauling his car. Which of her brothers was left to her?

Jakkie. Jakkie worked in his mama's garden, dressed in his new long khaki pants and shirt, and black doek tied round his head, his face smeared with red clay. Since he had been to the bush, he had changed. The girls told her that he had become a leader amongst his age-mates, they called him Jungle man or J-man. He seemed shy of her, as younger people are shy of older people that have suffered a deep sorrow. But she heard him and Bonsile laughing and talking as they sat round the fire at night.

Groote Schuur and Conradie hospitals could not help her husband, Poppie thought. It was not the igqira who killed him, it was the hard life in the Cape. Starting with the dairy work in Philippi, carrying on till she had to leave, even to the present. And the hardest for him was the burden *she* had to bear.

Don't harden your heart, Poppie, said mama. She took

238

her to the prayer meeting. She prayed for Poppie till the tears streamed down her face and she had to take a handkerchief to blow out her nose. Mamdungwana and mama supported Poppie when they left the meeting.

The old white boss Steyn at Standard House had told her: If it is the Lord's will that you must go, it is His will. You must accept it. You must not fight it. And now the Lord's will had led to tata-ka-Bonsile's death.

Her heart was filled with self-reproach. Was she right to refuse her in-laws when they had wished to take the body to the land? She let the preachers of her church bury him, because of her his tata and his mama did not see his corpse.

Dear Lord Jesus, did I do right?

57

After a few days, Poppie was strong once more. I have come thus far, she thought, and now, even with tata-ka-Bonsile dead, I can't turn back, for I must go forward. The year has begun, I must see that my children get schooling.

Buti Mosie came to Makhulu's house to see Poppie and said: Now the children are my children, 'cause why their pa is dead and the one oompie they have, is sick in his head and it's here we must put them to school.

We can't put them to school in Cape Town, buti, said Poppie, because they aren't registered here. I know this business well, I don't want to start struggling all over again.

We'll try, said buti Mosie.

Because Poppie was in deep mourning and had to remain in the house, Mosie went to auntie Violet, the auntie they had stayed with when she was a young makoti, and who wasn't working at the moment.

I'll give you bus fare, sisi, then you go to the school and say: These children were born here but their mama was sent away from the Cape. Can they get their schooling here?

This auntie Violet went, but the principal of the first school said: The children must first be registered at the office, and when sisi Violet went to the office they said: No, the children are registered in East London, they must get their schooling there.

We'll slip them into a school, said buti Mosie, and he sent auntie Violet to a principal that he knew, but the principal said: My school is full, how can I take them if their names are not registered on a house card?

Mosie was dissatisfied, but Poppie said: Then I must make new plans.

To mama she said: I decide one thing at a time, mama, and I have decided I must work for my children to keep them at school, and I am coming to work in the Cape. There is no money there in East London. With eighteen rand a month and five children, I'll get nowhere.

Bonsile must go back to school in East London, but the girls can't live alone in the house, they must go to my in-laws on the land. Even if it is far to the next ilali where I hear there is a school, they'll just have to walk.

Kindjie and Fezi can live with buti Mosie and I'll work sleep-in.

And your pass? mama asked.

I'll work without a pass, mama, and if I get sleep-in, how will the office know about me?

And if you come to the location weekends and there is a raid?

Then the Lord must take care of me, said Poppie. The money is twice as much here and I must keep my children at school. So it's not something bad I'm doing, mama.

She talked to Mr Kwinanu who was going with his lorry to Herschel: Take my children with you, I will pay you. When you get there help them to find a place in school, for the parents of my husband are old, they don't know about school. There are schools there, but it is far to walk.

He promised to help.

I am sending my daughters to the land as my in-law-people wished after all, Poppie thought, but there was no bitterness in her heart: What must be, must be.

You're going to Herschel, she told Nomvula and Thandi. I'll go back to East London first to fix up the house and get your school papers to send to you. Tell the teachers in the meantime that your father's death has caused confusion. Mr Kwinanu will help you.

Nomvula and Thandi did not want to go. They wept.

Let us stay with Katie and Baby, let us go to school here, they begged.

Poppie did not answer them.

Once more she felt the uneasiness come over her that she had felt before her husband's death. At night she slept restlessly, dreams darkened her sleep. She dreamed that she was searching for tata-ka-Bonsile. She walked past rows of old men sitting smoking their pipes. She looked for him but did not find him, and the old men turned their faces from her and would not show her the way to go.

Must I find the road myself? thought Poppie.

So she refused to listen to Nomvula and Thandi and packed their clothes in a bag and forced them on to Mr Kwinanu's lorry.

We don't know the land, they cried. We've never seen our grandfather and grandmother, we're afraid of them.

Then you must see them now, said Poppie. She wrote down the address for Mr Kwinanu; he put it in his pocket. She wrote on a piece of paper: Nomvula has passed Standard Six and must go to Standard Seven, Thandi must go to the Higher Primary to Standard Six. The sooner they get to school the better, she told Mr Kwinanu.

The girls wept as he drove off. We want to stay with Bonsile in Mdantsane, they had begged, we'll cook and do the housework and go to school. But Poppie had Xoliswe in mind: I won't leave my daughters unprotected in NU 7.

The owner of the garage in Goodwood where Stone had worked knew about his death and sent a message: If his son wants to come under contract, he can get his father's job.

But Poppie refused. To come under contract was for her

a harsh thing. Must Bonsile's life follow the road his father's had gone? No, he goes back to Mdantsane to complete his schooling.

Buti Hoedjie was drunk. He shouted at her: For what are you sending him away? Who told you about Mdantsane? Always Mdantsane, bloody Mdantsane.

Has buti not yet asked at the office who told me about Mdantsane, said Poppie. My people have never been to the Ciskei or the Transkei, Poppie thought. They hate the land, they don't want my children to go to Herschel or Mdantsane, but what other way is open to me?

A week later she said: I leave for East London on Sunday to fix up the house and to find people to rent it, then I will come back.

But before she and Bonsile could leave by train for East London, Mr Kwinanu's lorry stopped at the door of mama's house and Nomvula got out. Her face was streaked with dust and tears. She saw her ma and ran to her. She was unable to speak for crying, but hid her face behind her fist, and wiped her nose with her forearm.

And this now? Mr Kwinanu? Poppie asked.

Mr Kwinanu got down from the lorry and shook hands with Poppie.

Molo, sisi. He looked embarrassed. He looked at Nomvula, opening his hands to show his powerlessness. We couldn't get school for her. The little one got school at the Higher Primary, but the big school was full. Again he looked at Nomvula, at her uncombed hair, her dirty face. She fought, sisi. She wouldn't stay there. She got on to the lorry and we couldn't get her off.

I want to come back to mama, said Nomvula, I was too late for school.

If you're late there, you are late here too, and in any case they will not take you. I can't leave you here because already I am on my way to East London.

Nomvula arrived on Friday, and Sunday Poppie took her and Bonsile back by train.

I'm taking you back, said Poppie, because the law says you cannot stay here.

Poppie and Nomvula got off the train in the night at Stormberg, and Bonsile went through to East London. Poppie did not remember this part of the country, but by asking they found their way, from one train to the other, and at last by bus to Palmietfontein.

Since her first visit as makoti, the old people had moved to a trust village where the huts were built in rows, each one with a small mealie patch and a kraal. She asked her way of an old man who was half-blind and walked with a stick. It was tata-ka-Bonsile's father.

She said after she had greeted him: I brought the children here for their schooling, because I don't want them to live apart from one another. And tata-ka-Bonsile told me they are needed to look after you.

The old man nodded.

Now, if this one gets no schooling this year, she must stay here till next year, because I'm taking a job and she can't stay alone in the house with her brother in East London. I'm not looking for trouble. She must stay here with her sister.

Thandi was not expecting them. She was carrying water to the old people's hut when she saw her mother and sister coming along the road. She took the pail from her head and ran. She was crying. She tried to stop her mother from walking too fast and arriving at the hut too soon.

It's a bad place, mama, she said. I don't like staying here. I want to come back to mama.

What's wrong with it? Poppie asked. She talked roughly to the child. Are you too good for these people?

Ma, they don't even have paraffin here. To eat we must first make a fire outside. She pointed at the cooking shelter where the embers were still glowing and where the black three-legged pot had been pushed aside. Ma, I can't eat their food.

The trust village was far from the school and shop and post office. The old people had been given one hut only, and Miriam's small daughter from Johannesburg lived with them. The old woman was sitting inside the hut. It was dusk and she was wrapped in her blanket. She greeted Poppie, taking her hand.

While they talked Thandi went out to boil water on the fire and make tea in the little blue teapot and poured for them. Poppie tasted the goat's milk in the tea. She disliked the taste, but it was warm and wet, and she was thirsty after the journey.

What other work must you do? she had asked Thandi.

I must fetch the goats to the kraal, I must do my homework, I must cook for tatomkhulu and makhulu.

Go and help your sister, Poppie told Nomvula.

She sat beside her mother-in-law, close to her so that she might be heard.

It is good that you have come yourself, said her mother-in-law, because we are helpless. We are too old, we cannot walk to the school and speak. They did not take the child. We could not stop her when she got on to the lorry to go back to you.

She must stay here, mama. Because I must go out to work, and the money is not enough in East London.

They can stay here, said her mother-in-law. Miriam's child is too young to look after us, and the old man is blind and I cannot fetch water any more.

I will send money for their school and food, said Poppie.

Nomvula cried and pleaded when Poppie prepared to leave after two days.

Thandi goes to school, it is not so bad for her, she pleaded. She has her schoolmates, and even if it is far, they walk together and they play on the paths and on the hills, but I will have to stay here, every day. Ouma is too strict. They're raw people, mama, the hut stinks, I don't want to sleep here.

Poppie thought once more: If it is the Lord's will that you stay, you will stay, and if it's the Lord's will that you go, you will go. She was sorry for her child, and yet there was some

244

part of her heart which was not sorry for her. If this is what she was born for, then she too must carry her burden. As she, Poppie, had to carry hers.

You are still young, Nomvula, you will get used to it.

But I don't want to get used to it, mama.

They heard Thandi outside, breaking twigs and starting the fire. She was singing softly, a song unknown to Poppie. A new fear entered Poppie's heart.

She gripped Nomvula's arm. You are staying here, my child, but you must not forget where you have come from. You must not forget your ouma and your family in Cape Town. You must not forget your oompie Mosie. And don't allow Thandi to forget. You may visit your auntie Constance in the next ilali. Go to her for company. See that you get school next year. Keep thinking of next year, next year at school. Help Thandi with her schoolwork. One day, I promise you, we will live together again.

59

After two days with her in-laws, Poppie returned to East London.

She got off the train at Mount Ruth station, two stations before Arnoldon. She crossed the long railway bridge and waited in the shade of the station building for the bus to Highway. People who knew her by sight were loth to approach her, put off by the black clothes she was wearing. She heard someone sitting behind her in the bus, say: Which one of her family has died? But she did not answer him.

At Highway she got off the bus and took another. She held her handbag firmly under her arm, she felt strong, stronger than the other people on the bus. The illness of her husband, she knew now, had made her weak too; now that he was dead, it was for her to be husband and wife, father and mother to his children.

The only thing that still made her weak was the uncertainty about Bonsile's schooling. She had given him the money. Had the school taken him, or had he been too late? The school fees for Bonsile, Nomvula and Thandi had cost her more than seventy rand, and her train ticket and his and Nomvula's and the money for Mr Kwinanu took most of the pension money.

As she walked up her old street, she felt the heat again. It rose from the mealies growing green in the gardens, it rose from the red earth at the roadside, it pushed down on her from the low grey clouds packed together in the sky. Soon it will rain, she thought. Soon it will flash and thunder and the water will pour over me. She did not walk faster. Let it pour over me, let it soak through me, my body will dry out again.

She pushed open the door of her house. It was not locked. Bonsile was seated at the table, his books open before him.

Mama is wet, he said.

She shook her head, took a cloth and began to dry her face. Then she wiped her head, arms and hands, and bent down to dry her legs. She was glad about the rain on her face, because she felt the tears running over her cheeks with the rainwater when she saw Bonsile with his books.

It goes well with you, Bonsile?

Yes, mama.

They took you in at the school?

Yes, mama.

The next day she went to the office to pay the six rand rent, then to Majola and sisi Blaauw and Emily whom she told: I wish to rent out the house, but Bonsile must stay with the people who rent it; you must lend out your ears to find good people looking for a place to stay. I am in a hurry to rent, but I do not want to make a mistake and you must help me. She went to the people of her church and told them the same.

She waited a day. She cleaned the house and yard. The mealies were growing well. Bonsile helped her with the weeding until she felt her back could stand no more. Then she sat on a chair in front of the window and took Bonsile's clothes in her lap and patched and darned. She took her sewing machine for the last time and from the bits of material that remained she made dresses for Nomvula and Thandi and Kindjie and a shirt for Fezi. She tried to make something for each child, but at night her eyes ached, she could no longer use them, they were swollen and sore. After she had made food for Bonsile, she lay on her bed with closed eyes. Turn down the lamp in my room, Bonsile, so that I can lie in the dark, she said.

The morning of the third day a man and a woman arrived, sent by Majola. We are of his clan, they said, we are looking for a place to live.

She showed them the house and said: This room Bonsile must keep, and he will cook for himself in the kitchen. It is well, they said, and the money is right too. I will send the rent each month to the office from Cape Town, she said, then you will give the money you owe me to Bonsile, for him to buy his food.

We will look after him, sisi, said the woman. We have no children — he will be our child.

Then only one day remained before she was to take the train to Cape Town.

I want to see the child who was given to us when your father died, Bonsile.

The support of the child was another burden on her shoulders, but about this she did not complain. About the child she was glad.

I will tell Xoliswe to bring the child, mama, said Bonsile.

When Poppie got on the train the next afternoon, she had only a few cents left. Only enough, so she reckoned, to pay for the bus fare from the Cape Town station to Mosie's house. She had cut bread to eat on the train, for the rest she would drink water.

Not only had she to pay up on the train ticket, not only had she to leave money for Bonsile's food till the end of the month when the tenants would pay him, but the money that was over she had given to the mother of Bonsile's child. For the child was of the blood of tata-ka-Bonsile, of mama, of ouma Hannie. It was pitifully thin, the little legs drawn up to the body like those of a newly-born child, the belly was large, blown up, the skin lighter of colour.

I have not much milk, mama, Xoliswe said as she bent forward to loosen the blanket at her back and to take the child down and lay it on the bed. The child does not grow.

Xoliswe does not wear a kopdoek, she is not makoti. She is nothing but a schoolchild who has to carry a baby on her back, thought Poppie. She is thin, so slight of build that they had to cut open her belly to get out the child, as they did with my Kindjie. But for such a young girl. . .

Xoliswe stood with eyes cast down.

The child must have extra food. Did your people not give you money to buy food for the child?

Xoliswe did not answer.

Should I have let Bonsile come under contract at the garage at Goodwood, Poppie wondered, so that his child should not starve? But then she became obstinate again. And walk the road his father had to walk as contract worker? And let his wife walk that road?

She took out the money left in her purse. She counted what she needed for her ticket. She counted off cents for her bus fare to Mosie's house.

Take this, she told Xoliswe. I'll send more. Xoliswe put the money in the front of her dress, then she started wrapping up the baby.

But Poppie stopped her. Wait, she said, I made some clothes for your baby, too.

Heat water on the Primus, she told Bonsile, so that we may bath the child. She soaped the baby and bathed him in the basin. She sat down on the bed, and dried the baby on her lap. She dressed him in the little shirt she'd made, she folded a nappy.

Rinse the clothes he had on in the bath water, she told Xoliswe. It is so hot outside, they'll be dry before sunset.

She washed the blanket herself that Xoliswe had tied

round her body. Bonsile can bring it to you later, when it's dry. Take my blanket.

Now this has put an end to your schooling, Poppie said as she saw Xoliswe's eyes resting on the books lying on Bonsile's table. She felt sorry for Xoliswe. She had been a clever child.

And it is Bonsile who did this to her.

But then Poppie made herself strong again. What had to be, had to be. If tata-ka-Bonsile had to return to them in this child, then it was the will of the Lord. The child's name is Vukile, mama, Xoliswe had told her. Vukile means: arisen.

On these things Poppie's mind dwelt as she journeyed back to Cape Town.

For two days and two nights she sat up straight. She sat in the corner of the compartment, next to the corridor. The hard door frame and the backrest of the bench supported her body. She did not speak to the other passengers. At times her head dropped and she slept, to jerk awake as the train stopped. Children clambered over her legs, others pushed past her as they made their way to the toilet. When they wished to speak to her, she touched her forehead, as if she was in pain.

There was no strength left in her to share or to receive human contact.

She ate her bread sparingly, tapped water in the mug and drank it. When the others offered her food, she declined, because she had nothing to offer in return. At night she rested her body as best she could. She had given her blanket to Xoliswe, but she felt neither the cold of the night nor the early morning. The third day she ate her last piece of bread.

When the train steamed into the station and stopped, she waited till the other people got off, and then she took her bag and went down the corridor. She held on to the railing and carefully and slowly stepped down. As she put her foot on to the platform it seemed to rise up and rush at her.

What's the matter, auntie? a man asked her, a half-coloured because he spoke Afrikaans to her. He took her by the arm and led her to a bench. Only after she had rested, was she able to start walking to the bus terminus.

Buti Mosie's house was not far from the bus stop. The children seemed to have had a feeling that she was coming because when she got down, she heard Fezi shout: Mama, and Kindjie rushed up: Mama! But perhaps she was hearing other children shouting mama, perhaps it was not quite clear to her what she heard or saw. With the children round her, she walked on, neighbours saw her coming and recognised her. They left their gardens and came to meet her, took her bag and led her to buti Mosie's house.

She is sick, Rhoda told Mosie when he got home that night. She has suffered much. I think she is feeling buti Stone's death only now.

For it seemed as if her eyes did not even see her two children. She lay on the bed to which they led her and closed her eyes. That evening mama came.

Our sisi is sick, Rhoda had sent word. She has returned without telling us when to fetch her at the station. All these things have been too much for her.

Poppie lay for a week and then she got up and said: The children need money. I must go and work. Where else will my children get their food?

Six

The people of the land

60

One night I would sleep with my brother, the next with mama, or a night with Makhulu until the corrugated iron shack that we'd built was broken down and Makhulu taken to an old-age home, Poppie says.

It was then that I got work at Mrs Swanepoel's. The woman who took me to Mrs Swanepoel had worked twelve years for her, but she had to leave because of her legs — they were going to cut out her varicose veins. This woman told me: Come along and keep my job for me for the one month I am in hospital.

Mrs Swanepoel told me she would pay me thirty rand, but I told her I came to work for my children, I could not work for that money. I started working on Monday. Tuesday I told her I would work till Friday, then she would have to get somebody else. I cannot work for that money, I have too many children.

She was sick in bed and she asked me: Why can't you work for thirty? I told her, she seemed to understand and she said: You had better stay; I'll give you forty.

Later she asked me: Have you a pass, Rachel?

I have a pass, I answered, but the permits in it are not in order.

She didn't mind this and said: It is only for a month, I suppose there won't be any trouble. Don't go to the front door when the doorbell rings; the inspectors are making too much fuss in our street. If they catch you at the door and your pass is not in order, then I am the one that will have to pay the fine.

You are working for government people, Hannie, the servant girl from next door, told her. They don't like to get a bad name with the inspectors.

Mrs Swanepoel did not want to be bothered; she was a busy woman and went out a lot; and she liked Poppie's way of working.

I needn't tell you anything, Rachel, I see you know what to do.

She liked the way Poppie ironed her clothing and said: You have a neat hand, Rachel.

Poppie also did the cooking for Mrs Swanepoel's dinner parties.

You grew up among whites, Poppie. You cook well.

It seemed as if Mrs Swanepoel didn't mind the other servant not coming back after a month because her legs would not heal, and the doctor told her to work at a place without steps and staircases.

Then you will be staying, won't you? she asked Poppie. We get along well, I needn't tell you all the time what you have to do.

Thursday afternoons, her off afternoons, Poppie used to stay in her room; Sundays she was off all day and went home early.

And nobody had asked her about her pass.

But it worried Mrs Swanepoel that Rachel could not answer the front doorbell and she said: We must do something about this, I find it very inconvenient. What actually is the matter with your pass?

She paged through the pass but could not understand what she saw and said: We'll ask the master when he gets home tonight. He has lots of friends and maybe they could fix it up. Let's see what we can do about it. But then you must promise me that you won't leave me next month when Miss Susie and her baby are coming home. I will need you then.

Again she called Poppie: If I go to all the trouble of fixing up your pass and have you registered on my name, you must promise not to get pregnant, hey?

Poppie did not answer her.

She only saw the white woman's eyes travelling up and down her body.

Or are you pregnant already?

No, Poppie said, I am not pregnant, madam. I'm tied off.
Well, go get your pass and I'll show it to master tonight.
I really cannot get someone else before Miss Susie arrives,
and you know my ways by now.

I received back my pass, Poppie said, and on it was written:
No objection.

Once every six months I had to go to Observatory where
they would give me a closed envelope with a paper inside
to take to Langa. And at the Langa office they took my pass
book and read the letter which told them how many months
they had to stamp in my book. Every six months it was the
same again — go to Observatory, go to Langa, and they
stamped my pass book. The master had fixed up everything.

That is the way we know life. We don't mind about
justice, about whether a thing is right or not. We know of
people who came to Cape Town after 1960 who were given
permits and houses, and we who have been here much
longer, must leave. We don't mind any more. Our lives are
upside down anyway. We're used to it. One person gets the
pass, the next one doesn't. It's come to be so that we don't
care if we have a pass or if we don't. If we feel we want to
visit relatives we go. We don't worry about a pass. If they
catch you, well, they catch you. That's the way we know
life.

Mosie felt bitter about the permit given to Poppie. Bitter
about the years of struggle. To what purpose? This is what
we should have done long ago, sisi, he said. It's simple,
man. Go work for government people. 'Cause why, it's
them that like their comfort. It's them that make the rules.

If it suits the white people the law does not count, said
Jakkie. That's no law, is it?

Poppie showed her pass and her permit to mama.

When the madam's daughter and her baby come to visit,
I will be getting more money. I can send ten rand to
Herschel, and ten rand to Bonsile so that he can take the bus
to go to school, and five rand to Xoliswe and put money
aside for the children's school fees next year. And I can give
Mosie five rand for my children's keep. Then there's enough

left for bus fare and for some clothes for the small ones.

I don't want your money, Mosie said.

I had two feelings in my heart, Mosie explains. I was glad for my sister that she got a permit, but my heart did not want to swallow its bad feeling about all the rudeness of the policemen towards my sister all these years. And for what? It's like this, a black man in a uniform is protected like. They don't know what a human being is, they have no manners with a person, and you can't talk to them proper like. If they hear that my sister has no pass, they come knock us up, they knock at the front door, they go to the window and knock there, as if they are looking for a murderer. And all this only because of a pass.

And Johnnie Drop-Eye adds: In the 'fifties they told us we had better get pass books or else we'd be lost. That's right, if you haven't a pass you're lost. But man, you're more captive if you've got a pass, because the pass is not the end of everything. It's the stamp that counts. And it's the stamp that our sisi couldn't get.

It's good that you can now come home to us in the bus or on the street without being afraid they will catch you, mama told Poppie. And if you have to live with Mrs Swanepoel for ever, then you live with her for ever.

The only place where Poppie feels at home is in Cape Town, mama told Mosie. Poppie wants to be with us.

God Jesus Christ, Jakkie said. Do you forget all the years of hardship?

Poppie did not talk back; she only said: Mama, when is buti Plank coming home?

Poppie and mama's children sat around the table. They were singing; the whole night long they sang, church songs and other songs. Kindjie was on her lap, Fezi had crept in behind her back on the chair; Jakkie had left his friends outside and came to join in the singing.

Are you angry with me, Jakkie? Poppie asks. Because of the pass?

How can I be angry with you, sisi? I am angry because of the law.

256

Jakkie was back at school. After returning from the bush he said: I am not getting any place with my Standard Six. I am twenty-two and I can't get anywhere because of this education thing.

Katie, who was charring with Mrs Louw, the woman where mama once worked, was helping him with money, and the stepfather and mama too. Mama was glad Jakkie was going back to school. He wants to become a preacher, or even a teacher, mama said. Jakkie takes it to heart when people suffer.

Come Sunday maybe old Plank will be back from the sea, Poppie, said mama. Then you will be happy, hey?

This time of my life was not very good, says Poppie. I had lost my husband and I had to live without my children. But my family was my consolation. I was glad to return to my church, the Holy Cross, and meet the people whom I knew, like Mamdungwana and Mr Mata and his wife and the minister of the Guguletu congregation, and the minister of Langa.

At first I wore my black clothes, but when the time of heavy mourning had passed I put on the black skirt and white blouse to the prayer meetings on Sunday afternoons. Because I hadn't attended prayer meetings in Mdantsane regularly I had to be clothed again. If we stay away longer than three months we have to start all over. It's like a class, these prayer meetings — if we stay away we are marked absent. The woman who leads the meeting reads a portion of the Lord's Word, then she addresses us; thereafter each one may bear witness from the word, stand up and talk and sing if she wants to. Or we pray, we pray for the things close to every woman's heart — peace in the world and that war should stay away.

When the group has completed its three months, our great day comes. Then it is the time of umlaliso, or what the people will call the sleeping-over Saturday night's church, because the service lasts the whole night. We invite all the churches, the Methodists, the Dutch Reformed, the Presbyterians and the Roman Church and everyone that wants

257

to attend. From Langa and Nyanga East and Guguletu. All
the people come and the children bring blankets, and those
that work come directly from their jobs.

It will be about ten o'clock when the minister clothes the
people. The women to be clothed stand in a row. The
minister's wife and the women who help her have the
purple blouses each marked with its owner's name. Then
the minister reads what you must believe and what you
promise to do, and he reads your name and everybody
says from one throat: Yes, if the Lord will help us. The
women come and pull your purple blouse on over the white
one you are wearing, and you receive a card saying you are
a full member of the Mothers' Union. And the men are
treated in the same way except they receive purple waistcoats.

In the church hall the women have cooked a meal — meat
and vegetables and rice and soup, and outside they have lit
fires for making tea and coffee.

So then we are told: Now you must eat and drink.

All night long the candles are burning and the people
sing, and at about three o'clock in the morning the minister
leaves for home, as he must still be able to preach on Sunday
morning. When the day breaks, the candles are low and our
voices are gone because of too much singing, the children
sleep on their blankets on the church benches. Those with
cars will have gone, but those without cars have to stay
because they can't walk in the night, they have to wait
until the buses are on the road again.

Lord, your portals are opened to us. Your golden streets
await us. Lord, the wings of your angels enfold us. We will
shelter underneath your wings. We shall lack nothing, our
beakers overflow.

While she is singing, the worries that have clouded her
life fall from Poppie. When she is among the women who
have been clothed anew she is strong and safe. They are
her sisters and she is theirs. Singing, they walk down the
steps of the church, when they hear good news, they clap
their hands with joy, when the bad times are upon them
they take each other by the arms.

She sang until she was completely hoarse. When she had

to take the bus back to work on Monday morning her voice was still feeble. Her Bible lay next to her bed in her room.

No, there was no special portion of the Book that I read during that time, Poppie explains. When I read in the Bible everything I read is special.

61

When she had been working for six months she received a letter in a strange hand, but in the same blue envelope that her children in Herschel used to send to her. From the time of the telegram telling her of her husband's illness, Poppie was scared of a telegram or a letter in a strange handwriting. It was from Constance, buti Spannerboy's wife. Buti Spannerboy had been paid his insurance money from his accident and he had returned to Herschel. With this money they had bought the house in the ilali next to the one of the old people.

Dear Sisi, she wrote, things are all right with me, I hope that everything is well with you. Ma is a bit poorly, but she is in any case not lying down. Pa is not too well either although he is up and about. Tata says I have to let sisi know that Bonsile should return to go to the bush. Tata says he has no strength left and Bonsile should come before he dies. I close my letter by sending greetings to everybody, from Constance.

That afternoon, while Poppie was taking in the washing, Hannie the maid from next door, came to the fence to talk.

What's the matter, sisi? she asked, bad news or something?

Hannie was a coloured woman, about Poppie's age, with children of her own. Poppie knew she had also had her share of worries and troubles.

Poppie told her about the letter: I promised that my child

259

could go to the bush in the land, and now his grandpa calls to him to come.

Hannie knew about Bonsile, about the school and Poppie's hope for him.

She said: The child has done so well and his Standard Nine is going so well, you can't take him from school and send him away. For what are your people so taken up with this bush business?

That is our belief, said Poppie. It is our most important belief; he can go nowhere unless he has gone to the bush.

That evening Hannie came to Poppie's room: Sisi, you are such a loyal church-woman — she too is a church-woman, Methodist, like Poppie's mama — what's all this bush-going business?

Where did you grow up that you do not know about these things? Poppie had bitterness in her heart. She thought about the coloureds of Lamberts Bay and the Basters of Upington who held the bush ritual in respect. It's our belief, she said once again, not only of the raw people but of us all. The Lord made everybody, the Xhosa too. He takes us as we are; it's not sinful to kill a goat or a sheep or to make beer; it's good work. We are the amaXhosa, as they say, and we do our beliefs as amaXhosa, and above all we serve God.

She prayed about it, and then decided: Bonsile has not turned twenty yet and he must finish his year at school before going to the bush. Then she wrote to Constance: Bonsile cannot come now. Tell my father-in-law the time is not right, he will come later.

That night she dreamt one of her bad dreams. She was barefoot and walking on a dirt road. She was wearing a long dress, like when she was a makoti and the skirt was dragging in the dust, but she couldn't pick it up. She couldn't walk straight ahead, but was being forced to pass between old men who were all around her, wearing blankets and carrying kieries. And she saw them raise the kieries and point them this way and that. They came upon a herd of cattle and one old man told her: That is the ox that you must bring, then another old man spoke up and said: No, it is the other one. They were pushing her ahead in among the cattle, closer to the trampling hooves. She wanted to run away from all this, but the old men took hold of her, ugly old men. Mama, she cried, they are ugly old men.

The next day she received a telegram from Constance that tata-ka-Bonsile's father had passed by.

Mrs Swanepoel complained: When I come in late at night or if I get up during the night I see that your light is burning, Rachel. Now, Rachel, you're wasting electricity, or do you forget to turn off the light at night?

I don't sleep very well, madam, Poppie replied.

Must I give you a pill?

If madam would.

One Sunday she walked from buti Mosie's house to mama's, but mama wasn't there, she was in church. But in the back-yard she found buti Plank, sitting with his back against the wire of the fowl-run. He was carving thin palings. And he was sober.

If I had stayed on here in the Cape, buti Plank, she said, tata-ka-Bonsile would still have been alive.

She sat down next to him, but her hands were restless and she broke the shavings in ever smaller bits.

If I were here he would not have gone to that man for the strong poison medicine. I don't say that the herbalist was wrong, no; maybe it was only the medicine that was too strong for him. Or maybe I could have called a doctor. Maybe he would not have lain a whole night with his stomach running. Maybe I would have taken him to hospital earlier.

Well, it is now finished, little sister, Plank answered. Why does it worry you?

The old men come to me in my dreams, my buti. I can't sleep any longer. Tata-ka-Bonsile's tata died before I could send Bonsile to go to the bush at his place.

It's the fucking people of the land, said buti Plank. They must leave go of you; those things are finished for you.

They are against everything that I have to do with tata-ka-Bonsile's people, she thought. They are against the people

261

of the land. Later she talked to buti Mosie.

We are living here, buti Mosie answered. Bring the child to us; let him go to the bush here in Cape Town. We have never been on the land, we are not interested in what the people of the land have told you. Bring the child to us, we'll look after him.

It is my grandchild, mama joined in. Let him come to the Cape when he has completed his schooling; I'll help you with his going to the bush; I'll support you, Poppie.

The dreams did not stop.

She dreamt she was a makoti once again, sitting in the hut where she sat on her first visit with tata-ka-Bonsile. Now, however, the hut was full of people and she had no breath in her and they had to drag her outside by the arms. They took her to the big drums of beer boiling over the fires, they gave her a strainer and told her: Strain this. But however much she strained so the mtombo boiled up and she couldn't keep ahead, straining the beer. Eventually it was over the brim and running down her legs and feet.

Buti Mosie came to the house where she was working, and he remained with her in her room for a long time.

My sister, you take this thing too much to heart.

She lay on her bed in the dark. My eyes are hurting me, light the candle. She had got into the habit of lighting a candle at night when she couldn't sleep, so that the white woman couldn't see.

My sister, you must find peace, buti Mosie said.

It's the dreams, buti, she told him. Last night I went with the old men again, with one of them that I know, one who is alive, although I do not know who he is, the others are unknown to me. I dreamt I was in the land at my in-laws' place and there were a great many people coming to the place where they were taking me and there they sat around drinking beer. They had slaughtered an ox and the old men were talking about why they slaughtered the ox. And buti, it felt as if the slaughtering had been done to me, it was so bad I didn't even want to look. I saw the sides of life, like wings, moving, and fear came over me. Tata-ka-Bonsile wanted to take the child to the bush and my father-in-law wanted to fix the belief things for the child, and now they have both passed by.

She straightened up, her doek falling from her head, as she pleaded with her buti Mosie: I do not want to quarrel with anybody, buti. Buti Plank will be drunk and swear at me, and you, buti, will be against this thing, and a whole lot of talk-talk will follow on this, but I have decided. The child must go to his father's place for the ritual.

If that is the way you feel, then he must go. And we will help you.

She wrote to Bonsile at Mdantsane that he should finish his year at school and then come to Cape Town and work during the holiday at the garage where his tata used to work, so as to earn money for the new clothes he would have to buy when he went to the bush.

She went to Mr Brown's garage and asked him: Can Stone Nongena's child come to work here during the December holidays to earn some money? Good, he said, I liked Stone, his child can come.

She wrote to buti Spannerboy at his house in the ilali next to her mother-in-law's place and asked: I want to do as tata-ka-Bonsile asked me to, I want to send Bonsile to the land to do the ritual when he has finished this year at his school. Will you make the arrangements?

Buti Spannerboy answered: I have no son; Bonsile is my son, I will do as you ask.

But then she had to talk to mama, because mama would have to help her at her work. Mama was not for this bush business. You have had enough trouble with the people of the land, she said. Get some peace in you. Let the child do the ritual here in the Cape. Then we can all help you.

Poppie told her about her dreams: It has been decided, mama. And mama will see Bonsile when he arrives at Christmas time to work here. But now I need mama to help me.

263

Because she had asked Mrs Swanepoel: If I don't mind working during the Christmas and New Year, and if I help madam with the people who are coming down here to visit, can I have my leave at the end of January? I want to go home to my children.

How long will you be away? Mrs Swanepoel asked.

It will be longer than one month, she answered, but before Mrs Swanepoel could complain, Poppie said: mama will come and work in my place.

All right, Mrs Swanepoel answered, but I don't want to be bothered with all this, you'd better teach your mama what she ought to know.

Will mama help me? Poppie asked.

All right, I'll help.

Poppie began putting money aside for the bush business, and buti Plank gave her money, as well as Jakkie and buti Mosie who said: I am not for this, but I'll help, sisi. After all, we are the help-each-other people. It was a word that he had heard somewhere, and he liked the sound of it. Mama could not give much, because she had to save something for Katie who was pregnant by some city boy without people. But she gave what she could. Buti Hoedjie also brought her money. He had gone back to Muis and built her a house at Cross Roads. She was ill and buti Hoedjie worked during the day and looked after her at night.

Hoedjie has become like oompie Sam, said mama, he still drinks but when he is drunk he goes off by himself to sleep. Now he came to help Poppie too.

Are you feeling better now, sisi? asked Hannie as they sat in the backyard cleaning the cutlery of the two households.

I am now feeling better about everything, Hannie, she said.

At the bus terminus in Nyanga Poppie met a boy whose parents she had known at Lamberts Bay; he had been Bonsile's friend when he was still in the Cape.

Madolpen, she said, Bonsile is coming within a few months. Then, in the new year, he is going to the land for his bush ritual.

Madolpen answered: Then I am not staying home either, sisi.

His father, Malume, was a fisherman in Kalk Bay, his mother was working in Claremont. They were not living together any longer.

But how can you say a thing like this? You have arranged nothing with your parents.

That doesn't matter, sisi, I am not staying behind; if Bonsile goes, I go.

Get on the train and go and see your father in Kalk Bay, I will phone your mother.

I don't mind his going, his mother said. I can't leave my work, but if he goes with you he can go.

The next Sunday Poppie was at Mosie's place when Malume arrived there, somewhat drunk.

For what does my child want to go to Kaffirland? he said. Herschel is too far away. If he wants to go to the bush, he can do so here in Cape Town, just like his brothers.

Don't tell me that, Poppie replied, tell that to your child. Can I help it if your child wants to go along?

Madolpen's mother came to Poppie's work and brought money along. It was more than fifty rand. She was glad the child could go with Bonsile. Her eldest son didn't want to work, and the second one was a gaolbird.

I have too much trouble with the children all by myself, she said. If this last-born of mine can go to the bush where he is taught the proper things, maybe something can still come of him. Here in the Cape the ritual is just rush-rush and everything finished.

The boys left by train for Herschel one week before Poppie to start preparations. Sunday afternoon she went to the station with Fezile and Kindjie. Kindjie, six years old, would be going to school in the coming year; Fezi, at nine, was doing well and top of his class every time. They were going along with her to Herschel because she wanted all the children together once again, even though it would be for only one month.

They took the train to Stormberg, Burgersdorp, Aliwal North, the railway bus to Lady Grey, the bus to Sterkspruit, then they caught the next bus to Palmietfontein. The two children were tired and fell asleep leaning against Poppie. It was past noon and the sky was heavily overcast. There was dust all over the bus, on the seats and on the sills of the windows. The children were dirty, around their mouths the dust caked on the dried spittle of sweets and food eaten earlier. It was so warm Poppie felt the perspiration form in damp circles on her body where the children's heads leant against her.

Then the rain came. The water ran in dirty streams down the windows, the sound of the bus wheels on the road changed, the tyres seemed to cling to the wet dirt. The heat in the bus didn't cool down. Kindjie awoke, sat up straight and started to cry. Poppie comforted her and the child fell asleep again. The passengers were tired, they sat hunched, clutching their parcels. Through the dirty windows it was impossible to see whether they had reached the mountains.

When the bus stopped the back door was jerked open from the outside and coolness from the rain came into the bus. It was the stop at Sterkspruit. The two boys had come to meet them. Poppie saw them at once, Madolpen and Bonsile. They had thrown hessian bags over their heads and shoulders to keep off the rain. Bonsile took the two children down from the bus and tried to cover them with the hessian. Madolpen helped Poppie to take down her baggage.

My sisters stayed at home, because of the rain, Bonsile said.

That's all right, Poppie answered.

They watched the baggage being off-loaded from the roof. The driver got back in his seat and started the engine. From inside the passengers she'd talked to shouted goodbye.

We had a good journey, she told the boys.

The rain had gone from the sky, and the black clouds had cleared. They saw bits of blue sky appearing, and the pale glow of the setting sun. The land was still as green and damp-warm as Poppie remembered it. She felt familiar with it, not such a complete stranger as the previous time.

But Madolpen found everything completely new. He talked and waved his arms and stood in front of the two younger ones who were frightened by the passing cattle. They looked with huge staring eyes, just as Poppie, a long time ago, had looked at the naked bodies of the boys wrapped in blankets herding the cattle with kieries.

The bus from Sterkspruit to Palmietfontein that would drop them at her in-laws' ilali, Kwastorom, was waiting. In this bus there were raw people. Even in the heat the old men had blankets draped over their shoulders, although they were fully clothed.

Aren't the tatas very warm with the blankets over their clothes? Fezi asked.

Poppie told him to be quiet.

One of these days I'll also be walking around carrying a kierie, Madolpen boasted.

We have been looking around for goats to buy, mama, Bonsile said, but they are scarce and expensive; we're not going to have it easy.

Oompie Spannerboy will have to help.

The bus stopped at a rise where Nomvula and Thandi were waiting.

Poppie kissed them, the other children took them by the hand. The girls have grown up, Poppie thought. Their dresses were tight across their breasts. When they put the baggage on their heads and walked ahead of her she looked at the grown thighs, the firm buttocks. The dresses were thin from much washing, but clean. In her luggage she had new clothing which would be fitted and given to the

267

children later. But first of all the matter of Bonsile and Madolpen.

New houses had joined the others in the trust location since she was here a year ago. There was now a double row of houses and a dirt road ran between them. Some people had built square houses of clay and mud bricks next to their huts.

The old people were still living in their hut. It had been whitewashed a long time ago; the red clay underneath was showing through, and at ground level it was dirty where the red-brown earth had spattered up against it in rainy weather. The kraal was still there, but it was empty. Close by there was a small patch of mealies enclosed with sagging wire.

The girls took the baggage from their heads and made way for her to enter. She had forgotten how dark it could be inside a hut. As her eyes grew accustomed to the twilight she became aware of the people sitting there on the clay-smeared floor. She saw the blankets wrapped around the old men, she saw the high black kopdoeks of the women. There were between twenty and thirty people in the hut, and she caught the smell of many people in a small confined space.

Molo, my daughter, an old man said.

Since her previous visit her father-in-law had passed by. But to her it seemed as if he was talking to her, or maybe the old men in her dreams.

The old woman, her mother-in-law, spoke: Molo, Nonkosinathi.

The name that she had heard so long ago brought her some sense of peace. She forgot mama and buti Plank and buti Mosie. It was as if she felt the presence of tata-ka-Bonsile in the hut and the fear she had felt in her dreams disappeared. She felt the darkness surround her, but she no longer offered it resistance. She found rest in the hut within this darkness. If it must be so, then it is well.

How was the journey? the old woman asked.

It was all right, Poppie answered. Is there water to drink?

She knew that behind the hut, at the cooking place, a fire

would be burning and possibly water boiling.

Make her some tea, the old woman told Thandi.

Only water, Poppie said. She drank water from a tin mug which Thandi brought; she also gave some to the two young children. Then she told Thandi to take them outside.

But first Thandi took them to greet their grandmother. They were unwilling and had to be pushed to greet the old woman by hand.

They too, Poppie thought. Like Thandi and Nomvula they can cross to the other side of the hut because they are of the blood. I have to stay on this side.

When the children were outside Poppie looked around her at the people in the hut. The sisters of her father-in-law were there, also sisi Constance, all the old women of the ilali, and a few old men. In the villages of the trust lands only old people and children and the sick live.

Poppie felt better for the water. We must talk about the business of the boys, she said.

Goats are scarce, one of the old men answered. We are looking for goats for your boys, but so far we have found none. We can find small young goats, but they are very expensive, forty rand each.

Then we must take them, Poppie said, we take them so that the work of the ritual can be done. It is a long work and I must return to my own job.

We are ready, the old men replied.

Where then is buti Spannerboy? Is he ill?

He has gone to the other villages to look for goats. And he has gone to consult with the man who cuts the boys.

We looked everywhere, mama, said Bonsile who was sitting a little distance from the old men. We only found young goats.

That is all right, Poppie answered. I'll give you the money. She points at Madolpen. His mama also gave me some money.

We'll fetch the goats tomorrow, Bonsile answered.

Constance said: My sisi, we'll help you with the other work, but tonight you must first of all rest. Tomorrow we'll work. Are you satisfied?

I am satisfied. Tata-ka-Bonsile wanted to take the child to the bush; my father-in-law wanted to take him to the bush for the ritual, but they have all passed by before the work could be done. Now I have only one wish and that is to have the work done.

Let it be so, the old men answered.

We'll make the mtombo in the drums, the old women said. You can help us strain it.

Thus my dreams are coming true, Poppie thought. And she felt calm and at peace because she had not listened to her brothers and her mama. My blood and the blood of these people of the land flows together in the bodies of my children. They must not be children who lack something, they must not be half of a whole; I must make them a whole.

Early the following morning she rose from her sleeping mat, opened the door and went outside. The grey of the dawn was still in the sky and the mist lay over the hills, like white blankets over a body. Up in the sky the morning star was still shining. But she was not the first one to be outside. She saw women coming with bent backs from the low doors of the huts, a row of four or five figures taking the footpath leading to the fields below. She knew that these were the women going to cut the grass to thatch the hut for the two boys. She stared at them into the distance, until they disappeared behind a ridge. That afternoon or evening, they would return after having stored the grass at some distant spot. Before her arrival the old men had selected a place where the hut would be built. The boys had collected the side poles and palings and had hidden them in this secret place. The hut would be built today. She, the mother, would not know where it was. In this whole business of the man-making of Bonsile she had no part.

She thought about the huts built among the Port Jackson bush in the sandy flats near Cape Town, of the burning of the huts after the ceremony, or the sale of the huts to a new group when the abakwetha have finished with it. She thought of the women collecting wood who had to turn away their faces as they passed an abakwetha hut, so

270

crowded were things on the Cape flats. Here it was much better. My son has no father or grandfather, but here there are kinsmen who can take their places, she thought.

When night fell and they had eaten and everybody had come to rest she lay in the darkness listening to the singing of the boys and girls in a hut close to theirs. All night long they sang and drank beer, the boys courted the girls and pranced like proud birds in front of the young girls' eyes. It was the night of umguyo, the all-night party before the leaving to go to the ritual.

Buti Spannerboy got hold of a witchdoctor he knew, and he fixed up the hut the previous day, Poppie tells. He fixed it like so that dirty things could not enter it. We paid him twenty rand for his services. As they say, there must be a witchdoctor else the children get sick in the bush. He must place medicines and other strange things, so that sorcerers cannot come near to it. I am a woman, I asked my husband's brother to do the work for me. So when I arrived in the land I could not say: I don't want a witchdoctor. My husband died because of a witchdoctor. I did not believe. Now I kept myself to myself, but I was worried like. I didn't like the witchdoctors. Sometimes a child goes mad in the bush, and if my child became like that they would say it was because I talked against the witchdoctor. I did not know whether I had to talk or keep my mouth shut.

When morning comes, the umguyo for the boys comes to an end. The men go in the kraal with the boys, who are covered from head to foot with blankets, leaving only space for them to see where they are going. Then all the hair is shaved from their heads and from their bodies. Now the goats are slaughtered, one for each boy. The men start singing inside their kraal with the boys, and outside the women kick up a big noise, and it is a whole big business and everything inside is strictly private, no woman is allowed there. Then they all leave for the veld. All the grown men of the location go along with them. I may not greet the child. I last saw him the day before, he is kept away from me.

271

My mother-in-law wept when the boys were taken away: All my sons have passed by, my husband has gone, and now the only grandson I have is taken away. Buti Spanner-boy has no children.

On the first day in the bush the boys are cut. They cut the foreskin off their penises. A special man, an incibi, is hired to do it and we paid him three rand and a bottle of brandy. Some children die in the bush, that's why one is always worried. If the child is sickly, or if the father neglects to do all his duties, he can go out of his mind in the bush. Here in the Cape a child ran naked from the bush and ran to a vegetable farm near Philippi and the white man thought: He's mad, he wants to murder me, and he shot him dead. But it was the bush madness that got him.

Or his wound can become infected.

The bush ceremony is like baptism in the river. He must first confess, everything bad he has done must be told. If he keeps anything back, he'll get sick in the bush. Even if he has slept with his sister, he must confess. Else his wound won't heal. If he slept with other girls it's not so bad, it's not what the parents would choose, but it's not against the Xhosa belief. Other sins are worse, that's why this confessing is strictly private for the men alone. The women never hear what is said.

There's a big difference between a man who has been cut, and one who has not been cut. In the bush they are taught how to behave themselves as men, to talk like men. Even a mother can't treat her son like a young boy after he has been cut; I can talk to him, but as to a man, not a child. And his sisters must show him respect, they must call him buti. The man who teaches them, stays with them in the bush.

The first day they were there, a snake entered their hut. It worried me very much when the girls who took the boys their food, came to tell me about the snake. I couldn't sleep for thinking about them. I was upset even to see a man approach the house. I'd wonder: And now for what is he coming here, is he bringing me bad news? Whatever he said, I watched his face to see whether he was not hiding something from me.

The fire in the hut is never allowed to die down. If they fall asleep and kick their blankets off, they can set themselves alight. Or a flying ember can set the roof on fire, and the children be burnt alive. These things eat at you, you never stop worrying.

While the boys are in the veld, they must smear their bodies and faces with white clay every day. Now they walk in the veld with their naked white bodies, the blanket wrapped round them, kierie in hand. But the day they come home, they first go to the river to wash. Then they are smeared with red clay. Then the hut and the old blankets are burnt down.

The mother watches for the first sight of the smoke. But we were too far off and could see nothing till the men came along the footpath, the boys with new blankets wrapped round them, everyone carrying kieries and mock-fighting and singing. Ag, but you're glad to see the boys returning safely.

Before the big feast, the men go into the kraal and finish the work; they slaughter a sheep and give the boys gifts and the grandpas that could not walk as far as the hut, take their turn to tell the boys what kind of men they must become. And each bakwetha is given a new name which is kept secret from us.

I could not afford an ox for the feast, but I slaughtered two sheep, and we had enough beer and bread and stamped mealies and ginger beer and Kool-aid, and other cool drinks, our own home-made drinks. They feasted all night long.

The next morning the boys washed their bodies again and smeared on fresh red clay and put on the new khaki clothes they had brought from home, and small black cloths were bound round their heads. Then they sat down, kierie in hand, on a mat in front of the hut, and their relatives could see them and give them their gifts. But I could not go first, the ouma went first, and all the other old women. One gave matches, another tobacco, the next one money. But the mother must wait. When my turn came, I gave Bonsile my watch, because I had spent all my money on this ritual and had none left to buy a present. Others gave penknives or

273

pipes or anything a boy would like.

I was glad to see him, he'd got fat.

The feast lasted a few days and then it was all over. Madolpen was the first to return to Cape Town. I gave him bread and meat and a bottle of Oros to take along and the small gifts he had been given. Two days after he left, Bonsile left for East London. He went to look for a job. He couldn't go back to school, there was no money left for school, everything was used up. It was too late in any case, it was already March. The other children couldn't go back to school either, because there was no money.

The man-making ritual cost me a lot of money, more than a hundred rand, much more, with the two goats at forty rand each and the sheep and the new blankets. And all the new clothes, from head to foot everything new. The old clothes are given to the old men who are needy.

When Bonsile went back to East London to look for a job, I could see the difference in him. His born manner, his childishness was still there, but he was different. He spoke in a new way, and made his own plans.

63

The old auntie Nozazi, the witchdoctor-woman, the youngest sister of Poppie's father-in-law, called Poppie to her after the boys had left. Come sit here inside with me.

Poppie thought: Is it now about Thandi that she will speak?

Because she had seen at Bonsile's feast how Thandi danced behind the old auntie, copying her ways. She had noticed that Thandi went to the old auntie's hut and had been sent away.

Ag, dear Lord, Poppie prayed, don't let this thing come over Thandi.

The old auntie seemed to read Poppie's thoughts. Thandi is thwasa, she said, I saw it when she came here, but as yet I have not said anything to her.

I do not like your words, said Poppie.

If it must come, it must come, said the auntie. She can't pass it by. It's in the blood. Your husband's grandma was thwasa, as a child I knew I was thwasa and must do the work. You are thwasa too, said the old woman, but you fight against it.

Thwasa means to be able to talk to the ancestors, the izinyanya, thwasa is to have ears for words which others cannot hear.

I am a church-goer, said Poppie. Since childhood I have been in a church. My grandma told me I was born with a caul, and that's the only reason why I dream so much.

It's through dreams that you know you are thwasa, dreams force you to submit until you receive the inkenqe, the supernatural powers that take possession of you.

If it comes to me, Poppie told the old auntie, then I'll pray to the Lord to take the powers away from me. My church is more precious to me than to receive inkenqe.

It's an expensive affair, said the old auntie, especially for you as a widow. There are the goats to buy and the beads and the fees to study with the witchdoctors.

The child is young, said Poppie, it will pass.

I must get away from here, she thought. The work for Bonsile is done, I must go home.

But the old auntie did not allow it. I don't wish to speak about Thandi, she said. My brother's children passed by, and my brother passed by and all these deaths have taken my power. My powers must be returned to me, so that I can continue my doctoring. Beer must be brewed and an ox slaughtered and the hidden words must be said. We must do the ritual of ukulungiswa.

An ox slaughtered — and we could scarcely buy two little goats and two sheep, Poppie thought. Do you want money from me? she asked, money I do not have to give.

I sent word to my people to herd an ox from my husband's kraal over the border. But the ritual must be done here in the

275

kraal of my fathers. I ask you to help with the beer and the food. That is what I ask of you.

I had to agree, says Poppie. What else could I do? My daughters had no other place to live. In return I had to stay and help these people, only then could I leave.

She wrote mama a letter to ask for money with which to buy mtombo and stamped mealies and other food. And she asked mama: Stay on at work, keep my job for me till I return. Mama sent the money, but wrote to her: Poppie, don't go and forget your people here in the Cape. Remember, you must come back to us.

The mother-in-law and the aunties were old, they sucked their pipes, backs against the wall, legs stretched out in front of them. Constance had gone home to the ilali close by. Only Poppie and her daughters were left to do the work.

They made the beer. They fetched water from the cement dam in the centre of the ilali, but then the windpump stopped and the water dried up, and they had to go further away, along the winding footpaths down the slopes of the hill to the donga where the springs still trickled. They scooped up the water and filled the paraffin tins and hoisted them to their heads. The girls grew tired, but Poppie kept on till the drums were filled. She mixed the mealie meal with cold water, added the hot water and covered the dish with sugar bags to keep it close and warm. When the sweet-sourness had been reached, she added hot water once more, and then cold water. She carried water, collected kindling, bought firewood at the shop and stacked it at the fireplace.

The secret of beer, says Poppie, is the ityuwele, that is, to add the mtombo at the right moment, to close the liquid and start the fermenting. Time and again, in this hot weather, Poppie had to check and boil it up again. Nomvula and Thandi helped her, they dragged the drums nearer and filled them from the paraffin tins boiling on the fire. Poppie's thoughts went back to oompie Pengi and his beer-making at Upington. As she stirred the beer with a long stick, as she sifted the mtombo, pressed down the bran and added water to the dregs to make the after-beer, she thought: Ag, oompie Pengi, did you ever think your Poppie

276

would be making beer here in Kaffirland?

She cooked the food — stamped mealies and water bread. They knew they could trust her; when the others were tired and moved off, she stayed at the cooking pots. They called to her: Nonkosinathi, come here, or Nonkosinathi, go there. She worked for her in-laws according to the custom of the Xhosa. Towards evening she saw people coming along the hillside paths. Some carried tins of beer on their heads, some brought loaves of bread, others food. They were her in-laws' clansmen.

The ox is in another kraal, before sunrise he will be brought here.

Nomvula had gone to the veld with the other young people to gather kindling. She was sixteen years old, she laughed and joked with the young boys on her way to the spring. Poppie was not worried about Nomvula, but fears about Thandi ate at her heart. She knew that Thandi wouldn't leave the side of her auntie Nozazi that night, she'd come out of the kraal and dance till the others dropped. The spirits would take possession of her.

My daughters may go into the kraal, thought Poppie, but I may not enter. My mother-in-law may not enter either, women married into the family stay outside. When my daughters go into the kraal, they have left me, I cannot reach them.

More and more people arrived who must be fed and given beer to drink. The auntie had sent word to many of her kinsmen to come. The more of the clan gathered around her, the stronger would be the forces that are called up. The living kinsmen take the place of those that have died, their strength again gives to the old auntie the strength that she has lost, their life force fills the emptiness left by the dead, by those that have passed by.

Poppie stayed at the open fire to watch the cooking pots. She heard the noise in the kraal, the screaming when the ox was slaughtered. A special piece of meat is cut out first, they had told her, the piece behind the right flank where life shows longest, and given to the old auntie to eat. Then the meat is cut into pieces and the blood-family in the kraal,

277

my daughters, too, eat of the meat and they drink from the pail of beer put in readiness. The kinsmen share the same pail of beer.

Then the elders speak, the old men who know the words that must be said, the most honoured old man must speak up. He tells the ancestors the reason for the feast, he puts his request to them, he uses the very secret, very deeply hidden witchdoctor's words.

At the fire Poppie heard them stamp in the kraal and sing and preach and pray, she heard them all join in the chant, screaming, high pitched and shrill, the holy secret word: Camagu. It's a good word, it means: Bring to us what is good and beautiful. It is the word the witchdoctors use in their secret songs.

She saw the milling crowd in the kraal, the dust rising from their feet, dust not yet laid from the last violent trampling of the ox's hooves, the dust of her dreams, and amidst all this she could see the spot of blue of Thandi's dress as she joined in the stamping of feet, as she screamed the shrill scream: Camagu.

Tears ran down her cheeks. Words of the old Afrikaans hymn that ouma Hannie had taught her, mill through her mind.

> Heer waar dan heen, tot Uw alleen,
> Gij zult ons niet verstoten.

> My refuge, Lord, is Thou alone,
> You will not leave me helpless.

She thought: What will mama, what will buti Mosie think if they hear that Thandi has to wear the beads of a witchdoctor?

Again ouma Hannie's words came to her mind: It is a kind of faith, but it is not my faith. It's like an injection needle, it can cure or it can kill.

This work too, thought Poppie, is to help the old witchdoctor auntie, the other witchdoctors and the old men, they must know what the meat-eating and the beer-drinking and the word camagu does to the old auntie. But it is not for me to know.

After the eating and drinking the dancing started. The old woman came from her hut, fully clothed as a witchdoctor, beads round the neck, arms and legs, strings of beads tied round her head, hanging down her forehead. She joined the circle of dancers, started tramping with them, their feet shuffled, their heads bent down, their eyes on their feet. They stamped the ground till the dust rose. At first their hands were raised at shoulder level, palms forward, then they started to clap, slowly and softly, then louder and stronger in time with the beat of the drum. It was the midday hour, there was no movement of air, the heat lay heavy on them like a blanket, heavy with this thing they were breathing in and breathing out, drawing in and groaning while they uttered it. They called to the powers of the ancestors to heal the doctor-woman: The people who have passed by have broken our life force, restore it to us.

The sun stood quite still in the greyness of the heavens, it had melted into a pool of light to which no one dared raise his eyes. Their heads were bent, their eyes closed, they heard the thump of the stamping feet, smelt the rising dust. Their faces shone with sweat, their breasts heaved. As their hands met the hands of the dancers next to them, the sweat in their palms mingled, they strengthened one another, the life force flowed from one hand to the other.

Thandi was dancing in the front row. She stayed close to auntie Nozazi. The beat started to take possession of her body, she rubbed the sole of her foot in the soil, then the foot took the weight of her body, the other foot was raised, the movement crawled up her body like a snake, to the thighs, the buttocks, the hips. And then her arms jerked forward. Shrill sounds were pouring from her mouth.

This was quite different from the singing with Poppie in the house at Jakkalsvlei, the songs they used to sing with

279

Katie and Baby and buti Hoedjie and buti Plank. These were shrill sounds like birds taking flight with the flutter of black wings.

Poppie did not realise that these sounds came from Thandi, then she saw her hurl herself forward out of the row of dancers. She wanted to rush towards her to break into the dancers, to grab Thandi by the arm, to shake her and say: Thandi, Thandi come back from where you have gone. But she felt the hand of Thandi's grandma on her arm: Be calm, Nonkosinathi, there is nothing to disturb you. It's her age. It will pass. . .

But if she is thwasa?

If she is thwasa, she'll be taken care of. If she really possesses inkenqe, she must accept it. And if she does not, it will pass.

Thandi's dance had tired her, she panted, the sweat pouring down her face, her eyes were shut and she seemed to be in a trance.

Poppie pushed away the hand of her mother-in-law, but before she could go to Thandi, another old woman left the circle of dancers and joined Thandi. She was an old doctor-woman with a blanket tied over one shoulder, a kierie in the hand and strings of beads round the ankles. She danced with Thandi, taking the beat from her, and the life force flowed from Thandi to her. Thandi's dancing slowly subsided till it had become again just the slow shuffling of feet. The grip of the mother-in-law on Poppie's arm eased.

Do you see, she said, she is taken care of.

Thandi had gone back to the row of dancers, her eyes were open, and she was looking at the dancers in front and behind her, to get the beat again. She was once more the Thandi that Poppie knew.

Poppie was tired. She had been working since early morning. For such a long time her spirit had been fighting. She went to the pots and poured some beer to drink, to revive herself. But she spat it out again and drank from the cool water in the calabash inside the hut. She did not feel like staying in the hut, something forced her to go outside again where the drums still beat, where a single row of women still danced. Thandi was with them, but she was quieter now.

Like the other women, Poppie was barefoot.

My refuge Lord, is Thou alone.

The heat, the dust, the smell of the scorching meat on the coals, the beat of the drum, softer now, but still insistent, affected her. She felt as she felt the first day in the hut, if she could but submit to darkness, all would be well, peace would come to her.

She joined the older women in the small strip of shade at the side of the hut, her back resting against the wall, her legs stretched out in front of her. Her body, like the bodies of the other women, started to sway gently to the beat of the distant drum, something eased in her mind as she felt her body move, at times she touched the shoulder or buttocks of the woman next to her.

The children brought them meat and porridge to eat. She sucked the bones clean, putting them aside to be burnt with the rest after the feast. She drank more beer. It quenched a thirst she had never known before. She put down the mug and shifted to the other side of the hut where dancing had started again. The women with her started clapping their hands to the beat, they urged Poppie: Why don't you try?

The dancers are trained, Poppie told them, I can't just clap anyhow, I'll spoil their beat. And that dancing, it's like the quick step or the waltz or slow, how can I dance quick step if it's a waltz they're dancing? I can try to clap my hands, ja, if I get the beat, but if it's a song that I don't understand I must keep my trap shut.

The old women did not listen to her, but she kept on talking. She drank beer and she talked. With this thwasa business, she told herself, one must be very careful, ja, you fetch trouble on your back. If I start to dance and to clap hands, ja, man, then before I know, I feel I must join, because I can feel it is getting hold of me. I must not now keep on till I'm right inside the thing, if I feel I must keep out of trouble, and trouble I don't want, then I must keep away from them.

She talked to herself, the beer had loosened some tight

feeling inside her, the beat had taken hold of her, strange humming sounds came through her mouth and nose. She was being drawn towards the dancers and the hand-clapping, the dust and the drums. From where she sat, she started to crawl on all fours, she tried to come upright, tried to move to the beat. The pull was the same she had felt in her dreams. She had forgotten that she was Poppie, mama-ka-Bonsile, mama-ka-Thandi, mama-ka-Nomvula. She felt: If I can dance, I will throw all my troubles from me, I'll leave them behind, I'll be safe, I'll come to that dark land where I will feel no pain.

Fezi's crying brought her back to her senses. He did not get on with the ilali's children. He pulled her by the arm. Mama, they pushed me, I fell down, my knee is hurt, it's bleeding. Mama, I looked for you, where were you?

She wiped her face with her apron, got up, took Fezi by the hand, but it seemed to her that he led the way, not she. They entered the hut and she let him sit in the coolness. She stayed with him, and did not go outside again. She rinsed her mouth to cleanse out the taste of beer.

Late that night, when the drummers were tired out, when the dancers were overcome by fatigue and sleep, when the fire had died down to ash and the barrels of beer had been drained to the dregs, the feast came to an end. To be resumed from time to time, when a solitary dancer waking, still as if in a trance, felt the beat come into her body once more, and remembering the dance, sang in a low voice; when an old man moving to the fire, poked the ash to raise an ember for his pipe.

Only towards Monday did the last of the clansmen who had come from far, and slept in the hut with them, leave.

The old men didn't all return home. They gathered behind the kraal and spent their time talking. The youngest brother of Poppie's father-in-law, whom the children call old Koor, sent for her.

Mama-ka-Bonsile, he said, you have been with us for nearly two months and your daughters have lived with us for close on a year. Our headman has sent word that he wishes to meet you.

It is right so, kleinpa, said Poppie. I have some business with him too. Before tata-ka-Bonsile passed by, he told me it was his wish that Bonsile be given a plot of land by the headman. And that is what I must ask him now.

They started off early in the morning. The mist covered the green hills and lay thick in the valleys. At times the mist was all around them and they could hardly see the red footpath ahead. After sunrise it lifted and the mealie lands came into view. She heard birds calling and goats bleating. In a small kloof between the hills the old man put down his kierie at a spring, lay flat and scooped water to drink. She waited till he had walked on before she drank.

The house of the headman was high in the mountain, above the cultivated lands. They passed the women working the lands who lifted their heads to watch them. Their bodies turned as they gazed at the newcomers passing by. Molo.

The house of the headman was on a level piece of ground against the slope, four-cornered and built of stone, surrounded by smaller huts. A low wall enclosed the home yard, people were sitting on the wall, waiting. Poppie sat on the ground and her kleinpa on the wall.

After a while a young man approached them: The headman says he knows the others but this woman's face is strange to him, he is curious to meet her. You may come.

She wouldn't have known him to be the headman, she had expected a tall, strong man, and here he was a lean, puny little man, dressed in ordinary trousers and jacket.

Only when kleinpa started speaking to him in the way befitting a headman, did she know it to be him.

You have come on a busy day, the headman told them, and he pointed to the gathering place under a tree where more people were waiting.

She has come to ask for a plot of land for her son, kleinpa said. She is the wife of my brother's child who has passed by. When she is tired of the city, she wishes to build a house on the plot of land.

It is well, said the headman, but she must be given a letter to take to the chief. My small wife will write the letter for her.

The headman was a Sotho. In Herschel most of the people were Sothos. This headman couldn't write, so his small wife did it for him. He had two wives, an older one and a younger one, the younger one was even younger than Poppie. Their house was large, but with no furniture at all, only chairs and a built-in clay cupboard, nicely built, but all of clay. It was a busy place, a coming and going all the time, and they served Xhosa beer to everyone. The wives were very pleasant to Poppie and her kleinpa, they made them tea. The small wife chatted but the older one was quiet and held her peace. The young wife wore ordinary clothes, but the old woman wore a long old-fashioned style of dress.

Poppie's mother-in-law wasn't satisfied that she had asked for a plot of land.

This child of yours, Bonsile, is a man now, Nonkosinathi, the mother-in-law said. Bonsile must inherit our yard and the cultivated lands in the valley. He does not need other land.

Poppie remembered the dream she had in East London before she received the telegram telling of the illness of tata-ka-Bonsile. She dreamed about a lean dark woman who mocked her and said: Bonsile will never be an heir. . . Fear had touched her heart.

I don't want to cause trouble in the family, she said. Others must inherit the land, not Bonsile.

But the mother-in-law said: There is no one else but him.

Buti Spannerboy had no children, the eldest sister-in-law

in Johannesburg only had a daughter, the other brothers who had died, had been separated from their wives and their children had been lost track of. Only Lindiwe, the little sister-in-law whom she liked so much when she first came to the land, had a son.

I am not taking away the inheritance from Lindiwe's son, Poppie said.

Then the old woman explained it to her: It is because Lindiwe did not marry the father of her son. The headman wants a man to own the land. It must be put in Bonsile's name and Bonsile will take care of her, as he'll take care of his mother and his sisters.

The ancestors told me in my dreams not to take Lindiwe's inheritance from her, Poppie told the old woman. She showed her the letter from the headman. I'll apply for a plot of land, and that will be the inheritance of Bonsile.

Even against the wishes of your parents-in-law? they asked.

A great heaviness came over Poppie. Her own people were against her. Now the in-laws had turned against her too.

But she did not give in.

Tell me where to go, she asked old Koor. Tomorrow I will see the big chief.

She went alone. It was far and the way was hilly. She left before sunrise, in the dark, borrowing the torch Nomvula used when she had to fetch water at the spring in times of drought. The tiny beam lit up the footpath ahead of her; she had become used to the hilly paths, and walked fast. When the sun rose, she had covered a long way. Small boys were herding cattle, stick in hand, and she asked them: Where is the homeyard of the chief?

They pointed: Over there, in those hills.

She had brought some porridge along and ate on the road, and in the coolness of the small valleys she scooped up water to drink, and soaked her feet to refresh herself. She passed a trust village, and another small village and came

285

to a store where she asked: Where is the homeyard of the chief?

You can't miss it, they said, you'll see the hall and office at once.

She had some money tied in her kopdoek and bought a bottle of cool drink at the shop.

Do you have bread, white bread? she asked. In the shop she saw the shelves filled with familiar city goods and the sight filled her with homesickness like a pain in the belly. But they had no bread, so she bought a home-made griddle cake to eat.

It is not far now to the office in the chief's homeyard.

From far off she could see cars arriving, and people waiting at the gate. She was sent to an office run by a black girl wearing a wig. She spoke Afrikaans and some English. Sit down, she said to Poppie. She read the letter. Actually, I must give this letter to the clerk who collects the tax, but he isn't here today, his car broke down.

Must I come again? Poppie asked. The way is long, there are no buses. I knew nothing of a tax. What tax?

You pay a rand, it's a kind of tax, the girl explained, then when they divide up the land one day, you have claim to a plot.

Poppie was suspicious. Whose land will be divided?

Nobody's land, said the girl. The camps where the cattle and sheep graze will be made smaller, then they divide up the land and the tax is kind of your deposit.

The black girl was helpful.

Tomorrow morning I'm going to Sterkspruit, she said, I'll pay your rand; leave your pass book and the money with me. You can stand at the gate of your ilali and as I pass I'll give you back your pass book with the stamp inside. You can trust me. I'll write out your receipt right now. This is an office, this, it's not a bribery-place.

And the rand is all I pay? Poppie asked.

Next year another rand and the next year as well, then you can claim the land.

The time had come for Poppie to go home. Nomvula wasn't willing to stay behind. This is the second year I haven't had any schooling and had to work on the land, mama.

Thandi didn't mind. She had taken a liking to the life. She liked to work with clay and smear the floor of the hut with wet dung. She was of the blood, so she could smear the whole floor, including the men's half too where Poppie might not go. She was known in the ilali for the beautiful hand-patterns she smeared on the dung floor. She sang new songs which were strange to Poppie. At times when Poppie looked for her, she had disappeared.

Nomvula complained: Thandi leaves me at home, she wanders on the hillside all by herself.

But the old auntie Nombunguza reassured Poppie. Don't be uneasy, a child who is thwasa, is always taken care of.

Next year you and Thandi will both be at school, Poppie promised Nomvula. Your buti has gone to look for a job, he'll send the money. I spent all my money on him, so he now must pay for your schooling.

May I go and stay with auntie Constance when I get tired of staying with ouma? Nomvula asked.

Surely, you may visit her when you wish.

Poppie was taking Fezi and Kindjie back with her to Cape Town. She regretted that Fezi would have lost his year's schooling, for he was her cleverest child. When the bus stopped at the gate of the ilali, the whole village was there to say goodbye to her and the children. The ouma wept: I'll never see you again.

But Poppie was in a hurry to be gone. She was wearing her city clothes, and shoes and stockings. She couldn't think that she had spent two months in that place. From where she sat in the bus waiting for the driver to finish loading the baggage on to the roof, the ilali seemed to her to be small and dirty and poverty-stricken.

She paid extra money for them to travel back to Cape

Town via East London. Is it to see Bonsile once more? she asked herself, the son she had scarcely spoken to since the bush ritual, the son who had become a man, who must now take his father's place in the family, be her support, earn the money for his sisters' and brother's keep and schooling?

But it was not to see Bonsile that she went to East London. She had a longing for the grandchild sent to them on the day tata-ka-Bonsile passed by. The child is mine, she thought. It is completely mine. It does not belong to the people living in the ilali on the hill. They never talk about the child. It is only mine. The last time I saw him, I was in too great a hurry, I was not in my full mind, now I must see him in a proper way. She had forgotten the daughters left behind on the land. The skinny long-legged girl with the dark complexion and the hungry eyes, the puny baby tugging at her small breasts, had taken their place in her mind.

When she got there, the house in NU 7 was locked. They had had more rain here than in Herschel. The yard was overgrown. The mealies were full grown, but cramped by the weeds.

It's a good sign, she thought, that the house is locked up and the people gone. They are at work, earning money and Bonsile too has found a job. That's why he hasn't weeded the mealies yet.

She felt too tired to visit Majola's people and her other friends, so she walked round the house to find a sunny spot to sit, for the sun was sinking low. The children played about. Fezi remembered the yard, he rediscovered every stone and plant, and explored the street, but Kindjie was tired and sat down beside her. Fezi fetched them some water from the tap to drink. The city water tasted different to the spring water on the land. The taste of the city water, more than the sight of the house or the garden, more overgrown than when she left, made her feel at home.

The wife of the tenant was the first to come home, coming round the back to enter by the back door.

Hau, she said, when she saw Poppie and the children. Why do you sit here? Come inside with me.

She unlocked and they entered. Poppie sat at the table. She lightly stroked the table top. The tenants looked after the house and furniture well. She gazed around the room while the woman lit the Primus stove.

Is it well? Are you content? asked the woman.

It is well. I am content.

She put both hands round the cup as she drank the hot tea and she ate the white bread which the woman had cut with pleasure, doubling up the slice as she was used to before bringing it to her mouth. Hau, said the woman. You can be satisfied with buti Bonsile. He has found a job. He is getting ahead now.

Poppie lay down on Bonsile's bed, waiting for him to come home.

When they saw him coming, the children ran down the street to meet him.

If I'd known mama was coming, I would have bought meat.

The woman cooked · stamped mealies and beans and added some of her meat. The house was clean, Bonsile's room too.

I haven't got round to weeding the mealies yet, mama, said Bonsile.

Majola and his wife came to greet Poppie, the Blaauw family too.

Stay here in Mdantsane, they told her. Your son is working in the chloride factory, he'll get ahead. If you get work here as well, there'll be enough to keep you and the children. Let the tenants stay on as well.

No, said Poppie. I have it in my mind to get Bonsile back to school. And for that I must earn more money than they pay in East London.

How could she put it to them that she was sick with longing for the salty smell of the Cape, for mama and buti Plank and buti Mosie and buti Hoedjie, that she couldn't get used to the tribal lands and the people of the land?

Because it was against her custom to bring up the matter

with Bonsile himself, she asked Majola's wife the question that burned her: How is it with the child of Bonsile? It is not well. The girl was a cast-away child and the auntie has chased her and the baby away and nobody looks after them.

I sent money from Cape Town, said Poppie. But for the last three months I did not send. I promised tata-ka-Bonsile to do the ritual for Bonsile, it took all my money.

That is so, said Majola's wife.

Does Bonsile give her money? Poppie asked. But Majola's wife said: Hau, sisi, he's only been in his job for a week, where's the money he can give her?

I will leave the children with you, sisi, said Poppie. Tomorrow I must look for the child.

It took her a whole day to find them. First she went to the house of the people to whom they had paid the damage money. There was nobody at home, but the woman next door told her: Xoliswe is not here, she left with the child a long time back.

Mama, Poppie asked: Can you tell me where she has gone?

I heard, my child, that she works at a café in East London and she leaves the child with the old woman Makheswa who takes in small children to look after. I'll tell you the way to the old woman Makheswa.

So Poppie started walking once more. Now and then a lorry passed her, or a motor car and when she did not see to give way, water from rain puddles splashed against her legs on the dirt road. By now she was used to the heat and walking uphill and downhill, the long walk did not tire her. At a cluster of shops she stopped.

Where is the house of Makheswa, the old woman who takes in children? she asked a young girl standing on the stoep. The girl was wearing city clothes, long trousers, her lips smeared red.

How must I know, old mama? she said. I am not one to cast away my babies.

The young boys mocked her. Do you want to leave a child with her, old mama? they joked. They had hooked their thumbs into the bands of their tightly fitting jeans. Aren't you too old for that?

Who reared you, that you talk in this way to an older person? Poppie had in mind to say, but she kept her peace.

The girl lit a new cigarette and threw down the butt of the old one. A little boy playing in the mud in front of the stoep, snatched it.

Do you know where she lives, my child? Poppie asked him. He nodded.

Take me there, said Poppie.

What'll you pay me?

I'll give you a few cents.

With a dirty sign to the girl and the skollie boys on the stoep, the child got up to go. Poppie followed him.

As they walked away, other children joined them.

At Makheswa's house he stopped. Over there, he said. Then he pointed at her bag: Give.

Poppie counted out three cents, but when he refused to leave and shouted rude remarks at his friends, she added another.

The house and the plot were neglected, the grass over-grown, the doorstep dirty, and the closely drawn curtains were torn.

She knocked at the door. It was opened by an old woman who screamed at the children: Hamba, voetsek, which means: Get away, go. They were scared of her and backed a little way. When she turned to Poppie, they came closer again.

A cataract covered the old woman's one eye and it caused her to squint, she looked beyond Poppie while talking to her. She was wearing slippers, her dress was dirty and pinned over the chest with a safety pin.

Molo, said Poppie.

What do you want? she asked, looking at Poppie's clean clothes, her neat shoes. What do you want? Are you from the Welfare? Her body filled the door to keep Poppie from entering.

No, said Poppie, I'm not from the Welfare, but I have walked a long way. Can I sit down?

The old woman allowed Poppie to enter.

The floor and the walls of the room were filthy. As her eyes grew used to the half dark, she saw children of different ages crawling over the cement floor. She nearly trod on a child at her feet. She bent to pick it up and as she bent the old woman used her foot to shove him back to that part of the room where she had spread newspapers, where the children remained to urinate and defecate. The stench in the room was strong.

The old woman had cleared the corner of a settee and Poppie sat down on it. Next to her were two flat fruit-boxes and in each of them a small baby lay sleeping. One twitched in its sleep, as if trying to cough. Yellow mucus had hardened on its upper lip.

I don't take no more babies, said the old woman, if that's what you're after, they make too much work.

One of the children started to stuff bits of newspaper into her mouth. She choked. A girl of about nine years who was carrying a child on her back came from the kitchen and helped the choking child by smacking her on the back and digging her fingers into her mouth to get hold of the paper. The child started screaming.

Which one is the child of Xoliswe? asked Poppie.

She felt ashamed, guilt pressing down on her like a weight, because she did not know the child of her blood.

Bring the child here, the old woman called the girl who had returned to the kitchen and was busy at the stove. She left the pot she was stirring and came to the old woman, then bent down and unfastened the blanket tied round her back in order to lay down the child she was carrying.

The child seemed to be more or less a year old, but listless. It allowed itself to be taken down and put on Poppie's lap without making a sound or movement.

Is this child of my blood? thought Poppie. She felt no bond with him. He was dirty, his shirt ragged, he wore no nappy, his belly was swollen and his little legs skinny.

The child is makwena, said the old woman, he's backward. He doesn't crawl, he doesn't play, he knows no one.

Poppie kept the child on her lap. She settled him on the

blanket the girl had taken from her back. She touched the child's face with her fingertips, gently, trying to learn the shape of his face, stroking it, touching the high bridge of the nose. His eyes opened and gazed into hers. A feeling for the child stirred within her. She gave him back to the old woman. Then she took a rand from her bag and gave it to her. The old woman shoved it down the front of her dress. She owes me more, she said.

I'll bring her here tonight, said Poppie, then we'll pay you.

That evening in the house of Majola's wife, Poppie said: I am taking the child back with me to Cape Town. The child given to us in the place of tata-ka-Bonsile will die if he is left here.

Majola's wife told her: Fezi's teacher has heard that he's back. He told my husband if Fezi stays behind, he will take him up in his class. Fezi is clever, he says, he will catch up with the work. He'll help him not to lose the year of schooling.

Fezi had run down the road to meet her when she arrived home. Fezi was ten years old, but childish. Fezi was always close to her, wanting to know: Where is mama going, where is mama now? At the ilali, when she sent him to the shop, it was always: Where is mama going? When he came from the shop, he was restless, not satisfied till he had seen her again. More even than Kindjie, he was attached to her. He was the child of her heart.

Fezi. It felt to Poppie that bit by bit everything was being stripped from her.

So she would return to Cape Town with Kindjie and Xoliswe's baby. They would stay with buti Mosie. And if Rhoda couldn't cope, Kindjie would have to look after the baby. Kindjie was six years old. She would give up her schooling to look after the baby, as she, Poppie, had left school to look after Pieta, and as Bonsile left Sub A to look after his sisters when they were small.

But to leave Fezi behind. . .

If it must be, it must be, said Poppie. The Lord has given me a child, and He has taken one in return.

293

66

But Kindjie was no help with Vukile, Xoliswe's baby. Kindjie pulled the child off Poppie's lap, to sit there herself. When she was made to let go of the child's legs, she started pinching him. Poppie had to slap Kindjie to leave him alone.

Xoliswe readily allowed Poppie to take the child to Cape Town. I didn't want him in any case, she taunted Poppie, the child holds me back. She never sees Bonsile either. That's past, she said, I have other friends now. The thin body was better dressed than when Poppie saw her last, she wore boots and a wig.

Let it be so, I'll take Vukile.

Before leaving Poppie spent time cleaning and mending Fezi's clothes. She asked the neighbours to have eyes for the child; she spoke to his teacher: I will send the money for his schooling. She committed him to his care. After his first day at school where he saw his old friends again, Fezi was more willing to stay behind with his brother. But it ate deep into Poppie's heart to take leave of Fezi.

Back in Cape Town things didn't go as well as Poppie hoped. Rhoda had a job as a char and couldn't look after the baby by day. It was up to mama to help Poppie out, because mama was not working: She was looking after Katie's child, born while Poppie was at Herschel. Mama was willing to help, but the stepfather didn't like it. He bullied mama when she fed Vukile or picked him up to comfort him: This whore child from Kaffirland means more to you than your own daughter's child.

Weekends when she was off, Poppie fetched the children from mama's house or from buti Mosie's house or wherever they'd been left, and she went with them to Mamdungwana's house. She felt she was on the road all the time with the two children, but what else could she do? She bought food to take to mama and Rhoda's houses. She told them: Keep the washing for me to do on Saturday afternoon. She brought her own washing-powder and soap.

Vukile started putting on weight, and showed more life. Kindjie had got used to him. When you're not here, Poppie, mama said, she looks after him nicely. She feeds him and carries him around on her back, and I've shown her how to wash his nappies.

But when Poppie was there, she showed jealousy, dragging him from Poppie's lap to clamber there herself, pinching and slapping him. Poppie was careful to give attention to the child, to lay down Vukile and take the little girl on her lap. She did their washing, she took them on foot from one house to the other. She kept on. She sent money to the children in the country, she sent money to Bonsile and Fezi. She bought food for the little ones. Her legs started swelling from the never-ending work.

Hannie, Poppie told the woman who worked next door, I am working to put money by so that my children can get their schooling next year. It will take much money, but I must keep faith. The Lord will help me. And if it be the Lord's will, I have another wish as well. I wish to bring Thandi and Fezi back to Cape Town.

To go to school here? Hannie asked, for she knew the children would not be accepted there.

No, Hannie, for them to be blessed in my church, like Bonsile and Nomvula were blessed. I don't want to leave Thandi on the land. I have fear for what might happen to Thandi.

Poppie spoke to Hannie about her troubles. Hannie listened to her in a way that her own people did not listen any more.

When I talk about the land, she said, they show no interest, they have turned against me because of the tribal people.

She had told Hannie about Thandi's ukuthwasa. They were having tea together in Poppie's room.

Let us pray to the Lord that He should take it from her, said Hannie. Why shall the Lord be deaf to our prayers?

Poppie told her about Rosie, the staff nurse at the Guguletu Day hospital. The nurse was thwasa, said Poppie, but she would not pay heed. Night after night the ancestors appeared in her dreams and told her: We are speaking to you, you must listen to us. But she resisted them. Till she got so sick that she was taken to hospital. But the doctors of the Groote Schuur hospital could do nothing for her, their eyes were blind and their ears were deaf to what was wrong with her. So she went to a Xhosa doctor and he told her: You won't get well until you accept your ukuthwasa, you yourself are harming your body. There was no other way, but to accept the talent given her. She left our church and studied with a trained witchdoctor. But she wouldn't leave her job. Till it became too much for her, on duty all week long and dancing and singing with the witchdoctors the whole weekend. She got too tired and fell ill again. She was only cured when she left her job and studied full time with the witchdoctor.

Ag, but her heart was homesick for our church. But after her training as witchdoctor our church was too quiet for her, so she joined the Zionist where they clap hands and sing and stamp their feet, because this is what she had got used to and what the spirits in her head demanded from her.

I don't want this to happen to Thandi, Poppie told Hannie. That's why I want to bring her back to be blessed in my church.

But deep in her heart she knew: What has to be, has to be. If it could so happen to Rosie in the Groote Schuur hospital, how could Thandi go free?

On Sundays she was glad to be with her brothers again. Jakkie told her about his schoolwork.

Do you find your work easier now? she asked. Before Pieta died it had been a struggle.

It's better now, sisi, he said. He was wearing a green and red striped T-shirt, his long tufted hair brushed high and back, like an Afro-wig, his eyes shining as if wet. His face was pointed and his nose high-bridged like oompie Pengi's was. As he talked his head moved like that of a playful pony. He was full of fun like buti Plank when he was young. Only, thought Poppie, he doesn't drink, he loves his books. In that he's like Mosie.

Yes, sisi, how shall I put it, I think my brains grew bigger those years that I spent out of school. It's no bother to me now.

Jakkie had almost caught up with Bonsile. He was studying for Standard Eight.

Bonsile will go back to school one day, too.

Just give me one more year, sisi, then I'm neck and neck with Bonsile.

Jakkie is going to become a preacher, said mama. He loves his church more than any one of us. He's the best singer too.

Like them, Jakkie liked it best to speak in Afrikaans. It was what had stayed with him from his youth in Lamberts Bay.

I don't speak well, he joked, it's location Afrikaans.

The Nyanga children struggled to speak it, but Katie, working sleep-in with Afrikaans people, Mrs Louw, had become quite fluent. Mosie, on the other hand, still struggled with his Xhosa. Katie and Baby teased him when he made mistakes. Buti, they would say, that's not the way to say it in Xhosa. But his English had improved, because of working for English people all these years. And because of that the people in Cape Town took him for coloured or mixed rather than Xhosa.

Ag, I'm just an Afrikaner, that's all that I am, said Mosie.

67

Six months after she had returned to Cape Town, Poppie received a telegram from Herschel. She felt great fear. She was standing in Mrs Swanepoel's kitchen, but her fingers had no strength to open the telegram.

Please open it, madam, she asked. She forced herself to

read it. No, it's not my children, she told the madam. It's my husband's buti, we called him Spannerboy. He had an accident and went back to the tribal land, and now he's dead.

That afternoon she sent money to Herschel to help pay for the funeral.

This now has taken all the money I saved for the children's schooling next year, she told Hannie. I'm sorry that he's dead, because although he was sickly, while he was alive his wife had to be good to my children. I don't know if she'll turn against them now.

On Sunday she told mama and buti Mosie of his death and they started at her again: Tata-ka-Bonsile's only brother is dead. He had first right over the children. But now he's passed by and the children belong to us. They must come back here.

She paid no attention to what they said. I know the law better than they, she thought. They must go their own way, and I must go mine. I did not choose to go this way, but my feet have been put on this road and I cannot turn back.

Constance wrote a letter telling about her husband's death. He became weaker, she wrote. Afterwards he would not leave the house. Then the fits started, and cold fever. We took him by car to the hospital in Sterkspruit, and the doctor injected him, because he was getting fits all the time. The next day he died.

Poppie once again sent money to her. But she did not send for the children to come back.

You are too independent, my little sister, Mosie said. You keep your children away from us, you take your own decisions without discussing it with us. My heart is heavy for Fezi. 'Cause why I have no boy child of my own. He's older than my girl children. He's my son since the night he was born.

It worried Poppie to have misunderstanding between herself and Mosie.

I take my decisions because I have no husband, and because I don't want no quarrel with you, my buti. Because when it comes to my children, you turn from me. I was sent by force to the tribal lands, and my children must take the road their feet were set upon.

When speaking like this, she felt the strength in her. I am forty years old, she thought. I am stronger than buti Mosie or buti Plank or Johnnie Drop-Eye. I am bigger than them.

Because in her heart she knew that what she had undergone would come their way too. I have gone ahead of you, buti Mosie, she said. Your feet too will be set on the road that mine were put upon. That you cannot escape.

68

Sunday after Sunday in the afternoons when she was off and visiting the location they were discussing it — Mosie and Johnnie Drop-Eye and Jakkie, who, because he was still at school, knew more about politics than his elder brothers. It was the end of 1975 and the independence of the Transkei was not far off. Representatives of Sebe, Prime Minister of the Ciskei, and Matanzima, Prime Minister of the Transkei, came to address meetings in the location.

I'm worried like, Mosie told Poppie. They always hammer this homeland story: And if you're not Transkei, you're Ciskei by force. Even we who are city-born.

They were sitting in the front room. The front door was wide open, because of the heat. They could watch the people walking past in the street and the children playing in groups.

The people from the tribal lands, they don't mind, like Spannerboy and my brothers-in-law that passed by; they know it's their home place. But take myself and Johnnie and Jakkie, we've never been there. Now we don't know how to handle it. It's here we were born and grew up. We feel they are pushing us along a road we don't want to be pushed on.

ELSA JOUBERT

Another day Mosie said, after a meeting: The homeland boys, they are happy, ja. They're getting their self-government. But now I ask like: What kind of government is that? I know people who vote because they're bribed. The chief goes to him and says: Old man, you must sign here. The old man wants to sleep or wants to go out, and says: Man, sign for me where you like. Most of them don't know what they are voting for. For the homeland black, it's all right. They have land there, and their people live there, they are used to the Transkei. All right, they don't mind, but I, to tell you the truth, I'm somewhere else. Look, it's my home, this place, I'm not worried about the Transkei or the Ciskei.

Poppie was changing Vukile's clothes, she carried him to the front room.

Now you're upset, buti, she told him. I always said you didn't know what you were talking about when you went on at me about the land. *Now* you'll feel what it's like.

Johnnie was still living with Mosie. Once they tried to build him a house at Cross Roads. He and Mosie and Jakkie planted the corner beams, supporting and cross poles, and fixed a few corrugated iron sheets, but before they finished building, the stuff had been stolen and carried away. Now he was saving his money to buy more sheets and poles. The girl he married in the Xhosa way lived with them too.

This pass business is such a mess, the government can do what it likes, it doesn't bother me any more. But I've been working here for fifteen years, I qualify for a permanent permit, and God hear me, I'm going to stay. I'll try again to build at Cross Roads, ja, that's my plan.

They'll run you out of Cross Roads, buti, said Jakkie, who had been listening to the talk. They'll get you back in the homelands, before you can kiss your arse.

This made Johnnie laugh, and Mosie laugh as they forgot their troubles for the time being. We're the new homeland boys, they joked. We'll carry kieries.

But the thought gnawed at Mosie. If the government has to send you somewhere, he thought, it should send you back to where you were born. Send me to Upington and

300

Johnnie to Namaqualand, not to the homeland. And the people of Prieska and Britstown and De Aar, they don't know the homelands.

I don't know about the chiefs, said Jakkie, I can't get used to this chief story. I'm a city boy. I don't trust this chief business. That's what worries me, like.

Only after she had been back for several months, did Poppie tell her brothers about the claim she made in Herschel for a plot of land for Bonsile.

It was his pa's wish, she told them, that time he visited us in East London. I was forced to do it. But it worries me. It's a greater trouble than yours, buti.

Why, sisi, they asked.

It's all a muddle, she said. In Herschel I heard talk that Herschel and Glen Gray are becoming part of the Transkei. The people don't know if they want it or not, some want it, others don't. And what worries me, is: if Bonsile takes the plot in Herschel and Herschel becomes Transkei then he'll be a Transkei citizen.

So what, 'cause why, what's the difference?

But I've got a house in Mdantsane which is Ciskei, said Poppie. Now if Bonsile becomes a Transkei citizen, I lose the house in the Ciskei. Now I'd rather keep the house in Mdantsane, but I've paid the tax in Herschel, so where am I now?

You'd better be careful, sisi, said Jakkie. You're in more of a mess than what we are.

Jakkie tried to turn the conversation. He started joking.

You must come help me sing, my sisi. I said to buti Mosie, why didn't you come help me sing at the watch last night, man. The people they sang so out of tune, I said, but man, this woman is never going to get to Heaven. . .

Jakkie liked to go to the all-night watch, Poppie knew. Every Friday night if there was a funeral on the Saturday, he attended the watch. He prayed and read from the Bible. Mama had got used to him being out all night.

He was fond of Bonsile's child. He would pick him up and throw him in the air till he started screaming.

301

If I had a job, I'd give you money for this child, sisi. He pinched Vukile's cheeks. Just wait, his cheeks will soon be fat.

Don't worry so much, partner, Johnnie told Mosie, things will come right like. We'll force them to come right like.

But Mosie wasn't satisfied. I don't know where I am. I'm doubtful, I don't know what tomorrow will be like. The future is uncertain. I don't know what will happen to my children, tomorrow when I die. Will they be sent away, somewhere? What will become of them? Will they get a place to live, or just anywhere with people they don't know? There is no certainty, only unrest. I feel it everywhere. The people are restless like.

SEVEN

The revolt of the children

69

When we heard of the riots in Soweto, the black township of Johannesburg, says Poppie, it seemed a far away thing. It seemed not to come from the talk of Mosie and Jakkie and Johnnie Drop-Eye or their friends. It was not trouble about the homelands, Sebe or Matanzima or about passes and travel papers which they spoke now. We heard children were stoning the schools and refusing to go to classes because of the Bantu education law which makes the black children's schooling different from the white children's. We thought the trouble would pass, we said to one another: It is a matter for the teachers to show themselves stronger than their pupils.

But it did not pass. And the children were not children of Lower Primary or Higher Primary schools. We called them children, because they were still kwedin, but in fact they were young men and women. Like Jakkie who had left school to earn money for mama after Pieta's death, and then gone back after five years to start his Standard Six again. Or Baby's friend, Kathleen, whose brother had said to her: Go back to school, I'll pay for your books and uniform. Then you work as char on Saturdays and Sundays. You are too clever to remain a char for always.

There were large numbers of these older ones at school, who led the younger ones — twenty-two years old, twenty-three years, twenty-four years, young men already, but children because they were uncircumcised, kwedini, not yet a man.

So it did not die down in Soweto. Because the children were fighting for more than not learning Afrikaans or not having this special Bantu education thing. They were fighting because of their parents' unrest which came over

ELSA JOUBERT

them like a fever too. We heard on the radio that the children threw stones and burnt schools and stormed the administration buildings and we heard that they were shot for it.

Now that worked on me, because why, I have children too, and the thing that happened to those children in Soweto, tomorrow it could happen to mine. That's why it affected me badly. Because I read newspapers and listen to the radio too. Sunday in church the minister told us what had happened in Soweto and we prayed for the children that had been shot. A week later a memorial service was held. Then we knew the trouble would come down over us as well. There was no doubt in our hearts. We all knew it would come.

It had taken that course with the strike of 'sixty when the trouble spread from Sharpeville to Cape Town. It would take that course again.

Baby was the first to meet up with it. She went to the post office in Nyanga with Katie's child on her back.

I went to phone, she told mama later, I was waiting at the telephone booth when the school children came along, pushing and shoving me aside. I heard them phoning from the telephone booth: We want to talk to the School Board, they said. They must have got through because I heard the money clinking and one was more eager to grab the mouthpiece than the other, I heard them say: We don't want to learn Afrikaans no more, we don't want Bantu education no more. Everyone grabbing the phone said the same thing till the time was up.

Auk, what is this thing you are doing? I asked one of the children I knew, but he cheeked me: Shut up, sisi, you'll get hurt.

The same night they burned down the Nyanga post office. She saw the smoke rising from the school as well. She hid in the house, keeping the children with her, for she remembered the warning: You'll get hurt, sisi. But the next day she went back to see what had happened. The post office windows were smashed and the roof and woodwork burnt out, inside it was still smouldering, it stank of burnt rubber and paint, torn-up papers lay in heaps in the gutters and in the road. The telephone had been pulled from the wall of the burnt-out booth. She picked it up from the gutter by its cord, it swung from her finger till she threw it from her.

And the nylons drove up and down the streets, slowly.

Mosie heard about the trouble that afternoon at work. At lunchtime a man driving a Volkswagen van arrived, his face grey with fear. The windows of the van had been shattered.

What happened? Mosie asked him.

Things look bad, he said. The schoolchildren are marching, but the skollies have joined in behind them, I had to drive hard to get away. It's getting hot in the location, the children are rioting and they've started shooting at them.

But Johnnie Drop-Eye was the closest to the thing and could tell the best: The first thing I saw was private cars, white people and coloureds' cars pulling off the road. I left my dairy to have a look-see. It was about two o'clock. Now the children were all coming from the school and they told me: The other schools have sent word we must come out. They'll all be coming from other locations to our location, and the police vans are coming too.

The police drove slowly between the children, asking what was going on, and the children repeated: We don't want to be taught Afrikaans no more.

When the teachers asked why they said that, when they didn't object to learning Xhosa and English, the children said: We heard them saying that in the Soweto schools and now we say so too.

I stood listening to what the children said, they were young kids, Higher Primary School, then the police van came up. There was one white policeman and one coloured and the white policeman said: Then we'll have to shoot, and that's when I ran back to my milk dairy and told the people: Stay away from the streets, they're going to shoot.

But the police didn't shoot, they followed the children in the vans. It was when the children said: They're going to shoot, that they picked up stones and bricks. That was how the bottle and stone throwing and shooting started, ja, and then the police vans moved in to break up the groups of children standing around.

70

Poppie stood ironing in the ironing room and listened to the news on the wireless that Mosie had lent her.

It seems there's big trouble, Mrs Swanepoel said, you must listen, Rachel. She herself listened in the sitting room.

Poppie heard: The black people in the Cape Town locations are rising, they are burning down buildings, smashing the beer halls, overturning cars and stoning the buses. Fifteen buildings have been burned down — post offices, government buildings, three shops in Langa, the Guguletu hall. Ambulances and fire engines scream through the streets, the police use shotguns to disperse the crowds. The buses are not running, clouds of smoke hang over the locations, all exits and entrances to the locations are closed, only the police may enter.

The next day mama rang her up from the white woman's house where she charred.

Things look bad at the location, mama said, but we're all still alive. Mama's voice sounded as if she didn't believe her own words. We counted ten burnt-out nylons in front of the pass office. And the skollies cleaned out the K.T.C. Bazaars in Guguletu. No more bread or milk's coming to the location, so I'm taking food home this afternoon.

And the children, mama?

I don't let mine out on the street, Poppie. The children were one and all drunk yesterday. They burnt down the beer halls and broke the bottles, and it was brandy and wine running all over the streets. The police came and the shooting started. But by then the children had swallowed the brandy and gin as if they were cool drinks.

But the children that were shot at, mama?

We can't know to count, said mama. Mosie helped take pellets out of the children's arms. He told me many had been taken to Groote Schuur hospital and Tygerberg and the Conradie hospital. Some people say that five died, others say ten. How can we count? For myself, I don't know about anyone that is dead.

The riots were on Wednesday; on Thursday and Friday it was quiet and Saturday Poppie took her off day and went home. To Claremont by train and from there by bus to Manenberg. There the inspectors stopped the buses and they had to get down.

Look at the windows, the bus inspectors told the passengers, see how the children smashed them up. So now we don't go any further than this. It's too rough in the location.

So she had to walk the rest of the way, past the old St Joseph's home, skirting Guguletu; then on to Cross Roads, past the Snakepark squatters camp, past the shops beyond the crossing to Nyanga East, turning off at the Old Location. She walked for more than half an hour. Taxis passed, packed with people picked up at the bus stop. But she kept on walking. The Old Location showed the most damage: burnt-down buildings, blackened walls, roofs fallen in, burnt-out cars, laundry vans, bakery vans, even a big removal van smashed up, set on fire and then over-turned, left lying at the side of the road. As she passed a burnt-out bar the sour smell of spilt liquor came to her nostrils. She saw movement amongst the rubble, a number of men were gathered together, bending forward as if watching someone who was digging. Then they grasped at the bottles they had unearthed, covering them hastily with their jackets for fear of being seen. She was afraid that they would know she had seen them. She hurried on, not feeling at ease until she had left them far behind her.

The smells of the location were strong, when the wind moved it brought the stink of unemptied rubbish tins.

People seemed to be afraid. Even those she knew did not speak to her in passing, scarcely greeting her. Children walking along the street disappeared down the sanitary lanes when the nylons came past.

Nearing Zwelitsha Drive she saw the burnt-out centre and the post office. She trudged up the last steepness to mama's house. As she pushed open the gate, she felt exhausted.

The younger children were at home, as mama didn't allow them on the streets. Poppie sat down at the table, pulled off her shoes and stockings and soaked her feet in a plastic basin. Mama added hot water as it cooled. Pains of weariness shot up her legs.

I had to ride in a smashed-up bus with broken windows, she complained to mama.

All the buses are smashed up.

Now but why do they do it?

You could have come by car. I thought the taxis are waiting for passengers at the Manenburg bus stop?

I paid my money for the bus fare. From where must the money come for the taxi? Poppie was tired and dissatisfied. She had been working hard all week. Why must she have problems with transport home? Her legs ached. She watched her mother who kept silent.

One doesn't know how to talk to the location people, she thought, not even to your mother. Even after these few days. We who work sleep-in in the city, we don't know what happened here.

What is going on, mama? Poppie asked. What do the children want when they start smashing up everything?

We don't know, said mama.

Mama started weeping: Your troubles aren't the heaviest, not having your children with you. Pieta was stabbed dead, I only have Jakkie left at home as boy child. And Jakkie is part of this smashing-up business.

Poppie wanted to comfort her ma, but mama shook off her hand. She dried her tears. This is the burden parents must bear, she said. The parents want their children to stop this business, no one wants to lose his child. But the children keep silent. They come home at night and they don't speak a word to us.

We wait for them all day, Poppie, we are tired too, said mama. When they leave in the morning we don't know if we'll see them alive again.

Baby got a fright at the post office and stays at home, but Jakkie is the big worry to me.

When it was dark Jakkie came home to eat, but did not say much to Poppie, only: Sisi, we're not doing bad things.

Poppie couldn't accept this. The buses are smashed up and the schools are burnt down and the children are drunk on the streets and you say it's nothing bad?

But Jakkie wouldn't speak. After his meal, he left.

You see, mama said, that's how it is with Jakkie. Mama started crying again. And the children say he's their leader.

Later that night when he came to make sure his mama had not come to harm, Mosie stood outside the house with Poppie. He looked at the deserted streets, at the rows of houses, where the lights had been dimmed. He had left his motor car at home for fear of the stoning, he had far to walk to get back to Rhoda. But he didn't want to leave Poppie. He stood on the cement path leading to his mama's door and looked up at the sky which was black, for there were no clouds, just here and there the small light of a star.

Then he said: My little sister, I don't like these riots. You and I are of the Lord's people, his church-people. I don't like it that the children tease the government and get hurt, or that they stop my car with stones and shout: Donate! Donate! till I get out and tap off petrol for their petrol bombs. But little sister, I cannot help it, deep down in my heart I hear: At last! I suppress this thought 'cause why, this violence is not the way of the Lord. But then again I hear deep down: At last!

At work Poppie listened to the wireless for news of East London. Sunday the children of Wongalethu High School in Mdantsane marched. The police dispersed them, some were beaten up, but, thank the Lord, there was no shooting.

After that a few days of quiet in East London.

Later in the week she heard that the Higher Primary School had been closed until after the weekend. It was Fezi's school. Dear Lord, there has been no shooting.

I went by train from Cape Town to Heideveld station to get the bus for Section 3 on my off day, Poppie tells. As the train pulled in at Langa station I saw children crowding the platform. Some got into our coach. We were curious to talk to them, because a Standard Seven schoolboy, Xolile Musa, had been shot when they attacked the Langa police station and we guessed they had just been to his funeral. But when we asked them questions they hung their heads and spat on the floor.

Don't ask us, mama, they said, the police kept us from the grave.

Auk, the mamas said. Now for what did they do that? And you are all looking so nice in your school uniforms.

They robbed us of the funeral, said a schoolboy. The whole morning we practised our songs at the Langa High School, special songs that we made up for Xolile's grave, then we sang and marched down the street to his house. But his father came out and told us: Go home, see, the police jeeps are around us.

We don't mind the police jeeps, we said, but the boy's father kept on: The funeral is over. You're too late. Now this morning the police came: We bring you the child from the morgue, they said, he's outside in the van. Let us go bury him, quick. We don't want no trouble.

So we'll go sing at the grave, even if he's finished buried, we told his pa, but he said: Rather go home, you, the police chased the children from the grave with tear-gas, they'll chase you too.

We're not scared of tear-gas, we said. We bring bottles of water with us to wash the gas from our faces.

But the road to the grave was closed, we couldn't get near.

Johnnie Drop-Eye was at Mosie's house when Poppie got there. They wanted to hear what she had to tell. Nobody had news, everyone heard something different. But Johnnie at his milk dairy heard many stories. God man, one thing is true, he said. It was a black policeman who shot the child, they're too rough, man. The people were mad. So the next day, the people tell me, he was sent to another town, him and his wife and children, for the kinsmen of the child not to kill him.

You say the coffin was brought home in a police van, sisi? said Mosie. Now the kinsmen of the child will be insulted. Is it then something shameful, this child's funeral? they will say. For that is the way my heart will speak if it is my child.

And now this, she turned on Mosie, are you then on the side of the children?

I'm not on the side of the police, Mosie said.

But Poppie had no heart for what was happening in the location. It seemed to her that Mosie and Johnnie and Jakkie and everybody else was stirring up a trouble that would get too big for them to control. And God knows, more trouble she did not want.

Now you fight. Why didn't you fight for me when I was made to suffer so?

Jakkie was at Mosie's house that evening too. For the first time he spoke: I am fighting for you and your children, sisi. It's for you that I fight. When I throw stones it is not at the nylons that I throw but at the law.

Ten days later Mrs Swanepoel told Poppie: The trouble is close by. Hundreds of children are marching in the city and the police are chasing them with tear-gas.

And mama rang her: Jakkie has been caught. Yesterday he marched in the city. The police picked him out because they say he's grown up, what business has he got with the children, he must be a leader.

But many of the children were in their twenties, those that had gone back to school, and were the leaders. They kept Jakkie in gaol one night and let him go. He told the police: Ag, I just saw them marching and I went along. But they did not believe him.

When will this trouble come to an end? Poppie said to Mosie.

She held Vukile on her lap. The crèches were shut, the clinics were shut. Vukile had been getting on well, but now he was ill again. If the clinic could give him injections he would throw off this sickness, but the cough kept on, he cried and was listless like he was in East London. Rhoda was good to him, but couldn't do much and it was hard for mama to look after him. Kindjie was nearly seven. It seemed to Poppie that she walked permanently askew, from carrying the child on the hip. Vukile was nearly three but wouldn't walk alone, it was easier to pick him up and carry him around.

Mosie too kept his daughter at home, she was losing her school year.

It won't easily come to an end, sisi, he said. It's not only this Afrikaans education thing, that's an excuse. As we say: Bendifunanje inyathele ekonsini: I wanted you to tread on my corn. 'Cause why? If you tread on my corn I can hit you, not only for the corn pain but for all the other grievances as well. I think this is what has happened. The school was just the excuse and when they were beaten up, they got angry.

The children didn't want advice. They didn't talk things over with us, says Poppie. Their parents tried to stop them, but it was no use. The older people were afraid of the children and no one knew what they wanted.

71

The children didn't stop with burning down schools and administration buildings and beer halls. They got bolder. The older ones called themselves the Comrades and told the adults: Your time is past: When we speak, you must listen. For what do we burn down the beer halls if the bars and the shebeens still sell liquor in the private houses?

I was walking home with a woman, says Poppie, and I saw children digging in her backyard. I didn't know what was going on, but I heard them shout and then they started to smash up wine bottles they had dug up with their spades. So I knew the woman was a shebeen queen and she'd buried the wine in her backyard.

For my part, says Johnnie Drop-Eye, it was a good thing what the children did, I saw too many people killed by drink, and houses broken up and children outcasts.

And the children shouted at the people: For what we burn down bars if you sell drink in private houses? So they made war on the private houses.

Baby brought home notice papers that the children sent to people to tell them to stop buying and selling wine. Some will stop, mama, others won't stop, said the children.

The children stopped people on the streets and if they smelt of liquor, they would beat them up with sticks from the Port Jackson trees on the dunes. When the old drunks came out on the street, they ran from the groups of children, because the children wanted to know: Where did you buy the wine? Who sold it to you? The old men were scared to say we got it at such and such a house, because they knew they'd send trouble to that house. But they would be beaten till they told and then the children would go to the shebeen house and burn it down.

The children carried pails of water and chicken feathers. They'd make a drunk man drink the water, then push the feather down his throat till he threw up. Then they'd say: Old man, your insides are now clean, you must never drink wine again. Then they'd let him go home.

They caught buti Plank that way when he was staggering home, dead drunk.

That Saturday when I got to the location, I saw broken bottles everywhere, said Poppie.

The children were stopping people at the bus terminus and at the stations because people from outside were bringing in liquor, the women in their shopping bags and the men in their brief-cases. They stopped every man and woman getting down from the train.

315

Saturday afternoon they met every train at the Claremont station. They blocked the way, saying: Open your bags, mama. I carried a Checkers shopping bag and I opened it, I took out my stuff. They shook out my clothes, felt with their hands between the groceries I'd brought to my ma.

O.K. there's nothing here, you can go, mama.

I saw them searching another woman's bag, she had a bottle of whisky with her and they took it and threw it to the ground. The skollies joined up with the children, took wine from people, and drank it themselves.

They took chances, ja.

A skollie stopped me, but I said: I won't open my bag for you, you're not a schoolchild, you're an old man, I won't be searched by you. He was drunk, and his friends stopped him. I said: And from where do you get your wine? They must search you, not me.

But if he had been a schoolchild I would have given up what I had.

The schoolchildren went from door to door, searching for liquor and where they found liquor they threw it out, and they smashed up the house, broke the windows and chucked things about as a warning.

When Poppie got to Mosie's house he said: They searched my house too. They held a meeting and told us why they are fighting liquor. They hate it. One said: My pa drinks, and he robbed me of my education through drink. And another: My pa and ma don't go home on Friday nights, they drink at the shebeens. Or: When my pa pitches up, he's drunk and his wages are robbed. If he didn't drink, he would have money to give us. A drunk man gets hurt, gets mugged on a Friday night.

Rhoda sided with the children. They have experience of drunk people, she said. They have suffered in their homes because of drink. Look at the way you suffered with buti Hoedjie and buti Plank.

Rhoda was always against buti Plank and buti Hoedjie. She can't stand the drunken brothers of her husband, she thinks she is better than us, Poppie said to herself. Although Rhoda was good to her children, Poppie couldn't bear it

316

when she spoke against her brothers-in-law.

You can talk easily, she told Rhoda. Your children are still small. If they were on the streets now, burning houses and hitting older people, you wouldn't have liked it either.

And then one day Plank came home drunk again. Liquor was getting scarce in Zwelitsha and people went to buy liquor in Cross Roads. So Plank was on the way back from Cross Roads and the children were watching him. They pretended to be playing ball in the street, but they watched him. They followed him, kicking their ball this way, that way, but they watched him.

An auntie with a paper bag came along: Auntie, open your bag, we must see what you've got. But then they went on kicking their ball and watching.

They were following buti Plank and he didn't know he was being watched. They dragged him from mama's house where he lay on her settee asleep, they dragged him through the kitchen, to the backyard to the fowl-run. Some held him, others beat him with the sticks from the Port Jackson trees. They tore his shirt off his back and beat him till the strength had left their arms, and buti Plank did not make a move to start them off again.

Jakkie held down his buti Plank. Jakkie did not beat him, but Jakkie let the children into the house.

Mama had screamed at him: You bloody shit, leave your buti be! But Jakkie held fast to his struggling buti and laughed: Mama, we're helping my buti. Liquor has kept him asleep all his life. We are waking him up. It's our duty. We must liberate him.

Don't take it so much to heart, Poppie, Mosie said when he told her about it. Don't let it make you cry. Don't blame Jakkie for it.

When the children had done with beating buti Plank, mama went out to him and helped him back to the house and rubbed his back with ointment and let him sleep on the settee. He had a helluva fright, said Mosie. And he's stopped drinking.

317

Poppie walked to Mamdungwana's house. She met other church-women who had gathered there. They said: At last God has heard the prayers of the parents. The Lord is speaking through the children. The Lord is telling us: Liquor has ruined you, leave it be.

Mamdungwana comforted Poppie. Many parents know that their children drink, they're alcoholics, they're gaol birds. They are grateful that the Comrades have taken a stand against liquor.

My children don't drink yet, Poppie thought, but how do I know that they will not one day do like the other children do. I must join with the women in their gladness that the children have turned against liquor.

But she could not forgive them for what they did to buti Plank: first the white police beat him up in the chicken-run, and now it's his own little brother that did the same thing.

72

Why should it upset me? she thought, when she heard that more schools had been burned down, more children hurt.

This trouble is not mine, mine is behind me, I must forget it. It's not to say my children would not have a grievance if they were here. My daughters suffer because they have to live on the land, away from their mama, and their brothers must stay by themselves in Mdantsane. Perhaps their hearts are eating into them, perhaps in their hearts they also throw stones. I must be honest. I have my griev-ances too. If I had the strength I would try to do something to change matters but now I don't have the strength, I must now let matters rest as they are. I am tired. I want peace now. And I want my children out of it, so that they can have peace too.

But she knew Jakkie thought differently: I am not tired

yet, sisi. And we don't want peace to come. It's only you that are tired, sisi, it's only you that want peace. We are not tired, sisi, and it is for you and your children that we are fighting.

The Comrades went from door to door in the location and forced the children from all the houses to come to their meetings. We'll burn down your pa's house if you stay away, they threatened. When they heard of a mama whose children were on the land with their ouma, they'd say to her: See here, mama, when we come tomorrow, we want to see your children here, or the next day if they have to come far, we want them at our meetings. Our schools are burned down, we're not writing exams, so no one else must write either, here or on the land, that's why our children must come home.

The Comrades stopped Poppie in the street: Where are your children?

She showed Vukile and Kindjie: These are my children.

The Comrades said: You're an old mama to have such young children, hey, but they left her in peace.

Poppie felt: Even the people whom I know, I distrust. I don't know which one will say: That woman there has children on the land too. If *I* have to let my children come, why do you leave her alone? After Plank was beaten she did not trust Jakkie either.

I have had my share of trouble, said Poppie, I am not bringing my children into this new trouble.

73

Jakkie was spending his time helping Johnnie Drop-Eye in his dairy. The nylon stopped in the street and two policemen, one black, one white, came to arrest Jakkie.

Why do you cause so much trouble, why do you burn

down the people's houses? the policemen asked while they
put on the bangles.

Jakkie did not resist them. But he asked: Why is it me that
you run in?

It's not only you, many others are being arrested as well.

Mama wept once more, but Baby said: Mama, it's nothing
to be arrested. You get arrested if you sit and talk too.

Mama rang Poppie: The schoolchildren burnt down a
house in Nyanga East and Jakkie has been arrested. The
owner of the house and your stepfather go to church
together, but they had a quarrel and it's out of spite that he
told the police it was Jakkie who burnt the house down. He
told them Jakkie is the leader.

The night after Jakkie was arrested, the children held a
meeting in the church. We want to talk to the parents, they
said.

Mosie and Rhoda and Annie, the pregnant woman who
lived with them, went to the meeting.

When we got there, Mosie told Poppie, they were chasing
out someone with a tape-recorder. They said: You're a
traitor to us. That's 'cause why the children don't trust the
adults. They say they're working for us too, for the future,
that we've given in, we don't do nothing. That's why
they've taken over. Now we mustn't spoil their work.

A parent asked: Where's your chairman and your
secretary?

But they said: No, we don't have such things. It's such
people that are the traitors, they give the government the
list of names when they are caught.

Then the children shouted: You fathers and mothers, you
work for the white people, you make them rich, and now
their children are shooting at your children.

People became angry and a woman got up and screamed:
It's the truth they speak. We must join the children. We
must march on the police station and demand our children
that are locked up.

My little sister, said Mosie, that's where I didn't like the
idea any more. I knew Jakkie was sitting in the gaol, I
wanted to go demand him back, but I didn't like the idea

of marching in the night. We can't march in the night, I said to the people, they'll shoot the lot of us.

They didn't have a chance to listen to me, 'cause why a youngster had gone outside and said to the people crowding in the church: We're marching on the police station. And when we got outside the people were on the move already.

I tried to tell them: Go tomorrow, go demand the children in daylight, if you march on the police station at night, you ask the police: Shoot at me, 'cause why they don't know what's coming.

But there was no stopping them and I said to Rhoda and the pregnant woman: Look, the old people are marching too, and if the old ones go, how can I not go, we'd better go too.

But, my sister, I was worried like about my wife and the pregnant woman, and I said to them, when we pass the turn off at the tennis court at NU 7, you must take the side road and go home.

That's when we saw the rockets shooting up in the sky, and the crowd wanted to turn but they couldn't; some turned this way, some that, and then we heard the shooting, twiee-twiee over our heads and now if we wanted to we couldn't go on; they all turned back, they pushed us from the front, we all went back, with the police vans coming on behind us. We got back safely, but some people were hurt, others were picked up by the police vans and arrested.

The children were now satisfied. They said: Mothers and fathers, you can go home now. This meeting was due to us not knowing where you stood. Now we know you are standing with us. Now you can go home to sleep.

Every day for a week mama went to the police station to ask for Jakkie. After a week they took his fine and sent him home with mama.

Mama wept: Did they beat you up? Tell your mama, did the policemen hit you?

Jakkie did not answer mama. He took his path away from her. Two nights later he came home for the first time.

Mama talked to Mosie about Jakkie. She knew about the

321

meeting and Mosie marching to demand Jakkie at the police station.

Jakkie won't speak to me, Mosie, she said.

They're scared of traitors, mama. The children speak to no one. They say: I speak to my buti or my mama, then he talks to the neighbour and the neighbour is an informer and before we know, we are picked up. That's why they don't tell us what they think or what they plan.

But Poppie asked Jakkie when she got home on Sunday: Was it then you that burned down that house, Jakkie? Jakkie had got thin in the cells, but his eyes still shone. His hands were never still, his fingers kept twisting into each other. But Jakkie was still playful. He joked with her: No, sisi, I have a girl friend staying in that man's house, not his daughter, his brother's daughter. They are jealous that she goes out with me. So he gave the police my name when his house burned down.

You see, mama, said Poppie, that's what he's like. The children have no more respect for us. They mock us. They don't go to school, they hang around the streets. What about all the money we paid for their schooling?

We now have better things to do than go to school, mama, said Jakkie.

Going to gaol, yes, said mama.

Going to gaol, yes, till the police stations are so full that they must turn the whole location into a gaol. Then we'll all be in gaol together, mama, he teased her.

'Cause why, said Jakkie to mama, we're waiting to die.

74

So the children wrote big notices, says Baby, and stuck them up at the bus stops for the migrant workers who wouldn't stop selling wine. When the migrant workers didn't listen to the children, the children got mad and went to the special quarters and broke the windows and smashed the bottles they found. It was rough in the location that weekend.

Then the riot squads came and threw tear-gas to force the children to break up their groups. The children didn't run away, they carried bottles of water and washed the tear-gas off their faces. The police started shooting with pellets to stop the smashing up, white and black police and soldiers in camouflage clothes, the pyjama boys. So the children ran away back to the location but many were hurt and one died. The police took him to Groote Schuur hospital but he died there.

Sunday the migrant workers started fighting back at the city-borners, they killed two. One was still a schoolboy and the other, Mr Bisa, was beaten to death in his own house, then the migrants burned down the house.

So again the children came back, together with their fathers, to attack the special quarters where the migrants lived, burning their houses until the police with the riot squad came to stop the fighting.

The city-borners said: We are now fighting on the side of our children against the migrant workers from the tribal lands.

It worried mama, that first time the children attacked the special quarters. The children can't fight with kieries, mama said, and all the men who come from the country are trained to fight with kieries. The city-borners are stupid. Jakkie can carry a kierie in his hand, but if he fights a man of his own age from the Transkei, that man will knock him flat, because he is stupid about this kierie-fighting.

That's why the kids know karate and knifing, said Baby.

But mama didn't stop worrying. A man coming with a fist or a knife can't fight a countryman trained to use his kierie.

The migrants only think as far as their liquor, said mama. And the police tell the migrants: You fuck up the children for us too.

For the migrant workers say: We won't leave off the wine.

We won't be ruled by the amathole bonomokhwe, which means the children of whores.

When the migrant workers said these things the location-born people they got as mad as hell.

Do the folk who come from the Transkei or the Ciskei think they are better people than those who are born here in the city? Mamdungwana's husband asked Poppie when she came home on Saturday.

We location people, we are lawfully married, we don't have any whore children, Mamdungwana said, very cross. And many of those who live over there — she pointed to the opposite side of Zwelitsha Drive, on the other side of the trees to the rows of red brick houses where the migrant workers lived — many of them will leave whore children in the location when they go back to the land.

How many of the migrants know who their fathers are? Mamdungwana's husband asked. He was a heavy-set man with a beard; he worked in a car factory where they made spare parts; he came from Queenstown in the Ciskei, but he had been living in Cape Town since before 'forty.

Their mothers worked in Johannesburg and Durban and when they got whore children they sent the little ones back to the kraal for the grandmothers to raise; that is where they come from. *They* are the whores' children, not our children.

Poppie's thinking was going backwards and forwards about this matter, just like a swinging clock.

They are our people, she wanted to tell Mamdungwana; tata-ka-Bonsile lived with the migrants in those red brick houses when I was sent away. If Bonsile stayed behind, he would also have lived there. They marry our girls, there are location women and their children who lived with them in the special quarters. Why must we turn against each other?

There is going to be a lot of trouble between the city-borners and the homelanders, Mosie told his boss, Mr Green. If not now, in the time to come. The homelanders are the majority, and what they decide they are going to do, that is what they think I must do as well. Now our people won't stand for that. Sooner or later I will have to fight them. If the home-

THE REVOLT OF THE CHILDREN

lander votes, his voice also talks for me, and I don't like that, no.

I know I am an Afrikaner, I am here in South Africa, but tomorrow morning I can be told to go to the Transkei or to another country, and that is what I don't like. I will go to the Ciskei or the Transkei if I want something there, if I decide to go and live with my sister, but I don't like to be pushed around. No, man, no.

75

The children say this Christmas is a time for mourning, Poppie, mama told Poppie over the phone. No trimmings, no parties. No Christmas clothes must be bought. No sheep which the people are used to buying at Christmas time. They must only buy the meat at the butchers that they usually buy. Ordinary food. People must mourn those that are dead. No clothes, not even a shoe, nothing new.

Poppie was dissatisfied. Why was mama talking like this about the children?

Must we be frightened of the children, mama?

It is coming from Jakkie, mama answered. If the children say something, we must listen, he says.

Jakkie fought against the migrants, mama said. He has an arm that is all swollen; Mosie had to bandage it.

Mama, you must talk to Jakkie, Poppie said; he is wasting his life with the Comrades.

But when she was back at mama's on Friday he was there as usual, her little brother again. He came out in the street to meet her, took her carrier-bag with his healthy arm and, standing next to her at the table, rummaged through it with Kindjie, while Vukile tried to stand upright against the chair. He dug some sweets out from beneath the food

325

parcels, opened the wrapping and gave them to Kindjie and Vukile who sat on the floor.

How was your journey, sisi? Jakkie asked.

Your arm, it's very swollen, Poppie answered.

Ag, it's nothing.

I had a good journey.

She felt dusty, dirty, wind-swept. The children weren't looking for trouble at the buses. They waited at the bus stops and shouted: Here comes another TV. That is what they called the buses with broken windows. People streamed into the location, most of them carrying parcels of food. But they walked scared like, only using old carrier-bags so that everything should look worn.

But I'm covered in dust, I walked a long way, Poppie said. She was glad to find Jakkie at home with the children. It was his arm that kept him there. It is a good thing that you came tonight, sisi, he said. Things are going to be disturbed in the location, restless like. It seems to me the people want to fight. The city-borners and the amagoduka.

The amagoduka is the Xhosa name for the migrants that come to the cities for work and then return to the land.

The amagoduka are stupid for not wanting to help us.

Poppie had no presents for the children, no new clothing, only food. Here's meat, mama. She unpacked the bags and the children were all around her. It is only my sisi who brings me sweets, said Jakkie. When he said things like this she softened towards him and laughed, saying: What is all this, you making as if you are small? If I talk to you about going to school you have nothing to say.

As she was talking she thought: Long ago he sat on my lap, as Vukile is doing now. I brought him up for mama.

I promised Mamdungwana I would go to her on Christmas day, but tonight I'm sleeping with you.

That is all right.

Now it was mama and the stepfather and Baby in the bedroom, Poppie and the children in the living room and Katie, who had come from the work, and Jakkie and buti Plank sleeping on the floor of the kitchen.

I saw Hoedjie during the week, mama said, but Muis

is too ill to come here. It is too far for her to walk from Cross Roads to here.

They all sang together before they went to bed. Mama said a prayer, but all of them felt uneasy.

The next morning, while Poppie was dressing the children, mama asked: Are you going to church?

I might as well. Is mama not dressing for church?

The old man says we must stay. There is going to be trouble.

No, mama, I might as well go.

The stepfather is showing his bloody two-face, Poppie thought. Did he get his information from informers? It strengthened her will to go to church.

They won't come into the church to make disturbance, mama.

In church, which was usually crowded at Christmas time, there were few people. They all had to move forward to sit together, to make more people, a small crowd. It was not a church meeting which gave pleasure. The children wore no new clothes. Other Christmas times the church was bright with the new frocks and new shirts the children wore — yellow and pink and blue. Now everything was old and drab. Kindjie knelt on the bench to look around; Poppie dragged her down to sit properly. She had Vukile on her lap and quietly soothed him with a bobbing knee. The children were restless because of the empty church and because they weren't wearing new clothes and because there was no special food at home waiting. If they heard voices outside in the street they looked round while singing or peered with bent heads during prayers.

The minister shortened the service and Poppie left with Mamdungwana.

At about three, after the meal and washing up and the table clearing, they heard noises of the disturbance in the location coming through the windows and the open door. The small children were playing outside and they saw the men congregating in the street.

It is a kind of to and fro troublemaking, Mamdungwana's husband said. We do not know which way this thing is going to turn to; I don't like it, no, not at all.

And while he was saying this they saw the jeeps of the riot squad coming down the sandy road at the corner near to where the post office was burnt down. They called in the small children from outside and closed the door. Now it was quiet, for a little while. The jeep had gone down the street and was standing at the corner. Then another one joined it, and still another. It looked as if there was going to be a big fight at the bottom end of the street. They heard people talking very loudly and shouting.

Behind the houses they could see smoke going up into the heaven. Another house burning. It is not very far from mama's house, Poppie told Mamdungwana.

They pulled at Poppie. Come inside, you can't go there. You can see the riot squad going in that direction.

They sat in the house listening. They heard people running, then a few shots. Then they heard the quiet again. The children at the window suddenly cried: Come look, a house at the back of us is burning. They pulled open the back door and saw people rushing with pails of water. Boys climbed on to the roof and tried to put out the flames; the smoke went straight and black upwards.

It was a petrol bomb, a neighbour cried, but no one saw it coming.

The afternoon lengthened itself into lateness.

Mamdungwana's husband again came in from outside and reported: I heard that two men at the special quarters are dead. But the house wasn't burning in your mama's street; there it is quiet.

He brought another child to spend the night with them.

Now there were three adults and seven children in the house. Mamdungwana's last-born, Nofyn — Poppie had given her this name because she was so small and fine at birth and the name had stuck — she was thirteen years old, and Nomawetu and Fanie, a son and daughter of another working woman, were twelve and five years old, and Nomamasa, a crippled daughter of Mamdungwana's sister-in-law, was eight, and then there was the little brother of two who had just been brought along, and Poppie's

Kindjie and Vukile who were seven and two. That was without Mamdungwana's two youngest boys, Tera and Langa, who at thirteen and seventeen were both working. She had not seen them all the week. The elders cooked the food and made beds for the children.

You can't go home, Mamdungwana's husband told Poppie. You can't go out on the street, you must stay here.

Where are your two youngest sons? Mamdungwana asked her husband.

Are they women, are they girls that I should tie them to the house? he answered. They are with the group. Are they still listening to me?

Mamdungwana had grown tired during the past few days. Her boys had left school with the others. Both had already been caught. Some nights they didn't sleep at home at all. But they didn't talk to her or to their father.

You are really blessed that your children are not here, she told Poppie.

Poppie thought quietly: How is it that I catch blame for this; it is not of my will that they are not in the Cape.

Mamdungwana's house was on Zwelitsha Drive near the special quarters of the migrant workers. Only two streets removed from them were the red brick houses where the men lived alone, or lived with the women they had taken here in the Cape. These people had always lived peaceably with the location residents. Tata-ka-Bonsile lived and died there. When Poppie had gone down their street to Mamdungwana's place the men had looked up from their cooking fires and those that knew her made greetings — there was peace between them. Now they said war was coming. From behind those red brick houses standing between the eucalyptus trees they would leave their fires to come and fight.

In the road between the special quarters and the houses of the residents she saw the jeeps of the riot squad slowly going up and down. Behind the mesh wire in front of the jeep windows she could see the white policemen and the black policemen sitting; she couldn't see their faces, only the small holes in the mesh through which the guns would point.

329

The long dusk had become dark. Vukile was fretting. He had a fever and he was crying; he vomited his food. He was no longer satisfied with Kindjie, nor with the girl of thirteen holding him. Only in Poppie's arms he felt all right. Later on he slept in Poppie's arms, but she remained awake, looking up at the darkness.

She could feel the restlessness coming out of Mamdungwana like a smell.

Before the dawn she heard the two boys, Tera and Langa, coming in from outside and lying down on the kitchen floor. Mamdungwana was also woken by the quiet noise and she got up to make them tea. Poppie left the sleeping child in the living room and went to the kitchen. The boys didn't talk, they kept the mugs of tea close to their mouths as if they were cold and wanted to feel the warm moisture rising from the tea. The youngest one sat a little behind his brother, away from his mother. She cut them bread.

After the children had eaten and she lay down again, Poppie heard Mamdungwana going to sleep.

76

Sunday morning Mamdungwana said: Poppie, I don't feel that we can go to church. Not with all the children. We must keep off the streets.

Round about the middle of the morning Johnnie Drop-Eye and his girl friend arrived at Mamdungwana's house.

Sisi, we were at your mama's place looking for you and they said you were here. How are you?

All right, she answered. And it wasn't mama's house which got burnt?

No, sisi. But last night we were just as scared because the fighting was near my ma's house, the girl said. We ran away to Wili's house in Guguletu; there it was quiet.

Tell mama things are all right, Poppie said, but we don't know what is going to happen now.

We should have asked Johnnie to take us and the children away, Poppie said when they had gone.

And what about all my stuff in the house? My husband has been away from early morning; I can't leave everything here, Mamdungwana answered.

Things had again started slowly boiling up in the location; the men stood around in groups, they did not want to leave.

That Sunday, after Johnnie and his girl had left, the thing started, Poppie tells. I saw it all.

Now the city-borners were coming together one by one. They were gathering stones; the children and the young men and the old ones. It was now war against the men of the special quarters. In the distance I saw a bakkie off-load stones at the special quarters, but where they got the stones I do not know. Stones and broken bricks, and the migrants coming together like flies around dung. The migrants had strips of white cloth around their heads and around their bodies more white cloth; in their hands were their kieries.

They shouted like rain: Come, come let us fight. They were swearing, and the city-borners on our side, they also shouted and swore. Sometimes it looked as if the men wanted to break up and go, then they'd come together again. And all the time the riot squad rode between the groups.

Let us put your stuff together, Poppie told Mamdungwana. We saw how they burnt houses last night. You must try to put everything together, now. We can't stay here and look after the things.

Poppie had put her children's things in a plastic bag and put it outside so that she could take it at once if people wanted to burn the house.

She and Mamdungwana carried the furniture outside, because they saw other people doing the same thing.

While they were busy Mamdungwana's daughter, who worked in Kenilworth, arrived.

What's going on here?

331

We're carrying the stuff outside because it looks as if we are going to have bad fighting, Poppie told her.

No, the daughter said, I have only now come through the location, everything is dead, there are no people nowhere. Maybe it is better if papa takes away mama's radiogram, and the sideboard and a few things that mama wants taken away. We can store them at the place where I work.

As they drove away the fighting started up; stones and maybe a petrol bomb flew backwards and forwards, and there was terrible shouting, the men were like dogs watching each other. The throwing started, then stopped.

Now I could see the city-borners stand in a line in front of their own houses to protect them from the migrants. It was just like that, Poppie tells, like a hand dropping. Suddenly the riot squad was there, and we heard shots, and the special quarters men shielded themselves behind the riot squad to break through our lines.

The police came in, together with the men from the special quarters. They shot in between the people of the location, and that is why the location people had to fall back.

At the window I was looking through I saw the bottle coming. I saw the arm with the white cloth round it that threw the bottle which burnt Mamdungwana's house. I heard the bottle fall on the roof, then we ran out of the back door.

I had Vukile on my back, Mamdungwana carried the cripple child; she was seven but she had to carry her tied to the back. She had the other children by the hand and we escaped by a back way to other people's house behind us.

We saw men coming with the white cloth on them; they carried stones and bricks, kieries and other sharp things. Our people ran away because the police had shot at them.

I and Mamdungwana ran into another house and told the children they must hide under the kitchen table because the stones were flying this way, that way, from everywhere. Mamdungwana's block was burning because they had thrown a lot of petrol bombs at it. All her things, her wardrobes and chests, and her clothes, were burnt, everything but those things which her husband took away in the van; the roof of the house had gone too.

We were standing in the woman's house, Mamdungwana and I, when the first stone came through the window. Nearly in her face it was, but she only got glass over her chest because the curtains helped. We were going forward to her when stones came through the kitchen window. Our children were in the kitchen. They yelled out, very frightened, and I heard Vukile give a cry. I called the children to us but Vukile was still lying there, so I picked him up and tied him on my back, covering his head. I saw no blood. He just gave the one cry.

We thought then, what must happen, must happen. We did not know where to go because the streets were filled with men with the white cloths tied round them, and the riot squad was among them.

We must get out this house before the burning, I said to Mamdungwana, else we are going to die.

Where must we go? Mamdungwana asked.

Better outside, I told her. Better dead outside in the street than being burnt to death.

Outside the house, with the children in front of us, a man stormed at us with a kierie and I don't know what other sharp things in his hands. We'd already seen them chopping down children and one woman cried: They are chopping my child to death! Now we did not know what to do and we put our hands into the air, straight up.

This man said: Well, run away. He was taking pity on us.

But we have the children on the back, how can we run away?

I and Mamdungwana, we ran for a little way, the location people were all round us and the police were shooting again, when some other migrants came round the house, all wearing the white. They called to the man who'd stopped us first: Come, here are some more.

But he told them: Let them go.

Now I and Mamdungwana and the children started running, but she was so fat, much fatter than I am. We ran to the other side where it was quieter. We ran past a man lying dead there on the ground, and I do not know if he had been beaten to death or shot. We couldn't stop to look who he was, but Mamdungwana saw he had on a biscuit-coloured suit and her children hadn't any clothes that colour. At that moment you couldn't stop to look at a corpse, you couldn't turn round to see who it was, you just had to run for your life, you and your children with you.

Mamdungwana's eyes had been going everywhere as she was running because she did not know where her boys were. She thought they had been murdered.

Another woman ran past us, but she was completely mad in the head. She was shouting: They have chopped my two children to death; they threw the youngest one into the fire to burn. She ran into the bush; we could not help her.

I stopped and looked round. The police van came back in between the people. Then the location men used their heads and they put up a white cloth and told them: We can't fight any longer; our houses are burning and our children are being murdered. We can't fight against those other men because the police are helping them.

I saw one policeman from the riot squad sitting on the nose of the jeep with a gun in his hand. Then I saw them call the location men together, and also call together the men from the special quarters and tell them: Whoa! Whoa! Stop it now, just stop it!

My heart turned over in me because I thought why don't the police shoot the special quarters men? They are only shooting our men.

The police told the people to bring all the wounded and the dead out on to the streets so that vans could take them to hospital.

Mamdungwana's husband found us. His arm was covered with blood, somebody had slashed him. He couldn't drive the little van, a boy drove it. We can't sleep here, he said, the house is burnt. Everything is finished.

Everything that happened, the fighting around us, had made me so stupid I didn't even know how to get to Mosie's house from where we were, and the more they asked the less I knew. So we left Nyanga and tried to go a roundabout way to another section of the township. But at Section 4 black people with the white cloths stopped us and we sat inside the van, everyone had become stone because they had kieries and pangas in their hands.

Where are you going to? they shouted.

We're going to Section 4.

The boy who was driving understood how things were and said quickly: We come from Cross Roads, the squatters' camp on the other side of Nyanga.

So then they asked me: Sisi, and where are you from?

I am from the location, and I am going to my brother's house.

And from where come these people sitting in the van, because there were people in the back of the van who were hurt in the riots.

I kept talking: These people come from Cross Roads as well.

It is true?

I said: Yes.

If I'd said they came from the location those black people would have killed all of us straight away.

Well, that's all right. Don't go down this road; there at the bottom they are still fighting. Go round that way, and they pointed.

Now we had to turn back and enter at 102. Mamdung-wana wanted to go back and look for her boys, but we said, no, let us first go to Mosie's house and off-load everybody.

When we got to my brother's house everybody was out in the street.

The whole of Guguletu is on its feet, said buti Mosie. They want to go and help the people of Nyanga East. They heard that the police are helping the men of the special quarters. Is that so, sisi?

The people of Guguletu, Poppie explains, had taken out their sharp weapons to help their brothers. So now the police had to shoot to keep the people from each other's throats; they had to stop the people in the streets from going across to Nyanga because it would have been a giant thing if the Guguletu residents had got across.

335

Mamdungwana's stuff was off-loaded at my brother's house and everything was very crowded. We had brought the injured so that buti Mosie could treat them with his first-aid training. When we arrived he was busy treating a man who had been hit with grape-shot by the police.

As we unpacked the van he said to me: Sisi, why is your child so quiet?

I answered: Maybe sleeping. I have seen too much fighting to think of other things; my child is next to me, that is all.

Rhoda unloosened the blanket with which I had tied Vukile to my back; my arms had no strength left.

Rhoda took the baby and lay him down on the table in the living room.

The child of Bonsile is dead, Rhoda said.

There was no blood. If his head had been hit by a stone, maybe through the blanket, the skin would not even tear. There might be a little swelling and the bleeding might be on the inside of the head, travelling inside. The little head lay on the table, the neck limp. A little to the side the head lay, just as he had been put down.

I did not want to believe that the child was dead, but the little head was lying so quietly, the eyes were open, the lips a little parted and as I looked down at him I could see the greyness coming closer to him.

For what, I thought, all this for what?

77

Monday afternoon mama came with her load of things. They had fled into the bush the previous night. They fled from the people of the special quarters. Because the road to Guguletu had been cut, mama and her family slept amongst the bushes Sunday night. Mr Makasi and his wife who lived next to mama did not flee because they thought the war was over; then they got burnt out. Monday morning, at four, in the darkness Makasi's wife got up from her bed and dressed. She wanted to run outside. They threw a petrol bomb through the window and as she ran outside she was hit on the head by a brick. She had to get thirteen stitches for the wound. That was why mama was glad that they had fled into the bush.

Your youngest boys are alive, mama told Mamdungwana. They hid in a toilet when the police started shooting. Last night they fled and slept with us in the bush.

But the second eldest boy of Mamdungwana was hit in the neck with an axe; he died in hospital.

Buti Plank went out to look for Jakkie but could not find him.

Jakkie has not been killed, buti Plank reassured mama. His friends laughed and told us we must wait, J-man will be back.

And Jakkie came for the funeral of Bonsile's child.

Jakkie poured earth into the grave. He asked: Was it a stone or a bullet, mama?

It must have been a stone that came through a window; or maybe a stone that came while Poppie was running. It was not meant for the child.

Mama had become frightened of Jakkie.

But it was a stone, mama.

What could she do? She nodded slowly, yes, it was a stone.

78

After New Year Poppie returned to work for Mrs Swanepoel. She was two days late. We had first to bury my grandchild, she said.

The white woman did not say much. Only: I am sorry, Rachel. And then: I brought back a lot of washing from the seaside house. But don't try to do everything at once.

Poppie mourned the sickly little boy child who had passed by. She wrote to tell Bonsile and the mother about his death, but felt: They scarcely knew him, it was I and Kindjie who were the closest to him.

Kindjie can go to school now with my little girl, said Rhoda. She has lost two years of schooling with this looking after Vukile, the sooner she starts the better.

Ja, that's best, said Poppie. School took Kindjie's mind off Vukile, but Poppie's heart did not lift.

By the end of January Nomvula was also back at school and this pleased Poppie, as well as the good school reports of Fezi and Thandi. Bonsile had not saved enough money yet, and had to stay at his job for another year. Next year, mama, he wrote to her, then I'm back at school.

The children who had taken part in the riots in Cape Town were allowed to write their exams in March so as to pass on to the next standards. Jakkie did not write his exam. Bonsile did not lose much by having to keep his job, Poppie thought, these Cape Town children who stay away from school doing nothing don't make much progress either.

Jakkie's friends who had been locked up during the riots were brought to court. But the court cases were taken to be heard in the Malmesbury courts, because at the Wynberg and Athlone courts the schoolchildren gathered and made demonstrations and so much noise that the judge said: It's impossible to continue.

Jakkie and his friends hired cars to go to the court to Malmesbury, but there they were chased away.

All these years Mosie had worked for Mr Green, the boss of the wholesale firm, and now Mr Green asked him: Wilson, what now is it with the children, or must I say Comrades? What the hell do they still want?

The point is, said Mosie, a person can't know much about what they want. The youngsters don't talk to a person. No, they say our generation are the ones who gave the whites their chance to shove us around. Ja, they say, you are the ja-baas, the yes-men, so they don't trust us no more. They say the whites tread on us.

Do I tread on you, Wili? Mr Green asked Mosie.

Times are not the same, boss, said Mosie. They are more advanced than us. What I take from you, boss, they won't take. That now is what the truth is.

Another day Mr Green said: I can give your brother a job, Wilson. Tell him to come and see me. He can't lie around doing nothing.

He's not interested, boss, he wants to study, ja, he's always got his briefcase and his papers near to him. He wants to be a preacher, but his school is closed down. But he says: Just wait, the school will open again. But I'm worried like, because you never know what is in his mind. They gave in, they say, 'cause why, they're ruled by the gun, but if you're ruled by the gun, you'll run. Ja, you'll run, but you'll get tired of running and, boy, then you'll turn round. I'm not a youngster, but so what, I know what I feel, and I think this way, the youngsters they feel more than we, better or worse. Times have changed, boss, said Mosie. They make us feel it, ja.

It was during this time that they read in the newspapers that the pass books would be made away with and the blacks would be given travel documents.

Johnnie Drop-Eye told Mosie: Every time a new wrapping, but inside the same thing.

The way I figure it out, said Mosie, the travel documents will be stricter. You mustn't belong to this country no more, no man, you're from the other country now. That's what'll happen with the travel documents. You're forced to have them to get the job. And they'll force you to vote for someone. They say it's so simple, but they can't bluff me. When you've got the stamp, before you know where you are you'll be in the homeland.

I have the same pain that my brother-in-law had in his stomach, a hand that pushes into my stomach, just like my brother-in-law told me. 'Cause why, I can't think. If I think this way, I knock bang against something, and if I think that way, bang it's the same thing. I can't get no solution.

Mr Green talked to him about his own son who was going to fight on the border. Mr Green is worried too, Mosie realised.

Boss, he said. Just give me what is my right, here in this place, and I won't be frightened to go stand on the border together with your son. Give me a chance, just give me my rights like anybody else. Just let the Oubaas say: O.K. I give you your rights, and I'll say: O.K. tomorrow I go to the border with a gun. Give me a gun and watch me kill the skellums that come in here. My pa fought in the last war and see where I still stand today.

The big daddy who's in charge, he himself said: Unity makes strength, Mosie told Mr Green. Unity is like a bundle of wood, tied together. Now who comes to break up that bundle putting one stick here and one stick there, and then says we must be strong? No, man, that way my head can't work.

79

Going home on Saturday afternoon, Poppie tells, I saw a great deal of people on the street, coming from church. When I got home I asked Rhoda: What's happening, why are there so many people outside?

She said: We have all come from Mr Losa's funeral.

I don't know this Mr Losa, I answered, where does he live?

He's a man that was arrested with this riot business and then he died of a stroke in the Tygerberg hospital, said Rhoda. So it was a big funeral because everyone was curious to know why he died while he was held.

But the people were angry because a notice was read in church that only the family might go to the graveyard.

And when we left church we saw the hearse and the family's car drive away quickly to the churchyard.

But now the people refused to listen and kept on walking to the graveyard — it was the Roman graveyard close to the church — and all the time they sang and kept on walking and they followed the hearse by force, and while they were on the way to the graveyard the riot squad came and drove in amongst the people, but they did not stop, they walked on, singing, and made the black power salute on the riot cars.

But the crowd was too big, said Rhoda, so I came home.

Sunday morning in church I heard that a memorial service would be held that afternoon for all the people who had died in the riots, said Poppie. I had dinner with Mamdung-wana and did not feel like going. I felt more like going to the prayer meeting at three o'clock. After the prayer meeting I went to buti Mosie's house and there I saw Jakkie's jacket lying on a chair.

And this? So where is the jacket's boss then? I asked buti Mosie.

I think Jakkie has gone to mama's house, said Rhoda.

Now why would his jacket be here?

On Tuesday mama phoned me at the work and said Jakkie had been arrested at the funeral service. He and forty others, with three ministers and an old ouma and young boys and women and their men.

Jakkie was the one to speak at the graves of those that had died.

He said: In our minds we must be together with those that died, we must remember them.

A woman screamed: Those of you that are still Comrades, put up your hands. The youngsters raised their hands.

They sang hymns and then the police vans came.

Some were taken to Heideveld, others to the Guguletu police station, but they were all let out on bail, fifty rand each.

I don't know where the money came from, said mama, it's not us who paid. They say some white people started a fund.

341

Jakkie and the others were tried in the Wynberg court and the bail money was kept as a fine. The Catholic father spoke up in court.

80

At the end of the year Poppie went on holiday to the Ciskei. For two years she had not seen her children. She took Kindjie with her and they first went to East London.

Bonsile was earning well. But I'm not going back to school yet, mama. Give me one more year, then I'll have enough. I'll be twenty-three years old. That's time enough to go back to school.

Fezi was thirteen and had passed Standard Five. He was taller than Poppie. He turned his head away when he spoke to her, his voice was thick and it seemed that she was speaking to a strange child.

She cleaned the house and mended their clothes and cooked their food.

Majola's wife told her: If you take a Ciskei citizenship card, you are allowed to buy the house in which you live.

I decided to take the card, Poppie said, because I had had enough of the trouble in Cape Town. The children could help me pay off the house when they finished their schooling.

I've made up my mind now, Poppie told Majola's wife. Buy the house if it is to be bought. In 1971 the office said the house would cost eight hundred rand, then it belongs to you and you can build on if you like.

You don't get the citizenship card at the pass office but at the X.D.C. which is now called the C.N.D.C. The man asked me where I was born and wrote down my house address and I had to sign a form. I had myself snapped for one rand twenty and he gave me a slip so that I could fetch my card.

When he paged through my pass book, he said: I don't see one stamp on it that you're a voter. So I said, no, I had a stamp on my old book, but since then I've had no chance to vote, I've been working.

Neither mama nor my brothers ever voted. But I decided to see which way the wind blew. I had to think of my children. My decision was to get a house for them, an ikaya, where they could live after I've passed by. So that they need not be on the road like I was.

And if for that I had to vote for Ciskei people, so I would vote.

After Poppie finished her business in East London, she took Kindjie with her to Herschel.

The bigger girls were more content now that they were at school. Bonsile sent money with her to pay for the new year's school fees. It was more than eighty rand.

Nomvula told Poppie: The teachers have asked us to give the addresses of parents who don't live in Herschel. We heard from a man who works at the magistrate's office in Sterkspruit that children who are not registered in Herschel, but in the Ciskei, won't be allowed in this school next year. They say Transkei will not pay for schooling for Ciskei children.

And now I have taken out my Ciskei papers in East London, thinks Poppie. A person can be sure of nothing. When one trouble is solved, the next one is on its heels.

She spoke to the schoolteacher. Don't worry, he said, so many of the children's parents live elsewhere, the school will be empty if we send them all away. Just see that you send their school fees in time. Then we'll see what way the wind blows.

When will I have certainty? Poppie wondered as she boarded the train back to Cape Town. But you can't sit and wait for the day you die, it's now you have to do what you think best.

343

Sunday morning about twelve o'clock Poppie and Mamdungwana walked down the road from church. Poppie saw Baby coming towards her. She was running, but in the midday haze it seemed as if she was not getting any closer.

What is it, Baby? Poppie asked, shaking her by the arm.

They've come to fetch Jakkie, said Baby. You must come to mama.

Poppie's blood ran cold, because she had been expecting this. Now it has come, she thought. But Jakkie had been caught before, three times. Why was it now that her blood must freeze like this?

Come, let's hurry, she said to Baby.

I was getting dressed for church when Jakkie came into my room, Baby told her, but I said I wanted to finish dressing and he left. And while I was putting on my clothes the C.I.D. came in by the front door and the back door and asked my tata: Where's your child? So mama said: For what do you want my child? But he pushed mama out of his way and said: You speak like a woman, shut up. They were black C.I.D.

He's not here, said my tata, but the C.I.D. came into my room where I was dressing and looked under the bed and in the wardrobe.

They didn't find him?

No sisi, they didn't find him there.

Poppie and Baby and Mamdungwana arrived at the house. Mama was sitting at the table, the old man opposite her. Mama's voice was quiet, the way it was after Pieta's death, and Poppie saw a strange look in mama's eyes.

We won't see Jakkie no more, said mama. We'll see him when he lies in his coffin.

The neighbours were in the room with mama, other people joined them, children filled the yard and pressed in at the kitchen door. They made a way for Poppie to enter, then they closed up again.

Speak, mama, said Poppie, but mama could not speak.

Oompie Tata, the neighbour who lived two houses away, told Poppie: They didn't find Jakkie here, they searched door to door, and they found him in my house. I was working in my garden and I didn't see him go into my house, so when the C.I.D. persons asked me, I said: No, there is no child in my house, but they went in to search. So they wanted to pull open the door of the wardrobe, but Jakkie pushed it open from inside and I saw him sitting in the wardrobe on his haunches with a revolver in his hand. I screamed at him, but he didn't hear me. I heard the shot and the C.I.D. person clutched his stomach and fell down on the floor. Jakkie pushed me away from the door and so he's gone.

Now while the C.I.D. man helped the other one, Jakkie got away.

I won't see Jakkie in this life again, Poppie thought. The police will beat him to death if they find him, or they'll shoot him down, because now he's dangerous.

Mosie entered, the children had gone to call him.

Now what's this, mama? From where does he get the revolver?

How must we know, Mosie, said mama, they don't tell us nothing.

Poppie pictured Jakkie on the Flats, revolver in hand. The black police are angry when one of their men is shot, they'd throw the net wide, they'd find him.

He knows he won't get away, Poppie said to Mosie, so that mama didn't hear. He'll kill himself with the revolver, or he'll hang himself somewhere on the Flats.

Many people have been found who have hanged themselves on the Flats.

The ones who gave him the revolver will look after him, said Mosie, but that is no comfort to them, they know what it means. Leave the country and return to kill.

Jakkie, Poppie thought, my Baster-baby, what is this thing that has come to you?

She made tea. She gave mama some tea to drink. We must not grieve for Jakkie, she thought. That is behind us

345

now. He chose his own path. But I grieve for mama's sake. Pieta is dead, and buti Plank's chest is so bad that he can no longer work, and buti Hoedjie is drunk and what he earns he gives to Muis. There's only buti Mosie left to look after her. And the girl children. I must put Jakkie out of my thoughts, because if I think about him and grieve for him, I will take mama's strength from her.

As she poured tea for mama and stirred in the sugar and gave her the mug, it seemed to Poppie that she felt the strength flowing from her to mama.

Drink, mama, she said, we already know what life is like. We take what comes our way and then we go on. But we don't give up.

82

The black policeman recovered and was seen on the street again and that brought relief to the hearts of mama and Mosie and Poppie, but Jakkie was still missing.

A few weeks after Jakkie had gone, mama phoned Poppie. Plank is in the Groote Schuur, she said. He got sick yesterday, he seemed to get a stroke like, one side of his body is lame and his head doesn't make sense.

I'll go and visit him, mama.

She bought him ginger beer which he liked to drink because of its sharpness when he was cut off from his liquor.

It's me, my buti, she told him at his bedside, can buti hear me? But he didn't open his eyes because he was unconscious.

He doesn't talk any more, the nurses told Poppie, but he can swear, ja. He swears at us when we bring him the bottle and says: I won't pee in bed.

Two nights later he died.

THE REVOLT OF THE CHILDREN

It was a big funeral, with two motor cars and two busloads of people. Mama thought: Now that Plank is dead, Jakkie will come home but he did not come.

We were glad that Jakkie didn't come to the funeral, says Poppie, because when we looked round from the funeral car, we saw two plain-clothes C.I.D. among the funeral-goers. They also expected to find Jakkie here.

Mama took Plank's death quietly, just as she took Pieta's death. We expected to see Jakkie's corpse, she said, and now see, it's the corpse of Plank.

But mama wasn't mama any more, not like Poppie used to know her.

None of their family had seen Jakkie again. They heard people say: He was seen here, or he slept over there, this one gave him a rand for food, that one gave him clean clothes, but no one knew where he lived.

Jakkie is a man, Poppie told Mosie. He can look after himself, he can leave by one door in the morning, and it's only himself who knows where he'll sleep the next night, but the one I pity is mama.

Then Jakkie turned up at mama's house. It was late at night. Holding a lamp in her hand by the door, she saw that he had a girl with him and she was heavy.

I leave her with you, mama, said Jakkie. She's my girl friend. I bring her to you, mama.

Later when Poppie heard the story from Mosie, she was angry. I suppose mama can't help it that she's stupid. How could she let them come into her house, she should have said: You don't come into my house, you made your own trouble, you don't bring it over my doorstep.

But mama couldn't think fast enough. She wept when she saw how thin Jakkie was and she dished up some food for him. She said: You can sleep here tonight, and the step-father didn't go against her in this either. She gave the girl a jacket because she looked lost and cold and hungry too, and then she let her sleep behind Jakkie's back on the mattress against the wall.

But mama didn't sleep that night. All night she sat at the kitchen table in fear and she watched the dark slowly

347

growing less dark till the grey dawn broke. She sat in fear that the nylon would stop outside her door. She thought: There's no way that Jakkie can get out of this. And now he's stuck with a girl who's pregnant as well.

When the street came out of the dark and the houses could be seen, mama was not tired any more, but she was angry with the girl.

Before it was fully light she collected all the food she had in the house and stuffed it all into a plastic bag. Then she woke Jakkie up and said: You must get out of my house, and take your girl friend. I'm not keeping her.

That's where mama made her mistake, Poppie said to Mosie when she heard about it. She shouldn't have let them in, but once they were over the doorstep she should have kept the girl, because it's our custom.

Now Jakkie was in trouble two ways: first the shooting and then the girl whom he'd made pregnant but was turned away by his family.

My head thinks faster than mama's head, Poppie says. I suppose she can't help it that she's a bit thick in the head. Because now she has chased the girl away, she's got the girl's whole family against us. That family has now become our enemy. They're not going to let Jakkie come out of this thing alive. What's more, the girl knows all Jakkie's sleeping places and hide-outs.

Mosie agreed with Poppie. This thing of Jakkie rested heavily on him. Two, three times the C.I.D. had come to search his house, and during the day police vans went up and down the street outside. His nerves couldn't take much more.

And even if I knew where Jakkie was, he said, a man can't give away his own family like, I can't tell, even if I did know. But I don't know nothing. All I know is when a child tells me: He slept here last night, or another child says: No, he slept there. I never had his confidence like, and I didn't want to have it.

The girl has got two C.I.D. in her family, said Johnnie Drop-Eye. And if they now feel they got insulted like by your family, now they'll go tell everything.

THE REVOLT OF THE CHILDREN

We should have come together, said Poppie, and put our money together and told her family: We accept her. We take the girl and the baby.

No, mama did a wrong thing to chase away the girl.

Two weeks later Mosie phoned Poppie. The nylon came last night and took away mama and Baby.

Poppie was frightened, she felt her body go lame. Where did they take them?

Now, how must I know, I am not God, am I?

Mosie's nerves had broken. I walked last night, all last night, from one police station to the other, but I did not find them. I can't think of mama in the cells. She has never been arrested.

Mama does not know where Jakkie is? she asked.

I don't know what mama knows, Mosie answered, but I heard here in the location Jakkie wanted to dump the girl with mama 'cause why he wanted to go to East London.

When she heard Mosie say East London she knew what was coming. She felt everything in her die. East London meant he was going to Bonsile.

Why must my children come into this thing? She was shouting over the phone. Why can't he leave my children out of this? They have done nothing. They know nothing of all this.

Why are they watching me? Mosie answered, why are the nylons this way and that in front of me all day long, and nights they wake you any time. Rhoda can't take it any more, we are not criminals, did I marry criminals? she says.

Because of this Poppie wasn't surprised when she opened the front door of her madam's house to see the two C.I.D. men standing there, one black man, one white. She recognised their way immediately, she knew the way they stood, the way their hands never talked, the way they looked at you, the way the black and the white were always together. They want to know where Jakkie is, she thought. But how must I know? They can do nothing to me if I don't know.

349

But she wasn't expecting their question. I have had a lot of shocks in my life, Poppie said later, but this was a shock just as big as the others. The spit became dry in my mouth, I couldn't even talk, and when I had to take the pencil to write, my hand shook so much that I couldn't even make letters.

We want to know the address of your children in Herschel, the C.I.D. said.

She thought they wanted Bonsile's address, she didn't think of Herschel.

For what do you want to know the addresses? Poppie asked after a while.

Your mother and your sister are sitting in the gaol and you are making as if you don't know why we want the addresses, the white man said.

What has this to do with my children? Poppie asked. What have they done wrong?

They have done nothing, but we are looking for the one that is with them. And it isn't for nothing that we are looking for them, he is wanted for attempted murder and sabotage.

You can look if you want, Poppie said, because she had now regained her strength, you won't find him there.

And how do you know that? the C.I.D. man asked.

What will he be doing in Herschel? Poppie said. She was thinking of Bonsile in Mdantsane, and this address they had not asked for.

Rachel has done nothing wrong, Mrs Swanepoel said. She had come to the stoep, because she heard the talking and the dog barking when the C.I.D. came up the path to the house.

It isn't Rachel, the C.I.D. answered, but it is her brother who is the criminal.

What can I do about that, he is my brother, I can't cut him out of my life, Poppie said.

Mrs Swanepoel looked at Poppie in surprise. She had not heard her speak like this before.

The C.I.D. man turned round, facing Poppie, because he was leaving. He also heard the impudence in her voice.

And do you know about all the things he is doing? he asked her. Do you think it is right what he is doing now?

Poppie looked him in the eye. All children are not the same, maybe the mister has a brother who is not good as the mister is.

Let's go, the white C.I.D. said to the black one. We must phone to Herschel.

My children are safe, Poppie said to herself while she was working, while she did the dishes, and peeled the vegetables. They have done nothing, they are innocent. The C.I.D. have nothing on them.

But a day later Madolpen's mother touched at Poppie's room on her way home from work. The C.I.D. took Madolpen two days ago, she told her, and they released him this morning. They knocked him about and hit him so much I think his spleen is torn. He can't walk upright, and I must take him to the doctor tonight.

Madolpen who had been to the bush with Bonsile. Who had done nothing. Hit until he couldn't walk upright, hit until his spleen was torn. And there are some ribs broken, his mother said. They pushed him around and he fell against the side of a table, this is the way he was injured.

Poppie thought about the children who had been caught. If they come out again, they are not the same, the parents say. They have become hard. Nothing is the same again after they have been caught, they cannot forget what has been done to them.

Madolpen had done nothing. But he could have known where Jakkie had slept, Poppie thought. There might have been the reason to arrest him, to make him talk.

Bonsile knew nothing, Nomvula and Thandi knew nothing.

After finishing her work in the kitchen that night, she went to the bus stop and took a bus, then the train, then another bus to Mosie's house.

Are mama and Baby back? she asked Mosie.

There was something different on Mosie's face. He didn't

sound relieved when he told her: Mama is back, Baby is also back.

Were they hurt in the cells? she asked, because there was an expression on his face she didn't know. Did they hurt mama in the cells? she repeated.

If they have hurt mama. . .

They didn't hurt mama, Mosie answered, but his voice was strange, as if he was sorry for her, not for mama. And Rhoda was pitying her, because she brought tea and made her sit at the table.

They let mama go shortly after they left your place, Poppie, Mosie told her. As mama has told it to me, it looks as if they phoned Herschel and said: Go and look for that boy that we are having such a lot of trouble with, arrest him at the address of these people.

Did they catch him? Poppie asked.

It seems that he went first to Mdantsane, to Bonsile. They caught the man with the lorry and he talked. He told them Jakkie had asked Bonsile: Take me to Herschel so that I can cross the border into Basutoland. Like our sisi told us that old auntie of yours travelled on foot over the mountains and across the border.

The old witchdoctor woman for whom we did the slaughtering, whose kraal is in Basutoland, went through Poppie's mind.

And did they find Jakkie?

Let it be that he has been arrested, that this matter can come to an end, she now prayed. So that we can have some peace, so that my children need not be brought into all this.

No, Mosie continued, he had already crossed the border when the police arrived at this place. But they arrested Bonsile like, when he came back.

So they told mama in the cell: We caught him, you can leave. And while they were waiting in the police station before they could walk out, they heard like the man say over the telephone: It's the wrong one; you caught the sister's child, the other one has slipped through. But we hold this one now so he can talk.

352

The Revolt of the Children

And we also caught the sister; so she can talk too.

Bonsile, Nomvula, Thandi, Fezi, my little sheep, my lambs, my poor little lost sheep, whom I had to leave without a mama; has it finally caught up with you? What have I done wrong, where have I sinned? I who thought: You're free of it all, you have side-stepped the trouble; let the other mamas' children collect the troubles, let them burn the houses here in the city and throw stones and let them be shot and beaten up, you are free of it all. For you I have suffered hard times that you could live in peace and go to school, away from all this.

And now it has caught up with you. Now the time of troubles has come down upon us all, as Jakkie said to me: Let the roof of the gaol cover the whole of the location, let the whole of the location become a gaol, because, why, we are born to die.

Let them put you all in the cells: Bonsile, my child, Bonsile with the strong hands as soft as his father's as he strokes the young beard of the ripening mealies; Nomvula with the soft, full body, with a song in her throat as she sings in the school choirs praising the Lord; and Thandi who softly sings at the fire, softly singing while she follows the footpaths over the rolling green hills.

Fezi. . . Fezi. . . Poppie took fright. Fezi, she asked, Mosie, is Fezi in Herschel?

No, sisi, they did not talk about Fezi. Now why would he have left Mdantsane to go along? Hau!

Maybe he went along. Poppie's voice was so low, fear had nearly taken away the sound.

We'll send a telegram tomorrow, we'll find out what has happened, Rhoda said.

Rhoda poured some medicine into a glass and gave it to Poppie.

She had never seen her sister-in-law like this. It was as if her face had melted, as if the cheeks and the corners of her mouth could not stop trembling and would lose their form. But there are not tears. A little spittle runs from the corner of her mouth.

353

Come, sisi, Rhoda said. She took Poppie by the shoulder, shook her gently. Come, sisi, you must have courage. Drink what I have poured in the glass.

Poppie swallowed. As she swallowed she felt her body reviving. She felt as if it belonged to her again. She slowly straightened up in the chair. Kindjie who was standing next to her uncle Mosie, together with Mosie's child, went to her mother.

Come, child, Poppie told Kindjie, come and sit here; and she put her arms around her.

How are things with our mama and with Baby? Poppie asked Mosie.

Rhoda tried to make light of it. Baby says they weren't hurt, but the police swore at them; they took a chair and were like making to throw the chair at them; but they did not hit them. You black bitch, they swore at Baby, and lots of other swear-words that I can't repeat. That was before they heard that Jakkie had already crossed the border. Then they let mama and Baby go.

They will also let your children go, Mosie told Poppie. As soon as they see that the children know nothing about all of this.

The children will have to look after themselves, Poppie answered. Her voice sounded like her own voice again. But the hardness of heart that had come into her, she knew, would be there for always. I have found my way through everything, she thought, but through this I can find no way. Because this has been taken out of my hands, it has been given over into the hands of the children. It is now my children who will carry on.

Peace will not come, she told Mosie. Even those that wish for peace will be dragged into the troubles. We will have to grow used to that. About that we can't do nothing.

But God is my witness, Poppie said, I never sought out this trouble.

For a moment it was as if a weakness had come over her again. Her mouth started quivering, a small cry rose in her throat.

From the beginning it was not I who sought the trouble.

354

Lord, Lord, where, at what place, did I turn from your path?

She wiped her eyes, still dry, with her handkerchief, as if she wanted to wipe away the unclearness.

If the Lord wants you to go, you will go; if the Lord wants you to stay, you will stay, goes through her mind.

If the Lord wanted Jakkie to go, it had to be so, she thought.

And if my children had to be drawn into this thing, then that is what they were born to. And who can take from their path that to which they were born?

GLOSSARY

abakwetha	initiation rites; boys undergoing the rites
Afrikaans	Independent South African language derived from Dutch
ag	Afrikaans interjection, roughly equivalent to 'oh'
agterryer	attendant on horseback, after-rider
amafufunyana	hysterical condition
amagqira	witchdoctor people
A.N.C.	African National Congress (banned)
bakkie	open delivery van; small boat; small bowl
bakwetha	boy who has been initiated
bioscope	cinema
boer-meal	unsifted meal
buti	brother
C.N.D.C.	Ciskei National Development Corporation
doek	see kopdoek
dompass	identity document compulsory to blacks, in which is entered their address and employment; an abbreviation of Strydompass
erf	small plot of land
ewhe	yes
gogo	grandmother
grootma	lit. great mother, term for an aunt who is your mother's elder sister
grootpa	lit. great father, husband of your mother's elder sister
hauk	exclamation, roughly equivalent to 'wow'
igqira	witchdoctor who treats people for physical and especially psychological ailments, usually he is a herbalist as well

igqwira	witchdoctor who uses his power for evil purposes, such as to cast spells
ilali	village in the trust land
indima	traditional patterns traced by hand smearing in dung floors
inqodi	sour porridge made of mealie meal
Kaffirland	rural tribal areas
kierie	walking stick, also used as weapon
kleinma	lit. small mother; an aunt who is your mother's sister
kleinpa	lit. small father; husband of your mother's younger sister
klonkie	little coloured boy
kopdoek	head scarf: in the cities a square of material is folded triangularly, wrapped twice round the head, tied at the back of head with the point tucked into the knot; in the tribal lands, or more traditionally, the length of material is one metre or more, wrapped from the back of the head, folded in front and tucked in to form a bulkier, taller head dress
kwedini	uncircumcised boy
lobola	bride price
magou	thin sour porridge
mailer	man who carries drink illicitly to shebeens
makhulu	grandmother
makoti	young wife, the state of being one
ma-kwedin	pl. uncircumcised boys
mealie meal	maize flour
meisie	girl
mfundisi	minister in the church
molo	greeting: good morning
monkey-nuts	ground nuts
mqomboti	beer made from sorghum
mqomboti bran	sorghum bran
mtombo	bran
muti	witchdoctor's medicine
ndiyaphila	it goes well with me

ndiyathanda	I care for you very much
ngothando	with love
nikosikazi	married woman
nkokola	ground maize
nylon	location slang for police van, from the nylon mesh protecting it
oompie	diminutive of Afrikaans oom: uncle
ouma	grandmother
pondok(kie)	shanty
red baby	Xhosa expression for a baby under a month old
rondawel	round hut, usually with mud walls and thatched roof
sambok	horse whip
samp	crushed maize
sisi	sister
skellums	derivative from Afrikaans skelms: rascals
tata	father
tatomkhulu	grandfather
thwasa	talking to the ancestors; psychic
ukuthwasa	state of being psychic
um-kwetha	boy undergoing initiation
umphokoqo	crumbly porridge
X.D.C.	Xhosa Development Corporation